He who learns must suffer, and even in our sleep, pain
that cannot forget falls drop by drop upon the heart,
and in our own despair, against our will, comes
wisdom to us by the awful grace of God.

Aeschylus

When man dreams, he is a genius.

Akira Kurosawa

ACKNOWLEDGMENTS

There are some people that I must thank for their assistance in making this book a reality. First, from Peninsula Writers, Chris Henning, Carol Finke, Linda Peckham, Sarah McElrath, Kimm X. Jayne and many others who participated in countless writing group sessions. But especially these few. Also, the book was patiently read by many of my family and friends, including Maggie Stratton, Matt Bliton, Jim McClintock, Linda Cheeseman, Gail Walsh, and a dozen others. To my talented editors, Gina Patterson and Laura Matthews. Thanks for your feedback and good advice. To the many strong women I've been blessed to know, and admire, including Alice Mansfield, Sue Stratton, Meegan Holland and Patti Bates. I must mention my clients, who continue to amaze and inspire me. To my colleagues, Jane Roraback, Jean Brickman, and Tish Vincent, thanks for your encouragement. To Cathie Blumer, who gave Emma her lipstick and chocolate. To all those unnamed but much appreciated in recovery for whom this story will resonate. To my parents, Ben and Saralyn, passed away but very much in my thoughts and in my heart. This book is for all of you.

PART ONE:

A Book Of Lies

EMMA'S VOICE

This is a book of lies.

Every one looks to dreams for some deep truth and, after years of study, this is what I know—Dreams Lie. They distort, obscure, mystify and mythologize.

In my forty-fifth year, I formed a Dream Group. I thought this would settle a restlessness that began stirring when my son, Nathan, entered high school. A torment that erupted with the death of my parents. An explosion of misery once my son left for college. Left in a big Cape Cod in East Lansing, Michigan, alone (with my husband Frank, which meant really left alone), and running a private practice specializing in therapy with couples and families, I recognized my life was empty and sour. The irony of being a couple's therapist with a rotting marriage didn't escape me—the wounded healer.

Then the dreams started.

I was lost, I was stalked, I was chased. I found babies, I lost babies, I was falling, I was screwing, I had fallen, and I couldn't get up. I dreamed about doing therapy with a couple who morphed into my parents. I stopped breathing, and I couldn't stop bleeding.

Every night a new scenario of anxiety awaited me. Frank did what he could, he was tolerant. At first he would wake me up, hold me, try to reassure me. After a few weeks, he started to sleep in the guest bedroom. Then he told me to sleep in the guest room.

What did I do?

Ran more. Swam more laps. Biked further. Ate more chocolate.

No help.

So what else does a therapist do? I read.

I looked at all the theories on dreams. I started with Freud, then Jung, Adler, Gestalt, Native American, scientific research, and new-age dream dictionaries.

I read it all and kept a dream diary, with a crushed blue velvet cover with stars and a moon. I wrote in that journal like mad.

But it didn't stop the dreams. The dreams got more vivid. I lost sleep.

I decided two things. First I got back into therapy. After all, I'd faced major life transitions before and therapy helped. My post-partum depression, my decision to go back to school and get my Master's of Social Work (MSW) and start my own practice. When Frank and I had trouble years ago and I'd become convinced I'd made a bad choice, each time I went for help and each time I got it. I had found Claudia Silverstein, another MSW with years of experience. I'd grown up and Claudia had grown old, but I'd seen her on and off over the course of eighteen years.

The other thing, that second thing, I did was based on a quote by Hunter S. Thompson:

"When the going gets weird, the weird go pro."

So I decided, like the wounded healer that I am, to work in my wound, and not just with couples. So I started a Dream Group, to assist other struggling dreamers.

Remember—this is a book of lies. Fiction. A total fabrication. This is my voice; there will be others. Then again, that could be a lie.

CHAPTER ONE

"They each have a secret."

Emma Davis picked up her bottle of water and looked out her window, through the mirror that hung over her desk.

She took a moment before sessions, sometimes a minute or so of meditation or reflection, to still herself, to collect her thoughts.

This was her thought just before she conducted her first Dream Group:

"They each have a secret."

What a thought!

Emma looked out the window of her office and saw the stand of trees near the pond. The sun was setting, and it was early September. The trees were swaying in the late summer breeze. She caught a glimpse of herself in the reflection of the window and straightened a strand of her long black hair, which had a few stray grey streaks layered throughout.

"Wounded healer," she said aloud, looking at her face in the mirror. She saw the small wrinkles at the corners of her eyes, the slight worry lines on her forehead, and frowned.

Dressed in a dark long skirt and a plain white blouse, Emma looked younger than her forty-five years. She wore a wedding ring and a pair of turquoise earrings, which contrasted the blue of her eyes. Her office was neat and uncluttered, and there was a Georgia O'Keefe print on the wall. Some pottery and a dream catcher rested on her bookcase.

The clock ticked 5:58. In two minutes, the group would start. Emma had led a group in her practicum for her Master's Degree in Social Work. That had been a parenting group and had been educational in nature. This group was on dreams, and she wasn't sure what to expect. Except one thing: "They each have a secret."

Emma had interviewed each of the four group members individually, over the phone, prior to the group meeting. She'd found them each to be articulate, interesting, and open to looking at their dreams and engaging in a group process. Two in the group were older than she. Marianne was a fifty-five-year-old, single attorney who worked in her own practice, which specialized in estate planning. Mason was a seventy-two-year-old English professor from Michigan State University, whose specialties were in film. The other two were younger. Jake was a thirty-two-year-old psych tech, and Holly, a thirty-three-year-old Protective Services investigator for the state. Their common interest, as far as Emma could tell, was in dreams. She wondered if their dreams were as disturbing as her own. Emma shuddered slightly, opened the door to her office, and ushered in the group.

Mason and Marianne refused her offer for something to drink, but Jake accepted, asking if she kept any scotch in her desk. Both he and Holly took a glass of water, served in coffee mugs. Once the group sat in the comfortable chairs and a small couch in Emma's office, the therapist took a deep breath to begin an introduction. She was conscious of thinking, *Don't say, "You each have a secret."*

Emma said, "Welcome. This is a group about dreams." She took a breath and looked at the faces of the group members. She wanted to be concise and eloquent and answer any questions, yet also felt a strong need to explain what the group could and could not do.

"This is not a therapy group," Emma stressed, "though I hope that your participation in it will be therapeutic." She felt awkward, but continued on. "It's been a while since I've hosted a group. I mean, facilitated a group, so please bear with me."

"I thought we'd start with introductions," she went on. "Just go around the room and say something about yourself and what you hope to get from the group. Who'd like to start?"

The others were silent and looking at each other. Finally the silence was broken by the younger woman with red hair. "I'll start. I'm Holly," she said, shifting in her seat. She had a pretty face that bore little makeup, and wore khakis and a clean orange print shirt.

"Hi, Holly," said the young man, with an affected tone to his voice. Emma smiled at Jake's attempt at humor, while the older man, Mason, pursed his lips.

Emma calmly folded her hands in her lap. She had learned to not display her concern or anxiety during sessions. What she knew, that Jake didn't know, was that Holly was a member of Alcoholic's Anonymous.

As if on cue, Holly asked Jake, "Are you a friend of Bill's?"

"No, I'm a smartass," answered Jake, with a smile across his rakish face. Emma recognized that his humor had an edge to it. She caught the sparks that flew between Holly and Jake, and caught a blend of reactions from Holly's expression. She seemed both flirtatious, and almost defiant. There had been a moment of silence when Emma jumped in.

"I should have stated the ground rules. Try not to interrupt each other—"

"Sorry!" interrupted Jake.

"—and feel free to tell as much or as little about yourself as you'd like. You need to feel safe, and you need to know you can establish limits and boundaries with each other and with me." Emma nodded at Holly again and crossed her hands in her lap.

Holly started again. "Okay, I'm Holly. I'm thirty-three. I'm divorced. You might as well know I'm in recovery," she looked at Jake and smiled. "I haven't had a drink in five years. I don't have any kids. I work for the state."

Emma asked Holly if she'd like to talk about what she did for the state.

"Children's Protective Services. I investigate cases of child abuse and neglect. And that's what brings me here. I have dreams of dead babies."

Emma glanced at the other's faces when Holly mentioned "dead babies." Marianne seemed to squint, and Mason looked quizzical. Jake didn't respond.

Holly continued, "It seems too terrible to admit but that's what's in my head. I guess what I hope to have happen in group is to gain some insight, or maybe get them to stop. The dreams. Get the dreams to stop." Holly wiped her palms against her thighs, as though pushing something off her.

Emma looked back into Holly's face and noticed that she had good eye contact, but that admitting the content of her dreams caused her real pain. And Holly's cheeks had flushed. Emma said, "Holly, thank you for being so honest. It sounds like your dreams are horrifying. Is it safe to call them nightmares?"

"Yeah, I guess so," sighed Holly.

"We'll be talking about nightmares. In fact, we'll have a group session specifically devoted to them, and we'll look at their function. For now, just try think of your dreams as pictures of your emotions," said Emma. "Does that make sense?" Emma scanned the group for reactions.

There were general nods from the group before Emma turned back to Holly. She noticed a red cardinal light on the branch outside her office window.

"It sounds like your work is quite intense," offered Emma.

Holly admitted, "Yes, but I've never seen a dead baby on the job."

"Are you afraid that someday you will?" asked Marianne.

"Yes," said Holly. "I mean, if I mess up, the result could be a death of a child."

Emma noticed that Marianne leaned forward and scrunched her nose a bit. Mason remained cool but with a look of interest. She noticed that Jake was blushing, just slightly.

Emma decided to talk about her belief that dreams were essentially meant to be healing. Even nightmares could be helpful in revealing fears or shadow work. She talked for a bit, citing different theories and studies.

The therapist saw that everyone except Mason was beginning to glaze over. She turned again to Holly and remarked, "You know, Holly, I was thinking that even though your job can seem like a burden, maybe for now, you can focus on the good you do for the kids you help, as opposed to the fears you have."

Holly took a deep breath and sighed. She smiled at Emma and said, "Okay."

Emma looked at the other three group members and asked, "Okay, who's next?"

After a moment of Jake looking at Mason and shrugging, then Marianne waving towards the professor in an offhanded deferment, Mason declared, "I'll go."

Mason wore a turtleneck and wool slacks with a tweed blazer. His grey hair was cut close to his large, well-shaped head. He wore a wedding ring and a watch, no other jewelry. "I'm Mason Beobachter."

"That's a mouthful," said Jake. "Say again?"

"Just call me Mason. I recently retired from Michigan State. I taught film studies, from film history, to script writing."

"So, you're *Doctor* Mason?" asked Marianne. Emma noticed a slight flirtation.

"Yes, not a medical doctor, but a Ph.D. in the Arts. So," Mason continued, shifting in the chair and running his right hand across his brow, the wedding ring clearly evident, "now I'm retired and I'm interested in doing some new things. I'm interested in this group because I'm curious. I love film, I've always been a busy dreamer, and I love dream sequences in film. I saw the article in the newspaper, so I thought I'd join the group."

"Do you happen to know *Dreams*, the Japanese movie?" asked Emma.

"Very well. *Akira Kurosawa's Dreams* is the name," said Mason, sounding almost apologetic in correcting Emma. "I actually met Kurosawa once. Tall fellow. I love his work. *Seven Samurai* is one of my all-time favorites. I'll have to watch *Dreams*, again, just to see how much of it I remember. I've just started writing a book on the great film makers of the twentieth century, and there'll be a chapter on Kurosawa."

"Who's this Kuro-guy?" asked Jake.

Emma nodded to Mason and said, "Would you like to answer that, Professor?"

"Please, just call me Mason. Akira Kurosawa was a great film director. One of the really great and important directors, along with Ford and Hitchcock and Truffault and a few others. He's Japanese, or was Japanese He's been dead now for a while, since the early '90s, but he was a big influence on Western directors. Spielberg, Lucas, Coppola."

Emma smiled, listening to Mason. She glanced at the others in the group and saw that they were engrossed.

"Everybody knew his work and quoted from it," continued Mason. *Saving Private Ryan*'s storming of the beach owes a debt to Kurosawa's *Ran*, as do most modern films on warfare. *Star Wars* draws heavily on *The Hidden Fortress*. *The Magnificent Seven* is an Americanized remake of *The Seven Samurai*. There are many other examples. Near the end of his life, I think Kurosawa was eighty, he made a movie depicting several of his most significant dreams. It was like a cinematic dream diary. Not his best work. Interesting, though. The funny thing is, I read his autobiography, but I felt that I knew him better after watching his dreams than after reading his autobiography."

Emma saw an opening and went for it. "Thanks, Mason. You obviously know a lot about film. I'm looking forward to your input. Who wants to go next?"

Jake shifted and looked at Marianne. She gave a nod.

"I'll go," said Jake with a shrug of his shoulders. Jake was tall and thin in way that suggested the word "lanky." He wore blue jeans and a white T-shirt with a big denim shirt that was untucked. His hair was nearly shoulder length and it framed his handsome face. Emma noticed a one- or two-day growth of stubble and wondered if it was fashion or haphazard.

"I know what you mean about knowing an artist through their art more than you do through their writing," said Jake to Mason. "I know Miles Davis more from his music than I do from his book. Even though his book is fucking hilarious. Anyway. I'm Jake. I work at St. Lawrence as a psych tech."

"What's a psych tech?" asked Mason.

"A glorified psychiatric orderly. I'm a member of the nursing staff. I do rounds, make sure everybody's where they're supposed to be. Keep in touch with the patients, report to the nurses, run errands. Keep the peace."

Emma noticed that Jake spoke easily and openly, but also caught that his legs were crossed and he kept his fingers laced together around his knee. He seemed tightly wound.

"What brought you to this group?" asked Holly.

"I have bad dreams, too. Vampires and zombies, mainly."

"How old are you?" asked Marianne.

Emma made a note that Marianne had leaned into Holly's pain, while she was working to help Jake avoid his.

"I'm thirty-two. That might be a little old to be working as a psych tech," explained Jake.

"That wasn't my point. I just wondered how old you are. You look young," said Marianne. She smiled at him. Emma thought she might be flirting.

"Yeah, well, I don't feel young. I mean, I guess I'm young in this room." The group moaned as Jake finished. "I mean, I already explained that I'm a smartass. Sorry. I just meant that I feel like I'm old for my job. Most of the others are just out of college or working their way through. I think I'm done talking now."

"Just one question, would that be okay?" asked Emma.

"Sure."

"Maybe this isn't a question, just a reflection, but I'm wondering if there might be a connection between that sense that you aren't quite where you want to be in life, and the content of your dreams," said Emma.

Jake appeared thoughtful. He sighed and tossed his head, moving a shock of the brown curly hair from his forehead. "I'd like my life to change in some way."

"Do you know which way?" asked Holly.

"Well, I'd like to be rich and famous and improve my sex life, if you're granting wishes. But for now I'll just see if anything here works."

"Or helps," said Emma.

"Or helps," echoed Jake. "Anyway, I'm done. Next," he said, looking directly at Marianne.

Marianne straightened herself. She rested the heels of her hands against her knees and tugged at her skirt. Emma thought she recognized it as a business suit that she'd seen in a catalogue. Marianne was impeccably made up from nails to hair, a marked contrast to Mason's tweed, and the khaki and jeans that Holly and Jake sported. Emma noticed her legs were muscled and lean. She clearly worked out.

"I'm Marianne Walters. I'm an attorney. I work with estate planning. I have my own practice and a few employees. I guess I'm more like Mason. Curious." There was a protracted silence.

Emma wasn't sure if she was finished or just gathering her thoughts. Emma was used to silence. She often let clients sit in silence if they were comfortable with it, or if they were clearly trying to struggle with something or get something out. However, Emma also didn't believe in heightening anxiety for it's own sake. After it became clear to her that Marianne needed a little prompting, Emma broke the silence. "So you're curious. Do you have a sense of what you're curious about?"

It didn't escape Emma that Marianne had chosen to go last, that she had deferred readily when any of the other group members would have happily let her go first. *She's cautious. And she looks scared.*

"I have some strange dreams. And there was something in the article that Mason referenced," said Marianne, reaching down into her handbag and pulling out the clipped article from the paper. Emma noticed that it was folded, tightly and neatly, almost looked like it had been pressed or ironed, and that there was pink highlighting on the page.

"'Here is a way to know the deepest part of yourself,' is what you said, Emma. I thought that maybe I was hiding something from myself. I have strange dreams as well. They aren't nightmares, but I don't understand them. So that's what made me call. I'm glad I'm here. I think."

"You feel a little mixed," reflected Emma.

"That's right. I am curious. But—"

Emma thought, *I'm also scared to death to find something out.*

"—I don't know."

"So you're curious but also apprehensive," said Emma. She deliberately used a less threatening word than "scared." She wanted Marianne to feel safe, to reveal herself in her own time, not Emma's.

"I guess that would be true, even though now that I've said it, I don't quite know why I would be apprehensive. I guess this is just new for me."

"Have you ever been part of a group before?" asked Emma.

"No. I've never been in any therapy. My life is mainly work."

"Are you married?" asked Jake.

"No. I've never married." Marianne frowned and looked like she was picking lint off her skirt.

Emma noticed Jake glancing at Marianne's legs. She was probably twenty years older than Jake, but it was clear to Emma that she probably attracted a good deal of male attention.

"Is there anything else you'd like to tell us about yourself?" asked Emma.

"No. That's enough for now."

Emma thought again: *They each have a secret.*

Emma spent the rest of their time going over the group rules, discussing boundaries, cancellation policies, confidentiality, outside relationships. Then she talked more about dreams, stopping to answer their questions. She decided that this group wasn't going to get into their dreams tonight, but that was all right. They had fifteen more meetings.

The following morning Emma rode her bike along the trail that ran beside the river. She picked it up just a mile from her home near campus and rode towards downtown Lansing. Early in the morning there were few people on the path, and she relished the solitude, the sound of her bike's tires against the thunk of wood on the trail, the call of the geese. Emma thought about the poet, Mary Oliver, and her poem about wild geese, but couldn't recall a single line.

The path wound precipitously along the river and, after leaving the campus, Emma found herself in a quiet wooded stretch before pushing past the zoo and into the city proper. The air was cool against her cheeks.

She watched the water as she spun by on her bike, thinking how the color of the water was like a dark oolong tea, or some bitter blend of herbs that had been boiled until it had become a blackened stew. For the stretch of a couple of miles she left the sounds of the city, and heard the call of birds. By the zoo she heard lions roaring. *Wild things run fast*, she remembered, and pushed harder on her bike, her thighs burning as she cranked against the pedals.

Emma reflected on the previous night's group. She thought about her recommendations that they get a dream journal and write in it every day. She'd told them, "Even if you don't remember any dreams, write anyway." Emma had spoken about different theories, about how Freud believed dreams obscured the dreamer's intent, but how Jung held that dreams revealed rather than hid your feelings. Emma thought Jung might be right about that. Freud was so focused on pathology. When Emma read Freud she tried to read him as literature instead of as science. Jung fired her imagination.

Emma's thoughts became a crosscurrent, like the slipstream of the river she followed. She recalled a client, who was an expert in gliding, telling her about the earth's atmosphere being like a pot of boiling water. As the sun began to heat the surface of the earth, there would be spots that would heat unevenly and create updrafts, just like the bubbling on the bottom of the pot. Emma watched for birds looking for updrafts, but didn't see any. She wondered if consciousness was like the atmosphere, if your thoughts were particularly still in the morning. They didn't feel very still to her. She felt stirred up from the night before.

Emma contemplated each group member as she rode her bike. Holly was there to work. Emma admired Holly. Holly had seen Emma for therapy a few years before, after Holly had divorced her husband who'd been an abusive alcoholic. Holly had gotten into A.A. and therapy. Because of managed care, Emma had only seen Holly for a few sessions, but she'd been impressed at Holly's strength and resiliency. Holly was the only client in the group whom Emma had previously seen in treatment.

Emma pondered Holly's dreams about dead babies. She'd had some of those herself. What was it about? *A part of the self, that feels vulnerable, that's about the die?* Emma realized that she'd need more information. But Holly was struggling with something.

Mason was a treasure, thought Emma. But he would tend to intellectualize. He was a tourist. He would study the group, read and absorb information, and generally be an asset, but would likely not give himself over to any emotional display.

She thought, *They each have a secret,* and wondered about the secrets these first two might hold. Holly and her dead babies, rising to the surface, and Mason's cool intellectualism. *What could their secrets be?* The other half of the group was much more obviously anxious, almost afraid. Marianne had been more forthcoming over the phone, during their screening session, than she'd been in the group. She seemed to have worked hard over the years to completely depopulate her life. Her daily schedule was a tightly controlled regimen of work and working out. Marianne was gorgeous at fifty-five years of age, the oldest in the group next to Mason. She achieved that firm little body of hers at home by lifting weights, and doing Pilates, yoga and aerobics. All in the privacy of her finished basement. Her field was rife with opportunities to socialize. She had to meet eligible bachelors or widowers, yet Marianne did little of that, just the requirements of her practice. She seemed to get along well enough, had a successful business, and a solid reputation.

So, what's the problem? Emma reflected that if Marianne hadn't thought there was a problem, there wouldn't be a problem. If Marianne was content to live in solitude, why should that be anyone's business? But it seemed that solitude had slipped into isolation and now Marianne wanted to break out. She seemed scared, Emma thought. Beneath that professional veneer, all the makeup, her toned body, beneath it all was some fear. *Of what?*

Finally there was Jake. He was boyishly handsome, a self-confessed "smartass," a flirt, underemployed, and protecting himself. He might be a handful, but Emma remembered that he did quiet down after reminding him to not interrupt. He seemed less introspective than the others, but that attitude of his was covering up something real. Like pain.

As Emma rode her bike through the river trail into downtown, she passed a group of joggers and a couple of lovers holding hands. Emma wondered if she was out of her league with the group. Emma was meeting her colleague, Betty Williams, at a coffee shop in Old Town. Old Town resided on the north side of Lansing and, until a few years ago, was a slum. Recently Old Town had experienced a renaissance when business owners, artists, and various entrepreneurs had begun to buy up some of the old brownstones and lofts.

Betty Williams was African American and a little older than Emma, but looked like she could have been younger. She wore her hair in a tight afro and was dressed in chinos and a sweater.

Emma and Betty bought cafe lattes and sat at the table, where Emma could keep one eye on her bike locked up outside. They chatted about Betty's new car, then Betty's plans for teaching a course at MSU. Then Betty asked how the group had gone.

"Oh, not so good. I have my doubts. They were a pretty quiet bunch, and I'm not really sure of their motives," answered Emma.

"First group, remember, the forming, warming, storming, norming," reminded Betty. The women freely offered advice to each other, though lately it had been Betty giving more of it.

"Right," said Emma.

"Groups take time. More will be revealed."

Emma and Betty had gone to graduate school together fifteen years ago, and then opened a practice together, ten years ago. Emma kept few secrets from Betty and honored her feedback. Well, she did keep at least one secret.

That night.

Emma finds her bike in the garage, her smart little Honda parked alongside her husband's SUV, a vehicle she's always despised. The bike is unlocked, but stuck on something and hard to move. The garage is cluttered and dark. Emma loosens the bike and gets on it. The wheels seem to clank rather than whir. Emma rides down her street, towards the river. Reaching the river trail, in the dark of the night seems menacing. Emma is taking the turns of the trail too fast and can't seem to slow down. The stretch between the campus and the zoo, wooded and refreshing during the day, now seems impossibly long and also badly overgrown. It is more like a rain forest or jungle than anything else. The branches of the trees are growing over the path. Emma's face brushes against leaves and palms and sharp prickers, as she rides the trail—

Just as suddenly she is back in college, in graduate school, at MSU. She is sitting in the front row, something she never likes doing. The professor in front of the class is Mason, from the group, dressed in cap and gown. The chalkboard reads "Group Therapy 101." Emma's parents are standing alongside the wall of the class, watching and frowning. Emma feels terribly conspicuous in the front row. And then she remembers that her parents are dead—

And then she woke up.

Emma's husband Frank got up and began to get ready for work. *He pops up like toast*, she thought, while she lay groggy in the tumble of sheets. Emma reached for the journal next to her bed. She wrote:

> Riding bike
> Jungle
> Classroom
> Mason / cap and gown
> Parents

"I'm going to be late," called Frank.

"How late?"

"Eleven," he said and the door shut behind him.

Eleven means midnight, means I won't see him, thought Emma as she rose from bed. She felt relieved.

Their marriage had begun with a courtship as undergrads at Michigan State University. Emma was away from her home in Syracuse and was looking for stability and attention. Frank provided both. They shared the common interests of both being psych majors and runners, until Frank changed over to business. His father took him into the family insurance agency. After graduation, they got married, and after two miscarriages they had a son, nineteen years ago. After Nathan turned five, Emma went back to college for her Master's in Social Work (MSW) and now, fifteen years later, she was an established therapist who worked with couples and families. *Wounded healer*, Emma thought again, as she walked down to the kitchen.

Emma turned on the radio to the local public station. She was dressed in jeans and a big turtleneck. She thought, *No need to get fancy*, as she was just going to the gym for a swim. She ate a yogurt and had a cup of coffee before leaving.

The water seemed cold at first but her body warmed up quickly and, after the second lap, the water was refreshing. Emma flowed into interior mode, again reflecting on her dream, then her marriage. *I'm on a path that seems dark and twisted, yet I'm traveling fast. Maybe too fast, but I'm doing it. Then there is something to learn. My parents are a part of this lesson. They're smiling. And Mason is teaching. But I'm self-conscious.*

The slow repetition of her stroke, Emma's hand slipping into and under the water, moving and kicking herself through it, the otherworldly blue and quiet under the water became soothing and reassuring. She was able to put aside thoughts of her marriage, her work, the group, and her dreams. And her secret. There was only the water, her body, her breath.

Claudia Silverstein's office was plush with throw rugs, Tiffany lamps, and ferns. Emma sat across from the older woman on a small couch. After the opening pleasantries, there had been a long silence. Finally, Emma spoke.

"I've been thinking of quitting therapy. Or taking a break," Emma said.

Claudia was twenty years older than Emma. They had been meeting for the last few months, after Emma's nightmares began. Emma had gone to meet with Claudia, on and off in the past, once after her second miscarriage, and again during her postpartum depression, and a third time with Frank when they were working on their marriage. This time Emma had come to treatment after the death of her parents, just a few weeks apart, and her son leaving for college.

"What would you hope to achieve?" asked Claudia.

"I don't know that I want to *achieve* anything."

"Perhaps I worded that wrong. What's motivating this wish?"

"It has been months that we've been meeting. I just want to get on with my life."

"In what way?"

Emma paused and took a deep breath. She noticed Claudia's calm and envied it, how carefully she could pick her words, how clear she seemed.

Emma finally exhaled. She realized she'd been holding her breath. "I think I'm avoiding. Running or something."

Claudia asked, "How do you feel?"

"I feel blocked."

"What does it feel like? Where do you feel it in your body?"

Emma closed her eyes and frowned.

"Here and here," she said, motioning to her chest and her head. "I feel tight. Constricted. Maybe it was the chlorine."

The women discussed Emma's exercise regimen. Biking and swimming, running and aerobics. Claudia hadn't been aware that Emma was working out so rigorously. "That, or Prozac," said Emma.

Claudia asked Emma if she'd tried the spinning classes.

"Yes, I have, but the scenery doesn't change."

Claudia smiled.

"I'm looking for a change of scene. It always comes back to my marriage, doesn't it?"

"Before we get into that, how's your chest and head?"

Emma paused, closed her eyes. "Better," she said.

"So how's it going with Frank?"

"Not good. He's never home, and when he is we're either ignoring each other or arguing."

"How often is that?"

"Once a week. Every other week. He resents me. It is like I've stopped trying. I stopped going to the MSU games with him and we hardly ever make love. And I resent him because—"

"Because?"

Emma became aware of the clock ticking on the wall. She knew she was avoiding telling Claudia the truth. "Because he is who he is. As harsh as that sounds I'm just coming to that more and more. He can't help being who he is," said Emma.

"How do you mean that?"

"Who he is. Frank is—" Emma paused. "I'm feeling it again."

"What?"

"My head and my chest, constricting." Emma was frowning again and leaned back into the couch.

"You start talking about Frank, and you tighten up," noted Claudia, leaning forward.

"That's obvious."

"Is it?" asked Claudia, leaning back again.

"No. Not before you mentioned it to me," said Emma. "I'm sorry. I'm touchy about this stuff."

"No need to apologize. Just notice it," suggested Claudia.

"I tighten up when I think about my marriage. I'm snippy and defensive with you if you get me looking at it."

"So you believe that you're anxious, and your 'getting snippy' is a defense?" asked Claudia.

"I think so," answered Emma, calming.

"What are you anxious about, Emma? Do you know? What are you afraid of?"

Emma's answer was quiet, and almost imperceptible. "If I stay away from looking at my marriage, I won't have to do what I know I need to do."

"Which is?" asked Claudia.

"You're really starting to piss me off," said Emma with a smile on her face.

"I know, I know," answered Claudia. Her voice was like a cup of hot tea with honey.

Emma drew in a deep breath and closed her eyes and crossed her hands in her lap. "I'm afraid, Claudia." Emma began to cry.

"I know, I know."

"I'm afraid my marriage is over, now that Nathan is in college and my parents are gone. What reasons do I have to stay with Frank?"

"Why don't you sit with that? Your life has changed for you so much these past few years. Both of your parents dying, and even though it wasn't sudden, it was a surprise to have them both die so close to each other. You're out from under their expectations. And wrestling with your own grief. So who are you? You're no longer a daughter, your role as a mother has changed as well. And as a wife, you've complained about Frank's involvement with his work. You're doing a lot of questioning and also working out a lot of loss."

"Yeah, I guess so."

"You thought about taking a break from therapy, but it sounds like you'd like to take a break from your ambivalence, your losses. Of course, you can stop therapy any time you like.

But I'm not sure this is what you'd really like to end. And you don't need to decide anything today," said Claudia.

"No, I guess not." Emma sighed and opened her eyes.

"Shall we make another appointment?" asked Claudia.

Emma took a deep breath and then nodded in agreement.

Outside the office Emma kicked herself. Emma reflected that Claudia was a good therapist. Emma realized that it was her own failing, not Claudia's. Another week and she still hadn't mentioned falling in love with Dylan.

Emma's life revolved around working out, checking her email, getting ready for work, checking her email, getting to work, checking her email, seeing clients, and, in between, checking her email. She would see Frank some evenings and meet with Betty for coffee or some other colleague for lunch. And in between, she checked her blackberry.

Emma didn't work late on Thursday evening. After her last client, she stopped by the grocery store and picked up a few extras. Flowers, some fresh green beans, mushrooms, and a good red wine.

The Davis residence was an old Cape Cod that rested on the nook of a quaint street in town, shaded by oak and maple trees whose leaves had just begun to spin a cornucopia of color. After Frank's serious salary bump a few years ago, they had to decide whether to move to Okemos or one of the other 'burbs that was experiencing expansive growth, with steeple peaked homes and cathedral ceilings springing up like mushrooms all across the outskirts of town. Emma urged Frank to keep the house and the charm of the old neighborhood, and they had compromised by redecorating over the past few years. Emma loved her hardwood floors, the gas stove with electric convection oven, the graphite countertops, and hand-built cabinets. Frank had a large back deck built for himself, with a permanent grill. His den sported a plasma TV screen and home theater accruements.

By the time Frank came home, Emma was cooking. She'd called earlier and asked if he would be home by 6 p.m.

"Smells good," Frank said, as he walked through the back door at six on the dot. He wore a grey suit from work.

"Doesn't it?" Emma answered.

"Big game tonight on the Deuce," Frank said.

Emma frowned. She sighed, thinking *No one said it was going to be easy*. "When does it start?" she asked.

"Eight o'clock. Miami and—"

Emma didn't hear the second team, as Frank had left to go upstairs and change. He usually took a quick shower after work.

She made a salad and warmed the bread while Frank showered. She started to hum a tune that they used to listen to in college—Al Green's "Let's Stay Together."

"Nathan called and left a message," Emma mentioned when Frank retuned, wearing khakis and a green sweater over his T-shirt.

"Oh? What did he say?"

"Send money."

They both laughed.

"No. Really, he said that he was going to stay in Grand Rapids for the weekend. There's going to be a party Saturday. I think he's met a girl," Emma said.

"Good for him. I'll have to find someone to take the ticket for the State game. Want to go?" asked Frank. He poured a glass of wine for each of them. Emma was putting the chicken on a serving platter. She started to frown, but then smiled and looked Frank in the face.

"Umm, I was hoping to get the garden ready for winter but, you know what? I can do that Sunday. Sure. Who are we playing?"

"Notre Dame. It should be a good one. We're both ranked."

Emma didn't always serve Frank dinner. Quite often they ate separately, and he cooked almost as often as she did.

By the time dinner was ready, Frank had told Emma about Michigan State's chances in the Big Ten and how he'd met the defensive line's coach at the bar, and his concerns about the secondary. Emma listened and even asked a couple of questions.

Dinner was ready, and they were eating shortly after seven. Emma had a glass of wine with dinner and stopped after that. Both of her parents had been alcoholics, and since college, Emma had made a deal with herself to rarely drink and when she did, to limit herself to one. No exceptions.

Frank asked her about her day, during a dessert of apple cobbler, vanilla ice cream, and decaf coffee.

"The practice is full. That's good. And my caseload is the usual, couples and families. But my Dream Group met the first time last week."

"How'd it go?"

"Oh, I felt awkward and the group was—well, half of them seemed anxious and didn't say much. But they showed up. It is a start," she said. Emma looked at Frank and said, "So is this."

Frank smiled. "What? What are we starting?"

"Life after Nathan. Don't you ever worry that we could lose each other?"

"No. I never thought that," said Frank, smiling, and spooning the last of the pie into his mouth. "The game is about to start."

Emma told Frank she was going to tend to the dishes before joining him in the den. She looked at the wine, noticed that it was still half full, shrugged then shuddered before corking it and putting it back in the refrigerator. She joined Frank in the den. He had his brief case open and his laptop set up next to him.

"Working?"

"I just thought I'd get some paperwork done and look at our finances. The 401(k) has been taking a beating. I'm thinking about making some changes."

"Frank," Emma took a deep breath, "I really hoped to make this a special night."

"It is special."

"I thought we'd talk and make love."

Frank looked up from his lap top.

"I miss every cue, huh?"

"Yes, you do." Emma was wringing her hands.

"Want to make love now? In the den?"

"Frank," Emma said with a pleading look on her face, "I want to share my life with someone special. I want to have somebody I love and somebody who loves me."

"But I do love you. And you still love me don't you?"

Emma felt a sharp pang of disappointment. She thought about his question. *Do I still love you?*

"You're a good man and a good father," she said carefully, "and a good provider."

"You left out good husband," said Frank.

"I think *you* left out the good husband," said Emma. She immediately regretted her sarcasm. It was an old habit and a hard one to break.

"Ouch."

"I'm sorry," she said. "It's me. Not you. You're fine. I haven't been happy lately, and it's not your fault. I'm going to read."

"We still going to the State game Saturday?"

Emma considered the tableaux, her pleading, Frank's distractions. He seemed perfectly content, though. It was *her* dissatisfaction, once again an inside job. She answered his question.

"Sure."

"Emma?"

"Yeah?"

"What about making love?"

Emma bit her lower lip, holding back a sarcastic reply. *Don't say it, don't say it*, instead whispering, "Only if we do it right here, right now."

And they did.

And Emma barely thought about her new friend Dylan.

CHAPTER TWO

JAKE'S VOICE

I live in the night. I've worked midnights on the psych unit for years now and so when other people are dreaming, I'm working. I don't mind the work, but every now and then, I wonder if I'll show up for work and they'll tell me I can't go home. Maybe I'm the one who should get locked up.

During the day I try to sleep. You get used to it—close a room off and get some good blinds and keep a humidifier humming. Then I can sleep. Unless I have nightmares. Especially vampire nightmares.

I've always loved vampires. They scared the shit out of me as a kid. I mean, I guess I love being scared. Anyway, they don't scare me now. Not when I'm awake. I'll watch horror movies night and day. I used to read a lot of horror novels. I don't read that much any more. But I used to read Stephen King and Anne Rice and Edgar Allen Poe and H.P. Lovecraft and Wes Craven. I loved being scared. That seems crazy, because I obviously don't love being scared. I wouldn't have joined a Dream Group if I loved my nightmares. I don't know why I have them. I wish they'd stop. But I do love scary movies.

It wasn't always that way. When I was first scared by a vampire movie I was about eight years old. I was playing with my friend Dan and we went over to his house, and his older brother was home and was watching a scary movie. It was Lost Boys *and we watched it on videocassette. They were the first in the neighborhood with a VCR, and that seemed really exotic back then, being able to rent and watch a movie in your own house.*

The movie did a job on me. I could barely get home. I didn't want to see the color red for a month. I slept for the next few years with my neck covered by my sheets.

I still do that when I get scared.

Now, my dreams scare me. I do all right in the daylight. But I get nightmares, and they're often vampires or zombies. I blame my job. As a psych tech, I have to see some awful shit. When a paranoid schizophrenic is in psychotic mode, or even after, when they've been "zombified" by their meds, that's some crazy stuff.

I didn't mean to stay on the psych unit. It has been ten years. Somehow, I got stuck. I don't have much to do with my family back in Chicago. I fell in love with a girl at MSU, we got jobs at the hospital, we were going to go back to get our Master's degrees and open a practice in Lansing together, or maybe move away. But she left. I stayed at the hospital. And I left school.

I've just gone through another breakup. It doesn't seem to matter much to me. Something is missing. Anyway.

I love jazz. Somewhere down the line, I started listening to music that seemed to match what was going on inside me. Mingus, with his blue anguish, Bird and his super hyped intellect, Monk and his child like little ditties, Miles with his badass attitude, and Trane. Trane is something else. No matter how crazy my life seems, I can listen to jazz and it speaks to

*me. It calms me down and stirs me up at the same time. I don't know how
else to describe it. Anyway.*

*I wonder about the connection between jazz and horror movies. They
both make my hair stand up. Other than that, I don't know.*

*I saw an article in the paper on Emma Davis starting a "Dream
Group" and thought about my nightmares. I've avoided therapy like the
plague. I don't really know why. But there was a disclaimer in the article
that this wasn't going to be therapy. It might be therapeutic. I thought it
might help with my nightmares. I don't know. Anyway.*

Jake Harrison parked his car behind the main hospital and
walked into the building labeled "Mental Health Center." The
cool fall air felt good on his face and he was humming Mingus's
"Goodbye Porkpie Hat," as he approached the door. The door was
locked after 11 p.m., so he let himself in by punching up the code.

By the time Jake hit the floor where he worked, the nursing
report had started. The unit was quiet and Jake slipped by
the lone staff member in the lobby, a receptionist who was
lingering from the afternoon shift. She looked at her watch
and pointed to the clock on the wall, and ran a finger across
her throat. He was late again.

"I know, I know," sighed Jake, his lanky six foot, two inch
frame easing into the nurse's station.

The report was on and there were a dozen people in the
room, Jake joining the four others from the midnight shift
with the seven techs and nurses that made up the afternoon
shift.

They made a good-looking group, Jake reflected, looking
around the room. The nurses and techs tended to be in their
twenties, often working their way through college or nursing

school, some a little older. But someone with ten years of experience on the psych unit was considered a grizzled veteran. Jake didn't look that much older, with his shoulder length sandy hair framing his face and blue eyes.

"Art Jackson. No change, he slept after dinner for an hour. He's still in the day room. Dr. Lee has increased his Haldol," said the nurse reading from a list of charts.

Jake was in and out during the report. He had just started his tenth year working on the unit and was one of the oldest psych techs at age thirty-two. He attended MSU after taking "a break" post high school that stretched for years. His intent was to get a B.A. in psych, work for a year or two in a psych hospital to make sure he could do the work, and then move on to get his Masters and Ph.D. to set up his own practice. He still hadn't taken his first course to start his Masters. He hadn't even applied.

Once report was over the staff filed out. The afternoon shift was leaving and the charge nurse for midnights, Yvonne Webster, a squat African-American woman who was four years younger than Jake, gave him a clipboard with the names of each patient printed onto a graph along with the hours 11:30 through 7 a.m.

"First rounds are yours Jake. See to it that Mr. Jackson gets to bed, and I'd like to talk to you sometime after that," Yvonne said.

Jake took the clipboard and made a sour face after the nurse turned her back. Jake walked into the day room, the keys he carried jingling softly with each step, hanging off his belt over his khaki slacks. Art Jackson was sitting at a table moving a salt-shaker and a tab of paper so that they lined up with copies of *National Geographic* and *Sports Illustrated*. As Jake approached Mr. Jackson, he thought how much he looked like Jack Nicholson. *If McMurphy hadn't died, this would be him*, thought Jake.

"What's up Art?" asked Jake.

"I'm—I'm controlling the universe," said Art, carefully lining up the papers and magazines so that they were square with the edges of the table. He looked at Jake and placed a finger across his lips and issued a, "Ssshhhh."

When Jake spoke he did so in a low voice, almost a whisper. "Everything in the right place?" asked Jake.

"I think so," frowned Art, his hands held carefully over the table, as if a sudden movement could have disastrous repercussions.

"I was just out in the universe," said Jake.

"Oh?" Art looked up at Jake. His eyebrows arched, his mouth a large "O" amongst the stubble of his beard.

"Yeah—it's dark. Nighttime. Lights out. Time for bed," said Jake, quietly.

"Uh huh," agreed Art, looking out the window at the dark sky. Standing up, Art walked with Jake. The shuffling of cheap hospital slippers whispered across the floor, accented by the jangle of Jake's keys. Jake thought, *A percussion duet*, but kept that thought to himself.

After leaving Mr. Thomas in his room, Jake peeked in from room to room, putting a check behind each name as he saw them, mostly asleep, some needing a hushed reminder of "lights out," or "night, night."

Upon returning to the nurse's station he asked Yvonne, "What's up?"

She asked him to step in her office and close the door.

Uh oh, thought Jake.

"Jake, you were late again," Yvonne said.

"Yeah, look, I'm sorry, I overslept."

"Is there a problem?" she asked.

"No. I mean, I've had some trouble sleeping."

"Jake," Yvonne opened the drawer of her steel desk and took out a stack of time slips and said, "you've been consistently late since July—it's getting worse."

"I do a good job. I don't miss work," said Jake. He stopped himself, afraid of sounding like a whiner.

Yvonne looked at Jake and said, "Jake, you have a wonderful rapport with the patients and everyone on the staff likes you. I like you. You're likable. But you need to be here on time."

"Okay, is that all?"

"No. I'm wondering if I should make a referral to the employee assistance counselor. You did go through a breakup this summer—"

"And that is none of your business," Jake snapped, his lips drawn back. He quickly looked away, down at his lap, then the floor, and finally out the window. His reflection stared back at him. Jake sighed, and said, "I'm sorry."

"I'm sorry, too, Jake. If there's a problem let me know."

"I'm in therapy," said Jake.

"Oh. Well, good," said the charge nurse. "I didn't know. And like you say, it's none of my business. But I try to stay up on who is doing good therapy in the community. Do you mind me asking who you're seeing?"

"Emma Davis."

"Oh, I hear she's good," said Yvonne. She smiled at Jake and said, "Just be on time. This is a warning."

Emma was late finishing up with her five o'clock family session. Setting the next appointment with the nervous mother was taking longer than she thought, and she realized that she was making the Dream Group wait in the small waiting room of her suite. She took a quick look in the room and had seen all four of the group members. Mason and Marianne were talking while Jake was sitting next to Holly, leaning over her, while her body was leaning away from him. Emma told them to come back to her office and she took a quick break in the bathroom. *Well, at least they all showed up,* she thought.

Emma started by making small talk with the group members. This was the way she always opened her sessions. It helped her to connect a little with her clients before they got into the content of their therapy, and it also helped her notice what kind of mood they were in. The group seemed loose and interested in being there. Emma started to talk about dreams.

"So, this is our second group. Tonight what I'd like to do is see how everyone is doing on their journaling and maybe we can do some work on a dream or two," Emma said. She introduced the night's topic as a focus on "awareness."

"Focusing on dreaming is like focusing on consciousness," began Emma. "It's such a basic thing, but it's like focusing on your posture in yoga or on your breathing in meditation. It's something we're doing all the time, yet most of the time, we're not really aware of it. Does that make sense?" Emma asked. The group members nodded.

"So tonight what I'd like to do is to focus on awareness. And maybe do an exercise to help with awareness," suggested Emma.

Jake responded by saying, "I wasn't aware of having a problem with awareness."

"How could you be? Be aware of something you're not aware of?" responded Emma with a smile. She enjoyed Jake's playfulness.

"I was joking," Jake said.

"I was aware of that. And you're aware of being aware of joking," said Emma.

"And you're not aware of being a sarcastic—" interrupted Holly.

"Asshole? Oh, I'm totally aware of that," punctuated Jake.

Emma was surprised at this exchange. *What had been going on in the waiting room? It didn't seem like Holly to be hostile.*

"Maybe we could let Ms. Davis finish her point?" suggested Mason. He had leaned forward and was frowning at Holly and Jake.

"Thanks, Mason. And please call me Emma. I wanted to say that a lot of dream work is 'quick fix' kind of stuff. Dream dictionaries or charts that tell you what a dream means. I don't agree with that kind of an approach."

"Could you say more about that?" asked Mason.

"Sure," said Emma. "I think that we need to take each dream on its own terms. You can't just toss out a particular symbol and suggest that it means the same thing to everyone."

"Wouldn't that negate the idea of a collective unconscious? Sorry to interrupt. And what about archetypes?" asked Mason.

Emma was impressed that Mason seemed well-versed in Jungian terminology. She raised her eyebrows at him before answering.

"Not a problem. For those of you not familiar with the idea of 'collective unconscious' or 'archetypes'—I hate to use jargon—" Emma frowned while she searched for the right words. "I realize that Jung gave universal definitions to certain symbols, but I think that even those symbols have unique and individual meaning. For instance, let's say you dreamed of a bull. What does it mean?" asked Emma, looking around the group. To her relief, they all responded.

"Virility," said Mason.

"Bullshit," barked Jake.

"Strength," suggested Holly.

"The Market," injected Marianne.

"Great," said Emma. "Now, what if you lived in Spain?"

Mason said, "I see, once you consider the implications of societal context—"

"Huh?" asked Jake.

"Or India?" asked Emma. "What would 'bull' represent if you lived in India?"

Holly said, "Oh, I get it. A symbol has different meanings in different countries."

"Yes," responded Emma. "Often a symbol has different meanings from culture to culture, and not only that, it can have different meanings from family to family, from person to person."

"What does this have to do with awareness?" asked Jake.

"We did get far afield," said Emma. "What I'd like you to focus on, to begin with, is not so much what your dream means as how they feel."

"Why would we do that?" asked Marianne, crossing her legs and folding her arms.

Emma noticed that Marianne appeared uncomfortable talking about feelings. She had a choice to explore this with her or to keep things on a more surface level. Given the premise of this group, she opted to keep it light.

"To become more aware," said Emma. She wanted to get a sense of how Marianne would respond as the exploration of dreams gradually became more intense, and how Marianne would handle her anxiety. "One way this helps, when doing these exercises, is you start to notice more about your dreams. You begin to become more aware even while you are dreaming."

"Could I get to the point of controlling my dreams?" asked Marianne.

Could I get to the point of controlling my life? was the thought that Emma had, but discarded that as a response. "Some people have experienced a kind of awareness that they are actually dreaming while they are dreaming, and then have control, or some amount of control, in the middle of their dream. They call it lucid dreaming."

"What kind of control?" asked Marianne.

"Well, they might decide they can fly, or they can introduce another character into the dream, or even decide to wake up," said Emma.

Emma noticed that Marianne was interested in this notion of being able to control her dreams. Jake was leaning back, his long legs extended into the center of the group, but his head seemed barely into it. Mason was focused, his head resting against the palm of his hand, and Holly seemed pensive. Her lips were tight, and her hands were clutching the edge of her chair. Emma continued to talk about awareness, even while being aware of watching how the others were reacting.

"But for now, the first step is to just become more aware during your dreams, and one way to do this is become more aware in your waking life. Notice what you notice. Open up your senses. Take stock of what's going on around you. Do that a few times a day and when you dream, you'll start doing the same thing. You'll start to notice more colors, you'll start hearing and touching and smelling—"

"I never smell in my dream," said Jake.

"I find that hard to believe," responded Holly.

Jake opened his mouth to speak but no words came out.

Emma looked at them. Holly was clearly upset with Jake.

"Holly, do you need to talk about something regarding Jake?" asked Emma.

Holly took a deep breath. She said, "It's probably my problem, but I notice that Jake's been drinking."

Emma nodded. Holly was in A.A., she remembered.

"Hey, I had a beer with my dinner," said Jake.

"Well, you smell like it. And I'm not used to smelling alcohol in my face," said Holly. "Don't you all smell it?"

Mason and Marianne shook their heads. Emma hadn't smelled anything herself, but it explained Holly's snarky attitude.

"We didn't talk about this before, but it's probably a good idea not to drink before the group. Or do any drug, for that matter," said Emma.

Jake nodded. "Cool."

"Now, here's a list of questions I'll pass out, and you apply these to your dreams when you journal them," instructed Emma.

Mason sighed as he looked at the list of questions. "I'm concerned about this smacking of object constructivists," he said.

"Dude, I'm not getting anything you're saying tonight," said Jake.

Emma saw Holly flush and open her mouth, and she interjected before Holly could speak. "Holly," Emma said, holding out her hand in a "halt" motion before she could stop herself, "let me interject. I'm asking all of you to try something new. Put aside your biases, be they personal, emotional, political, or intellectual. Just try this."

"I'll try," said Holly, looking at the questions.

"Great," said Emma.

"I didn't mean to come off as resistant," said Mason. "I tend to make an intellectual inquiry into anything I do." Emma felt things were moving fast. She wanted to engage Mason on a discussion of object constructivism, but worried that it might just be an intellectual exercise. At the same time, something was cooking with Jake. She couldn't put her finger on it. The decisions made in interactions happen in the blink of an eye, and she made a decision to try to bridge the gap between her client's styles of working with this exercise.

"Of course," said Emma. "We all reply to something new in our own way. Jake's one way, you're another. I'm another."

Jake looked away from Emma, down to the floor and said, "That's a nice way of saying that he's smart and I'm an asshole."

"Jake!" exclaimed Emma. "I didn't say that nor even imply it. But the way you filter the world is through that sarcasm of yours. And you are provocative." Emma took a breath, saw her hands waving in front of her, and folded them in her lap. She'd hoped that she hadn't been too strong with him, but she hated being misrepresented.

"Provocative?" asked Jake. He appeared to be thinking it over. Emma decided to proceed.

"Yes," she answered. "You provoke people to either dismiss you or fight with you."

"Okay. That's fair," said Jake. "I get a lot of that."

Emma felt relieved that he'd taken the confrontation so well. She was surprised at her reaction. But Jake seemed to be doing okay with her interpretation, so she decided to take it another step.

"So, has that been working for you?" Emma said with a smile.

Marianne giggled and said, "Ooh, You're good. Remind me not to take you on."

"You'll get your turn," Emma said. She turned back to Jake and raised her eyebrows.

"I get your point," Jake answered. "And I already admitted I was an asshole."

"You're doing it again. Still. You're doing it right now."

"What?" Jake asked.

"Provoking us into—" interjected Holly.

"Dismissing you or—" said Emma, as though she were prompting him.

After a pause, Mason finished with, "—fighting with you."

"Okay, okay, okay! Stop already!" said Jake. His voice was raised, and Emma noticed that his cheeks were flushed.

"Okay," said Emma, unconsciously mirroring his use of the word. "I've pushed too far. Are we okay, Jake?"

"It's been a bad week. I'd rather not talk about it. And those are your rules," said Jake.

Emma was surprised how volatile his mood was. He appeared to be taking the feedback well enough, yet—

"You're right," said Emma. "Fair enough. Back to dreams."

The group took up her cue and looked at their handouts again. They were quiet for a minute. Holly finally responded.

"This third question: 'What is your role in this dream— active or passive?'"

"Yes," said Emma. Her blue eyes widened as she answered. "Are you the actor or the acted upon? Are you an observer? A victim? Are you watching the dream like it's on a TV screen or through your eyes?"

"Now, I always see my dreams that way, like they're on TV," answered Holly. "What does that mean?"

"That's my point. I'm encouraging you to not make it mean anything right now. Just be aware of it," said Emma.

"But I'd like to know what it means," said Marianne. Her demeanor was insistent, the tone of her voice demanding.

Emma wondered how far to push this point. She didn't want to just reflect; neither did she want to preach.

"Marianne, can I ask you a question?"

"Sure."

"Why? Why would you want to know what it *means*?"

"So I can understand."

"But why? Why is it important that your dreams *mean* something?"

"You're not taking *me* on now, are you?" asked Marianne. She had a coy smile.

"No. Well, maybe a little," said Emma. "Our dreams are profound works of art created by our subconscious. If we live with them and learn to appreciate them, I think we'll get more from them than if we just take a quick, instant answer. For instance, what does *The Mona Lisa* mean? Or *The Godfather* or *Citizen Kane*? Or what does Beethoven 'mean'? Does that make sense?"

Marianne nodded.

Mason said, "So your point is to encourage us to not be reductive about our dreams?"

"That's accurate," said Emma. Then she said, "Now, who has a dream?"

After a few moments of silence, Holly asked, "Would someone else prefer to tell a dream? Is anyone not having nightmares?"

There was a long pause. Emma felt herself sink. *Was this working?*

Mason finally said, "I'll go. I had a dream this past week I'll talk about. Many of my dreams are cinematic. They appear on a big screen but now that you mention it, Emma. I always see the dream from right here," he motioned to his eyes with his fore and middle fingers, "behind my own eyes. So I don't see myself in the dream, I am myself. So, in this dream I had this week I'm traveling. I travel a lot in my dreams and I've traveled a lot in life. But this week I was in London. The city wasn't familiar and London actually is familiar to me, but I had to get from one side of town to the other."

"And how were you trying to do this?" asked Emma.

"Oh, I was using the Tube, their mass transit system."

"And what was that like for you?"

"Well, as I said, this is not an unfamiliar dream," said Mason. "Traveling, usually in a big city, and I'm not certain how to get where I'm going, but I eventually figure it out."

"Do you ever get lost?" asked Jake.

"No, although sometimes I'm clearly searching."

"Anything different about this dream?" asked Emma.

"Well, it's something of a blur, and I guess that speaks to your exercises on awareness," said Mason.

"Mason, do you know how old you are, in the dream?"

"Now that you mention it, I always feel like I felt when I was younger," reflected Mason.

"Which was?"

"Well, when I was younger I felt a greater ease of movement, less aches and pains."

"Less?" asked Emma. "So you sometimes experience pain in your dream?"

"No, not often."

"Any other observations or questions from the group?" asked Emma.

"Yeah. Want to trade dreams?" asked Jake.

There was some laughter from the group.

After a pause, Emma asked, "No one else?"

There was more silence.

Emma finally said, "Okay, let's look at just one aspect of this dream. Travel. We could look at London, but the repeated theme is travel, right?"

"Yes," said Mason.

"So let's look at layers of interpretation," said Emma. "Mason, if a Martian were to ask you what is travel, how would you answer that?"

"Well, travel is how we get from one place to the next," Mason said, looking at the ceiling.

"For what purpose?"

"Business. Pleasure. New experiences."

"Now, if you were to describe the idea of 'travel' to someone from a foreign country?"

"I would imagine I would have to say it's a way to experience the 'other,' the unknown or less known," answered Mason.

"Now, how about a fellow citizen of the U.S.A.?" asked Emma.

"It depends. If the person is a fellow traveler, I'd just compare experiences. It's a way to relate. If it's someone who doesn't travel, I become aware of my privileged status."

"And what did travel mean to your family?"

Mason smiled before answering. "Oh, it was a big deal. I'm not a Michigander, but I am a Midwesterner. I'm from French Lick, Indiana, a tiny town—a village really."

"Larry Bird's home town?" asked Jake.

"Right, our claim to fame. I was already teaching at MSU when he came around. But travel was a luxury and something highly valued. My dad worked at the bank. He saved money and took us to Chicago on a weekend. That was a big deal."

"What did you do? In Chicago?" asked Emma.

"This was after the war. I still remember the headlines. We probably looked like a bunch of hicks because the main thing I remember is walking around downtown staring up at the buildings."

Emma noticed the group was enjoying Mason's story. "What was that like?" she asked.

"Amazing. It was so different than what I was used to. A whole new world opened to me. We went to a big store, maybe it was Marshall Field's, but I'd never seen such a big store. And we went to a museum. It was the Natural History Museum, and that was fascinating. And we went to the cinema."

"Oh, yes?" asked Emma. "What did you see?"

"A John Ford western. *She Wore a Yellow Ribbon*. And I fell in love with movies and always connected them up with that experience of the larger, outside world."

It didn't escape Emma that Mason's profession was teaching the study of movies, a childhood experience that left such a strong impression on him.

"You have siblings?" asked Emma.

"My little sister died. She was hit by a car when I was in high school. She was only ten. And my older brother, who's still in French Lick."

Emma noted Mason's sister's death, but decided not to comment on it. She asked instead, "How's your experience of travel different than your brother's?"

"He is a homebody. He decided to stay put in French Lick and took on a job in the hardware store. He's never even visited me here in East Lansing. He was a jock and his glory days were in playing basketball in high school. Kind of sad, but I shouldn't judge."

Emma looked towards Marianne, then Holly, and Jake. "So, do you see the difference now between dream interpretation and dream appreciation?"

"You're looking to find the layers of meanings here," responded Mason.

"You want us to make a soufflé instead of scrambled eggs," suggested Marianne.

"Or at least an omelet. Now, Mason's brother isn't in this dream and his dream isn't set in Chicago and the ideas of 'privilege' and 'relatedness' aren't specific. Once Mason begins to describe his experience of travel, do you see the shadings of these things in the dream?"

Emma spent a good deal of the rest of the group going over some of the awareness questions on her handout, answering questions and giving explanations. After a while she looked up at the clock.

"I'm noticing that our time is up. Try some of those 'dream questions' on awareness, and we'll meet the same time next week."

Emma was pleased that the group had seemed engaged and had gotten through the sticky exchanges with Jake.

"If we had more time with this dream, we could explore the layers of meaning with 'London' as a symbol. London as a place, as a state of the mind. See? So, let's do a quick check of how we're all doing before group ends. Mason?"

"I'm good. This was useful. I'm feeling a little nostalgic."

"Holly?"

"I'm okay. I'm still having nightmares and I'm not too crazy about becoming more 'aware' of them, but I'll do what I need to do."

"Jake?" asked Emma, hoping he had calmed down.

"I don't know," said Jake.

"How do you mean?" asked Emma.

"Well, I feel like I got put in my place tonight and you're pretty clever, but I didn't come here to be attacked."

Holly leaped in. "Jake, I don't think Emma was trying to—"

At that moment Jake stood up and walked out of the room. He didn't slam the door; he simply opened it and closed it behind him. Emma made it a rule not to follow clients out of her office if they made dramatic exits, but Jake's leaving was unexpected.

"I'll call him and get this straightened out. I think he'll be back. Marianne?" Emma kicked herself immediately. How could she have misread Jake so? Why hadn't she done more to connect with him after confronting him? And should she take the time to process this with the group, even though time was up? She'd already asked Marianne how she was doing, and Marianne was about to respond. Emma noticed that Marianne seemed upset.

"Well, I guess I have to decide whether I'm coming back, too. This isn't quite what I bargained for," said Marianne.

"Oh. Okay," said Emma. She really felt off balance now. "What's different?" she asked Marianne.

"This is upsetting, and I get enough of people being upset at work," replied Marianne.

"We're just getting started. I'm sure if you give it some time, you can be more comfortable. Would you be willing to call me, or we can talk after?"

Marianne said, "That won't be necessary. I'll give it another week."

The sun was setting as Emma drove down the tree-lined streets of her neighborhood. The angle of the sunlight illuminated the changing leaves to brilliant effect. Emma felt exhausted from the group. Still, she appreciated the beauty as she drove up her driveway. The shadows were long, the sun nearly down, the colors of the leaves a collection of oranges, yellows, and reds.

At home, Emma picked up a voice mail from Frank. He reminded her that he'd be in Detroit for a meeting, and that he'd be going to a Red Wings game. She knew it would be one or even two o'clock before he'd be back. Emma ate a salad from the fridge, drank a bottle of water and decided what to do for the night. She had three hours before she needed to be in bed to get her regular seven hours of sleep. She had three discretionary hours to use. She could watch a movie. There were a bunch of them that Frank had bought, which weren't even opened yet. Or she could read her new Barbara Kingsolver novel, or check the computer.

Emma changed into a fleece pullover and a pair of shorts. Then she threw in a load of laundry, a job that never seemed finished. She fed the big calico cat, Cleo, and decided she could enter her Dream Group notes on the computer. And check her email. The computer was on and the screensaver looked like an underwater panorama of brightly colored tropical fish. After writing her notes, she clicked online and saw the usual junk email. Advertisements to reduce debt, sexual enhancement drugs for sale, or offers on how to make money at home. Not the familiar address she hoped to see. Emma noticed a mix of disappointment and relief.

She clicked on "files" and then "notes from D" and read the most recent. It was from September tenth, now three weeks old. It read:

Hi Emma,

Really enjoyed our lunch yesterday. Thanks for introducing me to Ethiopian cuisine and Bubble Tea at the other place (?).

What we talked about over our tea has gotten me thinking. Of course, you have a lot more to think about than I do. You are attached, and I am not. I hope I wasn't pushy. I'd like to give this a month or so to sink in. I really don't want to act hastily or impulsively. I don't want to do anything we might regret. Or that you might regret. I don't think I'd have any regrets.

Are you sure Frank can't read your emails?

Take care,

Dylan

Emma typed:

Dear Dylan,

I can't get you out of my mind. I'm crazy about you, and I've been this way since meeting you at the conference. The lunches have been great and the trip to the lake was the best. I'm afraid Frank is history.

See Me Soon—

Passionately,

Emma

Instead of hitting "send," she hit "delete." She went to bed, thinking about Dylan, and then worrying about her marriage, then dreaming about Dylan.

The following morning Emma went for her swim. She saw an early client and then went to meet her friend and colleague, Betty Williams, for coffee.

The women talked about their children for a few minutes. Betty had a couple of kids who were away at college. She was widowed, her husband having died from cancer a few years ago. Betty worked and made money and took care of her kids, and did little socially.

They were comparing notes on early college experiences, when a tall man in an olive suit and tan rain coat walked into the coffee shop and ordered something at the counter.

"Check him out," Betty exclaimed in a low voice, motioning with her eyes before saying, "Oooh, I forgot you're married."

"Well," said Emma with a quick glance over her shoulder, "I can still look. Not my type."

"Look again, girl, he's pretty. *GQ* guy."

"Naw. Why don't you get his number?" asked Emma.

"Maybe I will," Betty said, and licked her lips. At that moment another man entered the coffee shop, waved at the first man and they hugged. "Oh, not another 'Friend of Dorothy'?"

"You don't know that," said Emma. "And if he is, so what?"

"Nothing. I just don't approve. Not that *that* makes any difference," said Betty. "Anyway, it's nice to see a woman so true to her man. How's it with Frank?"

Emma sighed, took a look over her shoulder again and said, "Maybe I was too hasty."

Betty laughed. "Is there trouble in paradise?"

Emma stared into the foam of her latte.

"I've fallen out of love. It's complicated. God, I sound trite."

Betty frowned. "I'm sorry Emma. Is it serious?"

"It might be. I mean, we've grown apart. We were a family, but now that Nathan's gone to college—I mean, I try, but—"

"Are you seeing someone?" asked Betty.

"What do you mean?" asked Emma. She fumbled with her cup, almost knocking it over, and wiped up some coffee with her paper napkin.

"I mean, are you getting some? Therapy?"

"Oh, yeah. Of course. The shoesmith's children need shoes y'know." Emma folded her hands in her lap.

"Okay," said Betty. She had a serious expression on her face. "Relationships have their ups and downs. I'd hate to see something happen to you and Frank, but mostly I want to see you happy."

"Thanks."

"You know, Emma, you've been through a lot. Your parents died, one after the other, and you never talked much about it. But I knew, I remembered."

"What?" asked Emma.

"That they were drinkers. Your relationship with them, it must have been hard."

"I moved away when I entered college and I never went back. But a lot of times I feel like I'm really, I don't know—" Emma rummaged through her purse for a chocolate, offered one to Betty who turned it down with a shake of her head, then finished her thought. "I've been alone. On my own. I've always been self-reliant, but maybe, too much. Sometimes, I think about how I have just never been able to trust. It makes me feel like I'm all messed up inside, sometimes."

"No, let me be clear," Betty reached over and touched Emma's arm. "It's not that you're messed up because of conflicts with your mom and dad. I'm thinking that maybe now—"

"What?"

"Maybe now that they're gone, you can make another choice for yourself."

"Oh. That's not what I thought you were getting at."

"Girl, you are so hard on yourself. Why don't you do what makes you happy?"

"Do you think I should leave Frank?"

"How the hell should I know? Yes, if it makes you happy. No—if it makes you happy."

"You know, Dr. Laura would disagree with your advice."

Betty snorted.

Emma whispered, "Actually, I did meet someone."

Betty asked, her own voice a whisper, "Who is he?"

Emma pointed with her thumb at the *GQ* guy, who was sitting at a table across the room, talking loudly on his cell phone. "It's not him. Seriously, I shouldn't have said anything. It's just a crush. I haven't even told my therapist yet."

"Ooh. I'm privileged."

Emma changed the topic by asking Betty how her practice was going. The two shared space in a suite, but it was hard to gauge how each other's business was going. After Betty described her struggles with managed care, she asked Emma, "How's the group?"

"Well, I'm surprised. A guy walked out of the group last night. I didn't see it coming. This guy is so incredibly sensitive, but he covers it up with his sense of humor. Then a woman said that it wasn't what she bargained for and she might not be back after next week. So I'm not so sure I have a group. Maybe I was too hard on him?"

Betty said, "Let me get this straight. You were 'too hard' on a guy in your dream group? What, was he having *bad* dreams?!"

"Yeah, I know. He's challenging."

"Well, maybe it was a good thing, then. I thought you said this group was going to be fun?"

"That's right. Once we got in the room I sensed a lot of pain and fear."

"People trying to get therapy by osmosis?" asked Betty. "Maybe they're getting more than they bargained for."

"Maybe I'm getting more than I bargained for. Look, coffee's on me. And next time we only talk about you."

"No way girl. Why would I want to look at myself when your life is so interesting?"

Mason poured himself a tumbler of water from his kitchen faucet, drank a quarter of it and walked past his wife, Mona, who was stirring soup at the stove. He entered his family room from the kitchen. His home was located on Sunset Street, a cozy neighborhood in the city of East Lansing, just a few blocks from Emma's home and just far enough away from the student population to be quietly comfortable.

Mason popped in a DVD of the Kurosawa movie, *Ikuru*. Black and white images appeared on the seventeen-inch television screen, and Mason cued to a scene of an old man sitting on a swing, rocking back and forth as he sings a Japanese nursery rhyme. The snow is falling in the picture and the man swings, apparently oblivious to the cold and the snow falling around him as he sings. Mason sighed as he watched the film.

His family room was cluttered with books and tapes and DVDs, most of them videos of classic and foreign films. One shelf held films of Fellini, Hitchcock, Bergman, Truffault. Many of the books were on film or travel, though some recent additions were Carl Jung's *Man and His Symbols* and James Hillman's *Dreams and the Underworld*.

Mason looked up as Mona called to him. "Mason, hey Buster, do you want some soup?"

He called back, "Okay, I'll be right there," and wiped away a tear as he turned off the TV and DVD player. He walked back into the kitchen, and Mona smiled at him. She was a handsome woman with grey hair and a fit figure, who had recently retired from her high school teaching career. "I recognize that tune," Mona said. "You're watching your new Kurosawa film, aren't you?"

"Yeah, one of the last scenes in one of his first movies. *Ikuru*. I don't know if I've ever seen a more poignant death scene. I've watched that movie, I don't know, dozens of times, but I don't ever recall crying at that scene before."

"Well, now that you're retired you can stop and smell the roses. Why not let yourself feel? It's probably good for you. I shed a few tears every day," said Mona, getting the bowls from the cupboard.

"You do?" asked Mason.

"Yes, and every day I laugh really hard. At least once. I bought some good bread. You want a slice with your soup?"

"Please. I'll cut it."

Mona ladled the soup from the pot into bowls.

"Chicken noodle. Homemade with those big Polish noodles you like so much, Buster!" Mona had been calling Mason "Buster" since their first meeting, when he'd hit her with a snowball by accident and she'd said, "Watch it, Buster!" After his apologies, he asked her out. Mason was so nervous that he forgot to tell her his name. So when he went to her dorm to take her to the movies she'd met him in the lobby with, "Hello, Buster," and had decided to keep it as a nickname for him ever since.

Mason opened the fridge and picked up an apple.

"This fruit is rotting," he said.

"Oh? Let me see," Mona said. "You can just cut around that part."

"No, thanks. The soup and the bread will be fine. More than enough."

Mason sat down at the simple wood table with Mona. They started to eat their soup in silence when Mona said, "We'll need to go to Chicago for Susan's fiftieth birthday party."

"My God! When is that?"

"You know when Susan's birthday is."

"April fifteenth—same as tax day. Her party's the same day?"

"Yes. Pete called to invite us, and he's trying to get people from all stages of her life."

"Great idea. 'This Is Your Life,' only for a birthday. He plans ahead, Pete does. But Mona, when did we get old enough to have a fifty-year-old daughter?"

"It was some time after you retired, Buster."

"Any excuse to go to Chicago is good. Why wait until April?" Mason ate more of his soup and then asked, "Say, what about Europe? London?"

Mona laughed. He watched her face as she laughed, and again reminded himself how lucky he was to be with such a beautiful woman.

"You research it, and we'll see what it costs and if we can afford it. We've got to remember we're on a limited budget."

"What if I publish the book on films, and it's a best seller?"

Mona smiled and blew on her spoon of soup. "How's your book coming?"

"Good. If nothing else, it's giving me an excuse to watch all my Kurosawa movies again."

"Are you writing?"

"No. Haven't started."

"Buster—"

"I think like Hitchcock. I'm getting the whole thing in my head and then when I actually write it, it's just getting down the tedious details."

"Whatever you say," she answered, shrugging her shoulders. For a few moments the couple ate in silence, and the only sound was the clink of spoons against bowls and the soft slurping of soup.

"No. I'm serious," said Mason. "The span of the man's life will be my main theme, and his influence on postmodern cinema."

"Okay. You're not eating your bread?"

"No. I guess I'm not that hungry."

"You still planning to volunteer for hospice?"

"Yeah. I haven't called yet but I will. Funny thing, being retired I don't feel like I have enough time to do anything. How did I ever find time to work?"

"Because you finally get to do what you want, Buster. And don't forget, we have tickets to the Wharton tonight to see the symphony."

That night Emma and Frank were on their way to the symphony at the Wharton. Frank had picked her up after work in his SUV, and was still wearing his suit. Emma had put on a dress and spent some time on her makeup. They'd caught a hurried dinner at a local restaurant before heading to the concert. Emma looked at her reflection in the small visor mirror from the passenger's seat, checking her makeup and freshening her lipstick.

"I know I said this before but thanks for doing this," said Emma.

"I thought it was quid pro quo Clarice," he said, in a fair imitation of Hannibal Lecter. Frank could be good at certain imitations, usually drawn from films. Emma always liked it when Frank was being playful.

She attempted an imitation of Clarice Starling, "I thought, Dr. Lecter, that if I'd go to the football game with you that you might go to the symphony with me."

"It puts the lotion in the basket," said Frank, imitating the Buffalo Bill character.

"Don't do that voice," said Emma.

"Why not?"

"That's too creepy."

"And Lecter is okay?"

"Lecter is funny. It's like imitating Dracula. No one takes you seriously."

"Okay. Whatever you say. I bet you had more fun at the game than I'll have tonight."

Emma bristled. "You know Frank, I really didn't want to go to that game, but I went because you wanted to go, and we've been so busy avoiding each other since Nathan went to school. I thought someone had to make the first move, and it clearly wasn't going to be you." She flipped the visor closed and shoved her lipstick into her purse, snapping it like an exclamation point.

"Okay, okay," said Frank. "Sorry. But we won."

"What?"

"The football game. In case you didn't notice."

"I noticed, Frank. That wasn't my point. My point was that I did what you wanted to do and didn't complain or whine."

"Until now," said Frank. They pulled into the parking ramp, and Frank gave the student attendant five dollars for parking.

"You think I'm whining?" whined Emma.

"That was an exaggeration. I'm sorry. I don't want to fight."

As they got out of their car, Emma noticed Mason from the group and a woman. *Probably his wife*, she thought, entering the Wharton. They were just a few feet away from them and Emma could see that Mason hadn't seen her, but she and Frank would be walking near them on the way to the hall.

She made a point not to initiate contact with clients outside of the office. If Mason saw her and waved or even stopped to introduce her to his companion, Emma would politely match whatever social contact he'd offer. But she would never initiate the contact. She saw Mason laughing at a remark the woman had just made.

"You know what I think?" asked Frank, angrily.

"No," said Emma. She hoped they wouldn't be having angry words in front of Mason on their way into the concert hall.

"I think you're unhappy, and I'm not blaming you. But maybe you should consider going back to Paxil."

Emma placed her hand on Frank's sleeve and stopped walking. She could see Mason get ahead of them in the crowd. She took a few steps away from the crowd and rounded a corner near the theater, still holding Frank's arm.

Emma flashed anger at him. Her blue eyes glistened, and she spoke calmly but insistently. "No, Frank. I'm not going back on medication. I'll admit I'm not happy. I'm struggling. I've gone through losses, but it's not pathology. It's life and I want to feel every goddamn second of it."

Frank seemed shocked. He didn't have a reply, and they were quiet during the rest of their walk into the hall.

Mason and the woman had entered before they did. Emma lost sight of them once they entered the foyer of the Wharton, packed with hundreds of people coming to hear the symphony. The auditorium was a jewel in the cultural landscape of East Lansing, and touring companies brought everything from musicals to dance performances, plays to chamber music. Tonight was a visit from the St. Petersburg symphony performing a program of *Prokofiev* and *Shostakovitch*.

After they sat down Emma mused, "This would feel more appropriate if it were winter. The Russians always remind me of winter."

"I was thinking it was frosty enough already," said Frank, and the lights dimmed.

CHAPTER THREE

MARIANNE'S VOICE

I always told myself to prepare for excellence. Ted told me that would be the end of me, that I'd die from overwork or miss the Big Picture. Ted was always good in reminding me of the Big Picture, while ignoring that almost every picture of him included one of his wife at his side. He was the attorney who hired me when I graduated from Cooley Law School. We worked long hours together, in the 1970s. At first he used me more as a paralegal than as an attorney. I ran errands and typed letters and did research. He always seemed so appreciative. Ted was always a gentleman, and after a while he began to do little favors for me. Sometimes flowers, or candy, or just little treats. Then came the invitations for lunch. And that turned to a drink after work, then dinner, and just as quick, a weekend away.

He kept saying he'd leave his wife, but he never did. The age thing didn't bother me. I've always had a thing for older men. I guess that's always been true. My dad was a realtor and made really good money. The way to get him to talk with me was to talk real estate. I thought about sales, but I was no good at sales. And if I couldn't be excellent, what's the point? I was good at organizing, always good at numbers, but I thought being an accountant might be too boring. And I was good at accomplishing goals. As time went on, I found out I was good at a couple of other things. One of them was building a practice, servicing clients. Ted told me I was good at the other.

So I climbed the ladder at his practice until I became a partner. God, I worked my tail off for that title. I attended trainings, got my designations, published articles on estate planning, and performed with excellence.

Ted wanted to keep our thing a secret. I accepted it. I gave him time. He always talked about there being one more thing that needed to happen before he'd leave her. Once he got enough money. Once the kids had left home. Once they had graduated from college. Once he retired.

I finally told him I had enough. I left him. It took years, I don't even want to count them. I don't know why. I don't regret it. He was a good man, but it became clear he could never leave her. I can't blame him.

But something is missing. I feel like I'm getting myself ready for it. But I don't know what "it" is. Would I know if I stumbled across it?

Work is stressful. No one ever found out about Ted and me, but this is still a man's field, and a female attorney has to work twice as hard as a man, let me tell you. I live by Covey's words—I sharpen the saw. I'm so sharp I can cut through steel. Not bad for fifty-five. I had no idea the years would go so fast. But I'm proud of what I've achieved. Total excellence.

Marianne Walters left work for home an hour after everyone else had gone, taking the highway beyond the town and suburbs to her home in the country just beyond Charlotte. She used the time to listen to motivational or business tapes. Once she reached her home, a sprawling ranch-style house, she warmed up her dinner in the microwave and ate after changing into her sweats. After eating, she went to her home computer and worked for an hour while digesting her dinner.

Her exercise regimen was one of the highlights of her day. Marianne began each day with a hard half-hour run on her treadmill, while watching the business report on her TV. She ended each day with a half hour of weights and a twenty-minute stretch. Marianne showered and was in bed by 9:30 p.m. where she would read for a half hour, usually nonfiction literature on law.

This night she dreamed.

Marianne is at work. Her secretary is telling her that her new "coach" has arrived. Marianne listens as the coach tells her she needs to change everything she does to be able to stay on top.

Marianne has the thought, "Be aware."

She looks at the coach—a white male, dressed in a dark suit with a bright yellow tie. He's young, and in fact he looks a good deal like that young smartass at the Dream Group. Then she notices herself. She watches herself as if on a screen. Her dress, she sees, is a kind of plastic wrapped suit. No one seems to notice or care. She asks the consultant to sit at the front of her desk and seats herself in the chair behind the desk, wondering what she is showing through her plastic suit.

Marianne picks up a legal pad and holds it across her lap, feeling a little less exposed. She wonders, "What can he see?"

She suddenly feels compelled to write on her legal pad. Even though she is supposed to be listening to the man sitting across from her, she has no idea what he's saying, even though he never stops talking.

Making the effort to focus, Marianne hears him saying, "so in the Reality Model to stay at the top of the pyramid you'll need to use this pen."

And as he stands and leans over the desk, Marianne sees that he is wearing a similar suit to hers, a suit of plastic. She covers her eyes with the pad, saying "Uh huh, uh huh."

She sees that she is holding a banana and thinks, "How am I supposed to write with this?"

Marianne decides to ask the consultant about his qualifications. "Did the bar hire you?"

He answers, "The bar has appointed me to be their legal manifestation. They'll be on vacation for the next year while I will work exclusively with you. You are my only client, you are my only employee."

"I don't get it," Marianne says,. "How can I be your client and your employee?"

"It's the Reality Model—I just told you but I'll tell you again."

"Well, you'd better because there's something I'm just not getting."

Marianne becomes obsessed with the banana and once again the young man, the living manifestation of the bar, drones on while the banana is more and more fascinating to her.

She puts down the legal pad and begins to peel the banana.

For a moment just before she bites into it, she recognizes that she is looking at the banana through her own eyes, not watching it on a screen. She is amazed and frightened and wakes up with a smile on her face.

Marianne opened her eyes. "I'm looking differently," she said. Then she picked up a pen, noticed it wasn't a banana, and wrote down:

> At Work
> Consultant/Coach
> Reality Model
> Plastic Suit
> Embarrassed

Pen is Banana

Shift from movie screen to own eyes

She then looked at the sheet of questions Emma had given the group. Marianne focused on emotions and awareness.

She wrote the words "Uneasy—Anxious—Unfocused—Embarrassed—Angry." She then asked herself if this matched the emotional states she experienced in her waking life.

"All the time," she wrote.

Marianne made her way down to where she stored her treadmill in her basement. Her ritual was to run before breakfast. She looked outside this morning and thought about going out, but it was a little dark, and so she decided to stick with the treadmill. After her run, she ate yogurt and a banana. She couldn't quite put her finger on it, but something felt good about this morning, and she related it to the dream. She showered, got dressed, and put on her makeup before driving to work, arriving one hour before her secretary arrived at eight a.m.

The bees outside the window of Emma's office caught her attention. Summer was ending. The work of the bees had increased and there seemed to be a cloud of them, busily working the blossoms on the sunflowers outside. She thought about what triggered their instinct to work, and if humans shared a similar urging. She got distracted from her thoughts by some squirrels that were chasing one another from tree to tree.

Emma had given Jake a call the morning, before the day of the next group. She'd remembered that he'd worked midnights and tried to call early enough to catch him before he went to bed. He was open and apologetic and expressed that he'd like to continue with the group. Emma related that the group was surprised that he'd left so suddenly and that if he felt defensive or even uncomfortable, it would be good if he could let her know it while it was happening. Jake agreed.

The next day, in the evening, the group convened again. Mason and Holly and Marianne all seemed happy to see Jake again. They addressed his leaving suddenly as their first order of business.

"It seems that everyone is pretty happy you're back, Jake," said Emma. "You and I had a chance to talk a little before tonight, and we talked about what you might do differently if you start to feel defensive."

"Yeah," Jake started, tossing his hair off his forehead with a quick nod. "I'll let you know if I'm feeling attacked."

"Is there anything we need to clean up before we start this week's work?" asked Emma. Jake thought not. Holly made a suggestion, and Jake denied feeling particularly upset about anything that was on his mind.

"I've just been kind of scratchy lately," he said. "But I wanted to talk about my dreams."

Emma looked at the other group members. They were open. "Great. That's what we're here for. I'm realizing that we may not have time for everyone but we'll try to make room so that everyone can share a dream."

"I didn't dream this week," shared Mason.

Emma explained that he probably did dream, he just didn't remember his dream. She crossed her hands in her lap and said, "When I can't remember a dream, especially one that feels important when I wake up, I always feel like I've misplaced something important. Like my keys or my checkbook."

Mason scratched his forehead, near the hair line of his short grey hair, and asked if there were ways that one might better remember one's dreams.

"For now," suggested Emma, "spend a few minutes every morning with your dream journal. First thing, even before getting out of bed. Even if you don't remember any dreams. Just write down anything you can think of."

Mason said he would happily let someone else talk about their dreams since he had had so much time last week.

Holly volunteered to go last. Emma noticed that this was the second time she had deferred in the past two weeks, and she felt a tug of concern. But she opted not to address it.

Marianne related she'd had a dream she'd like to work on as well, but deferred to Jake, since he'd been first to volunteer.

"You're all so polite and cooperative tonight," said Emma. "Okay, Jake, you're up."

Jake replied by saying, "Asia."

"Excuse me?" asked Emma.

"You said Europe, I said Asia. I thought we were naming continents. I'm sorry." Jake smiled at Emma, crooked his brow, and shrugged his shoulders. "One thing I recognized this week is that I'm a smart ass. All the time. Even when I'm trying not to be. And like you suggested, Emma, I probably use it defensively."

"Let's just say it works for you," suggested Emma.

"Okay. Anyway—"

"Your dream—" prompted Holly.

"My dreams are nightmares. Almost always vampires. Sometimes zombies. Mainly vampires."

"Is there one specific dream you could tell us about?" asked Emma.

Jake pulled a small notebook from his inside jacket pocket. Emma noticed his hand tremble as he flipped through the pages. "In my dream, the dream I had a few nights ago, there was a vampire in the house."

Emma asked, "What house? Where you live now?"

"Yes. But it changed. I rent a place now in Lansing, on the east side, but I grew up with my family in a house in northern Chicago."

"Really?" asked Mason, leaning forward.

"Yeah. So it was like both places," said Jake. He finally sat the notebook on his knee and gripped each of his thighs with a hand.

"How old were you when you lived in that specific house?" asked Emma.

"We lived in three houses while I was growing up. The one in the dream was the one I lived in, let me see, I was six, I think. And we moved when I was thirteen."

"Okay," said Emma, "what else did you notice about the house?"

"House? The dream was about a vampire not a house."

"Foreground/background," said Emma. "Let's pay attention to the details your mind is suggesting."

"Could you say more about that?" asked Mason.

"Is that okay with you, Jake?" asked Emma. She didn't want to interrupt the flow of Jake's memories.

"Sure," he said.

Emma looked at Mason, and then looked from group member to group member as she answered. "Okay, let's say a dream is a movie and your mind is the director. When you make a movie, how do you decide where the movie is shot?" She looked to Mason at the end of her question.

"Well, I'd like to say a movie is shot where the story is supposed to take place, but that isn't always the case. Cost is a big factor, but the art of finding locations that work, or building sets, that's a specialized area."

Emma asked, "So besides cost, why would a director choose one location over another?"

"To set a mood. Sometimes to suggest a character's interior experience by placing them in an environment that illustrates it. Like Cary Grant's vulnerability in a cornfield in *North by Northwest*."

"Right," said Emma.

"So you're saying my 'director' used my bedroom at the age ten to make a point?" asked Jake.

"Well, does it make a point?" Emma asked.

"Yeah. That was a terrible time of my life. My parents fought all the time, or they separated and then got back together. Yeah, it pretty well sucked."

"Okay, back to the dream. You were saying that it's your bedroom. Both where you are now and where you were when you were ten."

"Yeah. I'm not sure I want to continue," said Jake, with a sour look on his face.

"Why not?" asked Holly. "I think you're just starting to get somewhere."

"She's saying I'm like ten years old," said Jake.

"Whoa, whoa, slow down, Jake, I didn't say that," Emma clarified. Then she asked, "Is this feeling too scary? Are you feeling vulnerable, like you do in the dream?"

Holly added, "Jake, I'm sorry about that crack. I'm no one to talk. I have nightmares, too, and sometimes they're set in my childhood home. Dead babies, remember?"

Jake still hadn't answered, and Emma noticed that his eyes had moistened. She softly said, "Jake, I may be asking questions and probing but please understand, I am not trying to humiliate you or embarrass you or shame you. Can you believe that?"

Jake sighed and said, "I guess so. Anyway—"

"Back to the dream, or are you done?" asked Emma.

"Back to the dream," said Jake. "So I'm in my bedroom. In bed. And I'm aware there's a vampire in the house and that's it."

"You don't see it?" asked Mason.

"No."

"Do you ever see it?" asked Marianne.

"Sometimes."

"Let's stick to this specific dream," suggested Emma. "How do you know it's a vampire?"

"I just know."

"And you feel?"

"Terror."

Emma noticed that Jake was speaking more and more quietly and he had lost eye contact with anyone in the group. She thought he might be leaving the room without leaving the room, by dissociating, and made the decision to go after him.

"Jake, you felt terror, because—"

"Because it's a fucking vampire," he looked at Emma as though she were stupid.

"How do you know he's there to harm you?" she asked.

"Whadaya mean?"

"What if he's there to warn you?" Emma asked, "Give you a message? Or to protect you, or ask you for help? What if your vampire is there to honor you?" She waited while Jake mulled this over.

"I've never, for one moment, had any thought like that," Jake said.

Emma continued. "Did you know that certain Native American tribes believed that nightmares were powerful spirit messages, carried by beings of such terrible potency that they couldn't possibly be ignored?"

There was a stillness in the room. Jake was looking far out into the distance, through the window, yet seemed focused on something inside.

Finally, he spoke. "No. I didn't know that."

"Jake, one more question?" asked Emma.

"Okay."

"Do you have any idea why it's vampires?"

"I saw a vampire video when I was a little kid. A couple of them. *Lost Boys* was one of them, and the other scared me, too. I think it was *Salem's Lot*."

"David Soul was the protagonist," offered Mason.

"Blond guy."

"Yeah. That was a very chilling vampire film, even though it was made for TV," recalled Mason, "but the vampire is a true *Nosferatu*-type monster. Not a seductive leading man."

"Yeah. Well, for years after that I was afraid. I was always certain he was out the window or under my bed or in the closet."

"So you've known both, vampires and fear, for many years?" asked Emma.

"Yes," said Jake and deeply exhaled. He shook through his shoulders and then his neck and head, almost like a dog shaking the water from his coat. "I'm done. I don't want to talk anymore."

"Fair enough," said Emma. "Okay. Marianne?"

Marianne shifted in her seat and brought out her notebook. She'd highlighted sections that she wanted to talk about. Emma thought for a moment that she was surprised Marianne hadn't brought handouts and a PowerPoint.

"Okay, I'm at work and a consultant/coach comes to tell me about the Reality Model. I'm in a strange suit, like a plastic suit. He gives me a pen to write with, and it turns out to be a banana, and I get obsessed with this banana and start to eat it, and I can't focus on what he's saying."

"Anything else?" asked Emma.

"I also wrote down my feelings," said Marianne. She reported that she had felt uneasy, anxious, unfocused, embarrassed, and a little angry.

"That's a lot of feelings," said Emma.

"Yes, it was," said Marianne with a smile on her face.

She's done her homework, this one has, thought Emma. "One definition of dreams I recall hearing once is that dreams are pictures of feelings. What do you think of that, Marianne? What if this dream is a picture of how you're feeling?"

"That's good," she said thoughtfully. But Marianne quickly moved on to say, "There's one more thing I'm remembering now. Something I didn't write down. I asked him who sent him, the bar? And he said he was the 'living embodiment' of the bar."

Holly looked up from staring into the back of her hands. "That 'bar' thing always confused me. What's the bar?"

Marianne explained that in the legal field, as well as most other professions, there was an association that regulated practice and enforced rules and ethics. She went on about this in a fair amount of detail, until Jake interjected, "This may be more than we need to know."

Holly gave Jake a look, initially cross, and then smiled at him.

Marianne said, "That's probably true. There was another odd thing about my dream that I'd failed to mention. The consultant actually looked a lot like you, Jake."

"Really?"

"If you wore a suit. One more thing," said Marianne. "I noticed that at first I was watching the dream, from the third person, like on TV, but by the end I was watching it in first person."

"Once you started eating the banana," said Jake.

"Why, yes," realized Marianne, raising her eyebrows.

"Hard to eat something in the third person," shrugged Jake.

Emma had been taking notes. She asked Marianne whether she could ask her a question to clarify the role of the coach/ consultant.

Marianne said, "Sure. It would be out of the norm for the bar to assign someone to me, to teach me, or train me in some area."

"Like this time?" asked Emma.

"Yes. Well, I was going to be trained in the Reality Model. Whatever that is."

"So, the Reality Model. And you are in a plastic suit?"

"Yes."

"Can you describe it?"

"It was a lot like Saran Wrap."

"And you felt exposed?"

"Yes."

"Do you ever feel particularly vulnerable at work *vis a vis* the bar?"

"I suppose so. I mean, they police the work of attorneys. If you're in trouble, that's who you're in trouble with, in terms of your license to practice."

"Is it an 'old boys' business?" asked Holly.

"Very much so," said Marianne. "But not as much today as it was when I started."

"So the guy offers you a penis," Jake said.

Marianne blushed and said, "A pen. I said he offered me a pen."

"That's what I said."

Emma turned to Jake and said, "Jake, you did say 'penis.'"

"I know what I said."

"Jung and easily Freudened," mumbled Mason.

"It was a pen, but it turned into a banana. My gosh, you don't think these are phallic symbols? Do you believe in that stuff, Emma?" asked Marianne. She was still blushing and was sitting on the edge of her seat.

"Let's look at this," offered Emma. "Would it help you do your job better if you had a penis?"

"No."

"In your opinion," said Emma, "would the bar prefer it if you were a man? Give us your first thought."

"Okay, my first thought is yes."

Emma continued. "So, if those were phallic symbols, they might represent this power of the penis rather than the literal penis."

Jake couldn't resist. He chimed in, "'The Literal Penis'—I love it. The title of my next collection of short stories. The pen is mightier than the penis, don't you think?"

"I think I've taken up enough time," said Marianne, brushing some lint off her skirt.

Emma said that was fine. She took in a deep breath and smiled.

Holly asked, since there were only a few minutes left, rather than go into another dream, would Emma expound a little about dreams being "pictures of feelings."

Wondering if Holly was being inquisitive or attempting to avoid, Emma decided to just answer her question. She said, "People have intuitively felt that dreams were meaningful since the beginning of time. There's evidence of dream interpretation amongst the ancient Egyptians two, maybe three thousand years ago. The Old Testament of the Bible is loaded with references of dreams. So, there's a lot of historical and spiritual evidence of the relevance of dreams."

"But is there scientific evidence?" asked Holly.

"Well," started Emma, "outside of Freud's work—"

Mason chipped in. "I'd like to hear more about that, too."

Emma quoted from the neurophysiologist J. Allen Hobson from Harvard, who studied images of the brain awake and asleep and showed that the brain was using very different chemistry and wave patterns while dreaming. She related that Hobson also postulated that dreams appear to be assisting the brain in moving information back and forth between short-term and long-term memory.

"Like," said Holly, "filing away information?"

"Probably something like that," said Emma, who also offered the disclaimer that this wasn't an area of specialty for her. Then she wondered with the group whether or not the brain was trying to integrate information that it captured during the day. Could the brain be trying to explain new situations, data, emotions, and sensations and matching it to old to make sense of it?

"So that would explain Jake's bedroom," said Mason. "It's his room now, but also the one from his childhood."

"Exactly." Emma looked at Holly. "Does that make sense?"

"I think so. I mentioned to a friend that I was in this group, and she said it was nonsense and that scientists had proven that dreams were nothing more than a series of meaningless images."

"Well," said Emma, "I've heard that, too. And she might be right. Dreams may only exist as a series of images."

"But we experience them as stories," said Mason.

"Right. Perhaps we make up stories to explain these images, tie them together, make associations, and give them meaning," said Emma.

"How would we know what story to tell?" asked Marianne.

"I think it would be like a Rorschach Test," suggested Emma. "You know, interpreting ink blots? We tell ourselves stories at night that are similar to the stories we tell ourselves during the day."

"Oh, shit," said Jake.

"Exactly," said Emma.

Emma dragged herself to consciousness through the thick syrup of a heavy sleep. She woke up feeling groggy, almost drugged, yet aware that Frank had come in after she was asleep and left before she got up. She needed at least seven hours of sleep and Frank seemed to get by on much less.

Her morning bike ride was down to the river trail. There were patches of frost on the ground, but the sun had risen and it would thaw within the first hour of the day. In early October there might be a forty or fifty degree shift in the temperature within one day, the mornings chilly in the forties and dipping into freezing while the afternoons could feel like summer again. *Every season in Michigan gives you previews of coming attractions,* thought Emma. She decided not to think of Frank, Dylan, or work and last night's group, but to try to be present to the scenery, her bike, and her body. She opened her senses and smelled the water of the Grand River before it came into view. A damp, earthy smell mixed with the decomposing leaves off the trail. Following the concrete trail as it wedged between the river and the off ramp on I-496, she encountered the part of the trail that was her least favorite, because of its proximity to the rush-hour traffic. Paths soon diverged, and she was in the forest, leading up to the park and the zoo. The whine of the speeding cars receded, and Emma reminded herself that she was now in the garden. Although Emma rarely engaged in formal prayer, she did try to practice what she called "The Presence of God." It wasn't hard during moments such as these. She said aloud, "You're showing off," and smiled.

Emma turned a corner and saw the river from a new vista. She was in woods and recognized maple and oak trees, but there were so many she couldn't name. Emma could hear birds, more than she could see. Delicate twitterings, whistles, that could be robins and finches or blue jays, maybe sparrows, and the two-tone whistle of the Bobwhite, the deep caw of crows, and suddenly a cardinal, the red of his feathers standing out like a flame on the branch of a tree. Emma wondered about the language of birds. *Can they identify each other's calls? Do they know a welcome from a warning? Do they know each other any better than we people know each other?* The winding trail opened into the zoo, and Emma felt a fine trickle of sweat run down her back. She couldn't afford the time to take the trail through downtown to the fish ladder, which was her usual loop. Today she had her own therapy, and Claudia Silverstein would be expecting her.

After racing home and showering, Emma got into her Honda Accord and put in a Lucinda Williams CD. *"All I ask, is don't tell anybody the secrets,"* she sang absently along with Lucinda, and wondered again what life might be like without Frank.

She drove east and cut through Michigan State's campus, then traveled south to Mt. Hope and east again into Okemos before getting to Silverstein's office.

Emma hated being late, and today she arrived about five minutes after the hour. After Claudia ushered her back to the office, Emma took her usual seat. She was breathing hard. Claudia sat with her usual impassive expression. Emma took a moment and folded her hands in her lap.

"I've been rushing," said Emma, "I went on a bike ride this morning, and the time nearly got away from me."

"It's a beautiful morning," said Claudia.

"Yes, it is." Emma felt younger, though not in a physical sense. She felt immature.

"Last week you talked about your marriage, about Frank. You had some concerns."

"Yes," said Emma. "It hasn't been going well."

"How do you mean?" asked Claudia.

"I put a lot of effort into it. I spent time with him, I watched football with him, I even went to a game. I made dinner, I made love—"

"*I* made love?"

"I guess that was a slip. The relationship doesn't feel like it's working. It feels one-sided."

"He's not trying at all?" asked Claudia.

Emma looked out of the window and sat with the questions for a few moments before answering. "He did go to a concert with me. But we fought. He thinks it's my problem. He's happy."

"What do you think?"

"I think, that maybe he's right. I'm the one who's unhappy. But, here's the thing, I am happy. I enjoy my work. Even though it's challenging. And this morning on the bike trail, I felt real joy. But when we're together or when I'm even thinking of Frank, I'm terribly conflicted and upset."

Claudia allowed for some silence in the room before asking, "You don't feel he's meeting your needs?"

"No." Emma was surprised at how quick and definitive her answer was.

"Any of them?"

Emma sighed. "It's funny you should ask. Because I told him the other day, he's a wonderful provider. And he's a good father to Nathan." Emma felt her eyes fill with tears.

"What just happened?" asked Claudia.

"When I think of leaving Frank, I run up against what it would do to Nathan and I don't think I could live with myself if I hurt him."

After offering Emma a tissue Claudia said, "I hadn't realized how upsetting this is for you. Do you think Frank would, let me re-word that, have you asked Frank to go into therapy with you?"

"He might. I could. I'll try."

Jake is on the psych ward. He's late again and decides to skip the nurse's report entirely, just walk up and down the unit, but the halls are empty. The receptionist is gone. He peeks into the office. No ward clerk, no nurses, no psych techs. The clock is missing, too. Jake knows that there should be almost twenty staff here now, with the change of shifts. Jake is alone. He wonders, Where are the patients? In their rooms? Jake, starting to worry, decides to sit at the desk in the main lobby. From this spot he can see the length of the hallway. Each door is sheltered in an alcove so he can't tell if the doors are opened or closed. He listens for any sound and hears a low rumble from the end of the hallway.

Jake gets up from the desk, the light getting dimmer as he stands in the center of the lobby. There are twenty rooms on the "open side" of the unit. The opposite side houses the Intensive Care area, where the doors are locked, and the more disturbed patients kept in relative seclusion. Jake faces away from that side, looking down the hallway where the patients could be sleeping. He steps down the hall, slowly at first, and looks in the first room. The room is empty, and illuminated by a torch hanging on the wall. Jake can feel the heat and thinks, They've made some changes. *He'd have to tell the nurse that it probably wasn't to wise to keep a flaming torch in the rooms of psych patients. Right now his main concern is finding another human being. He steps back in the hallway and can smell the acrid stench of pure alcohol and human feces, and knows there is a mess nearby that needs to be cleaned up. Jake looks down the hall, but sees only darkness. He retraces his steps to the center of the lobby.*

Jake looks down the hall to the "open side," and the hall is lighter again. He doesn't want to look towards the locked unit. He can picture the steel door and the wire-meshed window at eye level. He turns and looks.

Jake knows that this is the area he needs to investigate. This is where the most psychotic patients were, the most suicidal, violent or just hallucinating and acting crazy. If there is any real trouble on the unit, it was always in the locked unit.

Jake thinks, They might be in there, the rest of the staff— the patients. *He knows he should look but the more he thinks about it, the more scared he is.*

"If I grow still it's because he's still here," Jake says aloud. He feels an instant of recognition and awareness, accompanied by a jolt of fear and electric tension running up and down his spine. "The vampire is still here. On the unit. He sure as hell is on the locked side. With the staff. He's killed the staff, but he's locked up. Will that door hold?"

On the verge of panicking, Jake wonders what to do. Leave the unit? Get out? The elevator door has disappeared and so has the stairway exit; there was only wall. Jake thinks about the panic button, but decides not to hit it. Besides, who would respond?

He has a thought, "That's passive. I'm always too passive. Maybe the vampire isn't going to kill me."

This thought lasts only for a few seconds, replaced by an even deeper fear. "Fuck that, I can't trust a fucking vampire." *Jake starts to calmly walk down the hallway on the open side, The hallway seems to stretch, the further he walks the longer it is, so he walks faster, until he is running and then sprinting and the hallway becomes endless.*

Jake stops running and finds himself standing where he began, in the main lobby. He is winded and sweaty. Jake turns to the locked unit. "I have go there," *he says out loud.* "Better the sooner, the beater the biter. Beater the Biter! BEATER THE BITER!" *He has started yelling in spite of himself and knows how he must look. Crazy.*

"Shit! Shut up!"

"Oh, it doesn't matter. He knows where you are. He's always known." *Jake walks over to the Intensive Care door. The heavy metal door has a window of thick glass reinforced with a cross thatch of wire, he can smell the metal and feels an impulse to lick it and see if it tastes like pennies on his tongue.*

Jake looks through the window before he opens the door with his keys, seeing no one, and slides the key in the lock. He looks at an empty hall and thinks, Just one look and just one look, *and listens to the wind, a white noise that seems like the absence of sound, an emptiness that calls from down the darkened hallway. At that moment a figure emerges from the seclusion room and Jake knows that would be the monster, and the figure turns in the darkness. Jake steps back, slams the door hard, and he feels a sharp thud on the other side. Jake looks through the window into the face of himself.*

My God, it's me. He's me. The monster is me, *Jake thinks, looking back at himself through the window. He sees the vampire looking back at him, not an exact mirror image, but definitely his own face, and for a moment feels comforted.*

The vampire is me. *Jake looks again, and sees that he is in the locked unit and looking through the glass. He watches himself starting to walk away from the steel door, holding a clipboard and jotting a note, and Jake thinks,* I'm at the window looking in but who's locked up who?

And then Jake screams…

He woke up, moaning out loud. Jake saw daylight through the crack of his curtain.

"Shit," he said, rubbing his eyes. He rolled out of bed, stumbled into the kitchen and poured a glass of water and drank it down. Then he opened his cabinet and pulled down a fifth of Scotch and poured half a tumbler. It was almost noon and getting back to sleep would be difficult.

CHAPTER FOUR

HOLLY'S VOICE

I stopped drinking a few years ago, about the same time I left my husband. He was somebody I loved like a mad woman, but my mother always said "Don't marry your drinking buddy." I'm afraid that's just what I did.

The funny thing is he put me out. He said he couldn't take it anymore. The crying, the hiding bottles, the getting sick, the excuses. My problem, I realized, is that I tried to keep up with him. He had more of a tolerance than I did. That's for sure. So he kept drinking at the same levels, and I just started to fall apart.

My first night alone in the little house I rented was terrifying. I locked the doors and slept on the couch. I couldn't bring myself to even sleep in my own bedroom for the first couple of weeks. I'm not sure what I was thinking. But I got therapy, from Emma, and she asked me how much I drank and I did a strange thing. For the first time in my life, I didn't lie about my drinking. And she suggested I look into A.A., and I did. And it clicked, right away. I felt like I was home.

Not everyone has that experience; in fact, most don't. But I did. And some good things started happening. I went from being a caseworker for Foster Care to switching over to Protective Services Investigator. I was pretty good at it. Assholes don't scare me much. Or maybe it was A.A. that helped. Sitting in a room full of people who were telling the truth—that seemed like such a relief. It was actually a shock. But once I got a taste for it, I wanted more. And telling the truth in my life helped me find the truth at work. I got a sponsor in A.A., and I made it a point to follow her suggestions. I stayed out of relationships for the first year, dated a little, but never too seriously.

I went out with my ex-husband a couple of times, but I couldn't stand his drinking and he couldn't stand me sober, I guess. Maybe, someday—

But then the dreams started coming. I wasn't in therapy with Emma anymore. I started having nightmares. Mainly dead baby nightmares. I'm not sure what that's about. I read about Emma's group in the paper and at first I was just kind of surprised, like "Hey! I know her!" Then I read the article and realized that I needed to do this group.

So far, so good. I actually feel shy in this group, more than I do in meetings. I'm not sure why. But there's something in these dreams, like something trying to claw its way out of me. Like I have a secret. And I don't think I do. I've done a Fifth Step with my sponsor, outlined all my resentments towards my mom and dad, my ex-husband, all the dirty little things I did when I was drinking. But I think there's something else. Something deep in the basement. I'm just not sure what it could be.

I asked Emma about that when I first called. She said she wasn't big on "hidden memories," and wouldn't usually go on a fishing trip to find anything that wasn't already right in front of you. I was surprised at how blunt she was about that. I've been a little quiet in the group. There's something about that guy, Jake, that really pisses me off.

Holly drove her state car through a stretch of streets on the south side of town, all industrial and commercial with strip malls scattered through, until she reached her destination. She was going to a trailer park to begin her investigation of an abuse charge. The child was an eight-year-old boy who had come to school with a handprint on his face. The school had made the referral, and Holly had already spoken to the boy while he was at school, the day after the charge was filed.

Since the most recent budget cuts by the state, Holly's job had gone from busy to hectic. She had twenty-six open cases and the amount of documentation and follow-up required on each file could provide her with a full forty-hour work week alone. But that was her job. Today she was supposed to visit the mother of the boy who had been hit. Holly looked down at the name again on her case notes. *Brandi Janes.*

As she approached the trailer park where Janes lived, Holly reflected on the players involved in this family constellation. The mom, Brandi, was twenty-five years old, just a few years younger than Holly. Jacob, who'd been hit by the mother's boyfriend, was eight and would be at school. Brandi also had a three-year-old daughter.

And then there was the boyfriend. His name was Gordon Thomas, and he'd been arrested before on a prior abuse charge. Domestic. Holly hoped she would not run into him today. He wasn't the parent of either child.

Holly had called to set an appointment with the mom. She didn't always make a call ahead. She would sometimes drop in. This first contact was to establish some basic goals. Confirm the address, names of the mom and boyfriend, establish his whereabouts, if possible, and let Brandi know that the state was involved. She would need to assess whether the child was currently in harm's way and end up making a recommendation as to whether charges should be filed or whether to file a petition for removal.

Holly usually felt secure with the knowledge that she had the power of the State of Michigan behind her. The court system often backed up her recommendations, and the police could be available if things became sticky. Sticky wasn't uncommon.

Holly did not often feel personal threat on the job, though she had been threatened in the past. She was no coward and wasn't one to back away from a confrontation. Her ex-husband's nickname for her was "Red," as much for her temper as for her hair.

She pulled into the trailer park on the south side of Lansing, knowing the layout of the park from earlier investigations. She'd find the trailer she was looking for near the back of the park.

Clouds had rolled in, and it had begun to rain. Holly saw the trailer and felt a chill. Jacob, the boy, had told her that the family didn't have a car, but there was a rust colored Cadillac parked outside the trailer.

Jacob had told Holly that his mom's boyfriend only came by at night and not every night. Holly wondered, *How would the boy know if the boyfriend came by during the day while he was at school?* She saw a curtain move in the trailer and made a decision. She could have driven by and come back later when he was gone, but her supervisor advised her to follow her gut. When Holly felt scared she was supposed to honor the fear, respect it, and leave a scene alone if needed.

Today Holly ignored her gut. She got out of her car and walked to the trailer, but the door of the trailer opened and a man stepped out. He was tall and lean, looked like he might be in his early forties. He was slender but wiry, his physique exposed by a tight white T-shirt. He wore a full mustache and had a pronounced overbite. He and Holly moved straight toward each other and the serious look on his face knocked the smile off hers.

"Look here, you have no right—" he began.

But Holly flashed her I.D. and called him by name. "Gordon Thomas, I'm Holly Masters. I work investigation for Protective Services, Department of Social Services for the State of Michigan. My authority is backed by the court and if needed I'll return with the police who can easily add 'impeding an investigation' to any other charges, and that's a felony, sir, so you want to keep yappin' or—" Holly stopped to breathe but watching Gordon fume she could see she'd knocked him off balance. *Not used to a woman standing up to him. Not this one. Thought so,* Holly mused as Gordon stood looking at her. She stepped around him and walked to the door.

"Brandi Janes? I'd like to talk with you.," Holly called, then felt a tug on her shoulder, was turned around and shoved once hard against the side of the trailer. Gordon stood with his right arm extended, gripping Holly's left shoulder tightly and pressing her against the dirty metal of the trailer.

"Let's get something straight. What I say goes," Gordon was hissing between clenched teeth. His face was a gathering of shades of red while the veins bulged in his neck. He was close enough that Holly could smell his breath, a mix of cigarettes and stale beer. Holly took a breath before she responded. Her response wasn't trained, but instinctive. She snapped and for a moment lost all vestige of professionalism.

"Look here, mister, I'm not some little mouse you can intimidate and I'm no eight-year-old boy you can slap around. Your touching me constitutes assault. Do you understand, asshole?"

Gordon took his hand from her shoulder, stepped back, and smiled.

"Little spitfire. I do believe you'd like to take me on. Okay, you talk to the little missy in there. She'll tell you I'm a good man who demands respect from youngsters. I have to take my leave now."

Gordon walked over to his Cadillac, climbed in, and blew Holly a kiss as he started it up. Loud country music blared through the windows as he pulled away.

Holly heard the door of the trailer close behind her. She got into her own car and called her supervisor who answered on the second ring.

"You know that new investigation?"

"Janes family?"

"Right. I'm here now. I just got into a tangle with the boyfriend. Gordon Thomas."

"Are you okay?"

"Yeah," said Holly. "He was full of bluster, and I gave it right back to him. He did put a hand on me, though. Shoved me."

"I can get a warrant. Why didn't you call this in before?"

"It just happened. Listen, I'll finish the interview with the mom then I'll come back in. He's a bad man, isn't he?"

"He's got a record. Couple of assaults, a DUI, tax evasion. Most of it old stuff."

"Okay, well, he's driving a big, older model Cadillac. Red, but almost a rust color. License is BFD609."

"I'll call it in, Holly. Be careful out there. Are you okay? Do you want me to send out an officer?"

"No, I'm okay, and he's gone. Just call it in. Thanks. I should be back in an hour or so."

Before Holly went back for the interview with Brandi she made one more call to her A.A. sponsor, Martha. Her sponsor wasn't home but she left a message.

"Hi. It's me. I'm having a rough day at work and I just got really mad at a guy and now I'm starting to feel scared. So, I'm not going to drink, actually I'm surprised it doesn't even sound good. Just wanted to call. I'll see you at the meeting tonight."

Later that night Holly walks through a house, looking for her cat. She makes a sound with her mouth, a high-pitched whistle caused by pursing her lips and drawing air through her teeth. It always cues the cat that it's time to eat. But the cat wasn't coming.

The house is dark and Holly turns a switch but the lamp doesn't turn on, and she looks to see if the lamp is plugged in. The cord, dark and coiled, begins to move like a snake. Holly gasps and walks into the next room but that room is dark, too. Suddenly she realizes that she's not even in her own house but in a customer's house. A perp's house. A victim's house.

"How do I get out?" *she wonders.*

Holly tries to evaluate what floor she's on. The first? She is standing in a hallway, and a group of doors that lead to rooms that she takes to be bedrooms, each door leading to another dark room. The floorboards of the old house creak with every step she takes. From what she can see there is junk, garbage, clutter, and the smell of decay, like a moldy sweater or old urine, and Holly thinks she should stop, but resists the urge.

"Don't panic," she whispers to herself.

Holly stops in a room. There are no windows. Then she hears it. The sound is a cry. At first it doesn't sound human, maybe a whimper of a badly wounded dog. Holly is thinking, Oh, God, no, *but instinctively she moves toward the sound, a pile of rags in the corner near the furnace. She reaches to pick up a rag to see who or what was under it—.*

Holly woke up. She was panting and sweating. She reached for her dream journal on her table before turning on the light. She prayed and picked up her pen.

Emma sat in silence during her session with a married couple in her office. She was observing the husband, who sat staring out the window, then she turned her gaze to his wife who was staring at the back of his head. Emma was reminded of a moment from a movie that Frank liked, a Clint Eastwood spaghetti western, where three gunslingers stood looking at each for an eternity before someone finally pulled their gun. Emma was sitting in her chair, a straight-backed, leather-bound piece of furniture that swiveled and gave her access to move and also good support. The couple sat across from her on the couch. They were close to her age, and both were on their second marriage. This standoff was over where to go on their vacation.

"We always visit your family. I just want to go to the ocean," said the husband. He was wearing a white oxford shirt and jeans.

"That's easy for you to say. Your family is here. You don't know what it's like not to live near the people you love," answered his wife, who was dressed in a sharp olive business suit.

"Yes, I do. I live with you, don't I?"

Emma had seen six clients before this couple. Two hours in the morning, after her own therapy, and then four after lunch. The last two hours of her day were couples, and she was feeling unfocused.

"Okay let's slow it down," Emma suggested. She squinted then asked, "Bob, you're not actually saying you don't want Lisa to see her family?"

"No," Bob said, "but I don't want it to be every—"

"Let's just leave the 'but' out for now. Lisa, can you see that Bob—" Emma hesitated and closed her eyes for a second before shaking her head and admitting, "I'm sorry. I've lost my train of thought."

Lisa looked at her watch and motioned at the clock. She said, "That's okay. I have to go now anyway and pick up the kids. Can you pay her?"

Bob answered, "I always do," and as Lisa walked out he said to Emma, "You can see what I'm up against."

"You know Bob, I really can't talk to either of you about the other one when they aren't in the room."

Bob was writing the check. "Well, I don't know if this is helping, but we'll be back next week."

"Thanks," Emma said as she took the check. She made a quick note in the chart and wrote the couple's names in her planner when she heard Betty's voice behind her.

"Ready for tennis?"

Emma looked up and saw Betty dressed in a beige tennis outfit. "God, yes. I feel like I've just been through a match," answered Emma.

"Rough session?" asked Betty, pantomiming a backhand while Emma locked up her charts for the night.

"Yeah. It wasn't them. Typical stuff. I just started to float away. I got so distracted, and before I knew it they were fighting again."

"Know what you mean," said Betty. "Let's go hit the ball."

The women drove separately in their own cars to the tennis club. After getting dressed and reaching the courts, Betty and Emma were soon lost in volleys.

Emma was reminded of the couple she'd just seen as they volleyed. Back and forth, back and forth, one shot answered by another. She pushed the memories of work out of her mind and got lost in the experience of being on the court. The sound of the ball pinging against the racket, the rhythm of volleys that bounced back and forth, the smell of the fresh tennis balls as she handled them.

Emma's father had taught her tennis years ago, and she had kept up the practice by occasionally playing with Frank. She and Betty had just started playing, after they discovered they'd both learned the games through their fathers.

Betty played aggressively and was winning the volleys consistently, though Emma found a rhythm that kept Betty running from one side of the court to the next. East and west.

After a few minutes of playing both women had broken a sweat, and Betty asked Emma if she'd like to play a game.

"Keep points? I'm having a better workout volleying but if you want to—"

They volleyed for serve and again Betty won. She revealed her secret weapon, an overhead slam of a serve, delivered with a grunt and giving her three aces out of the first four points.

The competition was friendly, and Emma was appreciating the exercise. She was impressed with Betty's strength. But when Betty said something after winning the first two games effortlessly, Emma started to bear down. She found the sweet spot on the court that put her in position to nail the rockets Betty sent her way. Her returns were hit with as much strength as possible, and Betty lost the next game.

Emma's serve continued to be weak, but she noticed by the fourth game that Betty was turning her entire body to hit as many shots as possible with her forehand. Emma started exploiting this by hitting cross-court volleys, forcing Betty further and further into a corner to compensate for her weak backhand. Emma chopped a volley straight down the opposite line which Betty couldn't reach in time.

Emma enjoyed the competition and found herself caring about whether or not she won.

Betty asked, "Win by two?"

Emma said, "We'll be here all night. How about next game wins?"

"It's my serve," Betty reminded her.

"I'm good with that."

Betty's first shot was another ace. Fifteen—love. On the next point her first serve was long, and her second was returnable. Emma softly slipped it over the net for a point. fifteen—fifteen.

"You're sneaky," said Betty.

"Hit it where they ain't."

The third point was another ace. Thirty—fifteen. On the fourth point Emma returned but Betty won a long volley. Forty—fifteen.

"Match point," Betty called and served a flash that Emma somehow returned, and another long volley, with Emma again exploiting Betty's backhand. Forty—thirty.

"Match point, again," and Betty searched for the opposite line of the rectangle she served into, but missed. The second serve was softer and led to another volley that Betty finally won, on a series of smashing forehands. Both women were dripping by the end of the game.

"You never give up, do you?" asked Betty.

"Betty, my dear, you trigger some primitive competitive streak in me."

In the steam room after the game, wrapped in oversized towels, Betty told Emma about the latest in her family, then asked Emma about how it was going with Frank and Nathan.

"Nathan calls once a week from college, but he hasn't been home on a weekend yet."

"That's probably a good sign."

"Yeah, I'm thinking there's a girl. And I'm going to ask Frank if he'd do therapy with me."

"Really? Well, good for you. Who do you think you'll see?"

"I don't know. Got any openings?"

"No way. Would Frank feel more comfortable with a man?"

"Only if he was a football coach," answered Emma.

"A coach isn't a bad idea. There are a couple of men who are adding personal coaching to their practices. Maybe Frank would do well with that approach?" suggested Betty.

"You know, I bet he would, but—" There was a long pause.

"That's one long 'but' you got there."

"When I think of it, I'm not sure this has anything to do with Frank. Frank is Frank. He's a good guy. I think it's me."

"You're going to leave him, aren't you?" asked Betty.

"I don't know."

"Well, if you work your marriage like you play tennis, you'll hang in there as long as you can."

"Yeah. I just wonder sometimes if maybe I'm in the wrong game."

Mason walks across a familiar field. He is holding a fishing pole and carrying a tackle box, walking towards a lake. As he walks across the harvested cornfield, he notices that he can see for miles.

"I've never fished before," he says, but he knew he had, as a boy in Indiana, with his uncle and then a few times with friends. Mason wore an old fishing vest and hat.

The landscape had a gentle roll, almost like a wave on the ocean. In the distance, Mason suddenly sees a Japanese Samurai in red armor. As the warrior gets closer Mason decides to keep moving. The Samurai might be harmless, but better to not risk it.

Mason commits himself to skirting the warrior in a kind of flanking maneuver and has to walk into a marshy area where there were a lot of cattails. Mason thinks, This is water, maybe there are fish here. *He knows this was not the lake where he's supposed to fish.*

Climbing out of the marsh, Mason sees a book on the ground, streaked with mud. Then another and another. He considers picking them up, but then notices that there aren't just one or two, not even just a few. There are dozens. Maybe hundreds.

"Still, they are just polluting this nice area. I should burn them."

Mason searches his pockets in his vest and finds a Payday candy bar, a compass, and some matches. The matches are damp from the marsh and won't light. Mason stacks the books so that they form a teepee-shaped heap.

"If I only had a lighter," *Mason says, before becoming aware that he is smoking.* "I haven't smoked in years. When did I start again? This is very disappointing."

The burning end of the cigarette is enough to light a corner of the pile on fire. The flames begin to consume books quickly.

"I wish I could have saved some of those."

Mason recognizes several titles, now that the books are burning. The Grapes of Wrath *and* The Sun Also Rises *and* The Great Gatsby.

"Is this my collection?" *he asks aloud.* "Why would I burn my own books?"

Then Mason realizes that the Samurai can see the smoke and will come to investigate. He feels a jolt of fear in the pit of his stomach.

He starts to walk again, across the landscape, looking back to see the smoke rising from the flames licking the pile of books. He doesn't catch sight of the Samurai. Mason looks towards the sky and sees geese pass overhead.

"I'm close," *he says.*

At the next rise Mason sees a painter, a young man with an easel set up, painting the landscape. Mason walks up behind him to see his work and notices that even though the painter is obviously studying the landscape of the lake, what he painted was an abstraction of black.

"That's the lake?" asks Mason. He sees the painter's face for the first time. It was the younger guy in the Dream Group, the smartass, Jake.

"Yeah. This is the lake, deconstructed."

"I wish you didn't have to do that. It's such a beautiful lake," says Mason.

"Do you really think so? You haven't seen it in a while, have you?"

Mason looks at the lake, a muddy puddle with a greasy film on top of it. Mason can see two fish floating on the surface, clearly dead.

Mason moans, "My lake, my poor, poor lake. What have they done to you?" Mason woke up crying, his wife Mona nudging him.

"Hey Buster, wake up, you're having another dream."

Mason looked at her and patted her hand.

"You want to talk about it?" she asked. Mason shook his head a picked up his dream journal.

"In the morning," he said to Mona, and she rolled over and went back to sleep as Mason started to write.

Gordon's Voice

First, it's dark.

Not the darkness of night, not that pansy dark. A darkness of your bedroom when you've just pissed your bed, like that little pisser of a boy does when I come home late. I swear to God.

So it's dark. It's like oil, greasy, or the shit that comes out of them octopussies if you was to slice their pie holes.

Dreams is dreams. Don't mean nothing.

Hardly worth a honk, you know what I mean.

Most a mine were about cars and ladies, all the things I'm good at working on. My new girl and her tight little butt—little missy is a good thing, cooks good, does everything good. Everything. If it weren't for that pisser of a boy of hers, we'd get along great.

Those dreams seemed like they'd be scary, but they ain't. Not really. The dark would just seem like it were sleep or something, but it's part of the dream. An oozy kind of dark.

Aw, screw it. Ain't worth talking about. Once I wake up and grab a brew and get out to my car and drive with the windows down and the air down my neck, I'll take ol' Betsy out on 96 and run her up and down to Wixford or Milford, running alongside them midnight running semis, just hearing those big wheels on the road seems like a purring cat and puts me back to near sleep. Reminds me of my trucker days. The times when I had a job, something to do, some place to go.

Once I've had the dream, I don't go back to her trailer.

Even though it ain't nothing. Just a dream. But it seems to get a hold of my imagination and I need to go shake it off.

If I can just get past the darkness.

See, the problem is the boy pisses his bed. And she won't do nothing about it. Even worse, once she blamed it on me. Stupid cunt. Said he never did it unless I was over. She'll never say that again.

So the dream always comes out of that oozy dark. The boy has pissed his bed, and the piss is all black. And for once I let him have it like he knows he's got it coming. And the piss just starts coming out all over. Not blood, but piss. I can smell it. Black piss. It comes out of his little dick, and his ass and then his mouth and nose, even his ears and his fuckin' eyes. All black piss. And the harder I hit, the more he pisses, and the more he pisses the harder I hit.

And then it's on me and the boy is gone and I've got it all on me and I'm just standing there, breathing hard and watching it move up my hands and covering my arms like it's alive, like that spider feller in the movies.

It ain't piss no more. It's more like skin. Ain't nothing going to wash it off, neither. Black, like oil. Dark.

Stupid to talk about it. Stupid to even think about it. Just running the highway helps. Counting the miles down. Down from each marker. Or following tail. Then I can breathe again. I'll go back to my place and get some rest, or back to her after that little pisser is gone off to school.

I swear to God, that little son of a bitch has it coming.

CHAPTER FIVE

Emma noticed the sound of her shoes clicking across the hardwood floors as she moved from room to room through her house. Cleo, the cat, looked up at her as she walked through the family room.

"At least somebody needs me," she said out loud. *Alone again, naturally,* is what she thought.

She fed the cat some dry food and put down some fresh water. She looked through the mail and tossed most of it out without opening it, and carried the bills to a small office that she kept just off the kitchen.

Emma checked her email. AOL, the news flashes, the president's latest address, another celebrity arrested, and the latest study on weight gain.

Emma looked over the email; it was mostly spam and nothing from Dylan. She was relieved and disappointed at the same time.

She typed "dreams" into the search engine (enhanced by Google) and up came Dr. Dream, "a man who can analyze your dreams on line, visit the Website, subscribe to the service, join the chat—"

She passed that up. There was another site devoted to poetry and dreams. She clicked on:

In My Dream

You were wearing
a yellow hat
and blowing bubbles
from a spoon
I called your name
and somehow knew French
knew Russian
no one else could hear

Emma thought of Dylan again. The poem made her sad and heartsick and lonely. She started to reflect on how she had met Dylan through a therapy list serve, where a group of therapists who did work with couples and families put forth ideas and questions and dilemmas. Dylan was in the midst of an argument with some other therapists over the use of medication. Emma had admired Dylan's courage and intellect, and they began to email off list.

Then Emma discovered that Dylan lived in Grand Rapids, just an hour away. They met in person at a conference last winter, and Emma was strongly attracted. They met at a retreat last summer, and Emma started to find herself falling hopelessly in love. She had begun to tell Dylan her feelings. Dylan had begun to tell Emma the same. Emma was married. Dylan was not.

"Go to bed," Emma said to herself, but looked at her email again.

No new messages.

> Hi Dylan!
> Just letting you know that I was thinking of you!
> Warmly, Em.

Emma hit "delete."

> Hey Dyl!

Delete.

> Hi Dylan—
> Hope you're fine. I'm miserable.

Delete.

> Dylan—
> What do you think?
> Emma

Send.

Shit! Send? What did I do? How do you work this goddamned machine? Can you get the letter back? Unsend? No?

Emma looked under old mail. No luck. Sent mail? Last letter was to Dylan. She tried unsend. It was too late.

She read the letter again. Four words. A question. Simple. Harmless. Open ended. But Dylan would know what she was saying, and what was behind it. Bold. Daring. Inviting.

Damn!

Emails are the worst of all worlds, she pondered, *the impulsivity of a conversation without the non-verbals, the permanence of a letter without a day to keep from sticking it in the mailbox.*

But it's worst than just an email. I'm about to cheat on Frank.

I'm in trouble.

Emma was in bed before Frank came in. She was awake when he came to bed. "Would you go to therapy with me?" she asked when he climbed into bed.

Frank was quiet for a moment. "Is it that bad?" he asked.

"Frank, I'm in trouble. I mean, we're in trouble. I'm not sure I can stay married to you. I'm not sure I can do it." Emma began to cry.

"What's wrong, Emma?" asked Frank.

"I just don't think I love you anymore. We've become so different. We never spend time together, and when we do it's one of us dragging the other someplace we don't want to be. I'm trying Frank, but I just can't keep trying alone."

"I know I've been gone a lot. Hey, Emma. I'll try to get home earlier. Is that it?"

"That would help," said Emma. Then she took a deep breath. "I think it's more than that. Frank, I think I'm in real trouble here."

"Is there someone else?" asked Frank.

"No. I mean, yes. But no," she said.

"What?!" Frank asked, insistently.

Emma took another deep breath and realized she had been holding her breath, then she said, as she exhaled, "I have a crush on someone."

"Who is he?"

"I'd rather not say."

"Do I know him? Does *he* know how you feel?"

"No and no. Not yet, anyway. Maybe." *Emma, shut up* is what she was screaming to herself on the inside. She couldn't believe she was telling him what she was telling him.

"Do you know him from work or from——"

"Frank, that's not the point. It's not my infatuation, which is harmless. It's us, Frank. The point is *us* and *us* isn't working for *me*."

Frank got out of bed.

"Where are you going?"

"I'm going to sleep in the family room. But I'm taking my pillow."

"Frank, don't go. Let's talk."

"You know what Emma? Fuck talk and fuck you."

After Frank left she could hear the voices of sports announcers downstairs. Emma had won the battle to keep television out of the bedroom but Frank retreated to the family room if they were fighting.

"Fuck talk!" Like a cave man. Or Tonto. Or Tarzan. "Fuck talk!" Put it on his gravestone. Fitting epitaph. "Fuck talk!" Well, at least he knows.

Emma tossed and turned most of the night. She wasn't sure if she was awake for most of it or if she was dreaming that she was awake most of the night. Either way, by the time she got up, Emma felt spent.

The TV was still on at 5 a.m. and Emma got into her sweatpants and a warm windbreaker over a long sleeved T-shirt. She put on sneakers and climbed on her bike. Even though it was dark, Emma was familiar enough with the trail and the gathering light was sufficient to find her way.

"Riding in the Dark: The Autobiography of Emma Davis," she thought. *The Wallerstein studies say divorce is bad for kids. Nathan will never get over it,* she thought.

Fuck Wallerstein, she thought.

"Please, God help," she said out loud.

When she got home Frank was getting dressed for work. He was sitting on the bed with his dress shirt on, his pants off, and was pulling on a sock. He looked up at Emma, and she could see that his eyes were red.

"Look, about last night, I'm sorry I got so angry. So, yeah. Counseling, Emma, whatever it takes," said Frank.

Emma felt an endearing warmth towards Frank, and a twist of disappointment at the same moment.

"Yeah, okay. Would you like me to call someone?"

"That would be fine. It's your field," said Frank.

Emma showered, and Frank went to work.

Emma dried herself and went into the study and checked the email.

Nothing from Dylan.

"What am I going to do?" Emma asked herself.

Go to work. Go to therapy. Talk. Fuck talk.

Jake stopped by a coffee shop on his way to his midnight shift on the psych unit. He felt tired and wired. Jake picked up a Starbucks with an extra shot of espresso, since he'd only slept four hours the day before.

Jake barely registered the drone of the nursing report. "Thorazine, 50mg bid—" *Blah blah blah,* and he slid over to the bathroom and tried to close the door without making a sound. He opened a bottle of extra strength Aspirin and took three of them. Then he took a swig from a bottle of antacid, then another long pull. He capped off his therapeutic regimen with two pieces of cinnamon gum. He looked at his face, puffy, bags under his red eyes.

Jake said quietly but audibly, "Who the hell are you?" He could barely recognize himself.

Returning to the nursing report room he noticed Yvonne, the charge nurse, shoot him a frown. Jake rolled his eyes.

Once report was over Yvonne was up in his face. Jake tried to avoid eye contact, but Yvonne's presence was insistent. It was clear she was going to confront Jake. He looked into her face and saw the "bad attitude" frown she wore beneath her tightly twisted corn rows.

"You don't look well, Jake. In fact, you look like shit. Should I send you home?"

"No," Jake answered.

"No, I won't. The only reason I won't Jake, the *only* reason I won't send you home, is because we're short staffed tonight. It's you and me, the new kid and Stella."

"Queen of the psych techs."

"She does just fine Jake. But that means I need you tonight. We have a new admission that you would know about if you were in report."

"I must have missed that moment."

"I know you did. I'd have Joe do it, but he's too new. And Stella is Stella so that leaves you."

"Got it," said Jake. "I can handle it."

"Be quick if you can, Jake. I want another male on the floor."

"Okay. Who's the admission?"

"Brandi Janes, white female, twenty-six years old. She'd made a suicide attempt after her kids were placed in foster care. There had been some Protective Services involvement."

"Kids? Where are the kids?" asked Jake.

Yvonne was handing Jake a clipboard with the assessment packet and a pen as she answered. "I don't know. That's something you can find out. I'm assuming if they're in foster care, they're doing okay. But I want a clear suicide assessment. The admitting doc is Chin and the provisional diagnosis is major depressive disorder, single episode. We're guessing there will be personality disorder as a secondary diagnosis, so watch for any 'games.' Don't let yourself get manipulated. And one other complication."

Jake looked at Yvonne and waited.

"Her boyfriend is with her, and he seems to be a pistol."

"Oh. Is that's why I'm doing it?"

"No, but he refused to leave until the interview was done."

"Why didn't afternoons handle this?" asked Jake. "They're always leaving us their shit to clean up. They have the personnel."

"I know. It's a dump on us. But these people didn't show until 10:45 p.m. and we're here just fifteen minutes later."

"Great. So on top of everything, they've been waiting an hour?"

"Yeah. You better get to it."

Jake entered the dayroom and saw a man and a woman sitting at a round table on the hard plastic hospital chairs. The woman looked haggard, with stringy blond hair, red eyes, big breasts in a tight black T-shirt and low hip-hugging jeans.

The man was a long drink of water. Red flannel shirt, unbuttoned and untucked, over a black T-shirt, jeans and cowboy boots. He also wore a straw cowboy hat with big aviator mirrored sunglasses. He was holding the girl's hand as Jake approached. Jake noticed something else about the cowboy. He was smoking.

"No smoking," said Jake as he approached the table.

"Well, that's a hell of a way to say hello," answered the cowboy.

"Sorry about the wait. You folks hit the shift change right on the button. My name is Jake Harrison, I'm a psych tech, and I'll be doing your intake interview. I take it you've been cleared by medical, over at the emergency room?" Jake was addressing the female, and was sorry that he opened the contact by confronting her boyfriend. Jake introduced himself to both of them and got their names, Brandi and Gordon, and made a point to shake their hands.

Brandi said she was cleared by the medical people and that she just wanted to get to sleep. She looked tired, but Jake noticed that her color was good.

"You have any medication to give her?" asked Gordon, taking another drag on his cigarette.

"I'm not the doctor. That would be his decision," said Jake. He pantomimed putting out the cigarette to Gordon, hoping a little humor might de-escalate his attitude. Gordon blew his smoke out towards Jake.

"Mr. Thomas, I'm here to interview Miss Janes and see she's gets what she needs for the night. Now unless you are in fact her husband, I'm going to have to ask you to leave."

Gordon sat in his chair and stared at Jake with his mouth open. Then he took another drag on his cigarette.

"It's okay, Gordon," said Brandi. "I'll be okay."

"Shut up," said Gordon. Jake heard the words like a slap. "This is between me and him."

Gordon never stopped looking at Jake's face, even when he spoke to Brandi. He was still sitting in his chair, but now pushed away from the table and let go of her hand. Jake shifted his stance in case Gordon charged him.

"First, you say you're a peon," Gordon said to Jake, "and then you start giving orders. Which is it?"

"I'm a peon with authority," said Jake. "Look man, I don't know what your gig is—"

"Gig?"

"Yeah, what your trip is, your gig, what you're doing now, your show, your act, but I'm just doing my job and—"

Brandi reached out and began stroking Gordon's arm, saying, "It's okay, Gordon. You can go now. I'll be okay."

Gordon never stopped looking at Jake, but the veins on his neck bulged. He said, "Fetch me a cup of coffee and I'll go."

Jake felt the blood drain from his face and resisted the urge to make a fist. Instead, he sighed. He looked at the stringy man, measuring his toughness. Jake didn't know if he could take him in a fight, and here on the unit he could only use restraint moves, nothing aggressive. He could call security. Call the guy's bluff, but that would be a big stand off and another mess.

"We don't have any coffee made. It's midnight. How about water—then you'll go?"

"Fetch me a water," said Gordon.

What an asshole, thought Jake. He realized that the guy looked a lot like Sam Elliott.

Jake walked in to the kitchen and poured water from the faucet into a styrofoam cup, walked it back to Gordon and put it on the table.

"Looks like your hands are shakin', boy," said Gordon with a smile. He stood up leaned over and kissed Brandi.

"I'll call you tomorrow, darlin'. Don't take any shit from these people."

The cup sat on the table, untouched.

Jake's interview with Brandi Janes was short. He learned that Protective Services had been called on Brandi after her eight-year-old son showed up at school with a handprint on his face, and that he'd admitted it was his mom's boyfriend who had slapped him. Brandi made excuses for Gordon, saying that he was a good man and that her son had been giving him "back talk" and "attitude." She'd been surprised when her son was taken into custodial care, and that had prompted her to take and overdose of Vicadan, but then got scared that she wouldn't see her son again. She called Gordon, and then the ambulance.

Brandi denied being suicidal, but Jake rated her as a risk, which meant he or other staff would be looking in on her every half hour.

Brandi said that the P.S. worker who had made the investigation was "a real bitch." Jake wondered if it could possibly be Holly from the Dream Group, and he asked if she remembered the investigator's name.

"Masters, I think," answered Brandi, but she couldn't remember the first name. *What are the chances*, thought Jake.

Marianne is at court.

There are several racks of women's clothing right outside the courtroom. She's thinking that she needs to get a really sharp suit, something in a new color before she meets with the judge. The meeting is in just a few minutes, so Marianne feels the need to hurry.

Marianne decides to look at the racks of suits. The suits appear to be lined up like the colors in a child's Crayola box, with white, then tans and light yellow to lime and forest green, pinks and reds, browns into black. I wonder if there are sixty-four, *she thinks, and recognizes Muzak was piping in the Beatle's song, "When I'm Sixty-Four."*

I'm supposed to have sixty-four suits, *she thinks.*

Where's the administrative assistant when you need them?

Are they all my size?

Doesn't matter. Time to try them on.

Start with the end in mind, *Marianne unsnaps her skirt and pulls down her slip.*

She gasps because she is wearing a dark skin-tight outfit that almost looks like scuba gear. She searches for a zipper and can't find one. Then she starts trying to peel it off.

"It's like it's a part of my skin," she says.

Marianne decides to grab a dark suit, but thinks, Isn't that just like the one I am wearing? How about the blue? No, I have one of those at home. *But then knows she needs something that accents the skin she is wearing.* Am I wearing it, or is it a part of me?

Marianne decides to put her clothes back on when she hears the bailiff intone, "All Rise." She hurries into the courtroom.

"Marianne, your brief?" asks the judge.

Marianne notices that no one seemed to care about what she's wearing. She looks at the judge, with his dark robes.

I'll play it straight, she thinks. Marianne begins to discuss the merits of her case, but realizes she has no idea what she's arguing. At the same time she is casually putting on her blouse and jacket and finally her skirt, doing a reverse striptease.

"Very good," announces the judge. Everyone in the courtroom claps. Marianne bows.

"For my next number, I'll perform a Spanish table dance."

Marianne is about to climb on the table to perform a dance, a bolero, with a rose between her teeth if she can find one. She notices dirty plates on the table, chicken bones and other trash on the plates that litter the room.

"I'll get someone in here to clean this up," says Marianne and steps out of the courtroom—into the basement.

"Not a good idea to be in here," she says in her ten-year-old voice.

That's when she woke up.

"We're not talking about that one. That's for sure."

She wrote the dream down. Then she went about her morning ritual of working out, cleaning up, and eating. But in the back of her mind she had begun to wonder if there was something so basic about herself that everyone noticed, that she never realized herself. It seemed to be a part of her.

By mid-October there was a distinct chill in the air in the evening. The Dream Group gathered, dressed in jackets and sweaters. Emma wore corduroys and a bulky sweater, her dark hair swept back off her forehead. Emma was also wearing her new bifocals.

The group filed into Emma's office and took their usual seats. Mason sat in the leather easy chair, while Marianne and Jake shared the couch. Holly sat on the straight-back wooden chair that Emma brought in for the group, and Emma used her desk chair, moving it into the circle rather than sitting at her desk.

Emma exchanged pleasantries with the group. She asked if they might spend a few minutes discussing what had happened since the last group. They talked about what it was like to write their dreams down, how the dreams stayed with them, how they were becoming more aware during their dreams.

After the topic of the awareness exercise was reviewed, Emma began to discuss the concept of "archetypes." She explained some characters or places or symbols are archetypal in nature. For instance, she explained, the idea of "mother" was understood internationally. So, then, was the concept of hero, though each culture created their own versions of a hero, be it Hercules or Indiana Jones.

Then Emma invited the group to discuss some dreams.

Marianne pointed at the others. Emma didn't take the bait.

"Marianne," she asked, "are you trying to distract me from asking if you've had any dreams?"

"I have no dreams to speak of," said Marianne.

"No dreams, or no dreams to speak of?" asked Emma.

They talked for a while about the difference. Emma gently suggested to Marianne that she might be uncomfortable discussing some of her dreams. Marianne admitted that this was true. Emma had learned long ago that a discussion focused on defenses or resistance could be just as beneficial as getting into the content of a dream.

"How would you feel if you told us your dream?" asked Emma, gently side-stepping Marianne's defenses. Marianne admitted that she'd feel embarrassed. Emma wondered out loud if she might even feel ashamed. Marianne asked Emma to explain the difference.

"We get embarrassed or guilty over what we do. We feel shame over who we are," Emma distinguished. "It's a deeper feeling and seems more rooted in our identity. It also feels more intolerable."

Marianne admitted that her sense was closer to shame, but couldn't explain why. Emma stressed that *why* wasn't as important as was being aware.

"I don't even know if you need to do more to get this. I mean I suspect you do a lot of *doing more*," suggested Emma.

"That's true. What's the alternative?" asked Marianne.

"Guys?" asked Emma, looking at the other group members.

"You could just notice it," suggested Mason, looking regally professorial in the leather chair.

"Notice how you feel," offered Holly.

"And lighten up, man," added Jake. "Stop taking yourself so seriously."

"So maybe you just become more aware of it, how you handle your feelings. Maybe you can become more accepting of it," said Emma.

"All right," said Marianne. She made a gesture with her hands, both of them waving in front of her, that indicated she was done and ready for the group to move on. Emma picked up on it and looked at Jake.

"So Jake, you have a dream?"

Jake related his vampire nightmare of being alone on the psych ward and having an awareness of another presence, from the locked side of the unit. As he spoke, Marianne was cringing and was leaning away from Jake on the couch.

Holly and Mason were leaning forward, and appeared spellbound.

When Jake reached the point where he was looking through the window in the door, and seeing that the vampire was a mirror image of himself, Holly put her hands over her mouth and Mason nodded slowly. Marianne looked like she was no longer listening.

"Now there's a twist," said Holly.

"So what was that like," asked Emma, "for you to see yourself in the vampire?"

"Frightening," said Jake. "It was actually horrifying." He had a faraway look.

"Okay," Emma turned to the group, "one way to give feedback on someone else's dream is to think about what you would think if *you* had this dream. What would you make of it?"

Mason was still leaning forward and answered. "For me, I would think that I was trying to keep part of myself locked away."

"So I'm trying to avoid getting in touch with my inner vampire?" asked Jake.

Mason laughed and Holly and Marianne smiled. Emma was glad that Jake had warmed up to the group again. His decision to share a dream, especially one where he felt vulnerable, was a good sign.

"Jake, give us five words that describe a vampire," asked Emma. She gave him a pen and a legal pad to write them down.

Jake wrote:

> Undead
>
> Killer

Mysterious

Nocturnal

Seductive

"Okay," said Emma, "write five things he's not."

Jake wrote:

Nice

Alive

Free

Friendly

Working with others

"So which list is more like you?" Emma asked.

Jake admitted, "The second list is more like me. But I'm also nocturnal. So what does that mean, I'm dreaming about what I'm not?"

"I don't know," said Emma. "What fits best? Let me ask you this. Which word on the first list, the one that describes a vampire, which word least describes you?"

"Killer," said Jake.

"Interesting," said Emma. After all of Jake's hostile humor that he'd displayed in the first few groups, "killer" was the way he least wanted to be seen.

"In fact, I'm a coward," said Jake.

"Takes a lot of courage to admit that," said Holly.

"Very funny."

"I'm serious," said Holly.

Jake smiled and their eyes met for a moment. Holly smiled back.

"So," said Emma, "what on the second list best describes you?"

"Not free," said Jake.

"So how is a vampire not free?"

"I don't know why I said that," said Jake.

"But you did," said Emma. "Listen, Jake, for a moment let's not make this about you. This is about vampires." Emma didn't want to move too fast for Jake. She didn't want him to feel threatened.

"Okay," Jake answered. "Vampires are not free because they can't be in sunlight. That fits."

"Make sure it's not about you," reminded Emma.

The group talked about vampires, vampire movies, *Dracula*, *Nosferatu*. Mason seemed to relish talking about vampire films.

"There is one other thing that vampires are," offered Holly, sitting with her hands clutched on the edge of her wooden chair, "that we haven't talked about yet. They're totally dependent."

"Dependent?" asked Emma. "That's interesting, Holly. Say more."

"Well, I mentioned before I'm alcoholic—"

"Hi, Holly—" said Jake.

"Very funny," said Holly. "I'm thinking that vampires are a hell of a lot like addicts. They're addicted to blood, and they live in darkness."

"The shadow," said Mason. "Carl Jung."

"So let's get back to Jake," said Emma. "What fits for you?"

"Well, it's a lot to think about. Why am I the vampire?"

No one answered Jake. Emma said, "You're right. That is a lot to think about. Do you feel okay about it?"

Jake nodded. "I'm done. We can move on."

"Okay," Emma said. She was relieved that Jake had shared something with the group and there hadn't been a conflict. "Who's next?" she asked.

Mason volunteered to tell his dream about going fishing, seeing the Samurai, trying to avoid him. Then he related how he had found a group of muddy and soiled books. "It was a surprise to me, but I piled them up and burned them with a lit cigarette, and I haven't smoked in years."

"Professor Burning Books," said Jake. "It's like your Indian name."

"Yeah, that sounds like the last line of a haiku, doesn't it? 'Professor Burning Books.' So I burn the books, because they're ruined, they're all soiled."

"Not wet?" asked Emma.

"No. Dirty. Muddy. Streaked. Wrecked."

"Okay, go on."

Mason told the rest of the dream, how he was concerned that he'd draw the attention of the Samurai, and then meeting Jake who was painting a landscape. Mason went into a good deal of depth about what it felt like to see the lake, polluted and poisoned, and how sad he felt in the dream.

"I paid attention to how I felt. Just like your exercise. And I felt remorseful and wished I hadn't burned the books." said Mason.

"You wish you hadn't retired." said Marianne.

"Well, I wondered about that, but I'm actually glad I retired."

"You're sad now, aren't you?" asked Emma.

"Yes," nodded Mason. His eyes were red and looked watery.

"So what's the sadness?" asked Emma.

"Dead lake. Burning books. Isn't it obvious?" asked Mason. "It's like, life is over. What's strange is, I don't feel that way. I love my life. I'm working on a book. My wife and I are talking about traveling to London. I love my kids. This doesn't match up."

"But it resonates, emotionally?" asked Emma.

"Yes."

"Maybe we should just leave it there."

Mason looked at her and said, "Emma, you seem to have a gift."

"Thank you, Mason. You're generous."

"No. I'm being honest. I was wondering if you'd just tell me what you see?"

"Well, first, what I see isn't as important as what you see."

"Just skip the disclaimer," said Jake.

"I understand that, Emma," said Mason. "but I want to hear you talk about it, if you would. And weave in what you told us about archetypes, earlier."

Emma crossed her hands in her lap. "Okay. Your dream is in three parts. First, a journey to find a lake, for fishing. Fishing is a symbol that can resonate in any number of ways. Maybe it's fishing for 'ideas' or 'experiences.' So in the first part you see a warrior, an archetype, and you want to avoid him. Warriors represent power or some fierce energy that you need to muster. You're running away from it; you don't want that archetype right now.

"In the second part you're burning books. Almost like a ritual, but not to destroy ideas but to clean up a mess. This is accompanied by remorse. Maybe grief. Something is ending, the ending of which might attract the warrior, which you don't want to do."

Emma took a breath. She noticed the stillness in the room, with each set of eyes engaged on her. She continued. "The third part is finding another archetype. The artist, who shows you that the lake is polluted," said Emma, slowing down, "and dead. If I had this dream, Mason, I'd wonder about the imagery of facing something I don't want to face, the fear of the thing, and the images of burning your precious books and being unable to fish your lake. This may seem like a strange question, Mason, but when was your last physical?"

CHAPTER SIX

Emma looked at the leaves changing in the early morning chill. She saw two black squirrels race from one side of her yard to the other, one chasing the other around the tree, up a fence, back across the yard again and again up the tree.

What are they doing, she wondered? *Fighting over food? Mating? Playing? It's probably food or sex. It's always food or sex.* Emma walked through her house and smelled her coffee brewing. Her footsteps were alternately sharp on the hardwood floor and dull on the area rugs. She walked from room to room and looked over the furnishings, the small mementos, the pictures on the walls. Her parents smiling at her through a black and white shot. Her mother looked beautiful and happy, her dad seemed to be trying to suppress a smirk. They were dressed up, at some formal affair. She'd never know now where they were. Did her mother ever tell her?

Emma wiped away a tear and looked over the landscaped yard.

"I love my house," she said out loud.

Frank has been generous, she thought. *He makes such a good living that it enables me to live in a beautiful house, work as much or as little as I want, and I can take chances, like the Dream Group.*

It's worth it to work on our marriage. Look at how my parents stuck it out. And they were miserable.

Emma went to the phone book and looked for Marital Counseling in the Yellow Pages. There were several names, including her own. Most of them were familiar to her. There was the therapist that she and Frank saw for three years. *When was that? We finished up two years ago. Or we thought we were finished.*

Emma thought to call Frank and ask if he'd like to go back to Janet Overton, but decided she didn't want to return to Janet Overton.

So that's decided. Good.

Food or sex.

What about love, Emma asked herself. *Squirrels—it's food or sex. They don't love, do they?*

Love is a decision. I remember learning that in the first marriage encounter weekend we went on. We were so high on that weekend that we got involved as an "Engaged Encounter" presenting couple. Frank was into it—God, we worked hard on it. What happened? We dropped out after a few months.

She looked back at the phone book.

This will be our third course of treatment. Is that good or bad, over a twenty-three-year marriage? Maybe it's neither. Two marriage counselors, a marriage encounter, a nice house in a university town, a son in college, good vacations. It takes a lot to keep a marriage together. If a boat has a leak, you start bailing, right? When do you know it's time for a new boat?

Food and sex.

The food's been good. And at first the sex was, too. Then it became, just sex. Emma looked at the phone book. *Love is a decision.*

If I can decide to love Frank, act "as if," can I be happy?

Would I be happy with Dylan?

Emma pushed the thought behind with another, *Love is a decision.*

Maybe that's what it takes—the decision to act loving when you don't feel it. But isn't that what I've been doing for the past—how many years? Ten, fifteen, twenty?

At first we were in love. It seemed like a good fit. Then Frank's affair with work started. I called it "emotionally unavailable," and once we did marriage encounter it was good again—for quite a few months. Then during my graduate school I became convinced that we needed to deal with our family of origin issues and a lack of intimacy. We attacked it for four years. Then life was okay and I started my practice and Nathan started school and we settled into a rhythm that was—what—satisfactory? No one else can make you happy. I've said that, what, hundreds of times to my clients.

Maybe Frank is right. Maybe I need to go on anti-depressants. Maybe that's what it'll take.

Keep bailing out the boat.

Food and sex. Mixing metaphors now. Food and sex in the boat with a hole in it. The hole won't seal so the food is all wet and sex is not desirable on a leaking boat.

I've gone over the edge, thought Emma.

She went up stairs to make the calls, but found herself standing outside of her son's open door. She looked into his room, untouched since he'd left, the posters of NBA stars on the wall, the soccer trophy on his desk. *Something is missing,* she thought. *Yeah, him. Nathan.* Emma choked up and then let herself cry. She surprised herself at the well of grief that opened once she started. She found herself sitting on Nathan's bed, wiping her eyes with one of his high school sweatshirts. She went back to her own bedroom, picked up the phone, and looked up the numbers she was seeking.

She made two calls: one to her doctor for an evaluation for anti-depressants. The second to a new marriage counselor for an appointment. His voicemail said he'd call back soon.

Emma sighed. *Help is on the way.*

Emma went back to click on to her computer and up popped an email. It was a message from Dylan.

Emma,
Maybe we should meet for coffee.
Let me know when and where.
Dylan

Holly is in a church. Which church, she doesn't know, only that she recognizes the building as a church. Christian, yes, because there is a cross and an altar and pews and stained glass windows.

She notices a man coming through a side door, all in black except for the white collar of priesthood.

He looks like Robert DeNiro, to Holly. He is attractive and has an air of authority. She can smell incense burning. Holly thinks that a service should be starting soon because other people are filing in. She notices several of her colleagues from work, and for some reason a group of cheerleaders.

Holly has the idea that it is up to her to start the investigation.

She approaches the altar and the congregation becomes still and the priest calls out, "Sister Holly, you've come before this congregation to repent for your sins." Holly replies, "I'm here to ask the questions, Father."

The priest looks at her and says, "I believe you would undergo the test against witches?"

The cheerleaders begin to chant, "Yes, the Test—Yes, the Test—Yes, the Test."

Holly reaches the altar and asks, "Who are you to test me?"

The priest looks at her and says, "I am the one who knows. You have nothing to fear, if you have nothing to fear."

"That's when I have nothing to fear," Holly says.

Several choir members in red robes approach Holly and place a dark robe and red piping on her shoulders.

"You who have nothing to fear will have nothing to fear."

"I have nothing to fear, and I am no witch."

The priest intones, "Sister Holly, you have a choice of nails or rope? What is your choice?"

"Wait, what does this mean, nails or rope? What are you asking?"

"For your test, your trial on the cross, your crucifixion. Shall it be by nail or by rope?" asks the priest.

"Well, neither! I never agreed to be crucified."

"Neither? The first test is over. It is to be trial by fire!" says the priest.

The cheerleaders shriek with glee and Holly notices the crowd is much larger than before. Now there are hundreds in the church, though it no longer even appears to be a church. It seems more like an auditorium.

"A witch will burn," says the priest and touches the palm of each of Holly's hands. Kneeling, he bows down and anoints each of Holly's feet with some kind of oil. Holly looks at her hands where the priest had touched them and watches the tiniest blue flame in the palm of each. There

is no pain, but some sensation, almost a slight tingle. She knows that the priest intends to crucify her.

Suddenly Holly is on a beach, wearing a simple, blue, terrycloth bathrobe. She is near the ocean and feels mesmerized by the pounding waves. Holly sees the water caress her bare feet. She looks to the palms of her hands. She sees the Stigmata, a white scarring across her palms. "I was actually crucified and somehow I survived," *she thinks.*

Holly was leaving work the following day. The temperature had taken a dip and the wind was blowing. Leaves were falling rapidly, like an evacuation. Holly walked across the parking lot to her Volkswagon Bug. She carried her brown leather satchel, loaded with paperwork. Holly's car was at the end of the row.

Holly got in and turned over the engine and threw a Bare-Naked Ladies CD on the player. She started to put the car into reverse when she saw the piece of paper on her windshield.

"What the heck?" she asked out loud. She stopped the car and leaned out to get the piece of paper.

"I know" was written across it in pencil.

Holly crumpled it up and threw it on the floor of her car.

"I know."

What? Who knows? What?

Holly's job of investigating child abuse cases naturally made her unpopular with a large segment of her "customers," but it was rare for her to be actively threatened. Holly thought back on her day to try to reconstruct it. She called one of her supervisors on her cell phone.

"Gene?"

"Yeah."

"This is Holly. Gene, I think I just received a threatening note."

"Where are you?"

"I'm driving away from work. I'm on my way to a meeting."

"So you're okay?" Gene asks. "What does the note say?"

"It just says, 'I know.'"

"Hmmm. Not really a threat," replied Gene.

"Well, I feel threatened," said Holly. She stopped at a red light and looked at the cars next to hers, and checked her rear view mirror. She hadn't intended on turning, but took a right turn, just to see if anyone followed her.

"Okay. Have you got any idea who sent it? Is it signed?"

"I'm assuming it's a man, but maybe not. No, it's not signed."

"Don't do anything to the note."

"I already crumpled it up," said Holly.

"Well, it could be evidence."

"Right. I won't throw it away." She looked again in her rear view mirror. Another car had turned right behind her.

"Any really emotional cases right now?" asked Gene.

"The only one that's been really charged is the Jane's case."

"The mom with the badass boyfriend, Mr. Thomas. If it's the boyfriend—he was the perp, right?"

"Yeah, slapped his girlfriend's son hard enough to leave a hand print on his face."

"Why'd he slap the boy?"

"The boy says it was because he talked back, but since then he's recanted his statement."

"Probably scared," said Gene.

"Yeah, well, I met the guy, and he is scary." Holly stepped on the gas and made a quick lane switch, then turned left at the first street.

"Where's Mom and the boy now?"

"Mom took an overdose, which looks like it might be a gesture rather than an attempt. She was hospitalized over the weekend for a psych evaluation and the son is at his grandparents. But get this—the E.R. notes that her boyfriend was with her right up to the time of admission."

"She's just digging herself deeper. Charges filed on the boyfriend?" asked Gene.

"Yeah, but an assault like that doesn't get an A.P.B." Holly noticed that no one seemed to be following her. She felt foolish for taking such chances with traffic.

"Well, if this guy is a narcissist and gets even with people who prick his self-esteem, he might be responsible for the note. Keep it around. We can hand it to the police and see what they can come up with at the lab. Holly, in the meantime, keep an eye over your shoulder. I'll call this in to the LPD and see if they'll try harder to find our friend."

"Thanks, Gene."

Holly ended the call on her cell and then hit her speed dial. Martha, her A.A. sponsor, picked up.

"Martha, it's Holly."

"Hey, Kiddo, how you doin'?"

"I just got a threatening note."

"No! Work or personal?"

"Well, I assume it was work. I assumed it was the jerk I had the run-in with last week."

"Okay. What do you need to do?" asked Martha.

"I need to call the supervisor and report it and I did that already."

"Good."

"And I'm on my way to a meeting right now."

"Good."

"And I'm calling you." Holly noticed she was calming down. She was driving slower, and she was nearly at the A.A. club.

"Right. Okay. I'm in for the night, so call me after the meeting and let me know how you feel then."

Holly said "Okay, I'm at the club now. Thanks."

Martha said, "You're doing all the right footwork, and guys who leave notes are usually cowards. He wants you to be scared. You know?"

"Yeah, you're probably right. The guy I thought it might be, well, this doesn't really fit his M.O. He's much more direct."

"Any other creeps in your life?"

"There's a guy in the Dream Group who is a jerk. But he's cute. I don't think it could be him."

Holly went to the meeting and then went out to eat at an old Italian restaurant on Michigan Avenue. She drove home alone and didn't think to check if she was being followed again until she was home for the night.

Just a few blocks away Jake's alarm clock went off. He had it set to the local jazz station and there was a duet of Archie Shepp and Horace Parlan playing "St. Infirmary's Blues." *Thank God for jazz.*

Jake sat up in bed and looked into the eyes of John Coltrane. There was a big "Blue Train" poster hanging on the wall facing his bed. Jake thought, *Coltrane looks like a saint.*

Jake got up and made coffee. His hands were shaking a little. He opened the freezer and took out a bottle of vodka and gulped down a sharp jolt of the clear liquor and felt it burn all the way down. He resisted the pull to vomit. Jake knew that if he had a drink or two now at 8 p.m., by 11 p.m. when he went to work he'd be fine. So he had one more slug of the bottle, then looked at how much was left and frowned. *How could there be so little left? I bought the bottle this morning and had a drink or two after work—*

"This is getting bad. I better slow down," he said.

Jake got a cup of coffee and a piece of toast and put on some music. He was playing a mix he'd burned on his computer: Billie Holiday's "I Cover The Waterfront," Miles Davis's "It Never Entered My Mind," and Coltrane's "After The Rain." Jake checked for any email messages and then took a shower. He made a sandwich and tried to decide whether he could have one more shot before work. He decided, *Yes.*

Jake gargled twice and put on aftershave. He got into his car and drove the two miles to the hospital.

It was 10:55 p.m.

Jake waited in the parking lot and smoked a cigarette before going in. He saw the new psych tech arrive and exchanged a minute of small talk, complaining about the Spartan's football team, and then got on the elevator together. They were in the nurse's station a minute before the change of shift report was supposed to start.

Yvonne Webster, the charge nurse walked into the room with a big smile spread across her face. She quickly frowned.

"What's that smell?" she asked out loud.

The staff from the afternoon shift was filing in, some making quick notes in charts, and they were joking and eager to leave.

One college age psych tech came into the nurse's station and said, "Dude, who's coming from the party?" and some of the staff laughed. The charge nurse looked at Jake, her eyebrows knitted in an intense frown.

"Let's start report," said the afternoon nurse.

"Brandi Janes checked out today. Her boyfriend visited, and she left with him. LPD arrived shortly after, looking for either one. They suspect he was threatening a P.S. worker and other charges or something. If either of them returns to the floor, we're to call the police—not 911, but a specific office. I have the number in the desk."

Jake remembered that he was going to mention something to Holly about this case. He'd been too distracted before and also knew it would be breaking confidentiality. Then he noticed the frown on Yvonne's face as she stared straight through him.

Yvonne said, "Judy, I'm sorry to interrupt but something needs to be settled before we go on."

She turned again to Jake and said, "I'd like you to join Judy and me in the office."

Jake rolled his eyes. He followed the two women down the short hall. Yvonne looked deadly serious, a frown etched across her dark eyebrows. Jake thought, *Never piss off a woman.*

Once in the charge nurse's office Yvonne said to Judy, "I want you here as a witness." Then she looked at Jake and asked him, "Jake have you been drinking?"

"No," said Jake.

"If I give you a BAC, your breath will show no trace of alcohol?"

"I gargle with Listerine," said Jake.

"Judy, do you smell alcohol?" asked Yvonne.

"Yes, I do."

Jake felt the blood drain from his face.

"I'm asking you to give me a breath test for fitness for duty."

"I had a drink before I went to bed at noon and another one a couple of hours ago."

"You smell," said the nurse, as she produced a small tube from her desk. "Blow in this."

"I told you I had a drink."

"But first you lied. You want to keep your job, you blow in this."

Jake blew.

Yvonne looked at it, then showed it to Judy, who nodded.

"Point oh eight Jake. You drank more than you're telling. Did you drive here, Jake?"

"Yes."

"You could be arrested for that. Do you think you have a problem, Jake?"

"I told you the other night. I'm in therapy."

"With Emma Davis, I remember. For alcohol abuse, Jake?"

"No."

"We'll need a release to speak with your therapist if you want to return to work. I'm writing you up. You're suspended, without pay, for three days. You can write your account of this interaction now, if you'd like, but I want you off the unit ASAP. Judy, do you have a tech who can work a double?"

"I'll check. Jake, do you want me to call you a cab? Or I can give you a ride home?"

"No. I'll walk."

Jake left the unit without writing anything. It was a three-block walk to the nearest bar.

Emma was enjoying the autumn weather on her drive to her office. The sun was bright, and she noticed plastic skeletons hanging on a neighbor's tree, pumpkins, and jack-o-lanterns on a number of her neighbor's porches. She wasn't sure why she was in a good mood. Was it the decision to get into marital counseling or was it that Dylan had emailed her, asking for a meeting? Emma knew the answer. It was Dylan.

She picked up cookies for the group that night. She bought a dozen, shaped like witches and black cats and ghosts, with orange and black frosting.

As she got back in the car for her drive to the office, Emma checked her voicemail, wondering why she always felt the compunction to call someone or check her messages every time she started her car. She noticed that there was a message from Jake.

"Hi, Emma. This is Jake. I need to talk with you. It's kinda urgent. Could you give me a call as soon as you get this?" He left his number.

Damn—he's going to cancel.

Emma called and Jake picked up on the second ring.

"Hello?"

"Hi, is this Jake?"

"Yes, it is. Hi, Emma."

"Hi. What's up?"

"Emma, I have a problem at work."

"Oh?"

"Yeah. I got written up, and I need a note from you before I can come back."

There was a long pause, as Emma tried to cipher what Jake was requesting.

"Emma, are you still there?"

"Yes, Jake. I'm not sure I understand. Why do they need a note from me?"

"Because I kind of told them you were my therapist."

"Well, Jake, we're doing a Dream Group."

"Isn't that therapy?"

"Well, Jake, I certainly hope it's useful. I hope it's therapeutic, even, but I don't think I'd call it therapy."

"I don't see the difference. They just want a note from you saying I can go back to work."

"Jake, I don't think I can do that."

"Why not?"

"Because it's not ethical. For the first thing, I would be lying."

"You'd be helping me though."

"Jake," Emma felt exasperated. She needed some clarity. "Why don't you tell me what happened at work?"

"I got written up."

"For what?"

"I came in late too many times."

"And you need an excuse from a therapist for that?"

"Yeah. My job sucks."

"Jake, I don't think I can help you."

"Oh, you have to! Can we set up a time where I meet with you alone? I'll pay for the session," Jake pleaded.

You bet you'll pay for the session, was Emma's thought. *Where was this going?* Emma decided it made sense to spend a little more time discussing what this was about. "I have a cancellation for the day after our group. Tomorrow. It's at 1 p.m. can you make that?" Emma knew her schedule by heart.

"Yes, I'll be there."

"And I'll see you in group tonight?"

"Of course."

"See you then."

"Bye."

Emma got to work and stored the cookies in the small kitchen she shared with Betty Williams. She checked her email before her first client was to arrive.

What should I do about Dylan's message? she thought.

Emma had let it sit for a couple of days without answering. She considered her options.

I'm so wrapped up in ethics with Jake, yet I'm on the verge of betraying my husband. Jesus, how can I live with myself?

It didn't stop her from answering the email.

Emma set up a new account online with a new address and a new password.

Then she emailed Dylan.

> Subject: Coffee with you
> Dylan,
> I got your message.

I'd like to see you.

Coffee? How about I come to Grand Rapids? You name the place. Since you know GR, send me an address. How's Friday? Four?

This is my new email address.

From now on, only send me messages here.

See you soon,

Emma

On the day before Halloween, the Dream Group met for the fifth time. Emma half expected someone to wear a costume, but the group dressed in their usual fare. Marianne was wearing a carefully coordinated casual business outfit, Holly had on a dark blazer and jeans, Mason was in a sweater, and Jake wore painter's pants and a green Spartan sweatshirt.

Emma had wished that she could have had a few moments alone with Jake before the group meeting, but decided that anything she had to say could wait until tomorrow's appointment. Besides, she still didn't know what the story was.

After ushering the group into her room, and hearing their enthusiastic response to her cookies, Emma began the meeting. She related that this meeting was intended to focus on Jung's concept of "the shadow," defined as all the parts of ourselves that we find unacceptable. Emma related that these parts of our selves could appear in dreams, particularly nightmares.

"This might be a good time to begin to delve into some of those more unpleasant aspects of your dreams." Emma looked to Holly and Marianne, who had seemed so reticent to share the content of their nightmares. She also contrasted some

Native American understanding of nightmares with Jung's idea of the shadow. That is, some believed the nightmare image to be a strong spirit with an important message. The message had to be important, why else send such a strong messenger?

Emma realized that she'd forgot to check in with the group as to how they were doing. She wondered if it was just forgetfulness or if she were a little anxious. Mason and Marianne related that they were fine. Mason admitted he hadn't had a physical yet, but had scheduled one.

Holly related that she was having a tough time at work and was wondering if maybe she had a stalker or if a perpetrator had become obsessed with her.

"He's one of the creepiest guys I've ever met," said Holly.

Jake frowned, like he was about to say something, then cut himself off. "Guy sounds like an asshole," he said. Then he went on to talk about how he'd had a hard week, that he'd run into a problem at work, but he was going to meet individually with Emma to work on it.

Holly asked, "What kind of problem?" Jake didn't seem to want to answer, and Holly asked him why he even brought it up if he wasn't going to be open about it.

Emma was concerned at the potential conflict. She saw how confrontational Holly was, and also knew Jake could be less than direct, but Jake talked back to Holly.

"Why are you always on my case?" he asked.

"You invite it," said Holly.

Jake related that he didn't know what he'd done to become a dumping ground for Holly's feedback.

"I think it's because, almost every time I see you, Jake, you smell like you've been drinking. You smell like alcohol right now," said Holly. Emma was surprised. She hadn't smelled alcohol when Jake came in, but she was sitting across the room from him. After her history with her parents, she usually had a pretty good nose for alcohol, but she'd missed it this time. She was also surprised since they'd addressed this previously, as a group. *Why would Jake take the chance and drink again before a group?*

Meanwhile, Holly had pushed on, "Are you drunk right now?"

Jake said he wasn't going to answer that question.

Mason suggested that the group should move on. But to Emma's surprise, Marianne thought maybe the group shouldn't, until Jake answered.

Emma wasn't quite sure what to do. They had addressed Jake's drinking a couple of weeks ago. She folded her hands in her lap and realized that she should push Jake, but found herself instead asking Marianne, "What are you thinking?"

Marianne answered, "This could be a key issue. Don't you think? Drinking before group?"

"Oh, I forgot. You're a trial lawyer.," interjected Jake, sarcastically, leaning back and looking away from Marianne. "I didn't know I was going to be on trial."

"Actually, I'm in estates," answered Marianne.

"Same thing," said Jake.

"No, it's not," said Marianne. "I think accountability is important. And you agreed with us that you wouldn't drink before group, and you also agreed to talk with us about whether or not you had a problem in the process of the group."

Emma found herself surprised at how forward and clear Marianne was being on this point. She was inwardly reproaching herself for not being more forceful herself, but realized that Marianne was making up for it.

Jake stood up and took a step towards the door.

Emma didn't stand up, but called to him. "Jake, remember, you said you'd stay and talk about it, if you had a problem."

"I've had it," he said.

Jake walked out of the office and the door shut behind him with a slam. The group sat in stunned silence. Then the door opened again and everyone looked up to see Betty Williams looking in, asking Emma, "Is everything all right?"

Emma answered, "Yeah, Betty, I'm fine. Everyone's fine. Someone just got upset and left." Betty apologized for interrupting and quietly shut the door of the office.

Holly finally said, "I pushed it. I'm sorry. He's a drunk, and it's really none of my business."

"What do you mean," asked Mason. "How can you tell that Jake is a drunk?"

"It takes one to know one, Mason," said Holly. "And I'm just going off. I don't know if he is an alcoholic or not. But he was drunk here, just now."

Emma noticed how tense every one seemed, herself included. She kicked herself for being so passive and letting things get out of hand. "Well, Holly, I feel like I'm the one who needs to apologize. I let things get out of control."

"We all did," said Marianne.

Mason said, "I like Jake." He looked absently at the back of his hands, his fingers splayed.

"So do I," said Marianne.

"It's not a matter of liking him or not," said Emma. "It seems that there is some trouble, maybe more trouble than this group is designed to handle, and Jake has a hard time handling his commitment to the group."

"Jake's in hell," said Holly.

"What do you mean?" asked Emma. Marianne and Mason both turned towards Holly.

"If he *is* an alcoholic," Holly offered, "his life is falling apart, he can't stop doing the thing that is destroying him, and he can't do the one thing that might help."

"What's that?" asked Mason.

"Stop drinking," said Holly.

Emma observed that maybe they should stop talking about Jake diagnostically, and focus on what the group wanted to do about his participation.

Marianne and Holly seemed bent on making sure Jake didn't come back, until he would address this problem with drinking before group. Mason seemed to feel that Jake needed the support of the group. He suggested that "Sometimes you people," looking at Holly, "are especially harsh on people who drink."

"*You people*," Holly asked indignantly. "What do you mean by that? Women?"

"No," said Mason, "I mean alcoholics. Recovering alcoholics. A.A. It seems like you think you have all the answers, whether people want to hear them or not."

"Is that what you think? That I'm a—" Holly had begun to sputter.

Emma wanted to help her out, but before she could speak Mason answered, "Strident is a good word."

Emma asked Holly how she was doing.

"A rough week. I dreamed I was crucified," Holly answered.

"Jesus Christ!" exclaimed Marianne.

"Exactly," said Holly. "It was a combination of witchhunt and high school and church. And I was confronting a priest, who had been accused of molesting kids, and I was suddenly the one accused. And he had me lay on a cross, it was in front of all these people, and he touched my hands and feet and this little blue flame appeared and I was nailed to the cross, in front of all these people."

"Trial by fire," said Mason, softly.

"Only it didn't hurt," said Holly. "I was more humiliated than hurt."

"Are you feeling like you're being put to a test right now?" asked Emma.

"Right now? This second?" asked Holly.

"Well, maybe," answered Emma. "I was thinking more generally, like at this time of your life."

"You said it was a really hard time," mentioned Marianne. She was leaning towards Holly.

Holly took a long breath. She leaned back on the couch and said, "I'm being squeezed."

Mason said, "Like orange juice. Not to be flip, but I remember hearing this metaphor: When you get squeezed what comes out is what's inside. You can't squeeze an orange and expect grape juice to emerge."

Holly said, "So what's inside me is anger, judgment—"

"Putting yourself on the cross," said Marianne, softly.

"I do that," said Holly. "I'm horrible! I'm hardest on myself."

"When you start to notice how much you judge," said Emma, "the risk is to judge yourself for it."

"How would I stop judging?" asked Holly, looking directly into Emma's eyes.

"I'm not sure," answered Emma, a little surprised at her own answer. "For now, just notice when you do it."

"Like all the time?" Holly said. It wasn't really a question.

The group spoke for a little while longer about Holly's dreams. Mason noticed that Holly didn't talk about her dreams when Jake was in the room, and Emma wondered if that was significant. Overall, the group related that they wanted Jake to stay in the group, if he was willing to not drink before the group. Holly related that she'd try not to confront him.

Emma knew she was scheduled to meet with Jake the next day, but hadn't related this to the group. She was wondering if she'd gotten in over her head on this case.

After the group left, Betty Williams stopped into Emma's office.

"Are you all right?" asked Betty.

"Yeah. One of the group members became disruptive. He'd been drinking and the group confronted him and he left. I'm not sure he intended on slamming the door. Thanks for checking on me."

"Hey, you'd do the same for me, right?" asked Betty.

"I'm supposed to see him individually tomorrow," said Emma.

"Why?" asked Betty.

"He said he was in trouble at work, and he needed a note from a therapist to return," answered Emma. She cringed at even saying it. She made a sour face and turned off her laptop where she'd been making her chart notes from the group.

"God, I hate that," said Betty, sitting down on the chair opposite Emma. "I refuse to do that kind of thing. Writing notes, the employer just looking for someone to sue if things go bad on the job. Not to mention this guy. So this is how he proves to his boss he's ready to return to work? Show up at his therapist's after drinking, slams a door, and storms out?"

Emma said, "Good point. But I'm not really his therapist. This group is just for fun."

"Who's kidding who? Emma, you're in and you're it. You might decide to refer this guy for a substance abuse assessment, but don't pretend he's not in your care."

"That's how you see it?"

"That's how he sees it. That's how a court would see it. And yes, that's how I see it."

Emma sighed and closed her laptop.

CHAPTER SEVEN

When Jake returned to see Emma the following day, he was stone sober and contrite. He was wearing an ironed dress shirt and a blazer over a pair of pressed slacks. He wore a sheepish look.

Jake explained to Emma that he knew he had a drinking problem and that he knew he had to stop. He showed Emma a book he'd bought on *Rational Recovery*, and another called *Control Your Drinking*.

He said that he'd taken the self administered tests and found himself to be a "problem drinker." He just needed some time to get a handle on his drinking.

"Alcohol is not my forte, Jake," said Emma. "I think you should see someone who knows more about it."

"But I feel comfortable with you."

"That's not the point. You should see someone who has expertise in this area."

"I don't want to. Most of the professionals in this community are A.A. Nazis. I'd like to work with someone who is open-minded."

Emma noticed Jake's flattery and wasn't happy in recognizing that it was working.

"Look," he said, "I have the books, we can go through them together. If I run into a problem, I'll do anything you say. I'll go to another therapist—A.A.—anything. Okay?"

"You seem to know a lot about A.A. More than I do, that's for sure." Emma felt a tug at her conscience. It seemed odd to her that she knew so little about alcoholism, after growing up in a drinking household.

"I went to a couple of meetings a couple of years ago and saw somebody for a few sessions," explained Jake. "I couldn't make it work in A.A. There was too much 'God' stuff. And the guy I was seeing recommended these books. I never bought them, and I never went back."

"Why don't you go back to him now?" asked Emma.

"Because I trust you."

"But that is not the nature of our relationship, Jake. We know each other through a Dream Group that I'm facilitating. I don't treat alcohol problems."

"Let me try this. If I can stop drinking, then I don't have a problem. If I do have a problem, then I'll go to A.A. and do anything you ask me to do. Is that a deal? I'd really like to work with you."

Emma said, "You are certainly a charmer."

She looked at the younger man and thought through her own resistance at working with him. On the one hand, she was correct to feel that Jake should see an expert on alcoholism.

And she should be suspicious of his apparent resistance. On the other hand, wasn't trust one of the most important features of a therapeutic bond? And maybe she was resistant herself, trying to distance herself from dealing with someone with a drinking problem, based on her own family history.

Jake was looking at Emma while she processed all of this internally. He finally asked, "So, what do you think?"

"Okay," answered Emma. "We meet weekly and you stay in the group, and apologize next week. Especially to Holly."

"I can do that. Now, about that letter—" said Jake, a large smile on his face.

"Who do I send it to?"

That night Jake was off work. He'd hand carried the letter to the personnel office at the hospital. He was scheduled to return to work the following night, on the midnight shift. He lived on the first floor of a rental house on the near east side of Lansing. Jake had lived here for several years, and his dwelling consisted of a cramped living room with a TV that he rarely used, and stereo equipment that he used often. There was a kitchen, a small dining area, a bedroom, and bathroom. The place was basically clean but cluttered.

After leaving Emma's office, Jake had replayed the conversation in his head. *Had he agreed to quit drinking or to moderate his drinking?* He couldn't quite recall. He'd told her that one of the books was called *Control Your Drinking*, so maybe that was okay. What was important, he decided, was that he was finally *going to get on top of this thing*. He picked up a bottle of scotch on the way home.

Jake decided to celebrate by playing his entire collection of Coltrane on LP. He stored his LPs on a shelf in his living room, and felt so proud of his collection that he'd mounted several of them on small wire holders, like someone would exhibit an antique plate or plaque.

Jake loved his turntable. He'd bought the turntable and the LPs used, both at the same time, from a college professor who was leaving town. Jake knew he'd gotten a great deal: stacks and stacks of old Blue Note and Prestige recordings from the 1950s and 1960s. As much as he liked Thelonious Monk and Miles Davis, his favorite was Coltrane. So for his first night of controlled drinking, he might as well share it with an old friend.

Jake started by playing *Blue Train*, then moved on to *Soultrane*, and then *Giant Steps*. He looked at a newspaper while he listened to the records. Then he picked up a paperback by Elmore Leonard.

By the time he reached *Live at the Village Vanguard*, Jake decided he could have one of his two or three drinks of the evening. He opened the bottle he bought earlier. He poured a stiff Scotch in a wine glass and sipped it slowly. *Just one sip per song*. He enjoyed the burn of the alcohol on his tongue and followed the sensation all the way down his throat. He could feel it in his stomach, and felt a warm sensation move across the top of his skull. He shivered.

Jake loved Coltrane's excursion on "India." He imagined what it was like sitting in the Village Vanguard in 1962 and listening to Elvin Jones and Coltrane and McCoy Tyner and Jimmy Garrison and even *fricking Eric Dolphy*. Jake took a long pull on the scotch.

Jake put on *A Love Supreme* and poured another drink. This one filled to the brim of the wine glass.

"I have to get more Coltrane on Impulse," he said aloud.

When he flipped over the LP, Jake poured his third drink. He was finished before the side ended.

"That's all for the night," he said aloud. He pulled *Ascension* out of its sleeve and dropped it on the floor.

"Fuck!" he yelled.

Jake blew on the LP and then wiped at it with the sleeve of his jacket before putting it on the turntable. He turned up the volume and heard the crackling surface noise from the vinyl just before the music started. Jake went back into the kitchen and opened the cupboard holding the scotch. It was more than half empty.

"Holy shit!" he said. "Well, no more! That's it," he slurred. Then Jake pulled the bottle off the shelf, unscrewed the top and took a long tug off the bottle. He put it back without screwing the cap back on.

It was then the phone rang.

Shit! Don't pick up the phone! It rang again. Jake looked at the phone like it might jump up and start running around. He appeared horrified and put his finger to his lips, as if to shush the ringing phone, or the music from the speakers, or the sound of his own thoughts. On the third ring the answering machine kicked in. Jake turned down the blaring Coltrane to hear who was calling.

"Hi, this is Jake," said the recorded message on the machine, "You know what to do." BEEEP.

"Jake? This is Holly. I'm sorry to do this on a machine. I think I owe you an apology. I hope you're okay. I mean it's none of my business but if you'd like to talk, we could, like, have coffee sometime. I hope you come back to group. Well, see ya." Holly left her phone number before hanging up. The phone beeped again as the message ended.

"Anyway," said Jake before turning up the Coltrane.

Jake awakens to the sound of someone at the door. "Don't let them in!" he cries, but he doesn't know who he's calling. He runs to the front door and sees the door itself shaking with each knock. He looks for something big and heavy to place at the door and settles on jamming a kitchen chair underneath the doorknob.

"They'll come in through the windows," *he realizes, and finds a hammer and nails. He gathers a group of planks and starts boarding up his windows.*

At each window he is certain someone is climbing through another window and he constantly looks over his shoulder. He keeps hearing a knocking. Jake finishes with the living room windows and takes a stack of planks into the bedroom, thinking that he may have a battle on his hands in the bedroom.

"Zombies," *he says aloud.* "Flesh eating, out of the grave, brain sucking, Night of the Living Dead zombies!"

But there are no zombies in the bedroom. Not yet anyway. He starts to place a plank over the window and before he can start hammering again a loud pounding starts. "I'll just have to hope that chair will hold at the door." *How can he keep them all out? Jake realizes that he should plank up the front door.*

When Jake returns to the front door it is wide open and he gasps. He considers whether or not he should leave his house. The street is jammed with zombies. That's when he sees that the windows are open as well, and he runs from room to room trying to find zombies, afraid to find them. Room after room, the doors and windows are wide open, and each room is perfectly empty.

Jake woke up sweating, with his head hurting and hands shaking. The little digital clock said it was nine o'clock, and for a moment Jake didn't know if it was a.m. or p.m. Then he remembered it was Saturday and it was light out, so it was the morning. He looked at Holly's number on the phone where she had left a message.

He poured himself a large glass of water and drank it with three extra-strength painkillers. He walked through each room to make sure no one else was with him. The front door was locked, and each window was closed tightly. He saw the fifth of Scotch on the counter and moaned when he saw that it was less than a quarter full. He put the cap back on and noticed his hand shaking as he did so. He sat down on the couch near the phone and saw the digital messenger reminding him of the one call. Holly's number. Holly's name. *Damn.*

"Take a chance," he said out loud.

He called Holly's number and got her voicemail.

"You've reached," and Holly mentioned her phone number. "I'm not available to take your call but if you leave a message I'll—"

Jake left a message.

"Holly, this is Jake. I got your message. I would like to talk with you. Get together for coffee."

Jake hung up. He said, "Fuck," out loud and picked up the phone and called her number.

"Oh, my number is—"

He hung up again, then swore again, and called her one more time.

"You have my number of course. You called me. The thing I wanted to say, Holly, is that you're not so out of line. I really think I have an alcohol problem and I am trying to do something about it. I tried to control it last night, and I just got drunk again."

"BEEP!"

"Shit." Jake said out loud. "I can't call again." And then, "Why did I say all that?"

Jake called again.

"Holly, never mind. I'm a little hung over, and I'm not quite myself. Please disregard these messages. I'm sorry."

He hung up and went back to bed.

Jake's phone rang within the hour.

"Jake?"

"Yes?"

"This is Holly."

"Oh. Okay. Did you get my messages?"

"Yeah, I just picked them up. I was at a meeting, and it just got out. I'm going to breakfast with some people. Would you like to meet us?"

"Oh, no, I wouldn't want to interrupt. But I was going to take you up on your offer for coffee."

"Jake, it's no interruption. These people are alcoholics. Like me. Maybe, like you."

"Uh huh."

"And they serve coffee at Sparty's."

"Okay. At Frandor?"

"Yeah."

"Okay. Well, I'm not really ready to take on the day yet."

"Where do you live?"

"Mifflin. 525 Mifflin."

"Perfect. You're right around the corner. I'll give you twenty minutes to get yourself together, and then we'll pick you up."

"I don't know if that's a good idea."

"Jake, if you're one of us, the last thing in the world you want is to meet some drunks in recovery. And it could be the thing that might do you some good. What have you got to lose?"

"Okay. Twenty minutes?"

"Twenty minutes. Is that long enough?"

"Yeah."

Jake hung up and took a quick shower and put on some clean clothes. He stood outside in the yard and watched leaves falling from the trees.

A car pulled up. Holly was driving, and there were two men about their age in the car. Jake didn't recognize either one of them and felt relieved. Holly introduced them. Jake didn't quite catch their names, but the one named Nick repeated his.

Jake got in the front seat with Holly. He felt like he was being led to an execution—maybe a Mafia hit, where suddenly he'd feel the barrel of a gun against the base of his skull, or a garrote slipped quickly around his throat.

Other than Jake, the other three in the car seemed cheerful enough. The guys in the backseat were talking Spartan football, how the team was away this week and would probably lose. Holly gabbed a little about how pretty the leaves were and how fall was her favorite time of year.

Jake felt miserable. They got to Sparty's and ordered coffee and breakfast before Nick asked, "So you think you might be one of us?"

"Well," said Jake, looking over his shoulder, "I don't know about that. But I'm taking a look at my drinking and trying to evaluate."

"Oh."

Nick and Chris both told him stories about how they'd tried to figure out their drinking, then tried to explain it, then tried to control it, but how nothing worked until they reached A.A. They talked through their eggs and bacon and pancakes.

Jake barely touched his food.

"Not hungry?" asked Holly.

"Hung over," answered Jake.

Nick stopped eating and asked Jake if he might like to attend an A.A. meeting.

"Oh, I don't know," said Jake.

"That's not *no*," said Chris.

"No, it isn't, is it?" wondered Jake.

He didn't know why, but he liked these people. They were so upbeat and open. They were strange, to be so cheerfully acknowledging their alcoholism, but there was something Jake admired.

"I guess I can go to a meeting and check it out," Jake said.

Chris said, "I have two questions. I've got to warn you they're a little blunt."

"Okay," said Jake.

"First, do you think you could stay sober for twenty-four hours?"

"Oh, yeah. I'm not that bad."

"Okay. Don't drink today or tonight and tomorrow. The four of us will go to a meeting."

"You said there were two questions," Jake prompted.

"Do you have any booze in your house right now?"

"Some scotch."

"Can you dump it?" asked Nick.

"That's three questions," answered Jake.

Gordon Thomas was trying to get it figured out.

How was it that *he* was it trouble? First of all, *didn't that boy have it coming?*

Out loud, Gordon counted the miles he drove from his odometer, backwards from 125,908, a countdown he never completed, just started or with the click of the next mile. Other times, he counted down from whatever mileage marker he had passed on the road, depending on where he was.

The counting seemed *necessary*, somehow, to keep himself from—*what?*

He'd abandoned driving the highways after that old man next door told him the cops were looking for him. A warrant for his arrest. *Arrest? For what? Giving the boy what for? Or telling that little slip of tail from the State where to get off?*

125,907...

Gordon drove the back country roads around Grand Ledge, Mulliken, Nashville, and he thought about the girl. The red head.

She'd turned him in for that little shove, he was sure of it. And as he thought of it, his anger grew like a bonfire out in these woods.

He remembered how he'd gotten back at girls before, starting with that *whore of a mother* who could never tell why she felt so sick on Sunday mornings, never guessing it was the little doctoring he'd do to her sour mash once she got lit.

Or his ex, the only woman he'd ever loved, *two timing bitch that she was.* He was never charged for the fire. She'd known good and well who was behind it and knew better than to talk. Then she up and disappeared, *Canada, maybe, all her talk of the Rockies up there, or back to her Daddy's family in Tennessee.*

125,906…

125,905…

Gordon watched his speed, made sure that no cops would have a reason to arrest him. *Unless they checked on a warrant!*

He'd never had a woman talk to him like that, except his mama, when she was sober, *God rest her soul.* That *bitch* from the State had turned the tables on him. *This is what it's like to be hunted.*

Well, not anymore. Little Missy doesn't know who she's messing with.

125,904…

125,903…

125,902…

She doesn't know who she's messing with. But she's about to find out.

Marianne is in a forest, walking with a group of people. She's in the dunes of Grand Haven, on the coast of Lake Michigan. Her family had a cottage on the north shore during her childhood and now she's back, walking in the woods. She remembers taking these walks as a girl, quite often with her sister but sometimes alone, and remembers that once or twice she got quite lost.

This time she is walking with several other people, and she's lagging behind. Then she knows why.

"You're going the wrong way," she calls ahead to the group.

"How does she know which way we're going?" asks another woman from the group ahead. Marianne recognizes her—it's Holly, from the Dream Group.

"I know these dunes, you can't get back this way," says Marianne and now she's stopped walking, but the group ahead of her keeps trudging along.

In spite of herself, Marianne begins to focus on her awareness of the images. She notices that there are four people walking in front of her—two men and two women. "Two by two," she says out loud. She recognizes them as the members of her Dream Group. But somehow they look different. And there's something else about them that doesn't make sense.

For one thing, Jake is leading them. And he's leading them deeper and deeper into the woods. Marianne remembers that this is the way she was lost as a child—going deeper into the woods, past the three hills she was familiar with. Jake is leading them into an area that is unknown. And everyone seems perfectly content to just go along with him.

Jake is dressed in buckskin, a fringed suede jacket, like Neil Young wore on that album she owned by him when she was a girl. In fact, Jake has Neil Young sideburns. Muttonchops.

Marianne looks for Emma and sees her walking next to Mason, intently listening to him, as he is reciting math equations. She seems so absorbed by what he's saying that she doesn't realize that they're getting further and further away from—

—from where? From home. Further and further away from home.

Emma, Marianne notes, is wearing a beautiful gown and high heels. She looks too formal for a walk in the dunes, Marianne thinks. And Mason is dressed in a black suit. And Holly, who is walking behind Jake, but in front of Mason and Emma, is walking nonchalantly in a two-piece bathing suit. Yellow. It goes nice with her hair, thinks Marianne.

Back to the concern at hand. "You're going the wrong way!" shouts Marianne. The group still walks in front of her. Marianne becomes furious.

"NO ONE IS LISTENING TO ME! LISTEN TO ME— I KNOW THIS AREA AND I'M A LEADER! LET ME LEAD YOU!"

The group keeps walking.

Marianne runs to catch up with them and grabs Emma saying, "You've got to stop them. Make them listen. We'll all get lost."

Emma looks at her, with a blank expression and says, "How can we be found if we don't get lost?" She turns and walks away.

Marianne watches them walking down the trail and focuses again on the details. She can feel the heat of the sun, smell the pine from the nearby trees. The lake is probably a half mile away, but she can still hear the waves. She watches the group continue to walk deeper into the forest.

Marianne thinks about her choices: keep with the group and get lost, or turn around and go home, alone.

Home is not even home, *she thinks.*

I've been lost before, *she thinks.*

She runs to catch up and finds it easy to run in the sand. She remembers the line she heard about politicians and dogs. What they have in common. They find out which way the group is heading and then run to get in front.

She wonders if she can catch up to Jake. Waking up, Marianne found her legs churning in the sheets.

"Whew," she said aloud. And then reached over to her night table for the pen and paper. It was 3 a.m.

It was a rainy morning in November. Emma had an early workout at her gym and then drove to meet Betty at the coffee shop.

Emma made small talk with Betty regarding her weekend plans. Betty was planning on volunteering for the Council Against Domestic Assault's silent auction, and asked Emma if she'd like to help.

"Sure, what do you need me to do?" asked Emma.

"Stand at the tables, answer questions, encourage bidding, look pretty. You know, just be your own charming self," answered Betty.

"I'm not feeling very charming these days," said Emma.

"What's up? Is it Frank?"

Emma sighed. She blew on her coffee to cool it before taking a sip.

"That bad?" asked Betty.

"Yeah. Where would you like me to start?"

"How about at home, and then we'll work our way back to the office."

Emma sighed again and said, "Frank and I had a fight the other night, and I told him that I have a crush on someone else."

"Wow! Nooo! Who?"

Emma looked over her shoulder, frowning. She pantomimed that Betty should be quiet. Then she nearly whispered, "That doesn't matter, does it? I haven't acted on it. Well, a couple of emails. And we're supposed to get together for coffee."

"Emma, I'm not acting as a therapist here. Not as a colleague. But as your friend, Emma, as *your friend* I have to tell you I think this is a terrible idea."

"But…"

"I don't care *who* he is. He could be Denzel Washington, and I would say the same thing. *Don't* meet him. Bad idea. *Baaaad* idea."

"You really think?"

Betty raised her eyebrows as a response. Emma looked around the coffee shop. There were some college kids tapping away at their laptops and three women in raincoats with notebooks, focused on some project.

"Does your therapist know about this?" asked Betty.

"No," said Emma, looking down into her coffee.

"Do you know why she doesn't?" asked Betty.

"No," said Emma, now looking up.

"Because you're ashamed, Emma," whispered Betty. "You're ashamed and you *should* be ashamed, because you know what you're about to do isn't right. You're married. If you decide you and Frank can't make it, if you come to that agreement, then you make any arrangements you need to make. Get separated, get a divorce, have an 'open' marriage, whatever that is, but have it come out of an agreement with Frank. *Do not* meet this other man."

Emma looked her friend in the eye. She held eye contact for several intense seconds before asking her, "Betty, don't hold back. What do you really think?"

They both laughed. Emma added, "So, we are going to get some counseling. And I've set an appointment to talk with my doctor about anti-depressants."

Betty looked at her friend and said, "That bad, huh?"

"That bad."

"This is going to sound terrible, 'cause I'm just giving you advice right and left, but I would hold off on the anti-depressants for now."

"Really?"

"Are you suicidal?"

"No."

"Can you function?" asked Betty.

"Yes."

"I think you shouldn't block your emotions. If you were really in trouble with your feelings, I think I'd make a different recommendation."

Neither of the women had any clients until the afternoon. They spoke about Betty's children and whether or not she should go back to school to get her Ph.D. Emma reflected how lucky she was to have a friend like Betty, and wondered why she'd been so reticent to tell her what was going on in her life. And Claudia. Why should she be keeping secrets?

Because she knew, come hell or high water, she was going to meet with Dylan.

The first week of November carried a shift in the weather. The skies seemed naked and exposed once the leaves were off the trees. The bare trees looked vulnerable, stark. Emma felt on edge on her way to the Dream Group. She knew that Jake had agreed to come back, but she wondered if she should disband the group. Maybe she'd gotten in over her head.

She made some tea in the office while waiting for the group to arrive. She noticed that Betty was still in her office, doing paperwork. Emma wondered if she was just hanging around to offer support if Jake stormed out again.

Jake and Holly were the first to arrive and both seemed to be in good moods. Mason joined them in the waiting room. As the group was scheduled to start, Emma brought them all into her office. She had just started when Marianne joined them, a few minutes late.

Emma shifted nervously in her seat at the outset of the meeting. She was aware that everyone was watching her, so she deliberately settled herself, made eye contact with each member of the group, and folded her hands in her lap. Finally, she spoke.

"Before we get started, we may need to process a little about what happened last time," Emma remarked.

Jake was the first to speak. "Yeah, I'd like to say I'm sorry."

Emma was careful to facilitate this part of the group. She wanted Jake to hear how he'd impacted others in the group and give them a chance to share their feelings.

"Well, I appreciate that Jake, but I think people in the group may need to talk about their reactions."

Holly was the first to speak. She'd been sipping a chai and set it down on the table next to her.

"I can say I was really mad at Jake for coming in after drinking. I've talked about this outside of this group. I think I've mentioned it before, but I'm in A.A., so I have a sponsor, someone I can confide in, someone who gives me some spiritual guidance. So I've already had a couple of chances to talk about this. I think that, for me, it made me think about my childhood: Dad coming home drunk, mom and dad fighting—"

Emma asked, "And you felt?"

"Scared. Scared and then mad," said Holly, looking towards Jake.

Emma wanted to make sure she attended to Jake's reactions as people shared, so she turned to Jake and said, "I'm a little concerned about how you're hearing this, Jake."

Jake was contrite. "I've got it coming." His face was pale but his throat was flushed a deep red. "Maybe I should tell you guys something. I mean, I will tell you guys something. I called Holly, well, Holly called me first, then I called her back. Anyway, she took me to an A.A. meeting. I think I can admit now that I've got a problem, and I'm ready, with her help, to do something about it."

Emma and Holly both started talking at once. Emma deferred to Holly.

"Well, I don't think this is the place to talk about that part of it," said Holly.

Emma said, "Usually I discourage outside relationships in the group, while the group is being conducted."

"How come?" asked Jake.

Mason added, "I would think outside contact might be helpful, but—"

"I'm not sure I'd like to have outside contact," said Marianne. Then she added, sheepishly, "Not anything against all of you, of course."

Emma said, "Well, I can see we have a few things to discuss tonight. One thing is what's happened in the past week. But there are certain things that naturally occur in a group that it's my job to monitor and facilitate."

"Such as?" asked Marianne, straightening her skirt.

"A group needs to be clearly defined. The goals and the boundaries. These are different matters. Do you mind if I explain?"

Mason asked her to do so.

"When a group comes together, they come together for a very specific reason, usually. For instance, in A.A., the goal is—" Emma looked to Holly and tilted her head.

"To stay sober," said Holly. "First to get, and then to stay, sober."

"Exactly," said Emma. "In A.A., you don't decide to become involved in politics."

"No," said Holly, "in fact, it's forbidden for the group to endorse anything like that."

"Good," Emma said. "Now, that helps the group define their goal and stick with their goal. So our goal was to do some dream work. And you all came here—"

"To understand dreams," said Mason.

"To change my dreams," amended Marianne.

"To stop having dreams," interjected Holly.

"To make a mess of things," said Jake, to the laughter of the others in the group.

Emma smiled and said, "I may need to join you on that count, Jake."

Marianne asked Emma what she meant by that.

"I need to take responsibility and be accountable to you all, for keeping the goal of the group clear and predictable. You need to know it's safe to be here, to share what your dreams are, to know it's confidential, to know I'm competent," said Emma. She felt her throat constrict in saying it, but at the same time felt relieved.

"I don't doubt your competency," said Mason. It was clear his delivery wasn't complimentary, just matter of fact.

Marianne nodded in agreement, but then said, "I do appreciate you mentioning safety, Emma. I have felt a little threatened at times. Not specifically. But it's gotten a little—"

"Heated?" offered Jake.

"Yes, that's a good word for it. 'Heated.'" Marianne smiled at Jake, in a stiff manner.

Emma went on. "So there is a hierarchy of concerns a group needs to address. Safety is very important. And a shared purpose is another. The matter of things getting, 'heated,' let's say, is a matter of process, not intent."

Jake frowned. "I think you've just lost me."

"I hope I don't get too esoteric here," replied Emma. "A group has several factors that I need to monitor. Intent is the reason we're here. Our goal. One reason I'm spending a lot of time talking about this is that I think the goal we first set has shifted. Process, on the other hand, is about how the group is going. Not why we're meeting, or what we're doing. I need to keep a check on the emotional thermostat of the group. Make sure everyone is comfortable. And feels safe." As she spoke Emma made a point to keep eye contact with one group member after the other, to make sure they were tracking what she was saying. Mason was the first to reply.

"But they are related, aren't they? Process and intent?"

"Certainly."

Jake still appeared perplexed. "Can we slow this down even a little more?"

"Yes," said Emma. She leaned forward. "Let's look at our group. We got together to look at our dreams. The group was going to explore some theory, maybe get a little insight."

"And I took us over the waterfall," moaned Jake.

"I don't think you did it alone, Jake. Let me finish. So the idea was a Dream Group, not a therapy group. A therapy group is likely to be a little more intense, the level of sharing may become more personal, the need for trust is higher, so the boundaries need to be clearer."

"That's why you don't like fraternizing," said Mason.

"Exactly," said Emma. "An outside relationship could complicate the process of the group."

"So I should decide between A.A. and the Dream Group?" asked Jake.

"No," said Holly, abruptly. "I mean, I haven't. I didn't want to say this in the group, but maybe I should."

"Go ahead Holly," encouraged Emma.

Holly looked out the window and back at Emma. "I trust you, Emma. And I trust my sponsor, too, and she's told me pretty clearly," Holly shifted her attention towards Jake, "that I can't be your sponsor, Jake."

Jake laughed. "Look, man, I wasn't asking you to be. I don't even know, really, what a sponsor is."

"Like I said, a guide, a mentor, someone who shows you the ropes of the programs."

Jake smiled at Holly and said, "So, you have ropes?"

"You know what I mean. You need a man to do that, so the relationship doesn't become blurred. Like Emma is describing. Clear boundaries."

"I've heard this word 'boundaries' a lot from the psycho-babble circuit. What does it mean, precisely?" asked Marianne.

"It means who can participate, to what extent, and in what ways, and with what kind of relationship. We all get to choose that. Who we let in, who we keep out."

Marianne looked for clarification. "So boundaries are good?"

"They're not good or bad," said Emma. "No more than a wall is good or bad, or a door is good or bad."

"But those things you mention are good," said Marianne.

"Until there is a change," said Emma. "A wall can protect you, until you no longer need protecting. Then it becomes a barrier."

Marianne appeared satisfied with this answer, but Mason interjected, "So how does this relate to our group? You've said our purpose has shifted."

"Well, I think we're sliding from a Dream Group to a therapy group."

"Oh, my God," said Marianne and the rest of the group laughed. Emma tried to keep a straight face. She wasn't sure if Marianne was joking or not.

"What do you mean, Marianne?"

"My dream. I dreamed we were all walking in the dunes of Grand Haven, a place close to where I grew up. And Jake was leading us and we were getting further and further lost, and you all were following him. And I was trying to convince you to turn back and you wouldn't."

Jake said, "Oh, man. I'm a bad influence."

"Well, yes, sometimes I think so," said Marianne. "So I ran up to Emma and tried to persuade her to turn back, and, do you know what you said, Emma?"

"'How can we be found if we don't get lost'?" asked Emma, raising her eyebrows.

"That's exactly what you said. How did you know that?"

"Sounds like something I would say. But that is strange," said Emma.

"So how did the dream end?" asked Holly.

"You all kept walking," said Marianne. Her voice choked with emotion. "And I had to decide whether to stick with you or not."

"I wondered if you might leave the group," said Mason.

"I wondered that too," said Holly, softly.

Emma tried to suppress a sigh. It was her worst fear—she was losing the group. She asked, "Has anyone else wondered whether or not to leave the group?"

After a few moments of silence, Holly answered first. "To tell the truth, my sponsor has suggested I look at whether or not I should be doing the group."

"Because of me?" asked Jake.

"Well, ultimately because of me," answered Holly. She blushed, the red on her cheeks accenting her red hair. "Because of what I may need or not need."

"Hmmm. Obviously, I've been in and out of the group," said Jake.

"One foot in," said Emma.

"And the other foot out. Yeah," finished Jake.

There was a moment of awkward silence and then Mason said, "Interesting."

Emma looked to him for some relief. She wasn't quite sure where to go next. "Care to expound, professor?"

"No," Mason answered. More silence.

"Well," Emma began again, "I wondered if there was a little ambivalence about what was happening with the group. And frankly, I've also wondered if we should continue."

Marianne was the first to respond. "What?"

"No!" said Mason.

Jake started to apologize, and Holly looked alarmed.

"Let me finish," said Emma. "I've wondered if we should continue, if we can continue as strictly a Dream Group. We seem to have opened up a deeper level of concerns. I've wondered if we haven't crossed a boundary into being more of a therapy group. And that is not what any of you signed on for."

"I feel like, if it would make things better for all of you, I'll quit the group," offered Jake. He slumped over and said, "I never meant to put you in this fix."

Mason answered Jake first. He leaned over and, for a moment, Emma thought he was going to put his hand on Jake's knee. "Jake, I should have said something before this. I wanted you to know, last week, we all said we were sorry you left. I was sorry you left. I've known people who have drinking problems, I've worked with people at the college who talk about going to their 'meetings,' and I think they're fine human beings. I guess what I'm saying is, if the group continues, I sure hope you're a part of it."

Jake looked at Mason and smiled. It was clear he wasn't sure what to do with this type of compliment. "Thanks, man," is what he said.

"Mason," said the older man. "Call me Mason."

"Thanks, Mason."

Holly looked at Marianne and asked her how her dream ended.

Marianne said, "Well, I wrote it down." As she searched through her purse she said, "I was aware of being angry and frustrated that none of you were listening to me. It was terribly annoying. It was even stronger than that. So I had a decision. You were all walking deeper and deeper into the woods and I knew we'd be lost. I asked Emma to get you to turn back, and then she said, 'How can we be found if we don't get lost?' And you kept walking. So I decided to follow you."

The group was silent for a few moments.

"So you're with us," said Holly.

"Yes," answered Marianne. "But how is it I see Jake as leading us? Nothing personal, Jake."

"No, I understand."

Emma answered, "Jake is significant to the group in many ways. And one of the ways he's significant is that his issues have surfaced earliest. So maybe Jake's, shall we say 'crisis'? Jake's crisis felt like getting lost. And when people first begin to address a problem in their life, it often feels like getting lost." She looked at Jake to make sure he was hearing this interpretation as supportive, that he wasn't about to bail out on the group again. Jake nodded to Emma in understanding.

"I see," said Marianne. "So I'm not seeing him as a leader in the traditional sense. I hope this doesn't mean I have to start drinking."

Everyone laughed. Emma felt relieved. The tension in the group had broken.

Mason mentioned, "You know, it's funny, but Jake was in my dream, too."

"I'm the man of your dreams," said Jake.

"Let's not get carried away," groaned Holly. And then she blushed again.

Emma looked to the group members to make a clear commitment towards still being in the group. To her surprise, they were all still interested in continuing.

After they left, Emma wondered about what happened in her office and how she had been surprised by people again and again. So often people weren't what they seemed. They made choices and decisions that surprised her, encouraged her, disappointed her, elated her. And just at the point she was certain the group was on the verge of disintegrating, they had made a commitment to continue.

CHAPTER EIGHT

It was the second week of November, the morning after the group. Frank and Emma were leaving the office of their marital counselor after their first appointment. Emma suggested they drive together.

After getting back in Frank's SUV, the couple sat in silence for several long moments. Emma finally asked, "So what do you think?"

Frank sighed and said, "I guess I hadn't realized it was so bad. I had no idea you were this unhappy. And, I hadn't understood why up until now."

Emma said, "It seems worth another appointment, don't you think?"

Frank answered, "Yeah, absolutely." Then he shifted the car into gear and began to drive. The couple rode in silence down the East Lansing streets towards their home. Leaves blew across the streets, and the trees were growing bare.

Frank asked, "Why didn't you tell me before?"

"I kept hoping my feelings would change. I kept wondering if it had something to do with my mother's death. I thought I could just ignore it. I just don't know. Look, I'm sorry. I can't keep pretending."

"I don't want you to pretend. I just want us to be happy."

"What if that's not possible? What if it's possible for only one of us to be happy?" asked Emma.

"I don't want to think that. You're the one who's always reminding me not to think in terms of either/or," Frank said.

"Yeah, I guess. I just mean, maybe sometimes it is either/or. Like a person drinks or they don't drink. Sometimes it's just one or the other."

"And you would really leave me?"

Emma was silent for a minute. A minute, in these circumstances, seemed like a long time. Frank maneuvered through the traffic carefully. Emma was aware he was driving a little slower than usual, making the ride home take longer. Finally she spoke.

"Frank, I don't know. That's as honest as I can be. I don't know. There's a part of me I've denied and shut off—"

"You make me sick!" Frank exploded. "Do you know that? I'm repulsed by you, and I didn't think that was possible. But it is. You make me sick!" His face was a grimace and Emma looked away and out the window, passing by a school with children playing in the playground.

"Maybe we shouldn't talk about it right now. The therapist suggested we talk about it in the room but focus on where we get along."

"Where's that, Emma? Where do we get along? How can we possibly get along with your newfound *feelings*? Answer me that?"

"We've always been good friends, Frank."

"I don't care about that. I want a wife, Emma. Not a friend. A wife."

Frank drove into their driveway, stopped the car and reached across Emma to open her door.

"Get out."

"Frank—"

"Get out. I need some time. Get out. Now. Please. Get out."

Emma could see that Frank was on the verge of tears and felt torn between trying to comfort him and stepping out onto the driveway. She got out of the car, and before closing the door asked him, "Let's do dinner together, okay?"

Frank answered, "Shut the door, Emma."

Emma shut the door. Frank drove out of the driveway and pulled away towards the direction of his office.

Emma felt numb.

She went into the house and looked at the clock. 10:15 a.m. She had a light clinical day. Appointments from 1 p.m. through 6 p.m. Time enough for a run.

Emma slipped out of her jeans and sweater and into running pants and a sweatshirt and started stretching. Her mind felt like a blur.

At least that part is done. At least he knows.

Emma glanced over at the computer as she stretched. She considered whether or not to turn it on.

What do I say to Dylan? Do I meet for coffee? I want to more than anything. Can I possibly make it work with Frank? Am I crazy or just terrible?

Suddenly Emma felt too tired to run. Too tired to do anything. She went back to the bedroom and laid on the bed for a few moments, just to catch a cat nap, and was asleep in moments.

Emma dreamed of two snakes crawling across the floor of the bedroom towards her. One was red and one was black. They were small snakes. Vipers. Emma knew that one was poisonous and one was not, and she knew that it was up to her to choose.

She awoke with a start, a gasp. She looked at the floor of the bedroom and even peaked under the bed. No snakes. She'd only been asleep for ten minutes. She wrote in her dream journal:

> Today I dreamed of two snakes
> One was red and one was black
> One was poisonous and one was not…
> …Some choices are too hard to make.
> …When is love not a choice, but destiny?
> …Maybe some choices are too hard not to make
> …Maybe we'll end up like a couple of snakes.

Then she turned on the computer and checked her email. Looking again at the message from Dylan suggesting they meet for coffee in Grand Rapids, Emma wrote back:

> Dylan,
> Looking forward to coffee. The sooner the better.
> Emma.

Mason recognizes London from the view of Big Ben and the Houses of Parliament across the river. He knows he must be on the south bank and wonders if he should take a cab, find the Tube, or just walk. He decides to walk, aware of walking west along the bank, but wonders if he shouldn't have a map. He always carried a map in London but couldn't find one. In fact, he usually carried his passport and couldn't find that either. He was a little concerned. I'll get there when I get there.

Mason thinks about Shakespeare as he walks the south bank, passing the bridges to his left, and wonders what the city looked like 400 years ago. He passes the London Bridge and heads towards the Tower of London. He remembers feeling ghastly when he stood on the spot where Ann Boleyn, one of the wives of Henry VIII, had been beheaded.

He wonders if he is going to be staying at the Tower. He realizes that he can't remember where he is staying. He can't remember if he is in London alone or if Mona is with him on this trip. What he can remember is that it was important for him to reach the Tower of London.

As Mason walks on, he quickens his pace. He realizes there are few people on the streets. It is getting cooler and he isn't dressed for such cool weather. And it is also beginning to get dark.

He feels a need to hurry.

He can finally see the Tower and begins to walk towards the open front gate. He sees a crow standing in the entrance way, recognizing it to be one of several that tradition held be kept in the Tower, wings clipped to keep them from flying away. He expects the bird to move as he walks past, but is surprised when it actually takes flight.

Mason enters the Tower's courtyard, and finds it empty. He feels colder and wonders what he was doing here. Then he catches a glimpse *of red and hears footsteps. A Samurai emerges from a building directly across from him.*

It all seems to happen in slow motion. Mason's mouth, forming a wordless shout, an "O" for the terror he sees approaching him. He turns to run, as the Samurai walks with determined deliberation towards him.

He wants my head.

Mason only hopes that if he can reach the gate, perhaps the Samurai won't walk past the barrier.

In a panic Mason runs as fast as he can. He doesn't dare turn his head. Suddenly he is out of the gate and then walking towards the Thames, where he sees a small rowboat tied to a dock on the bank. He climbs into the boat and notices there are no oars. The boat is tied by a thick rope and the momentum of his weight in the boat has allowed it to pull away from the dock. The rope is long, twenty-five or thirty feet, and Mason worries about getting close to the shore again because the Samurai must be near.

And he is. The Samurai stands on the dock next to where the boat is tied. Mason freezes and looks up at the warrior. The Samurai looks at Mason without any expression whatsoever. He doesn't recognize the man, but can see he's Japanese, with a dark mustache and dark almond shaped eyes. He tries to keep himself from appearing scared, but he is scared, cold, and has started shivering. The Samurai draws his sword from its scabbard, the red of his armor still reflecting light in the gathering dusk of the day.

Mason wonders if the warrior might throw the sword at him. He makes eye contact as the Samurai as reaches down and pulls at the rope.

Mason is about to scream when very suddenly the Samurai's arm flies up and down, the sound of a whisper as the sword cuts through the rope swiftly. He gasps and looks at the Samurai as his boat is set adrift on the Thames. The Samurai looks at Mason with the same impassive look as before, betraying nothing of his intent, no anger, no disappointment, no smile. The boat is moving fast away from the shore. There are no oars, the boat adrift and in the middle of one of the largest rivers in the world. Mason wonders if he might swim to shore. He looks into the water and sees a film of oily scum on the surface. The water is polluted. Badly polluted. Dead fish and ruined books float by. Mason notices something bobbing in the water, and as he gets closer sees that it is a human head. Mason looks into the face of Ernest Hemingway and recoils in disgust. As Hemingway opens his eyes, Mason tries to yell, and wakes up with his wife shaking him.

After telling his wife his dream he wrote it down in detail in his dream journal. He did not go back to sleep.

That night Jake began writing a story. He was working hard at not having a drink and decided this was his chance to become a writer. He sat down on his front porch with an iced tea, a pad of paper, and a pen. He wondered what to write. And then he wrote this:

THE GOLF KILLER

Ohio Donahoe slipped the rifle from its case. He was not a young man, but neither was he old. He was a marksman, and he enjoyed his time on the range shooting at targets. His family told him he would really be something if he would take up bowling, but bowling did nothing for him. In fact, he hated bowling. He came from a family of bowlers and had decided that, no, the bowling life was not for him.

The only thing Ohio hated more than bowling was golf. And the only thing he hated more than golf was golfers. He hated polyester pants and golf shoes with spikes or cleats or whatever the hell they were, and, God did he hate golf shirts! He hated the sight of overweight white men with their cases of beer, holding business meetings on the golf course.

You see, Ohio Donahoe lived on a golf course. His family had lived in a home that was close to a course and they'd always felt 'less than,' being bowlers and all. Ohio had grown up mistrusting the golfer and feeling like he should become a bowler. But he had no aptitude for the big ball. He hated the sounds of a bowling alley. Again, the shoes made him want to barf. In fact, and this may be significant, he did barf in his own bowling shoes the very first time he went bowling. He was a child. Barf, he did, right in his shoes, and that started his hatred for bowling.

Now, as an adult, he lived on a golf course. Unlike his family, who lived near a golf course. When I say that he lived "on" a golf course, I don't mean that he lived "near" one, or that he lived "adjacent" to one. He lived between the ninth and tenth hole. Golfers were always asking to use the bathroom, the polite ones, and the others would just sneak around back and pee on his tomato plants. Ohio hated that. And the windows, my God, the windows that would be broken!

Ohio, however, learned to shoot at a young age. His first gun was a BB gun, a Daisy, and he'd become adept shooting at the flags on the golf course. As the years went by and the windows broke more and more, and his tomato sandwiches had that familiar tang of piss, he decided to up the ante. He bought a rifle with a scope, and would go to shooting ranges all over the state. He was told that he was good enough to compete, but that wasn't what he was interested in. No, he wasn't. He wanted to shoot live game. But not deer, nor fowl, nor varmint. Not the four legged kind, that is.

Ohio took the rifle out of its case, just like I said at the beginning of this story. He laid on the ground and viewed his prey some 300 yards away. As silently as he could, Donahoe fitted the rifle with its telescopic sites, and brought the rifle up to his shoulder. It was late in the day and Ohio Donahoe thought the hunting would be good. The golf course was abandoned except for this twosome, dressed in bright yellow golf shorts and driving to the ninth hole, far from clubhouse and close to the woods where Donahoe hid.

Now, Ohio wasn't stupid. He never hunted at his own golf course. Not that he owned the course. He didn't. He just owned the house on the course. But he knew that he'd be a suspect if he hunted at his own course. So he'd drive miles and miles to courses around the area. Sometimes he'd even visit another state. But tonight, he was just a few dozen miles from home.

Donahoe had his standards. Never shoot at a foursome. Too difficult. It was very possible to hit two of them, but the third or also certainly the fourth would be capable of waddling to the golf cart and disappearing over a rise before he'd get them all.

And never shoot the lone golfer. It reminded him too much of himself. He was a loner by trade. Never made any money at being a loner, but it kept him from having to deal with friends. Or family. Don't ask how he lived or provided for himself, because I never found that out myself.

Never shoot women. That was another rule. Only men, and men who were driving golf carts and were too fat to run back to the clubhouse. There were plenty of targets.

Jake put down the pen. Writing, as it turned out, was hard work. He'd love a drink. He looked at his hands, and they were shaking slightly. He'd been to an A.A. meeting the day before and was considering whether or not he should go back. He decided to call Holly. She picked up on the third ring.

"Holly?"

"Yeah?"

"It's me, Jake."

"Oh, hi Jake."

"I was wondering what you were up to."

"Oh, not much. I'm just doing my dishes, and I have load of laundry going." Jake could hear water running in the background, and the clanking of dishes and silverware.

"Sounds like you're busy."

"How are you, Jake?"

"I'm fine." Jake heard the water turn off.

"Do you know what FINE stands for in recovery, Jake?"

"No."

"Fucked up, Insecure, Neurotic and—I always forget what the E stands for."

"Oh. Well, guilty as charged. Maybe the E stands for Empathic. Or maybe it stands for Egghead, since everyone in recovery is smart. Or maybe Elephant, as in the Elephant in the room we're not talking about. Or maybe just Egg salad, as in sandwich."

Holly laughed. "So you're okay?"

Jake imagined her drying her hands on a towel. He wondered what she was wearing. He didn't ask.

"'Is he drinking,' you're wondering? No, I'm not."

"Cool. Good for you. How's it going?"

"Okay. I'm a little twitchy. I'd like to drink, but I haven't. And I'm not going to. I went to a meeting today, at the A-Lo-No Club."

"Great. The Alano East Club?"

"Yeah, it's not far from where I live. You know."

"How'd you like it?" Jake heard Holly slipping into the trained empathic responses of a social worker.

"It was okay. There was a guy who talked about being in a car accident last weekend. He just got out of the hospital and the police didn't even know about it."

"Jake, everything that's said in a meeting is supposed to be confidential."

"I didn't tell you his name."

"It's Alcoholic's Anonymous, Jake. 'Who you see here, what you hear here, let it stay here, when you leave here.'"

"See, you're full of good advice. I knew I'd learn something if I called you. So, Holly, what was it like for you?"

"What?"

"Your first meeting."

"I was scared to death. I'd left my husband and I had gone to see a therapist. Oh, Emma, I saw Emma."

"I didn't know that."

"Yeah. She came highly recommended. I was still hoping to save my marriage, as miserable as that was. And I was very focused on my ex's drinking, and she asked me about my drinking. Imagine that. And for some reason, for the first time, I was honest. I told her how much I was drinking. And she said, 'Your assignment is to go to an A.A. meeting.' And I went. And I'm still going."

"Did you stop drinking right away?"

"No. Not right away. But A.A. will fuck up your drinking."

"Oh."

"So how was it for you, Jake?"

Jake walked from the living room into the kitchen, then back into the living room. He looked out the window, then caught himself being restless. He sat down and answered Holly's question.

"Well, it was okay. I expected there to be more, you know, kind of street people."

"The homeless?"

"Not quite 'the homeless,' but some skid-row types, yeah, sure. But it seemed, mostly, like a bunch of pretty nice people. I kept looking for the alcoholics."

Holly asked, "How was it for you emotionally?"

"Uhh, I don't know. Like I say, I guess it was okay. But I have to ask you, people, some of the people, were putting slips of paper in the basket when it went around. Should I know something?"

"Oh, those are slips for the court. A lot of people get sentenced to attend A.A. meetings."

"Really? Oh, that's interesting. Hope that doesn't happen to me. A lot of them just passed when it came their turn to talk."

"Did you talk?"

"Yeah. A little. I said something about being glad to be there and thanked them for the list of phone numbers."

"Is that what you felt?" asked Holly.

Jake hesitated, wondering what the hell he had felt.

"Jake? Are you still there?"

"Yeah. I'm just thinking. No, I didn't feel 'thankful,' or, what's the word you guys use all the time?"

"Grateful? Gratitude?"

"Yeah. No, I didn't actually feel that. I actually felt kind of pissed off that I had to be there. I actually felt like I never really wanted to be an alcoholic. I felt ashamed of myself. I actually hated being there."

"Do you know what that is, Jake?" asked Holly.

"Denial?"

"No. It's honesty. And that's half the battle. Just speak your truth at the meetings, speak the truth to your sponsor. Speak your truth in therapy. The rest will follow."

"Really? Huh. Go figure. Listen, Holly, I was wondering if you'd like to get together for coffee."

"Oh. I don't think that's a good idea."

"Oh. I think it's a great idea. Let me turn the tables on you and just be honest. Outside of what Emma says, or your sponsor, or anyone else, would you like to get coffee with me?"

"Honestly, I would. I really would, Jake."

"Then let's do it."

"But Jake, there's a bunch of things that I don't do that I'd like to."

"Like what?"

"Like drinking, for one."

"But seeing me won't get you drunk."

"I doubt that it would, but there's such a taboo about dating someone in the first year when they're getting clean," said Holly.

"Who said anything about dating? We're talking on the phone. We could just as easily talk over coffee, couldn't we? What's the difference?"

"Okay. Beaners or Starbucks?"

"Beaners. Always support the local business."

"When?"

"I knew you'd see it my way. I can be there in half an hour."

"Give me an hour," answered Holly.

"Okay. See you then. Bye." Jake put some Mingus on the stereo and cranked it.

Holly put down the receiver, sighed, smiled, then frowned. She picked the phone up again and started to dial her sponsor's number, then stopped. She put the phone back on its cradle and went to wash her face and put on makeup.

It was a short drive for Holly to get to the coffee shop in East Lansing. She made sure to take her time, and considered walking, but decided it would be good to have her car in case she needed to make a hasty retreat. It was mid-November and the air was very cold as she stepped out of her apartment. The trees were bare and some leaves were still blown about the street. She got into her car and put in her Kasey Chambers CD. The twangy rock filled the small space and, as she got close to the coffee shop, she turned down the music, as if Jake could hear it while she parked her car.

Holly was disappointed she got to Beaner's before Jake. The place was near campus and had a number of young people, probably college students, hanging out and drinking coffee. Holly didn't recognize anyone in the shop. There were a number of Korean students in the back and a few singles on their laptops. One young woman was reading a textbook on criminal justice and an older guy had a copy of the *New York Times* spread out in front of him. But there were several empty tables. She got a double skinny latte and sat at a table near the back of the coffee shop when she saw Jake. He was wearing his dark winter coat—double breasted, over a beige turtleneck and jeans. He looked pale. He got a cup of coffee and joined her at the table.

"How are you?" asked Holly. "I thought for sure you would beat me here."

"I'm okay. I just saw someone outside who I know from work."

"What is it you do again?"

"I'm a psych tech. That's like a glorified psychiatric orderly. I work at St. Lawrence."

"Oh. So you saw another tech, or a nurse?"

"No, usually I see patients in East Lansing, but this was a relative of a patient. A real nasty guy."

"And he's here? In the coffee shop?" Holly lowered her voice and leaned across the table.

"No. He was out in the parking lot. Sitting in his car. That's why I took a minute to come in. He was just sitting there, across the lot, like he was on a stake out. I thought he was waiting for someone in here, but after five minutes no one came out so I circled around and came in the back."

"You take a lot of precautions. Patients aren't supposed to know you drink coffee?"

"No, it wasn't that. This guy was kind of a badass. He was threatening towards me at the hospital and I just wouldn't want to run into him out here. In the real world."

"I know what you mean. I ran into one of those myself recently."

"Now that you mention it," said Jake, "I was wondering if we might know the same people. Now and then we get someone on our floor who's had some Protective Service involvement. Actually, the patient I'm thinking of mentioned that you were the investigator on the case. This guy was a perpetrator."

Now Holly's face went pale.

"Who did you see out there?" she asked.

"Well, his name is—I can't remember his name. His girlfriend was checked in a while back after a suicide attempt. I think I mentioned it to you at the group, didn't I? He had a real odd name, though. Like he was named after a vodka, or a gin? Like Beefeater, or Popov, or something—"

"Gordon? Was it Gordon Thomas?"

"Yeah, that's him. You know him?"

Holly took a moment before answering. "Yeah. I had a run-in with him. I think he left a note on my car. You say he was here, like waiting outside before you came in?"

"Yeah, I think so. Do you think he might be tailing you?"

"Stalking me? I wouldn't put it past him. I should call the cops. He has a warrant out against him."

"Let me take a look and see if he's still there."

"No, don't. I'll just call the cops. I have my cell phone right here."

Holly put in the call. She knew some of the Lansing police but wasn't as familiar with the East Lansing cops. She described her situation but realized she couldn't tell them what kind of car he was driving.

Jake jumped up. "Let me look," he said and walked over to the big glass door, which lead to the parking lot. When he came back he said, "I think he spotted me. As soon as I looked at his car the headlights came on and he drove away."

"What kind of car was it?" asked Holly.

"I couldn't tell you."

"I'm sorry for wasting your time," Holly said to the dispatcher on the phone and clicked her cell phone closed.

"This is really weird," said Jake. "This guy, this Gordon guy, he gave me a hard time up on the unit. I thought he was going to get violent."

"That's his M.O. Intimidation. He pulled the same shit with me."

"What did you do?"

"I told him I wasn't an eight-year-old boy."

"You're tough," reflected Jake.

"Why, what did you do?" asked Holly.

"I got him some water," he said, sheepishly. "Guess that showed him."

"The world is full of bullies. Appeasement doesn't seem to work."

"Anyway. We're here, huh? I wasn't sure you'd come," said Jake.

"Yeah," answered Holly, followed by a long pause. They couldn't help but look out the window from their table, but they only saw their reflections looking back.

"Had any dreams lately?" asked Jake.

"Plenty. Usually nightmares."

"You don't talk about your dreams in the group. Have you noticed that? I think you tend to be a little quiet."

Holly didn't respond right away. She took a pull on her latte, and Jake noticed the silence between them and the soft reggae playing over the speakers. Eventually, she said, "I actually tend to be a private person. I talk with my sponsor, share with a couple of friends. I tend to keep to myself. Why? Are you an open book?"

"Not at all. I used to be more open."

"Now you have something to hide."

"What do you mean?" asked Jake.

"Well, your drinking, for instance."

A group of students walked into the coffee shop and Holly and Jake looked up as a rush of cold air blew in.

Jake looked back at Holly. "Boy, you guys never stop talking about the drinking, do you?"

"Do you ever stop thinking about it?" asked Holly.

Jake sighed. "No. I guess not. Not for long. Ever since I saw that guy out in his car I've wanted a drink."

"Jake, that's okay. So do I."

"What are you saying?"

"I'm not suggesting we drink. I'm saying that if you talk about what's on your mind, you're less likely to do it."

"Oh. Well, then, I better not talk about the other thing on my mind."

Holly blushed. "I think I should go home. I certainly don't need any more caffeine."

"I'm sorry. I didn't mean to make you feel—"

"Embarrassed? You didn't. I'm flattered. I just think we should watch ourselves."

"Someone else is watching you," said Jake, nodding out the door. "Can I follow you home? I mean, I won't come in or anything. I'll just make sure that guy isn't following you."

Holly thought about it for a moment. "Okay. I guess that makes sense. Actually, I'd like it if you came in with me, just to make sure no one's there."

"Sure, Holly. Someday, you'll do the same for me."

"I'm sure I will. But Jake, do me a favor, and yourself a bigger favor."

"What's that?"

"Get a sponsor. And talk with him. Every day. I can't do that for you."

"Okay. Anything for you, Holly."

"Great."

Holly blushed again and the two of them went out to their cars and drove into the darkness of the Michigan night.

In Claudia Silverstein's office, Emma was talking about her week.

"It's been busy. I had a really good talk with my friend and colleague. She told me—let me start over. I realized that—"

"This is hard for you to talk about," offered Claudia.

"Yes, it is. But I have to."

"Don't rush by this. What is in the way?"

Emma sighed. Then she began to cry.

"What's in the way? My marriage. It feels like my entire life. The last twenty years. Trying to make it work with Frank. So much is in the way. My career. My role as a mother."

"You feel like there's something so big, it will effect every area of your life."

"Yes. I—the reality is—I'm in love with someone else. Or maybe it's just a crush. But I haven't been talking about it to anyone. I mentioned it to my friend. And she really, she really let me have it," said Emma, blowing her nose. "And she challenged me to start talking about it and I think she's right because I've just been all fucked up inside, pardon my language."

"You're fine."

"And as long as I held on to this secret, the more distant Frank and I became, and my boundaries started slipping at work and now I'm not sure I can stay married."

"Let's slow this down, shall we? First of all, tell me about this other relationship."

"It's someone I met at a conference. Dylan. I met Dylan at a conference and we had a great time. I felt like I'd met someone who really knew me, who was a real match for me, someone I was totally turned on by, physically, emotionally, intellectually. God it feels great to say this out loud! And I discovered, it wasn't hard to see, that it was totally mutual. And we've been emailing, and the feelings have gotten stronger and now we're going to meet again, in Grand Rapids."

"When?"

"Soon."

"Does Frank know about Dylan?"

"I told him in our session with the marital counselor. He took it hard, which makes sense. He won't talk with me now."

"A lot of married women have had crushes on other men. It doesn't mean you have to act on it."

Emma sighed and clutched the Kleenex she was holding.

"But I want to."

"I know," said Claudia, empathically. "You've found someone who represents all the things that feel missing. And there's been so much missing. With your son moving away, with your parent's death."

"Are you suggesting that I not go to see Dylan in Grand Rapids?"

Claudia shifted in her seat. "Emma, this is not about what I suggest or not. You sound like a teenager who's mother suggested she be home by midnight."

Emma slumped in her seat. "I guess I do. I'm just convinced I have to meet Dylan. I have to let myself explore this."

Claudia said, "Okay. Let yourself have this for a while. In here. Let yourself fully explore this idea of meeting with Dylan. What do you think will happen?"

"I'll fall in love," said Emma. Her face softened, her eyes held a far away look, their focus on something beyond the consultation room.

"Great. You fall in love," said Claudia, shifting in her chair. "And what will that be like?"

"It'll be great. I'll feel fulfilled. I'll feel whole. I'll stop denying myself."

"And then what?"

"Then I'll have to choose."

"Between?"

Emma regained her focus, and looked back at Claudia. "Frank and Dylan. Staying married or getting a divorce."

"And?"

"And that will be hard. And, like I said, I could lose everything."

"So there are a lot of possible consequences to making this visit? Consequences you may or may not be ready to face?"

"I'm ready. I'll just—" Emma didn't finish. She began to cry again.

"You're really at a crossroads. And you might not be as certain as you think. There's no rush. This 'Dylan,' is he married?"

"No."

"I suppose it matters less about who Dylan is than what he represents."

Emma looked at her hands. She started to pick at the skin around her nails, then took hold of them and folded them neatly in her lap. When she looked up at Claudia she was angry.

"I'm sorry, Claudia, but I think that's bullshit! There's something here I just feel like I need to do."

"Oh, Emma. Of course, you'll do what you need to do. I have to tell you that I have the utmost respect for your ability to make your own decisions. I just need to remind you, that with each choice come consequences. And you must be prepared to live with those consequences. You must be prepared to embrace them."

"Yeah, well, I'll let you know how it goes."

"I have a good guess," said Claudia.

"What do you mean?"

"I'm sorry. I shouldn't have put it that way," countered Claudia. "It's just that I've been in this line of work long enough to have seen this before. So have you. In fact, why don't you tell me how this is likely to go?"

"Claudia, you're getting on my nerves."

"You don't want to look at it, do you?"

"*I look at nothing else!*" Emma was shouting. She quieted her voice and said with great deliberation, "I look at my future without Frank, without Nathan, without my career, every day. I run, I bike, I swim. I try to make it all go away, and it haunts me every step I take, every dream I have. I realize now what my dreams are saying to me. That I'm a snake, and it's time for me to realize my snakey ways. It's time for me to find someone who can worship the ground I slither on. I'm going to meet Dylan because I have to. I'm going to meet Dylan because I'm ready to burn it all to the ground if I need to. I'm going to meet Dylan because I won't be able to go on if I don't."

Claudia looked at the clock. "We're going to have to stop. Can you come in again tomorrow?"

Emma drew a deep breath.

"No. I'm busy. I'll see you next week."

Emma dropped her check on her seat, instead of giving it to Claudia and walked out of the office.

CHAPTER NINE

Marianne woke from her dream with a start, gasping for air. She looked around the room and sighed, "Thank God." She turned on her light next to her bed and then began to write:

I just dreamt about nothing. I was in a place that was no place. There wasn't any color, there wasn't any sound, there was nothing to look at. It wasn't dark. It wasn't light. It was nothing. And I couldn't make any noise. I was just in this landscape where there wasn't anything at all.

Marianne looked at her clock. It was 5:45 a.m. She was usually up by now and through her workout, so that she could be at work before 6:30 a.m.

How did I sleep through my alarm? She looked at her clock and realized that she hadn't set the alarm.

Marianne got up and put on her terry cloth bathrobe. She walked across the floor of her bedroom and looked out the window. It was dark outside and the sun wouldn't come up for another hour. She thought about getting a quick workout in, but decided against it. She went to take a shower, then got ready for her day at work. Her TV was in her bedroom and she decided to turn it on. The morning news blared about budget cuts, a missing girl. She got back into bed and closed her eyes. She dozed off again, with the sound of the television acting as a white noise. The sound of voices in the room was reassuring.

Marianne opened her eyes with a start and looked at the clock again. It was 7:49. It was light outside. People would start arriving in the office within the next 10 minutes. She was always the first one there, but wouldn't make it today.

Marianne picked up her phone and called her secretary's number.

"Hi Macy, it's me. I'm going to be a little late today. I'm getting a late start. I'll be there by nine." Marianne hung up.

She went into the bathroom to put on her makeup, looked at herself in the mirror, glanced at her watch, and walked out of the bathroom. The commute to work was about a half hour, and if she got dressed now she might make it by 9:00 a.m.

On the way to work Marianne realized she hadn't checked her planner, nor had she checked it the night before going to sleep. She fought the urge to speed to work. She looked at her clock in her car and saw that it was 8:20 a.m. She'd be at work before 9:00 a.m. Then her cell rang.

"Marianne? It's Macy. I was wondering if you'd forgotten your eight o'clock appointment with your new clients? They're in your office."

Marianne frowned, swore under her breath and said, "Tell them that I had some car trouble. I'll be there in just a few minutes."

Marianne started speeding.

Jake stood in the frosty air of the November night, breathing out a long sigh while looking up at the second floor of St. Lawrence. He noticed his breath in the air, plumes of frost emitted with every exhaled breath. He walked to the door and keyed himself in with his security card. It was a half hour before he was supposed to come in. He'd told the charge nurse that he'd meet her at this time.

Yvonne was already on the unit, chatting with the charge nurse from the afternoon shift, when Jake got up to the floor.

"Jake, won't you come in?" asked Yvonne, as though she were inviting him to her home instead of the nurse's office.

The other nurse left as Jake stepped in, and he couldn't help but notice her inhaling deeply through her nose as she stepped past him.

"So," asked Yvonne, "how are you?"

"I'm good. As you know, I've been off for a week and I've been doing a lot of thinking and I want to apologize for my drinking."

"Okay, let's get to that in a second. I first and foremost wanted to know, you know, I just wanted to know that you're okay."

"I'm okay."

"Because, Jake, I have a role to play and so do you, and the hospital requires certain things of us."

"Like what?" interrupted Jake.

"Just a second," Yvonne shuffled through some papers on her desk. "They require documentation, mainly, but before I got into any of that, I just wanted to know that you're okay."

She looked up from the desk, and caught Jake's eye. She was holding a file with his name on it.

"Uh oh."

"It's not that bad, Jake. I'm speaking now as a 'human being.' I like you. I authentically and truly like you as a human being, and it pains me to see you in pain. You're a good worker and we're better off with you on the unit than off it. But I also want to make sure you can get any help you need and that you don't self-destruct."

"Yeah, I understand," answered Jake. He resisted an urge to sink in the chair.

"So, were you able to follow through with what we required of you?"

"I got a letter from Emma Davis, if that's what you mean." Jake pulled an envelope from inside of jacket and handed it to Yvonne. He noticed his hand was shaking. Yvonne looked at his hand for a moment, looked him in the eye again, and then took the letter.

"Good," she said. "We'll enter it in your personnel file and you can get back to work. I'll read your letter and you read mine, and then we can talk about them."

Jake and Yvonne read the letters. Jake's letter from Emma stated that he was in her care and she felt it was safe for him to return to duty, that he wasn't a threat to himself or others. Yvonne's letter indicated that Jake was suspected to have an alcohol abuse problem and recommended that he seek out therapy and an evaluation. It asked for his signature.

"I have sought out help, but I haven't gone for an evaluation. Do I need to do that?" asked Jake.

"Yes. That's what we're requesting of you. I don't know if you have a problem or not. But a professional evaluation should help to indicate if you do or not, and what steps should be taken."

"Can Emma do that?"

"You'll have to ask her that, Jake. I think it needs to be a licensed substance abuse counselor."

"Oh. I don't think she's that. In fact, I know she isn't. There's something else I want to say. I've finally admitted that I do have a problem. And I'm ready to do something about it. I mean, I'll go for the evaluation if you want, but I'm already going to A.A. meetings."

"That's good news. I have an uncle who goes to those meetings and they've made him a different person."

"That's what I'm afraid of."

"What?"

"Nothing. So do I do the evaluation here?" asked Jake.

"No, you don't have to. I mean, you could do it at the substance abuse clinic we have in the main hospital, but I think you'd be more comfortable going outside of this organization."

"I wonder why. There's going to be documentation on me either way, isn't there?"

"But if you stay out of our system, the only documentation is in your personnel file." Yvonne picked up the folder and waved it over the desk. "Only myself and the human resource staff have access to that information. And it's listed as 'confidential.'"

"Okay. I'll get some recommendations from Emma for an eval. So can I return to work?"

"Yes. If you're going to A.A. and you can get an evaluation scheduled tomorrow, you can start work tomorrow night. I'd like to have you start tonight. Our midnight crew is pretty green. I could use you tonight, but we have to follow formalities. Get the appointment scheduled tomorrow and start tomorrow night."

"Okay. I wish I could start tonight. I could use the money, I don't get paid for this time."

"I know. Nothing I can do about it."

"Okay. I'll do my footwork and get it all lined up. So I'll plan to start tomorrow. It's funny how I missed this place."

"Isn't it? I know what you mean. Even though it's—"

"Crazy?" asked Jake with a smile.

"You said it, I didn't. There's something you should know. Art Jackson died yesterday."

"Oh, man. That's terrible. Here? On the unit?"

"No, he may have froze to death. He was discharged a few days ago, and it looks like the after-care was lacking. He was found down by the river. No winter coat."

"He went off his meds," said Jake.

"Probably."

"Yeah. Wow. Art. What a shame."

"I didn't mean to burden you, but I thought you'd like to know."

"Yeah, thanks. I noticed Brandi Janes when I came in. She's back?"

"Yes, she took another overdose. She left her boyfriend and then took all of her anti-depressants."

"Wow. I saw that guy the other night."

"Really?"

"Yeah. I think he's stalking this woman I know who works for Protective Services."

"You know, this is a weird coincidence, but I get used to them in a town this size. Miss Janes was talking about that— that her boyfriend had some vendetta against Protective Services. He was going to get even. Blah blah blah."

"Duty to warn?" asked Jake.

"Nothing specific enough. People make threats all the time. Unless they're specific, we can't jeopardize a patient's confidentiality."

"Wow."

"And neither can you, Jake. You can't technically tell this woman that Miss Janes is here."

"I know."

"Not technically, anyway. See you tomorrow night."

"Yeah, thanks Yvonne."

Marianne dreams of voices.

She hears them and at first thinks they are from somewhere outside, down the road. Her house is on a long stretch of an isolated county road. She wonders where people might be gathering. She looks out the window to see a full moon in the sky. Closing the window, she listens again but the voices are still there.

She feels her skin prickle and goose bumps raise on her arms. Marianne knows the voices are in her own house and now that she focuses she can hear other sounds, almost like a party.

Marianne puts on her robe and steps out in her hallway. She remembers what it was like as a child, when her parents would host parties and she was to go to bed and stay quiet, but one night her father's friend had come upstairs, and—

I really don't want to think about that tonight Marianne thought, but she feels a lump in her throat and a knot in her stomach. She hears the voices more clearly. She recognizes them as people from work.

As Marianne walks down the stairs she sees her living room has transformed into the main room of the office. Desks are moved in, and her couches and chairs displaced. Her employees are acting just like it was a typical workday. John is on the phone, planning a meeting. Macy is at the copier, set up where her piano had stood.

"What are you doing here?" Marianne asks. No one looks at her. She stands at the foot of the stairs, and where first she had been cautious and self-conscious, she becomes boisterous. "What are you doing here?" she repeats.

Still no response. Marianne steps out into the room and approaches Macy. "Macy, what are you doing here?"

Macy doesn't respond. In fact, she acts as though she didn't even hear Marianne.

My God, I'm invisible. I'm a ghost. Marianne walks over to John and passes her hand in front of his face and he doesn't even blink.

Marianne went back upstairs, then heard steps coming up the stairs behind her.

And she woke up.

Emma drove her Honda Accord along the long, straight patches of I-96, from Lansing to Grand Rapids. She remembered taking this drive often to visit friends at Aquinas, and later, on vacation along Lake Michigan. There was always a feeling of escape, of freedom, that she felt while on this road.

She passed Portland and crossed miles of farmland and open field. If she'd been taking her time, she would have gone along Grand River Drive, the two-lane highway that paralleled the expressway. It was slower, but the scenery was better—huge oak and maple lined the road, and big red barns and century old farmhouses popped up with regularity. As you got closer to Grand Rapids, the road started to twist and run up and down hills as it traced the route of the river. *Maybe next time,* she thought as she passed the exit and increased her speed a little, while setting the speed control.

God, what am I doing? Emma thought. It was a momentary jolt of trepidation. She felt antsy but at the same time very much alive, noticing every color in the fields and sound of her car speeding along the highway.

The sky was grey; the leaves from the trees mostly down. The trees themselves appeared nearly skeletal. The harvest had been taken and the fields looked barren. Emma thought it was the most beautiful sight she'd ever seen. She remembered that deer season started just a couple of days before and thought she might see a field dotted with the safety-orange of hunters, or a deer carcass draped across the roof of a truck. Emma's thoughts went to the deer. *Courage. Be safe.*

She drove into Grand Rapids and took a downtown exit to find the coffee shop where she was to meet Dylan. It was dark by now, but it was after work-hours and it wasn't hard to find parking. Emma noticed her hands sweating as she approached the coffee shop. She was a few minutes early. *Would Dylan be there already?*

Emma walked into the coffee shop and noticed a few occupied tables. It was dinner hour and there were only a few people scattered around the room, mostly with their noses stuck in laptops, but she didn't see Dylan. She ordered a decaf latte. Feeling more than fully caffeinated already, she sat and waited and watched the door. She got a newspaper from a nearby table and began to look through it, realizing she wasn't seeing a single word.

When Dylan walked through the door, Emma felt her heart skip. She smiled broadly before rising. Tall, blonde, dressed in black jeans and a black turtleneck, Dylan was even more attractive than Emma had remembered. Dylan walked over to Emma and gave her a hug before sitting down at the table next to her.

"Hi," said Emma.

"Hi, yourself," answered Dylan.

"Don't you want some coffee?" asked Emma. She was trying to slow her heart, and found her eyes misting with tears.

"I didn't come here for the coffee," answered Dylan.

"Whew. You're right. You get right to business, don't you?" Emma laughed a little. It felt forced, and she wished she hadn't.

"I'm sorry. Am I too abrupt? I can get a bottle of water, if you'd feel better." Dylan motioned to stand up before Emma answered that she was just feeling a little nervous.

"I know what you mean," answered Dylan.

"You too?" asked Emma, smiling.

"Not so much. But I remember."

Emma noticed the door open and several women walked in, laughing. She realized she was trying to see if she recognized them, and then reminded herself that she was not in East Lansing. She looked back at Dylan and smiled.

"Yeah. We're in different circumstances," said Emma.

"Yes, we are," said Dylan. "I'm not married. I'm not seeing anyone. I'm a free agent, so to speak."

"Right. And I *am* married." Emma grabbed her coffee cup. She felt a little chilled.

"How's that going?" asked Dylan.

"I've told Frank. I'm thinking of a separation."

"Okay," said Dylan slowly. "Are you sure? Because, that's a big step."

"I know. I've seen it with dozens of my clients."

"And," Dylan hesitated before saying, "I don't know how to say this, but you can't, you can't leave Frank for me."

"I know," said Emma.

"Because you don't even know me. You know the idea of me. But you have no idea what a relationship like this would entail."

"I know. I've given it much thought. But I'm tired of living a lie."

"You've done therapy?"

"I've been doing individual, and Frank and I had a single session with a couple's counselor."

Dylan looked straight into Emma's eyes.

"Okay. As long as you've thought this through. 'Cause I can't be with a married woman. I tried it once and it was hell, on all of us. But, Emma, I have to tell you, I'm really attracted to you. And I'd love to explore something with you and see what's there. What's here."

Dylan took Emma's hand.

Emma drew it away. She looked briefly around the coffee shop. No one was looking. Emma felt embarrassed.

"I'm sorry."

"No," said Emma. She looked down into her coffee and raised her eyebrows. "Don't apologize. I want the same thing, Dylan. Ever since we met at the conference, and we just talked and talked and walked and then—that kiss. And those emails. You're a beautiful writer." Emma looked Dylan in the eyes.

"So are you. I've saved those."

"Me too."

"So, we kind of jumped into things." Dylan smiled and said, "So how the hell are you, Emma Davis?"

"I'm good. Confused. My heart is beating out of my chest."

"I know. Work is good? You mentioned your Dream Group."

"Dream Group is good. It's challenging. Every one of the people has more going on than they first indicated, but that's par for the course, isn't it?"

"Do you interpret the dreams?" asked Dylan.

"I help the clients appreciate them. But I do seem to be able to help them find some meaning, yes."

"Good. I brought you some of mine," said Dylan. "I wrote them down."

"Really? Do you have them here?"

"Absolutely. I have a whole purse full of dreams. Here they are." Dylan reached into her own purse and pulled out three pages of writing. "I'm not going to ask you to interpret them here, or anything. But sometime, if you get around to it, take a look and tell me what you see."

"Okay," answered Emma.

"Dylan, I want you to know, I've never felt this way before."

Dylan was silent, but her eyes were moist and attentive.

"I wanted to come here and ask you to be patient. I have to deal with my marriage, I have to tell my son, and I have to tie up a number of things. I just want you to be patient."

"Emma, you do what you need to do. And I'll be here. Waiting, on the other side."

They made small talk, looked at each and smiled, and then Emma noticed the time.

Emma got up.

"Gotta go. I'm glad I came," said Emma.

"Me too. Let me walk you to your car."

They left the coffee shop together. Emma felt an impulse to grab Dylan's hand, and resisted it. She was aware of every person walking by. What if she saw someone she knew?

They reached the parking garage.

"You ready for this?" asked Dylan.

Emma looked at a couple emerging from a car a few spaces away.

"Emma, are you okay?" asked Dylan.

"Yeah, I'm just—this is so new." She unlocked her car and opened the door. The couple walked past, and Emma felt a wave of emotion well up in her chest.

She reached behind Dylan's neck and pulled her face close.

"I'm ready, Dylan. God, I'm ready. And I'm so fucking scared."

When their lips met Emma lost her breath. She heard Dylan moan quietly, deeply in her throat. Her heart percolated as Dylan kissed her back, more deeply, a brush of her tongue against her lips. They pulled apart and Emma wiped a tear from her own eye.

"You'll hear from me soon," Emma said.

"I better," said Dylan. She turned and walked away.

PART TWO:

A Purse Full of Dreams

CHAPTER TEN

The next Dream Group was held the week of Thanksgiving. Emma looked out the window at the dimming sky. The late fall landscape of barren trees as the earth prepared itself for that winter blanket of snow that felt inevitable. In spite of how depressing it appeared outside, Emma found herself looking forward to the group. She'd developed a sense of attachment towards the different members, and reflected on her thought *"They each have a secret."*

Jake, it was clear, had a secret. He'd been drinking alcoholically. Emma thought about the connection Holly made between Jake's vampire dreams and his alcoholism.

Holly, Emma thought, *is still a bit of a mystery. She judges herself harshly. What's she feeling guilty about? She's in recovery; she divorced the man who was so abusive towards her.* Emma reminded herself to pay more attention to Holly.

Mason planned to be a tourist in the group, yet his dreams were so compelling. Emma wondered if her intuition was correct about there being a connection between his dreams and a physical problem. She hoped she was wrong.

And Marianne. Emma wondered why she was in the group. Even more than Jake, Marianne seemed highly ambivalent about participating in the group. Yet she still came and shared and seemed scared to death. *Scared of what? Marianne seemed elusive and, if not quite fragile, then brittle.*

The group arrived on time and took up their regular seats in Emma's office. Emma started with a "check in," inquiring how the week was for everybody.

Mason started by reporting he'd had a disturbing dream. Emma said they'd make sure they talked about it, after everyone else checked in. Mason nodded and leaned back in his chair, and Emma noticed the look on his face. He seemed bothered.

Emma asked how the week was for the rest of the group.

"I thought this was a dream group. Why would we talk about our lives?" asked Jake.

Holly chimed in with, "Right. As we've seen so far, our dreams don't relate to our waking lives whatsoever."

"I was joking," said Jake.

Emma asked Mason, "So Mason, you were the first to answer, and we'll get to your dream, but how was your week?"

Mason said that he had scheduled an appointment with his doctor and was going to see her within the week. He was lucky because he went to the health center on campus, and many of the students were gone over Thanksgiving break. He mentioned his hope to visit London.

"And that's interesting," Mason said, "because my dream occurs in London."

Emma reflected that he was really eager to talk about the dream and Mason said, "I guess I am," almost sheepishly.

Emma continued her check in with the group and asked Marianne how she was doing.

"It's been, it's been an odd week for me. I've also had some dreams, but I've also been a little off. I don't know how to describe it."

"Off in what way?" asked Holly.

"Well, I missed an appointment, for one thing. And I missed a couple of workouts."

Emma asked if she'd felt preoccupied.

"I wish it was that. Maybe so. I just feel like, almost apathetic," said Marianne. She frowned.

"You're starting to get into my territory, Marianne," said Jake. "Next thing, you'll be procrastinating. Then unable to get out of bed in the morning."

"Yeah, maybe you're right. I should try that next," she said.

"So you're noticing something shifting," said Emma. "Do you feel sad, or depressed?"

"I'm not sure. More like, just not caring."

"And that's unusual for you because you really care, very deeply," said Emma. She leaned over so she caught Marianne's eyes, which had been focused on a spot on the floor.

"That's true," said Marianne.

"You almost look like you could cry, if you let yourself," said Emma.

"Once you said, that I *care*, it just hit me as so true. And what has it gotten me?"

Emma said, "Now that is a good question. What have you gotten as a result of caring?" She waited in silence while Marianne thought it over.

Finally, Marianne answered. "I've got a good career. But it almost feels like it doesn't matter."

"Something's missing," suggested Holly.

"What do you mean?" asked Marianne.

"I don't know," said Holly. "But if everything's good in one area of your life, like work, but suddenly it doesn't seem to matter, maybe it's not the work. Maybe it's somewhere else."

"My personal life is not what I'd like it to be," said Marianne, looking out the window.

"And this is news to you?" asked Jake. "We may have a lot more in common than you've realized."

"No, I haven't really seen it," she said. Marianne looked at Emma. "I probably should have talked about this before, but I haven't been dating anyone for a long while. And before that, I was involved for years and years." She started to cry. Mason handed her the box of tissues that sat on an end table between them.

"I mean, of course, I've known, but, work has always kept me so occupied I never really spent much time thinking about being lonely."

Emma pointed out that she was about to reveal something to the group and wondered if Marianne might feel safe enough to tell the group something about her life.

"I guess I should. I was involved with a married man for years and years. And he kept saying he would leave his wife, but in the end he never did. And sometimes I feel like I've just wasted my life. I feel like I've just put all my eggs in one basket, like they say."

Emma gave Marianne some encouragement over sharing her feelings and sharing such an intimate part of herself with the group. After a few moments, she continued her check in with the group.

Holly said that she was doing well, except she was concerned with being stalked. Everyone expressed some concern, and Marianne appeared particularly frightened by this news. Emma asked if she knew who the stalker was.

"I think it's by someone who I've had contact with through work. A perp."

"Perp?" asked Marianne.

"Perpetrator," said Marianne. "He's hit a little boy, now his girlfriend has left him, and he's focusing on me."

Emma asked if Holly had called the police. Holly said, "Yeah, but they haven't picked him up, yet. Jake saw him in the parking lot, when we were having coffee together."

"Oh?" asked Emma. She thought about confronting them about the "outside relationship" issue she'd raised the group before. Then Emma thought about Dylan and felt like a hypocrite, and let it go. She looked over at Jake and crossed her hands in her lap.

"Yeah, I know him. Or I've met him once, because the same woman was on our psych unit," said Jake. "And he, well, he's an intimidating guy. I had a little run-in with him myself."

"So, Holly, are you still involved in the case?" asked Mason.

"Only as a witness. The kids are in temporary foster care, until the mother pulls herself together. So if it goes to court,

MICHAEL STRATTON

I may have to testify." Holly noticed she was beginning to wring her hands and forced herself to stop.

"So why's he focused on you?" asked Marianne.

"I think he's nuts, myself," answered Jake. "That would be a reason, wouldn't it?"

"Well, it sounds like he's obsessed," said Emma.

"He gives me the creeps," said Holly, looking like she'd tasted something bitter. "People know about him, so if anything happens, it's likely him."

"Don't even say that," said Marianne. "You don't think he'd—"

"Well, I try to be realistic. It doesn't happen very often, but Protective Service workers are assaulted pretty regularly. And occasionally, one of us gets killed."

"Are you afraid for your life?" asked Emma.

"Honestly? No. This guy's M.O., like Jake said, he's an intimidator. He mainly wants to scare me."

"Okay," said Emma. "Jake?"

Jake reported that he'd started to go to A.A. meetings. Mason and Emma congratulated him, and Holly smiled and blushed.

"And I started back at work," Jake said. "And I haven't drank in ten days now."

Holly said "I thought it was twelve days."

"It may have been," said Jake. "Who's counting?"

"Well, Holly seems to be," Mason observed.

"Yeah," said Jake. "Maybe you need an Al-Anon meeting, Holly."

"How do you like it so far?" asked Emma.

"The meetings? Or staying sober?"

"Both."

"I'm not sleeping for shit," said Jake. "Pardon my French. But the meetings are okay. I am surprised at how happy most of the alcoholics seem to be. Most of them tell these horror stories; then they all laugh."

Holly nodded and shrugged her shoulders.

Emma looked to Mason and said, "Okay, Mason, your dream."

"Well, I was in London."

"The city of your dreams," said Jake.

"Yes. And, as usual, I was trying to get from one place to another. But this time, I was trying to get to the Tower of London. And there seemed to be a curfew, because the city was almost deserted. And once I got there, the Samurai was there, and I've seen him in a couple of dreams already. And he chased me down to the river, where I got into a boat. Once in the boat, he cut the rope, because I was still tied to the dock. And then, I was floating and I saw books in the river, and I realized they were my books. Then I saw the head of Ernest Hemingway floating in the river."

"Eeewww!" exclaimed Jake, pulling his feet off the floor like it was contaminated.

"Yes. And Hemingway opened his eyes, and I woke up. What do you suppose it all means?" asked Mason.

"We've been doing this for a few weeks now," said Emma, looking around at the other group members. "What do you all think?"

"I think you're scared," said Marianne.

"Say more," encouraged Emma, leaning towards Marianne.

"I think it's a nightmare, so it's a dream about a fear you're having that you won't let yourself confront."

"Marianne, if you had this dream yourself, what would you be thinking?" wondered Emma.

"That I was scared."

"Okay. Anything else?"

"No."

Holly interrupted the exchange by saying, "I was thinking the Samurai is a symbol of strength. So what if the dream means Mason is running away from one of his strengths? Because, even though you're running away from the Samurai, he hasn't done anything to you, right?"

"I suppose that's true," said Mason.

"And even when you get in the boat, he sets you free?" asked Holly.

"Yes," said Mason. "He could have had me. All he had to do was pull the line in. But he cut me loose."

Jake wondered about the books in Mason's dreams, and reminded him that in his other dream there were books burning. "So what if it's a reflection of your life work? You feel that maybe you have to burn what you've done already, or you're all washed up? Or Hemingway is trying to steal your ideas?"

Mason didn't think it fit for him.

"What do you think of when you think of London?" asked Emma.

"It's a wonderful place. I've talked about that before," said Mason.

"And the Tower of London?" she asked.

"It's a daunting place. People went in and didn't come out. I've visited there several times. The ghosts are palpable."

"And the Samurai?"

Mason said "He looks like the Samurai in Kurosawa's film *Kagamusha*."

"What was that film about? Specifically, what was the Samurai's role in the film?" asked Emma.

"He was an imposter, hired to fill in for the Emperor after he'd been killed."

"And Hemingway? What does he mean to you?"

"He was a boyhood hero of mine. When I was a teenager, in high school, I loved his books and the story of his life."

"So if you look at the layers of meaning in this story you've told yourself, what comes up?" asked Emma.

Mason looked reflective. He stared into the back of the fingernail on his right thumb. Then he said, "London is a place of promise and possibility. And I'm always busy trying to get myself there, or to get from one part to another. The Tower probably does represent fears. So if I juxtapose those…"

"What possibilities do you fear?" asked Emma.

"I don't think I'm afraid of being a fraud. I think, I hate to even say it, I think I'm afraid of death."

"Why do you hate to say it?" asked Emma.

"I'm aware of getting closer to the end of my life. But I like to think I have another, maybe, twenty years left. And maybe a chance to do some more writing or commit more time to projects that I'd like to do, now that I'm not teaching."

Marianne asked Mason about Hemingway and what it was about his life that fascinated him.

"His life, his story," said Mason, "was always fascinating to me. How he'd travel from one place to another and write a novel out of his life experiences. Where my life has been spent watching movies, not to belittle that, but I sometimes wonder how much of my life I've actually 'lived' instead of, you know, having been a bystander."

"So Hemingway opening his eyes—" said Emma.

"He is looking right through me. It's a challenge. A frightening one."

"What's frightening about it?" asked Emma.

"I'm not sure," said Mason. He looked down into his thumbnail again. "Do I have the right stuff?"

"You're kidding," said Jake.

"What? No. I have my doubts."

"Well, I hate to get all serious and stuff, but you're great. It's hard to imagine you'd be wondering," said Jake.

"Sometimes I *do* wonder, Jake, if I have enough talent, if I am smart enough. That doubt, I guess, you never lose. Or some of us never seem to."

Marianne asked, "So, Mason, do you think the Samurai had decapitated Hemingway?"

"I suppose he could have, but that wasn't my sense in the dream."

"And what does the Samurai want from you?" asked Emma.

"I think, I have always thought that he wants my life. But now that I'm thinking about it, I've always made the mistake that he wanted to kill me. Now, I'm just wondering if he wants my life."

Jake sat back in his chair and nodded, looking up into the ceiling. Emma was aware that the time for the group was getting short and she wanted to work with Marianne's dream before the group was over.

"Marianne, you said you'd had a dream."

"Two of them, actually. And both were disturbing. One dream, well, I'll tell them in reverse order. One dream was about somebody in my house. But it turned out to be people from work. They had set up my living room like the office, and people were working. But I couldn't be seen by them."

"Work is taking over home," said Jake.

"That's what I thought," Marianne said to Jake, conspiratorially. "But at work, I know what I'm doing and, here, I was invisible."

"Could you be heard?" asked Holly.

"No, I was imperceptible."

"What do you think?" asked Emma.

"I think it was creepy. I think that, it's what you mentioned before Emma. That I care, very deeply. And I don't think I matter. And I'd always had this very tight boundary, I think that's the word, between work and home. And now I'm wondering if any of it makes a difference."

"Does it?" asked Emma.

Marianne looked thoughtful. "I'll have to think about what I heard here tonight. About something missing."

Emma reminded Marianne that she'd had *two* dreams.

"The other dream I had the night before the one I've just talked about. It was a dream about nothing."

"Sounds like a *Seinfeld* episode," said Jake.

"No, this was literally nothing."

"How do you mean?" asked Emma. "How do you know it was a dream?" Emma hadn't heard of a dream like this before.

"Because I was aware of dreaming."

"You knew that you were dreaming. Could you affect the dream?"

"I didn't consider it."

"How did you know you were dreaming?" asked Holly.

"I'm not sure. I just knew."

"And could you sense—?" asked Emma.

"Nothing. I couldn't see any colors. I couldn't hear any sounds. It was just nothing."

"Talk about something missing," said Holly.

"Oh, my God," gasped Marianne. "Everything is missing."

"In this dream, yes," said Emma. "In the other dream, it seemed like your impact on other's lives was missing."

"I see," said Marianne.

Emma took a moment to notice how different the group seemed. Every one was participating and seemed authentically interested in each other. She felt humbled and wondered again at how therapy seemed to work, even at times when she felt lost.

The rest of the group was spent discussing everyone's plans for the Thanksgiving holiday. Marianne was going to be visiting her sister in Chicago, Mason said he and Mona were hosting dinner for family and friends, and Holly said she would be volunteering to work at the A.A. dinner.

Jake said, "Cool, can I come to that? I don't have any other plans."

Holly said that would work fine. Emma made a point to tell her they would have to make sure to work on one of her dreams next time. She also looked at Jake and said something supportive about his attending A.A. "We didn't even get to one of your dreams this week, Jake. We'll have to look at that next week."

"Yeah, sure. Remind me to sleep first."

"You have to learn how to fall asleep all over again," said Holly. "Most alcoholics know how to pass out."

Emma laughed. She saw a spark between Holly and Jake and it worried her.

On Thanksgiving morning Holly thought that the sky was as blue as paint, as she drove to the Alano Club. The back of her car was loaded with pies she had made the night before, pumpkin, mincemeat, and apple. She was struck by the clarity and the blueness of the sky.

It seems so unusual because it's been days since I've seen it, she thought. The grey skies over Lansing could last for weeks at a time, during fall and winter. Holly hit the button of her radio and flipped through the stations and rested on a piece of classical music for her short drive.

She pulled up in front of Jake's house and saw him out front smoking a cigarette, wearing a jean jacket and an orange sweater.

"Happy Thanksgiving," she said as he got into the car.

"Yeah. Bird day. The local DJ is doing three hours on Charlie Parker this weekend."

"Charlie Parker?"

"Yeah. Jazz saxophone. I'll have to play you some. Great stuff. Anyway, his nickname was 'Bird.'"

"Oh, yeah, I think I've heard of him, but I've never heard his music."

"You'll have to! He's amazing. Bebop, you have to hear it. Man, it smells great in here."

"Pies. I've made three of them for the dinner."

"Should I have brought something?" asked Jake.

"No, you're fine."

They drove the few blocks from Jake's to the Alano Club, down abandoned streets on the east side of Lansing. The smell of pies was now mixed with the smell of cigarettes. *The smell of addiction,* thought Holly, but she didn't say anything.

After they pulled into the parking lot, they found a space behind the building. The club itself had been a bar and restaurant at one time. It had a parking lot that could hold sixty cars, and today the lot was probably half full.

"Wow, all these people came on a holiday?" asked Jake.

"Well, a lot of people don't have anyplace else to go. I'm here. So are you."

"Yeah, I noticed. I wasn't judging. Just surprised."

They walked through the doors of the club, Holly holding two pies and Jake holding one. "They'll have meetings around the clock on holidays in the meeting rooms, but the dinner will be buffet style here in club," explained Holly as they approached a group of tables, with people setting out steaming dishes of mashed and sweet potatoes, green bean casseroles, plates full of rolls and breads, a large ham and a large platter of turkey.

"Howdy, Holly," said one of the men who was cutting the turkey and placing it on the platter.

"How's it going, Jim? Look like we have enough food?"

"Yeah, I think so. What do you have there? Pies?"

Holly and Jake put the pies towards the end of the buffet line, where they had to make space amongst stacks of cookies, cakes, and brownies.

"At an A.A. party, there is never any want for sweets," explained Holly.

"Yeah, I noticed that," said Jake.

"There's a ton of sugar in alcohol. Most of us crave sugar once we've stopped. Especially early on."

Jake recognized a few of the people from meetings he'd attended, and nodded to acknowledge a group gathered by a TV. The Lions were on television and some guys were watching. Jake stayed close to Holly.

"Why don't you go talk to those guys," Holly suggested. "Or watch the game."

"Oh, I'm all right."

"Jake, you're not all right," said Holly, quietly. "It's okay to feel awkward and uncomfortable. We all do at first. Go over and watch the game. It's okay. Besides, I left my serving utensils in the car. I have to go get 'em."

"Okay. You know where to find me."

"You'll be fine. They don't bite."

"Not yet," answered Jake as Holly walked across the floor to the front door.

Stepping outside she felt the cool brisk air hit her face like a slap. Crossing her arms across her chest, Holly rapidly walked around to the back parking lot, face down to protect her cheeks as much as possible, and got to her car. She opened the back door and heard a voice speaking right behind her from outside the car.

"I was hoping to meet you again."

Holly gave a quick 'yip' before leaning back out of her car, this time with her serving blade in her hand. She slammed the door shut before turning to see who was behind her.

"Gordon!" she gasped. Holly had been startled. "What are you doing here?" Holly asked. She felt the air rush out of her lungs and the blood rush from her face.

"Just wanted to talk a little."

She looked around, and saw no one else in the lot. "This isn't the time or place to talk," Holly said, brandishing her utensil like a knife.

Gordon laughed. "You're not going to do much with that. But I can see you're scared. You oughtta be. You cost me my woman and you cost her custody of her own kids. I just thought you should know that. And I wanted to know what you're going to give me to replace them."

"Gordon, I'm not the one you need to talk to about this. I don't have any power; I was just doing my job." Holly knew she was panicked. She wished she felt calmer. She looked around and saw no one else in the parking lot. Gordon stood between her and the building, and she'd have to get around him to turn the corner to get to the front door. No one could see them here.

"My car or yours?" asked Gordon.

"Excuse me?"

"Do you want to talk this over in my car, or yours? It's cold out here and I just want to have a talk."

"Let's talk in mine," said Holly, her eyes darting back and forth. "I have to go back inside though, I need my keys."

"You just let yourself in the car, you already have your keys. Hand them over and get in the damn car!" said Gordon Thomas, more forcefully.

"Hey, what's going on?" It was Jake, who had just walked around the corner of the building.

"I can't believe it," said Gordon. "You two, together? Little chicken-shit boy and his bitchy chicken-shit girl. We was just having a talk is all."

"Leave her alone," said Jake, taking a step towards Gordon. Gordon took a step in close to Jake and shoved hard with both of his arms, knocking Jake down onto the asphalt of the parking lot. Jake grunted as he fell.

Holly took the moment that Jake bought by putting her key back in the car door. Her hands were shaking and she had a hard time getting the key in, but then it went in, and she opened the door to the car. By the time Gordon turned around Holly had locked the doors, and was honking her horn. She turned the key in the ignition, pulled it out of her parking space, and aimed the car at Gordon, still with the horn blasting.

"Shit!" said Gordon as he jumped out of the way.

Several alcoholics had come around the corner by now and were watching.

"Call the cops!" yelled Jake, still on the ground. Gordon was running toward his own car, with Holly driving behind him, honking the whole time.

"Call the cops!" yelled Jake, now up on his feet and running towards Holly's car.

Gordon got into his car and screeched the tires as he pulled away.

Holly kept the horn honking until she noticed Jake motioning to his ears. She stopped honking, put the car in park, and unlocked her door.

"Let's go get him," shouted Jake as he got in the passenger side.

"No. No, Jake. It's over," Holly said, beginning to cry.

"Bullshit. Let me drive your car, Holly, and give me your cell phone. I'll tell the police where he is."

"No, Jake. Let it go."

Jake took a deep breath and looked at Holly. She'd started to cry, and he noticed her shaking. She wouldn't stop, even as he held her.

Emma had spent the day at Frank's family, visiting. Their son, Nathan, was there, and Emma saw him for the first time since he left for college. He didn't stay the night, though. Emma couldn't sleep that night. She got up late and wrote in her journal:

Went to the Davis's for Thanksgiving tonight in G.R. Nathan was there, but didn't stay the night—visiting his girlfriend again. I still haven't told him about my plans to leave his father. I haven't told anyone except for Betty and Claudia. And I still haven't told them the whole story.

I can't believe I'm about to do this, take this step, but I've been denying my feelings for too long. I heard Dr. Laura on the car radio the other day, talking about how we shouldn't go by our feelings. That obligations are more important, and responsibility. More important than feelings. More important than love? She said it's okay to be gay, but not to act on it. I can't believe I let myself listen to her, let alone rent any space in my head. I must feel guilty. Maybe that's the feeling I should learn to suppress. I'm tired of living in a world without love.

Frank decided to stay overnight at his parents. They must think something is up. He said it's up to me to tell them. I will. I'll tell whoever needs to be told. I dread telling Nathan. I wonder if he knows his parent's are in trouble. He didn't ask for this. How can I live with this guilt? But if I don't take this step—

And now I'm thinking about the finances. I work, but Frank has always provided the income. Can I really make a living off my practice? I'll have to see an attorney. It really doesn't matter. I'll live in a shack if I need to. I have to leave. I have to let myself be who I am. It sounds selfish, but what can I do?

Tonight, when Frank cut the turkey, I thought about this being our last Thanksgiving together. I was thinking about the last year Dad was alive and how much he always hated holidays. He was so depressed through his life. I think I became a therapist to find a cure for him. And my mom was an enigma. I never knew her. I can't believe they're gone. Would they understand? I'd like to think, they'd want me to be happy. What if they knew this was my choice? They stayed together through all kinds of hard times. Alcohol held them together.

Sometimes I wonder how this will affect my livelihood. I guess there are gay therapists, but do they work with straight couples? Do they work with families? What kind of hypocrite will I be, to try and keep families together, when I can't even keep my own?

What a mess I am! I go back and forth—guilt, remorse, tears, but also certainty. I have to do something—to live into my own truth—to live in the possibility of love. I'm sorry for what happens next. I'm sorry for all the hurt I'll bring to those I love. I'm sorry for the consequences of my being who I am, and my choice to stop hiding. Yes, I'm sorry, but I'm also angry—angry at the years of denial, the hiding, the lies. I did what I could. It's no one's fault. Now I need to focus on my work and see what kind of life I can build.

Emma put the pen down and went to bed. She turned out the light and counted her breaths. Down from one hundred. She stilled her mind and she was asleep before she reached her own age.

And she dreams, of being on the side of a mountain, climbing through the snow, the snow blowing into a blinding blur, until she can't see where she's climbing, and then she sees exactly where she is as the wind stops suddenly, the snow stops blowing and she stands at a precipice, a cliff edge. She stands on the edge, wondering if she can go back, take a step back before she falls, and then, too late, as the edge below her collapses and she is falling, free falling down the mountain side, hitting a hill and sliding in the snow until she reaches another edge and again falls, and falls, and falls and—

She awakened with a start. Heart pounding, sweating, panting. It was only two in the morning. Emma got up for a drink of water and then went back to check her email. It was going to be a long night.

Mason was walking through the doors of the Michigan State University medical clinic. He'd let Mona out at the door and had parked the car and walked through the lot to the clinic. Mason was thinking about the results of the blood work, the other tests, and why his doctor asked him to come in immediately to discuss the results. Mason was keeping his hands in his pockets to keep them warm and found his wife, Mona, waiting in the lobby.

"Internal Medicine is on the second floor," he said, and they took the elevator upstairs. There was a sterile quality to the building; the paint on the walls looked like a half-hearted attempt to make the place appear cheery. Mason thought there was the aroma of antiseptic, which seemed to mask a much more human smell. The lobby seemed dingy to Mason after he checked in. There were magazines spread on the table, some worn furniture, and a television that no one in the room was watching.

"Want something to read?" asked Mona.

"No. Thanks."

Mona patted Mason's hands and smiled at him.

"I think I'd like to go in alone."

"I don't think so, Buster."

"Don't tell me what I like," he snapped at her, quietly.

"I'm not doubting that's what you'd like. I'm just telling you that I'm going in with you," said Mona.

"And what if I don't let you?" asked Mason.

"Then there's going to be one hell of a scene."

Mason sighed. "Have it your way." A moment later he apologized. "I'm sorry, Mona. I guess I'm a little nervous."

A young nurse opened the door and called Mason's name and the couple rose to their feet and walked through the door.

Mason's intern was a young woman from India, whom he'd been seeing for the last two years. Dr. Naraji had a pleasant smile and led the couple into a small conference room. She had Mason's chart with her, as well as X-rays.

"How are you today?" Dr. Naraji asked, her face a template of open acceptance.

"A little nervous," said Mason and Mona nodded.

"I'm here to take notes," said Mona, as she took a pen and a pad of paper from her purse.

"Oh, good," said the doctor. "Ask any questions you'd like. You are here to learn the results from last week's tests. I'm afraid I have bad news."

Mason could barely focus as the young doctor made some remarks about his diagnosis, his prognosis, and the treatment options. He looked at Mona's face and saw the tears in her eyes as she scribbled away on her note pad. He looked back at the doctor and asked, "Cancer? I have cancer?"

"Yes, I'm afraid so."

"Treatable? Did you say something about treatment?"

"It is at a stage of advancement where I cannot give you any hope. It is too late for surgery. Chemotherapy could give you some extra time, but we are at a point of discussing the quality of your life, versus the quantity."

"Oh, God," choked Mona. She was writing furiously the words "quality" and "quantity."

"Such a cliché, but I need to ask. How long have I got?"

"We don't like to give specifics. Studies have found that they become self-fulfilling."

"Or maybe accurate. I'd really like to know. Do I have a year?"

The doctor showed the X-rays to Mason and Mona, showing how the cancer had started, probably, in the kidneys, moved to the liver, and was now most likely progressing to other organs.

"I've got to ask again, doctor, do I have a year?" asked Mason.

Dr. Naraji shakes her head. "I am afraid not."

"Six months?"

"At the most. We are probably talking weeks, perhaps a few months. As I said, it is very advanced." Dr. Naraji turned her attention again to the test results and began to explain the cancer. "It is amazing you've had so few symptoms. But the cancer is developing at a very rapid rate, and we can do everything possible to relieve your pain, when it comes."

"I haven't had an appetite, but other than that, no pain. But my dreams—"

"Yes," answered Dr. Naraji.

"My dreams were warning me. A polluted lake, a Samurai, that I now think was death stalking me. Somewhere in my body, I knew there was a problem."

"Yes. There are amazing tales of self-awareness. In India, some yogis give amazing self-diagnosis that medical tests later confirm. Perhaps we all have such self-knowledge."

"So, what's the next step?" asks Mason.

"You may need some time to think over whether you wish to pursue treatment," answered the doctor. The clock on the wall seemed to be ticking louder.

"Time," answered Mason. "What would you do?"

"That is impossible to say, because I am not you."

"I know, but I'm not asking you to predict what would be best for me. What would you do?"

The doctor seemed hesitant, but then she spoke.

"I would visit the Taj Mahal and take a pilgrimage."

"I see."

Mason looked Mona in the eyes. Hers were full of tears, but she held his gaze.

"London?" he asked.

"Whatever you want, Buster."

It was just outside of town, a few miles out, someplace they weren't likely to be seen, in a place that was one of their favorite restaurants. It had been Frank's idea to meet there, and Emma hadn't seen him since the day before, Thanksgiving Day.

The décor was homey, and there were reminders of the holiday season, Christmas lights and faux snow around the bar area.

When Emma arrived Frank was already seated at a table, looking at the menu. He waved her over, and she sat down in the chair across from him.

"I wanted to meet you in public, so we would be invested in keeping this civil," said Frank after greeting Emma. It was late in the afternoon, too early for diners, and there was only a scattering of servers and guests in the dining room. The waiter came and Frank ordered a martini.

"Only one," he said to Emma, when he saw her raise her eyebrow.

After the waiter left they exchanged a little small talk about the holiday and how long Frank had stayed with his parents after Emma had left. Emma asked if he'd told his parents about their troubles. He had not.

"Emma, have you had a chance to really think this over? Maybe changed your mind? Maybe changed your heart?"

Emma smiled at Frank and then frowned. "I've given it a lot of thought. I can barely think of anything else. And I think I need a separation."

"I was afraid that was what you were going to say."

"This isn't easy for me, Frank. It's not anything I ever—" Emma hesitated. She sat quietly as the waiter brought Frank's martini and her tonic water.

"Are you ready to order?" asked the waiter.

Frank ordered a steak, rare. Emma asked for the soup of the day.

After the waiter left Frank drank the martini in two quick gulps and said, "I'm going to ask you to do something for me."

"What is it, Frank?"

"I want you to get a full psychiatric work up. I want neurology reports, psych testing, the full gamut. Would you do that for me?"

Emma sat with her mouth open.

"Why would you want that?"

Frank looked into her face like he was looking at a puzzle.

"Because, Emma, this is so unlike you, I just want to make sure you're all right."

"I think I've been confused. I think I've been torn. I think I've been obsessed, ambivalent, depressed, angry. I think I've been a lot of things, Frank. I also think I'm gay. But I don't think I'm crazy. I'm not mentally ill. I'm not insane."

"Will you do it for me, Emma?"

Emma could tell he was serious. She could barely catch her breath. She felt dizzy. *My God, I'm on the verge of an anxiety attack!*

The waiter brought out the salads and took some time preparing them at the table.

"You can just leave that," ordered Frank. The waiter left again.

Frank picked up his fork and stabbed a leaf of lettuce. He looked at Emma without eating a bite.

"You want to know if I can do that for you? Can I submit to tests? I—I don't think I can, Frank."

"What's the hurt? If we have so much on the line, there's so much for us to lose— for you to lose."

"I—I think I'm stunned you would suggest that. Do you know me at all, Frank?"

"I thought I did. That's why I want the tests. What if it's something really horrible, God forbid, like a brain tumor?"

"A brain tumor that turns a woman into a lesbian? I've never heard of such a thing."

"Well, you might be right. But will you do this one thing? For me? For us? For Nathan?"

Emma sat in silence. The waiter returned with their meals and this time served them quickly and without comment.

"Let me think about it," said Emma.

Frank started to eat his steak and they talked about Nathan. Emma asked if Frank had spoken to him since yesterday. Frank had not. Emma had a few spoons of soup and felt some warmth return to her hands. She started to feel better. Finally, she answered Frank's request.

"You know, Frank, I'm not going to get those tests. There'd be no point. I understand it is difficult to accept. Believe me, it has been so hard for me to try to accept it myself. If there were any other way—"

"But maybe there is."

"But maybe this is what I need to do."

"Emma, do you even love me? Even a little?"

"Frank, I do love you. Almost like a brother."

"Is that it? If only I were a woman, you might be able to get excited for me? God, I must repulse you."

"Frank, let's not do this." Emma looked over her shoulder at a family that had entered the restaurant and were being seated just a few feet away from them. She was startled by the sound of Frank's voice, which came out as a snarl.

"Here it is, then. If you don't want to look into this, try to fix this, get therapy for it, because there are people who are, you know, 'that way', but they learn to live with it, like living with a disability—"

"For God's sake, Frank, I'm not disabled, I'm not crazy," answered Emma, with the same intensity in her voice. "I am what I am," she said, her voice softening. "I am what I am. Can't you accept that?"

The waiter was approaching, and Emma couldn't tell if it was to ask about their meals or to ask them to quiet down. Frank headed him off.

"Another round, please," Frank said.

"I thought you said 'just one,'" whispered Emma, as the waiter left.

"Fuck you," Frank whispered. "Here it is. If you won't do anything for me, not the simplest thing, I want you out of the house."

"I wondered when it would come to this." Emma leaned back in her chair and tossed her napkin onto the table.

"I want you out."

"When?" asked Emma.

"As soon as possible. Before Christmas. And you have to tell Nathan."

"He doesn't know?"

"Not from me, he doesn't. And he won't."

A tear ran down Emma's face as the waiter brought the drink. "I'll pay the check here, as well," he said, glancing at Emma.

"I have to live my life," said Emma.

"Yeah, well you can live it somewhere else. You're going to regret this, Emma. You're the one making the mistake here."

"It's not a mistake. I'm sorry to hurt you. I'm sorry it's come to this. I'm sorry. But it's not a mistake."

Frank gulped down the drink in two quick slurps and then threw a wad of cash, too much cash, on the table. "I'm out of here. I'll be staying at a hotel until you move out. Please, don't take your time." He stood up and left Emma at the table. She waited for him to go out the door before she got up to leave.

Outside it was snowing and Christmas carols played from speakers strung up on the streetlights, along the street. Emma felt alone in the world.

The following day, Jake was sitting in the big smoke of an A.A. meeting at the Alano East Club a few blocks from his home. He'd arranged to meet his new sponsor, Nick, whom he'd met through Holly.

Jake was sitting at a booth, one of a number that ran along the east wall of the club, framing the large room. There were a number of small tables arranged across the linoleum floor, each equipped with an ashtray and a *Big Book*. There was a bar on the opposite end of the room that served coffee and soft drinks.

Nick walked into the club. He brushed the snow off the shoulders of his winter coat, looked around and saw Jake. Nick smiled and waved and pointed to the bar, returning in a minute with a styrofoam cup filled with black coffee.

Nick had a high forehead and wavy brown hair, which was graying at the temples. He looked ten or fifteen years older than Jake. His demeanor was happy and, to Jake, he looked almost jolly.

Nick asked, "Cold enough for ya?"

"Yeah," answered Jake. "Early winter."

"I understand you were involved in some excitement the other day," said Nick.

"That was crazy. Holly has a stalker, and he showed up here and threatened her."

"Did they get the guy?" asked Nick. Jake noticed he kept his hands on his coffee to keep his fingers warm.

"No, and I'm pretty discouraged about it. We called the cops and then, if you can believe this, he did, too. He said Holly assaulted him with a deadly weapon."

"I heard she was chasing him around the parking lot in her car."

"Yeah, she was."

"Well, that's more excitement than we've seen around here for a while. You and the guy fought?" asked Nick.

"He knocked me down. Shoved me." Jake held up his hands so Nick could see the scabs on his palms where he'd fell.

"I'd heard he knocked you out," said Nick, looking at Jake's scars. "Funny how fast and inaccurately news travels. So what's going to happen?"

"I'm not sure," said Jake. "The police told us Holly is best suited to file a personal protection order. They're trying to get the guy on an assault charge against her, to begin with. He's all excited because she investigated his case with Protective Services and he ended up losing his girlfriend and she ended up losing her kids, and the police are looking for him. So it's a real mess."

"The police are involved, so that's good. Maybe they'll handle it."

"Yeah," answered Jake and pulled out a cigarette.

"Would you mind not smoking while we're meeting?"

"Oh, okay," said Jake, putting his cigarette back in the pack. "But I bet you're smoking a couple of cigarettes just by sitting in this place."

"Yeah, the smoke is pretty bad. I don't come here for the atmosphere. I come to stay sober. And that's what we're here for today. You've been hitting meetings for a couple of weeks now, right?"

"Yeah," Jake nodded, "I've been going to a meeting every day."

"Cool. Any drinking?"

"No," answered Jake. "Not that I haven't thought about it."

"Great. It's not easy. Especially early on," said Nick. "What do you think of the meetings?"

"They're okay. At first I wasn't sure. But the more I come, the more—I don't know—I guess I feel welcomed."

There were a few moments of silence between the men. Jake felt uncomfortable. Then Nick asked him, "Does it fit?"

"What do you mean?" asked Jake.

"I guess it's a two-part question. First, do you have a drinking problem? And second, do you want what we have?"

"I am pretty sure I have a problem. I'm not sure it's a disease. But my drinking is really, well, it was getting out of control."

"That's the First Step, to 'Admit we're powerless over alcohol and our lives had become unmanageable.'" Nick looked at Jake with his eyebrows raised to check and see if he was following him. Jake nodded.

"I always like to break that down, being powerless can be a matter of degree," said Nick. "Most of us could control our drinking at times, in special circumstances, but it became like Russian roulette. My drinking became unpredictable, and I'd end up binging at times that I didn't plan on. Some of us had a more serious problem and drank around the clock."

"That's what surprised me. I thought that was all alcoholics. That's why I thought that I couldn't be an alcoholic, because sometimes I did seem to have control. Like right now, if you paid me, I could drink a beer and stop." Jake looked at Nick and wondered if he'd challenge his assertion. Nick stepped aside from it.

"This is an important question. Because, if you're not convinced you have the problem, there's little likelihood you'll stop. So the second part of the First Step is 'Unmanageability.' I like to substitute the word 'misery' or 'consequences' in its place. Were you happy when you drank, or did it cause problems in your life?"

Jake thought it over. "I guess that's pretty obvious. It's funny now that you ask about it. I used to get really happy when I drank. It used to be social. Lately, most of my drinking has been alone, and it doesn't make me happy."

"So why do you drink, then?" asked Nick.

"I don't know." Jake fumbled for his cigarettes, then put them back in his jacket.

"Look at the First Step again," Nick suggested. "Maybe you're a little more powerless than you'd like to think. Maybe you drink, because it's not so much a choice."

"Maybe."

"And the consequences?"

"Well, I almost lost my job. I almost got kicked out of a dream group I was in. That's where I met Holly," said Jake. "So I guess there were consequences."

"You drank at work?"

"No. Never at work. But I worked midnights, so some days I would drink and sometimes I wouldn't stop in time, and sometimes I would drink a little before work. Geez, I guess this sounds pretty bad, doesn't it?"

"Does it?"

"Yeah, it sounds bad." Jake looked out the window at traffic in the street and realized he was just trying not to look at Nick.

"Sounds bad?" asked Nick, "Or is it bad?"

"What do you mean?"

"'Sounds bad' seems more like, 'just a misunderstanding.' Or is it more than that? Is it a real problem? Is it out of control?"

"I see what you mean. I guess it's a problem." Jake looked Nick in the face.

"Are you certain? Because if you're not, you'll be tempted to do more research," said Nick.

"Research? What would I read?"

"Research, the way I'm using it, isn't reading. It's drinking. To see if you can control it."

"Drinking is out. It's not an option," said Jake. Some people laughed at a nearby table, and Jake felt annoyed. He knew they weren't laughing at him, but for some reason it pissed him off that people in A.A. seemed so jolly.

Nick explained, "So, the second thing is, 'Do you want what we have?' And that means sobriety, recovery, and doing the steps. And what we're doing, the whole sponsorship thing."

"What exactly does it entail? The sponsorship thing, I mean? Are you like a boss?"

"No, not at all. I'm more like a guide or a mentor, or someone with experience who can help you get through the steps."

"So you won't tell me what to do?" asked Jake.

"I'll make suggestions, at times. But mostly we'll just talk. Here's a suggestion: Give me a call every day, while you're going to your meetings every day. Not from the meetings, but at some time of the day, just give me a call and let me know how your day is going."

"Why?"

"To let me get to know you. So you can get to know me. Most of us are fairly isolated by the time we get here. Do you have many friends?" asked Nick.

Jake looked down at the table. He started to reach for his cigarettes again but then stopped. "No. I guess not."

"Neither did I, when I got here. I have lots and lots now. But not at first. So if you call every day, you get used to reaching out and talking and maybe even asking for help."

"I see. Listen, I've got to go pretty soon. Are we close to being done?"

"Sure. So, in conclusion, you're working on Step One, officially, with me, right now. Okay?"

"What you say makes a lot of sense. But I still don't get 'why.' Why am I an alcoholic? Why are you? Do you know the answer to that?" Jake looked Nick in the eye, watching to see if he might flinch.

"Absolutely," answered Nick. "I'm an alcoholic because I'm an alcoholic. Just like I'm a man because I'm a man. I'm fifty-two because I'm fifty-two years old. It's just a fact. I'm left handed because I'm—"

"Okay, I get it. It's just wasn't something I ever wanted."

"You think any of us wanted it?" asked Nick.

"No, but you all seem, like in the meetings, people say they're 'grateful' alcoholics. I'm not 'grateful' to be an alcoholic. And everybody seems so happy. It just seems phony."

"The gratitude and the joy you see are, trust me, authentic. Once you realize a quality life is available, possible, even likely, without drugs and alcohol, the lift to your spirits is pretty profound."

"Yeah, well, I'm not there," said Jake, taking a cigarette out of his pack and holding it in his hand. His fingers began twirling it back and forth.

"Not yet. Second Step, and we'll end here. Second Step suggests there is hope."

"Can't wait," said Jake with a scowl.

"We'll talk again soon. Call me anytime, day or night. Just make sure you do it before you drink, because after, I can't do anything for you," said Nick.

"Drinking isn't an option."

"Cool. Call, call, call."

Nick took Jake up to the bar and bought him a *Big Book* and told him to read two pages a day. He also bought him a small brass coin that had "24 Hours" stamped into it.

As Jake got into his car, he lit up his cigarette. Starting the engine he flipped on the radio station to hear Lester Young playing "Lady Be Good." As he drove away he wiped away a tear.

The weekend passed slowly, hour by hour for Jake. He was staying in his place, almost afraid to leave home, except to go to meetings or to work.

He spent time switching between football games on TV. The Michigan/Ohio State game was worth watching, and Jake felt ambivalent about who to root for. Later on there would be the MSU/Penn State game, and he thought about walking over to the campus and purchasing a scalper's ticket. It was cold, and television gave him a great seat. He decided instead to turn his attention to his record collection.

Jake had purchased a ready-made collection from a professor at MSU who had to move out of town and had no desire to transport hundreds of LPs, as well as his turntable.

So Jake owned LPs from the fifties, sixties and seventies, some great blues and R&B, but mainly jazz. He'd had a windfall of cash from his great aunt's estate when she died and he'd been able to purchase the collection at a dollar a disc. Even though he'd spent a few hundred dollars, it was a steal. Dozens of records by Miles Davis, Thelonious Monk, Charles Mingus and Jake's favorite, John Coltrane. Jake decided to work his way through the Monk stack today, while keeping the TV on.

Jake watched visions of maize and blue vs. crimson and grey, while Monk plunked his peculiar variety of genius from his earliest recordings. The songs were only three minutes long. Jake made some coffee and started to do the dishes, stopping every twenty minutes or so to flip the record over, or to carefully replace it in its jacket and put on the next album.

He looked at the phone and decided to call Holly, but there was no answer at her home number. He didn't leave a message.

Jake called for a pizza and watched the end of the game. By this time, Monk had Coltrane in his band, and one of Jake's favorite ballads, "Ruby, My Dear" was playing. Jake looked through his fridge, found a can of Vernors, and poured it into a tumbler over ice. He looked with some satisfaction at the color of the fluid through the glass. Without the carbonation, it almost looked like scotch.

Without understanding why, Jake began to weep.

The pizza delivery guy interrupted him by ringing the doorbell. Jake threw on some sunglasses to answer the door. He paid for the pizza, and the guy didn't ask why he was sniffling.

Jake gorged himself on the large pizza, sipping the pop, stopping only to turn the station for the next game, and flipping a new album onto the stereo. *Misterioso*. With Johnny Griffin on sax.

At the halftime of the MSU game, Jake thought about calling Nick. He realized he'd just talked to him a few hours before and decided against it. But Nick had said he should "Call, call, call." "Naw, he doesn't want to be disturbed," said Jake out loud. He looked at the clock and realized he'd only have a few hours before work at 11 p.m., so Jake curled up on the couch and soon was asleep.

Only to fall into a familiar dream. In this dream Jake is outside of Nick's house. He barely connects with the idea he has never been to Nick's house. He only knew this is it. He notices a hotel nearby and thinks maybe he could spend the night there. He walks into the hotel. There was nobody around. There seems to be no lights and no electricity. Jake looks around at the desk and sees no one. He walks into the first hallway and thinks, This is where the zombies are.

Wait, what am I doing inside? It's light outside. *He can see the zombies milling around down the darkened hallways. Jake turns slowly and sees the opening of the door to the outside, and now sees that it is dark outside.*

Shit. Have to go out there, because I'm sure not staying here. *And he's out the door.*

Outside he sees himself near a lake, and Nick's home is near the shore of the lake. Jake thinks he shouldn't take a direct route to his sponsor's home, because the zombies would follow him.

Jake walks across the street from the house and along a route of trees that line the street, looking for a way to circle around. Turning, he sees zombies emerging from the hotel. The hotel, which before had appeared clean and modern, now looks dilapidated and rundown. He is amazed by the number of zombies. There appears to be a few strays in the hallways, maybe less than ten. Now dozens and dozens are emerging from the doors of the hotel, like bats flying from caves, or rats escaping a burning building. It is sickening and disgusting and fills Jake with a hopeless type of dread and despair. Usually he is inside fighting off the zombies, and now he's outside and hopelessly outnumbered. The zombies are moving slowly; he can only see their forms in the darkness.

Jake watches to see if the zombies are following him or if they're spreading out. He sees them begin a direct path to Nick's home.

My only hope is to join them, because I don't stand a chance out here. Once I can get in the house with them, Nick and I can fight them off together.

Jake starts to walk slowly towards the house, doing his best zombie walk imitation. Even in his sleep, he resists the urge to start doing Michael Jackson's "Thriller" dance, though it crosses his mind. Jake notices the front door is open and he can see the warm illumination of the house shining out onto the front porch of the home.

Jake enters the front door, now appearing to be huge, flanked on either side by zombies. He is careful not to look at them, trying not to inspire close inspection, and so far he hasn't been attacked. Upon entering the front of the house he sees a large circular stairway, and Nick at the top of the steps, his arms held open expansively and smiling widely.

"Friends! Welcome!" says Nick as he sees Jake and the others entering his home. "Let me take your coats! I'm so glad you could come!" Jake looks around at his fellow zombies and notices other men and women. Are these the zombies? *He recognizes some of the faces and realizes these are people he's seen at the A.A. club, people he'd recognizes from meetings.*

Waking up, Jake said out loud, "Geez Louise," before grabbing his pen and his dream notebook.

At nearly the same time Jake was waking up for work, Holly was having dinner at her sponsor's home. Martha lived on Lake Lansing, and as they set the table for dinner Holly said, "I can never get over how beautiful it is here."

"It is," said Martha. "Watch this." She turned off the lights and the two of them could see the lake from the double glass doors that led out onto Martha's deck. The snow fell and was illuminated from a light outside the doors. Holly saw the pristine condition of the snow on the porch and, in the distance, the ice on the lake.

"When it first snows, it's just so beautiful," said Holly.

"Yes, it is, isn't it? I always think the outdoors seems like a big room when it's snowing. You know what I mean?" asked Martha.

"I think so. There's something about it that seems, kind of, contained?"

"Yes. Watch," Martha said and turned off the outdoor light. Initially it seemed much darker, but then their eyes got used to it and the lake outside became outlined, the ice reflecting light.

Martha lit some candles, and they began to eat their dinners. Martha had made a stew from a chicken and some fresh vegetables. They also had fresh bread.

"I love to come home to the smell of fresh bread. I don't know what I'm going to do, now that we're hearing how bad carbs are for us. I guess I'll stick to the high fiber stuff."

They ate for a few minutes in silence, treasuring the dark. Finally Martha said, "So what's up with this guy stalking you?"

"I told you the story about our run-in. He called the police on me, but the police said they weren't going to press charges."

"Isn't that interesting? He's the victim? I guess that fits, doesn't it? The whole victim/perpetrator continuum is where he lives. He's on one side or the other," said Martha.

"Yeah, I guess you're right. I hate to say it, but if he hadn't been so fast, I would have hit him. I would have run him over."

"I don't blame you. The A.A. literature talks about how we can't afford anger, but on the other hand, we're not doormats either."

"Could we turn on the lights?" asked Holly. "Just talking about that guy gives me the creeps."

"Sure," said Martha, rising to flip on the inside lights. She took their bowls to the kitchen and said, "Now, what kind of ice cream do you want?"

Holly asked for a small bowl of Cherry Garcia, but declined the offer of hot fudge.

"Where are you with the new guy, Jake?" asked Martha.

"He's got a sponsor now, Nick. So he's in good hands, and I think I should probably watch getting too involved with him while he's so new. But, Martha, I swear to God, seeing him come around the corner of the building when Gordon was threatening me, I've never been so happy to see anyone in my life."

"I bet," said Martha. "He really bailed you out of a jam."

"I hate to think how it might have gone without him being there."

"Do you think that big bully would have done something?" asked Martha. "I mean, you said yourself that his M.O. was to bully children."

"Women and children," said Holly. "Although he didn't waste any time knocking Jake over, and Jake is a big guy."

"So he's dangerous. You have to treat him that way, anyhow."

"I wonder," said Holly.

"What do you mean?" asked Martha

"I wonder how dangerous he really is. I mean, what would have happened if he'd gotten me in his car? Would he have pulled anything? He doesn't have a record for rape, much less murder."

"Well, you have to assume he is dangerous. Just because he doesn't have a record doesn't mean he hasn't done those things. Maybe he just hasn't been caught. Maybe you're the first one to confront him."

"I've been giving him what he wants. I've been afraid. He seems to feed off that," Holly acknowledged. She pushed her bowl of ice cream away.

"Sure, that's how he gets off. He loves to see the fear in people's eyes. That's why he keeps following you around."

"That's what I mean. What if I stop being afraid? What if I confront him and let him know, as calmly as possible, that I'm not afraid of him. In fact, maybe he should be afraid of me?" smiled Holly.

"Yeah?" asked Martha. "One problem I can see with this is the fact that you really are scared of him."

"You know your problem, Martha? You're always so practical."

The women laughed and changed the subject but Holly continued to feel tense. After a cup of decaf Holly decided she'd better go home. She put on her parka, and waded out to her car, taking a few minutes after starting the car to clean the snow off her windshield, rear and side windows before driving away. Martha waved at the lights disappearing down the street before returning to her seat by the fire, next to the double glass doors. She flipped off the light inside again and sat down and lit a cigarette and watched the snow in the dark, when suddenly she said, "Shit!" out loud.

She turned on the outside light again, lighting her deck to see a pair of fresh footprints that lead to the glass doors, the footprints indicating that someone had walked up the porch, onto the deck, and stood outside the glass, looking in, while the two women had eaten their dinners. Martha called Holly, and then the police.

That night, after going to sleep, Holly slept fitfully. She kept imagining Gordon breaking into her place. She had called the police, and they had told her they'd routinely drive by, and they were still looking for him, but she had given up hope they were going to find him before he found her. By now, he knew where she lived, where she hung out, he'd followed her to the A.A. club and to her sponsor's house, the coffee shop she frequented.

In her dream, Holly is swimming in warm waters. She's in the Caribbean, maybe Key West, a place she had visited as a child. She dips her face underwater and watches a man swimming underneath the water. He looks familiar to her. She notices that he is swimming towards her, from the bottom of a reef. Holly watches his face change. Gordon Thomas is smiling at her as he swims closer. Not the sinister, sneering smile she expected, but an innocent kind of smile. And he became younger, more boyish, then a child, even a baby, but still with his mustache, underwater, a baby, smiling at her, waving, then swimming away.

Jake wanders through the halls of a large building he knows to be either a hotel or a school. Or both. He was attending a training, but can't find the room where the training is to take place. There are people of every sort milling through the halls. Children, older people, people his age. And we're all here to learn, *thinks Jake. He sees turbans, Indian feathered headdresses, a priest, but mainly people dressed like him.*

The further he wanders down the hall, the taller the people get. So tall that he appears to be a child. Every so often someone looks directly at him. The sensation of being seen makes him feel peculiarly conspicuous. No one is saying anything.

Jake enters a room off the large hall. The room is filled with a clutter of many old things, dusty globes and a mounted moose head piled in the far corner, a map, a flint lock rifle, a saxophone that seemed tarnished, and a drum kit with a broken bass drum. Jake was alone in the room.

The sax seems interesting, so he walks over to it and picks it up, but the mouthpiece is filthy. There are cobwebs and dust all over the metal. He looks around the room for something to clean it with and sees a red, checkered handkerchief, sitting next to a bottle of scotch.

Jake notices the scotch is a single malt, one he's been searching for, and the bottle is dusty and unopened. Jake picks up the bottle and opens it, and then holds the handkerchief over the mouth of the bottle, tips it up and feels the liquid spill out onto the cloth. Jake rubs the wetted cloth over the sax mouthpiece and then slips the mouthpiece into his mouth. He can taste the scotch. The warmth reaches over his tongue and pulls on his throat, his lungs. He feels a glow cascading over the back of his head, over his forehead, and over the lids of his eyes, which now feel as sleepy as Lester Young's.

"What could possibly be wrong with this?" asks Jake as he lifts the bottle to his mouth. He begins to drink it and look down to find that the bottle is half empty. He doesn't feel drunk, just ecstatically happy, and he just knows that he could play the shit out of the saxophone. He starts to inhale into the mouthpiece, and then to full-out blow, and produces at first nothing more than a breathy hum. Jake inhales deeply, and blows again, this time producing a sqrawk that fills the room. He feels happy and loopy and drunk and says out loud, "Archie Shepp," before the door of the room opens and several men enter.

One of the men is Jake's sponsor, Nick. Jake says, "Oh, shit," and tries to pretend to be sober. He stands in front of the bottle. Nick has seen it all, and clearly understands Jake has been drinking.

At a long table Jake is sitting, and the men sit on either side of the table with Jake at the head. A light shines from the opposite end of the table, directly in Jake's eyes.

"What we want to know, is why you are an alcoholic," asks one of the men, who Jake had never seen before.

"I think that—"

"We don't want to know what you think. We want to know why."

Jake clears his throat. "It's because of my genetic predisposition."

"We know about the genetics. We want to know why you are an alcoholic," said the same voice.

"It's because of my parents. They didn't love each other. My home was unhappy," says Jake, feeling himself starting to cry.

"We know about your home. We don't care about your home. What we want to know is why are you an alcoholic?"

"I—I don't know."

"We don't care about what you don't know, we want to know why are you an alcoholic."

"Nick. Tell them, Nick. Tell them what you told me." Jake searches the darkened faces to find Nick's. He finally sees him, standing next to the man with the voice, and he notices that Nick's eyes are wet and tears are running down his cheeks.

"We don't care what Nick told you," replies the voice. We want to know why you are an alcoholic."

"I'm an alcoholic because I'm an alcoholic" answers Jake.

Jake woke up crying, saying these words out loud. He looked around him, looked around his room, looked for the bottle of scotch that he was certain would be nearby. He didn't see it and felt relieved. He didn't know why he was crying.

CHAPTER ELEVEN

Marianne had driven to Lake Michigan and was watching the sunset while sitting in her car, a new model. She was listening to music, some station she happened to tune into, a Christian station, and she was hoping for a little inspiration. It was early in the evening. The sun had nearly set. She sat and watched it dip below the clouds in the distance, a crack of space between sky and water, the sun's rays began to reflect up off the water, so bright that Marianne needed to squint.

Marianne spoke, and her own voice, speaking aloud, startled her.

"How dark is dark?" is what she said.

The sun broke through the clouds, the white of the snow on the beach reflecting it back, and Marianne tried to focus on colors, the colors in the sky, the clouds, the beach. She named the colors out loud, like a little girl, and then counted them, each one in a singsong voice.

"Red—one," she recited, "yellow—two, orange—three, pink—four, and there's white and blue and grey, five, six and seven, and purple. Eight."

Marianne stopped, the silence in the car pronounced. She was parked in the driveway of her family's former cottage in Grand Haven, a building that her family sold years ago. It was sold, twenty years ago, to a dentist from Chicago, and as far as Marianne knew, he was still the owner. *The property value has probably tripled, twice again,* she thought as she sat in her car outside the building.

Marianne was wearing a winter parka over her slacks and a sweater. She didn't bathe today and had made the decision to leave work early to drive up to see the sunset.

"Something has to change," she said, out loud again.

Her decision came after a dismal day at the office. She found herself spending half the day looking at her emails, and feeling so totally unfocused that she would catch herself staring at the screen of her computer. Her secretary had interrupted her isolation twice to ask if she were all right, before Marianne asked her to not interrupt her anymore and to stop putting calls through to her office. Finally, she noticed the snow had stopped outside and she decided to leave work early and head over to Grand Haven.

"Something has to—" she said.

Marianne noticed her breathing, exhaling plumes of frozen breath, each one she took, exposed in the air, almost as though she were smoking. "Cancer would be an answer," she said.

She watched the sun go down and realized that it would become very dark, very fast. She thought about going to eat, but realized that she wasn't hungry. And besides, the thought of sitting in a restaurant, alone, seemed to be too much. She reflected that she could check in to a motel. The drive back would be treacherous.

"I should drive fast," she said out loud.

And then another thought hit Marianne. She should drive her car straight into the lake. Here? Or wait a little while, when it was completely dark and drive without her lights on, so she would stand less of a chance to be interrupted. Would the water be cold? Of course. And would she freeze to death before she drowned? And drowning, how much pain would be involved in that?

"Just a little bit. I'd just need to be patient, and brave," she said out loud.

How long before she was missed? Tomorrow they would miss her at the office. Her car would be found by then, of course. Who would care? *Who would care?*

Marianne startled herself out of this trance by saying, "What the hell am I thinking?"

She started the car up and backed out of the driveway, out onto the deserted two lane road that was North Lake Shore Drive.

"I'll take my time. I don't need to do it today. This shouldn't be impulsive. I know how to plan. I know how to do things right. Maybe I'll wait, just until after the holidays. Just a little longer. I can hold on just a little longer."

Marianne took her time returning home.

In the last week of November Emma hosted the Dream Group. She'd lost track of exactly how many times they had met, but knew that they'd agreed to meet until the first week of January. Maybe then they'd want to continue, or maybe not.

Emma really didn't feel like working, but found herself relieved once she was in her office and returning phone calls, talking to a new referral, rescheduling an appointment. Anything to get her mind off her own life for a few minutes.

She heard the door down the hall open and heard Jake and Holly's voices. She could hear them greeting Mason. And a minute later she heard the door again and heard Holly saying hello to Marianne. Emma took a moment and looked out at the stand of trees, now snow on their branches. She took a breath and walked down the hall.

After the group had taken their usual seats, Emma joked that it looked like they'd all survived Thanksgiving. Mason gave a weak smile, and Marianne had a look of surprise on her face, but said, "Yes, I guess so."

There was the usual check-in that Emma conducted. She was experienced enough as a therapist to sense something big had happened, but she couldn't tell what it was. The air in the room seemed heavy. But then Holly started.

"Yeah, well, my week sucked. That stalker I mentioned before is still around. In fact, he confronted me, tried to get me in his car, like tried to kidnap me."

Mason and Marianne both expressed shock and Jake nodded his head. Emma was in wonder at how calmly Holly told the story.

"This happened on Thanksgiving day, and he caught up to me when I was alone in the A.A. parking lot, and started to threaten me, like I owed him and he wanted me to go someplace with him, like to 'discuss' it, and just that second, Jake walked around the corner—"

Everyone but Jake was asking questions all at once, and Holly told the story again without leaving out any details.

Emma asked about Jake's involvement. "And you say that Jake helped you?"

"Yeah, she said I 'distracted' him," said Jake, quoting Holly. "I distracted him by letting him knock me on my ass so Holly could escape. I was surprised, because after he knocked me over, I looked up and there she is, bearing down on him, chasing him up and down the parking lot."

Emma was surprised Jake could joke about it. She asked Holly if anything like this had ever happened to her before.

Holly brushed back her red hair. "I've had people on the job not be happy with me. I've had verbal taunts and insults. But I've never had someone so persistently come after me."

Then Holly frowned and told the group about the other night, when she was at her friend's place, and afterwards the friend had noticed footprints in the snow of the deck.

"This is really unusual," said Emma.

"How so?" asked Mason.

Emma explained that stalkers usually were well-acquainted with their victims. She looked nervously at Holly when she said the word, and amended it to say "intended victims."

"It's usually old boyfriends or ex-husbands," she said, "or current husbands. It's just unusual for a guy to get fixated on someone who he just knows peripherally."

"You sound like you have experience with this," inquired Marianne.

"If you're a female therapist the chances are, sooner or later, you run into someone who—let's just say, I do have a little experience in this."

"What happened?" asked Holly.

"Well, it's not anything we can talk about, but eventually he stopped. But this was years ago. Maybe, oh my gosh, maybe ten or a dozen years ago."

"I'm sorry to ask this, Emma, but you look so tired," said Mason. "Are you well?"

Emma smiled and said she was fine. She turned the focus back to Holly and asked her if she were afraid.

Holly looked out the window, and it was dark outside. She looked like she wanted to melt into her chair.

"It's funny, when I first met the guy, I was afraid but also really mad. Then I got afraid, because, it's like it became his job to start following me around. And he's good at it, because I don't see him. Jake saw him once, and my friend saw his footprints."

"He feels in control that way," offered Emma.

"Yeah, I think so. I had a dream the other night about him. Well, it wasn't about him, it was about me. That's something I'm getting from the group, dreams are always about me. So, he went from being a man to a little baby. And I think I was seeing the child inside of him."

Holly sighed and then continued to talk. "He's really terrified, you know? He's really terrified to be in the world. He must have lived through some terrible shit. And that's my job, to keep kids safe from the kind of stuff he went through, and the kind of stuff he is continuing to perpetrate."

After the group had talked about her dream for awhile, Emma noticed they weren't relying on her for an interpretation. She thought that was a good sign.

Holly finished up by saying, "Anyway, I don't mean to monopolize the group. But, I thought it was kind of cool, that for once I had a dream and the baby wasn't dead."

"Can we do anything?" asked Emma.

"I don't think so," said Holly, then, "I could use an escort in the parking lot. For all I know he's out there now."

The group looked nervously at each other, and Emma got up and walked to the window and looked out at the lot. There weren't any extra cars parked.

Jake offered to talk next. Mason said, "It sounds like you were quite heroic."

"All I had to do was land on my butt."

Jake told his version of the events. The group asked questions and Emma noticed how pleased Jake looked, having some attention that was positive.

Emma asked him, "So you were at A.A.?"

"Yeah."

"And you're still not drinking?"

"No, I'm not," said Jake. And then he smiled and looked at Holly. She smiled back.

"Congratulations," said Mason.

"Thanks. I feel pretty good about it, too. I've gone to a bunch of meetings. I've gotten a sponsor."

Emma thought Jake sounded healthy and optimistic. She was concerned, since what she remembered about the odds for recovery over alcoholism weren't very positive.

"And so far so good," said Jake. "I'm not sure I want to stop for my whole life, but people say, 'Just stop for today,' and so far it's working."

"So you're liking it?" asked Emma, smiling at Jake.

"That might be pushing it. Let's just say I'm not drinking, and I'm going to A.A. every day, and I'm dreaming like crazy."

"Great. Anything making sense?"

"I think my dreams have become amazingly transparent. The zombie dreams I had been talking about?"

Mason commented that Jake's description of his zombie dreams had stayed with him.

"Well, I had another one, but this time, I was on the outside of a house. And it turned out to be the house of my sponsor, and I thought, 'Oh, no, he's going to be attacked by zombies, just like me.' So I think, 'I'll sneak in with the zombies and then, together, we'll fight them off,' only something funny happens."

"What?" asked Emma and Mason, simultaneously.

"Once I get inside, I look around, and all the zombies are regular people, and this sponsor guy is welcoming them into his place."

"Wow. And you felt—" said Emma.

"Uh, surprised. I was glad they weren't zombies."

"Relieved?" suggested Mason.

"That's a good word for it," Jake agreed.

"You said that the dream felt transparent. How so?" asked Emma.

"Well, I think it's pretty basic. I've been treating people like intruders. Like they're going to take my life, my soul, my mojo. And, it turns out, they're just people."

Mason leaned back in his seat and looked at the ceiling, then back at Jake. "I like that. I like that quite a bit. That's the 'shadow' element you were talking about, isn't it, Emma?"

"Yes," said Emma. "Our fears, or those parts of ourselves that are dark or unacceptable."

"So Jake has welcomed them in. Through his newfound recovery," said Mason.

"I had another dream where I was drinking," said Jake. "It was weird. I thought for sure I had actually drank. When I woke up I was looking around for the bottle. It was so realistic."

Holly told Jake that drinking dreams weren't uncommon among recovering alcoholics.

"So it doesn't mean Jake will drink," said Emma.

"Jake will drink if he wants to drink," said Holly, "but a dream won't make him do it." Holly was looking into Jake's eyes as she said this and Jake was looking right back at her.

"And you two are—?" asked Emma.

Jake and Holly looked at each other and back at Emma, and said simultaneously, "What?"

"Are you becoming involved?"

"No," answered Jake. Emma took in the look of relief on Holly's face when Jake said it. "We're just friends and we go to meetings together, sometimes."

"Right," echoed Holly. "No. No way. Jake's in his first year of recovery, and I don't believe its right to start dating someone when they're first sober."

Emma moved on to Marianne. Marianne looked different to Emma and she just realized why. She wasn't wearing any makeup. Marianne related that she had almost called in to cancel, that she hadn't been feeling right lately. In fact, she was beginning to wonder if she'd keep coming to the group.

Emma felt discouraged. This seemed to be one of Marianne's issues, committing to something that might benefit her.

"Still trying to figure out if it's helpful, or—?" asked Emma.

"No, I'm just busy."

"You look a little different to me," ventured Emma.

"Marianne isn't wearing make up," said Holly. Emma wondered if the men had noticed.

"That's it," said Emma. "Too busy for makeup, also?"

"I, uh, I've stopped wearing it recently. I also, uh, I've also stopped exercising."

"So the group isn't the only thing you've been thinking of quitting lately."

"I guess so. I've been a little disorganized. I just, I think I've just been tired."

Jake suggested she might need a vacation.

"I go to conferences," said Marianne. "Usually that's as much vacation as I take."

"Maybe you need a conference," he suggested.

Emma noticed the circles under Marianne's eyes. The makeup was doing a good job covering up her exhaustion.

"I think I need a break. Maybe that's why I'm thinking of leaving the group."

"It would be unusual to quit the group after working so hard. Don't you want to see it through? We were going to meet into the New Year, and that's just a little more than a month away now." Emma was trying to think of a way to convince Marianne to stay. It occurred to her to try the other direction.

"Of course, it's always your decision. You really didn't even have to come to the group tonight. But you did. Maybe you feel two ways about it."

"I guess that's true. Because I did think about not coming tonight."

"So what helped you decide to come tonight?" asked Emma.

"I guess," Marianne said, "I guess I'm not sure. I—"

After ten seconds of silence Emma saw she was really lost. "Marianne?"

"I'm sorry. What was I saying?"

"Have you been feeling sad? Depressed?"

"Hopeless?" asked Jake.

"I'm sorry. I just got lost. I've just been tired, that's all. I think Jake's right. I need a break. I didn't mean to take up a lot of time. I'll be okay. I just need to take a little time for myself. I'll be okay. And of course I'll finish the group."

Emma noticed the silence that followed and the rapt attention that each group member was paying to Marianne.

"You didn't answer my question," Emma reminded her, gently.

"What was it?"

"Have you been depressed?"

"I think I've been mainly tired."

"Would you be able to stay a little after group and talk?" asked Emma. She realized that the check-in for the group was taking up most of their time, and she really wanted to ask some more probing questions to assess Marianne's depression.

"Well, I usually go right home. I guess I could."

"There's a simple screening for depression and anxiety that I'd like you to take," explained Emma. "It'll just take a few minutes."

Marianne agreed and the group looked at Mason. Emma realized that he looked tired, too.

"Well, I guess that leaves me. I'm afraid I have some news. I'm thinking I might be leaving the group, too." Then he smiled. Jake was the only one who smiled back.

"Really?" said Emma.

"Yes. I mean, I've really enjoyed it immensely. And, if we'd gotten to the date when we were supposed to stop, I would have voted to keep going."

"There's a 'but' there," said Emma.

"Yeah, a skinny academic 'butt,'" said Jake, still smiling.

"Well, it's about to get even skinnier. I've just been diagnosed with cancer."

They all gasped. Emma asked about the type of cancer and the prognosis.

"I'm afraid it's very advanced, and the doctors really think I just have a few weeks or months left. It's amazing, isn't it? I think my dreams were trying to tip me off. You were on it, though, weren't you Emma? You were the first one to recommend that I get a physical."

"Oh, Mason," Emma said, "I'm so sorry. What a shock." She had tears in her eyes.

"It is," Mason agreed. "It's really a shock. My wife and I are talking about going to London for Christmas, if I can still travel. I've been lucky, because there's been no pain whatsoever. And that's why this has been so advanced, because there were no symptoms to speak of. It's a very aggressive form of cancer, though."

"How you doing?" asked Jake. Emma could see that he was shaken. Even Marianne seemed concerned.

"Well, I think I'm okay. I mean, I'm dying, but aren't we all? I just have the insight to know that it's any day. Like you said Jake, 'One day at a time.'"

"You've very philosophical about it," said Emma.

Marianne began to cry. "You're so strong."

"I don't know about that. There have been plenty of tears. It's almost touching to see people react to the news, because, people have been very kind. Generous. But, you see, I realize that this isn't about dying. It's about how I want to live. The dying part, well, I think that will take care of itself. But I'd love to see London again. And London at Christmas is London at it's best."

Jake said, "The dreams really made sense, didn't they? The Samurai."

"He was my warrior. Almost a grim reaper. I thought he was trying to kill me. I think now he was trying to warn me."

"The burning books, the polluted lake," remembered Jake.

"All symbols of the cancer growing inside me. How did you know, Emma?" asked Mason.

"I'm not sure. Well, I didn't know. I just thought—I just remembered that the Greeks used to believe that dreams were diagnostically significant. I think Aristotle used them to help diagnose illness. Greek oracles used to do the same thing," Emma said. Then her eyes filled with tears. "Oh, Mason. I'm so sorry."

"So am I," said Mason, smiling. "But I'll be with the group as long as I can. And then, if I can travel, go to London."

"London's Calling," said Jake. He didn't know whether Mason would get the punk reference.

"It is," agreed Mason.

Emma and Betty were sitting in the sauna at the gym. They were talking about the weather and the tennis match they just finished. Betty spoke about her mother's health problems, how her sister was pregnant again, and how her niece was running around with thugs at high school.

For a few moments the women sat in silence. Emma was enjoying the scent of cedar, and the warmth soaking into her skin. After a while, Betty asked Emma how the group was the night before.

"I think it's a mess," Emma answered, with her eyes closed. "The group seems a little more engaged, but there really is trouble."

"Tell me about it," suggested Betty.

Emma opened her eyes to make sure they were alone.

"Well, first of all, and most devastating, is that one of the group members was just diagnosed with cancer."

"Oh, Emma, I'm sorry to hear that. The alcoholic kid?" asked Betty.

"No. It's a professor, a retired professor from MSU. It's just heartbreaking. He's such a sweetheart. And the suggestion is that it's a very aggressive type of cancer. He may only have weeks."

"Wow. How is the group taking it?"

"They were supportive. They took it well. But the rest of the group is, well, one woman is being stalked. At the same time, the 'alcoholic kid,' as you refer to him, is beginning a courtship with her."

"Is he stalking her?" asked Betty.

"No, not him. But he's starting to fall for her. That's clear. And she's keeping some boundaries so far, but—"

"But still you don't want that in a group setting. So is the kid still drinking?"

"Well, he's not exactly a kid," said Emma.

"You know what I mean."

"Yeah. I do. He's not drinking. He says he's going to A.A."

"Well, that's good news," said Betty.

"I suppose it is. I'm still worried about him. And the other woman in the group is severely depressed."

"Uh oh. What are you going to do with her?"

"I saw her for a little while after the group. She's almost non-functional. She registered as 'severely depressed' on the screen, but, this was curious, she completely denied suicidal ideation. I'm getting hot. Are you getting hot?"

Betty shrugged and said, "Keep an eye on her. She might be trying to go underground."

"I know. I asked her to see Dr. Morenas for a med consult. She seemed willing."

"Good. Keep your eye on her. Are you going to meet with her individually?"

"I didn't set it up. I offered it."

"What do you think it is?"

"The depression?"

"Yeah. What triggered it?"

"She was reporting some dreams that were upsetting. But then she had a dream that was, well, it was nothing."

"The dream was nothing?" asked Betty.

"Yes. That's what she says."

"How does she know it was a dream?"

"I'm not sure. She seemed sure," said Emma.

"What do you think that means?" asked Betty.

"I'm getting too hot to stay here anymore." Emma felt herself getting dehydrated in the sauna.

"Okay. I'll meet you for coffee upstairs in a half hour."

"Okay," said Emma.

After taking showers, Emma and Betty met for coffee upstairs. The club was busy after work, and Emma chose a table that was far away from the front of the café.

"I feel better," said Betty.

"So do I. Betty, there is something I need to tell you," said Emma.

"Oh, no. This doesn't sound good."

"No. It is good. Well, it's not good or bad; it just is. I wanted to thank you, first of all, for kicking my ass and getting me on board with getting honest."

"Sure. What are friends for?"

"Well, I haven't been entirely honest with you. And you're my closest friend."

"I'm not going to like to hear this, am I?" asked Betty.

"I don't know. I know it's hard for me to say it. You know, I've been mentioning that I've fallen for someone else?"

"Yeah. You told me that."

"Well, the person I fell for is 'Dylan,' and, this is hard to say, but Dylan is a woman."

"Sweet Jesus. You're turning on me?" said Betty, looking over her shoulder to see who might be listening. They were almost alone in the coffee shop.

"Turning? I don't think I'm 'turning' on anyone. I'm just learning who I am."

Betty was silent for nearly a minute. Emma waited her out.

"Emma, I've lived long enough to have seen a lot, and I've been surprised a lot, and I've had to learn to accept a lot. I know you are a strong woman, an honorable woman, a really good woman. We've worked together for years now and you're my best friend. If you're straight, I'm good with that. If you're gay, I still love you, girl, just not that way. But I accept you, I accept your choices, I accept your struggle. I may not like it. But I accept it."

"Thanks Betty. That means a lot." Emma felt enormously relieved. She took a sip of her latte.

"I'm just a few years older than you, Emma. But I remember different times. I remember having to sit outside of restaurants and even bathrooms when we visited our relatives in the south, waiting for Pops to find out if they let colored people use the facilities. I remember little white boys calling me 'nigger.' I remember being ashamed of the color of my skin. I remember hating myself for something I couldn't help. And I've learned, never be ashamed of who you are."

Emma sat in silence. Her eyes were filled with tears.

"So what are you going to do?" asked Betty.

"I've been looking for apartments."

"Are you going to live with this woman, Dylan?"

"No. Not at all. Maybe eventually. But not for a few years. I don't want to jump right out of one thing and into another. That wouldn't be good."

"I agree. You're wise. So when do I get to meet her?"

"Once we hit that point of our relationship, you'll get the first visit."

"Great."

Jake left his shift on the first day of December and started his drive home. It was still dark this early in the morning; the days were growing shorter and shorter. There was rain and the snow was melting away, and some Christmas lights were on in the windows and porches of homes along busy Saginaw Street. He turned right on Capitol Avenue, to drive past the big lit-up Christmas tree, in front of the state Capitol. The dome was dark, and he turned left on Michigan Avenue. The jazz radio station was playing some pop bullshit, and he was utterly disappointed that they were beginning to play less jazz. Jake was tired.

The lights along Sparrow Hospital were cheery, but Jake didn't feel cheered. He could see the light in the eastern sky, but knew there wouldn't be a sunrise today, too many clouds. *Another day without sunshine. Typical Michigan winter.* "Whatever," he said out loud, and lit a cigarette. Maybe he should call Nick. Maybe not.

Jake pulled into the parking lot of the Quality Dairy. He thought about Holly and stayed in his car before getting out. *She's so cool*, he thought. He pictured her in her jeans and the blue sweater she was wearing the other day at group, the last time he'd seen her. Or at the meeting before that, in the tight black turtleneck, her red hair, a splash of freckles across the bridge of her nose, cute as a button.

Jake was hungry. Hence the QD. He rarely stopped for doughnuts but thought today might be different. He went into the store and was struck by how depressing it all was. The wet slush on the floor needed mopping, but the two people behind the counter looked up to their ears in work, selling a quart of beer to one guy, the next woman buying a loaf of Wonder Bread and a lottery ticket.

"One way or the other, get me out of here," said Jake under his breath as he traced the outline of the store, walking past the magazine rack that shouted the messages of "Cars Cleavage Muscles Fame," before getting to the cat food and past that, to the ATM. He slipped in his card, punched in his code and withdrew forty bucks.

I don't need forty bucks for doughnuts, he thought, but that's what he withdrew. *Oh, well.*

Jake walked by the beer and wine and noticed that the Canadian brews that he favored were on sale. They looked good. Maybe one.

"No," Jake said out loud and walked over to the doughnuts. He picked out a couple of chocolate covered doughnuts and slipped them in the waxy paper bag and took his place in line behind a couple of other people, one guy buying a Detroit Free Press, another with a box of Sugar Pops cereal and a quart of milk. The guy immediately in front of him looked vaguely familiar.

Jake felt lonely. He thought of Holly again and wondered if she was going to work today, if she were okay, if she'd seen Gordon again, if she were going to a meeting tonight, and when he might see her again.

The Sugar Pops guy in front of the line had finished his transaction and the second employee was now mopping up the front of the store. Jake watched the traffic whizzing down Michigan Avenue. People were going to work now while he was on his way home from a quiet night on the psychiatric ward, a page written in his journal, another chapter read in his novel, and another meeting to go to tonight. He felt dreamy, lost in his own thoughts, when he caught the words of the guy in front of him.

"Fifth of Popov," Jake heard the guy say. He looked at the guy from behind, then looked up at the screen of the black and white monitor that recorded every moment, seeing the back of the clerk's head. A little paper QD cap pushed down on a thick Afro, Jake looked her in the eye and saw a quiet discouragement as she reached for the bottle and put it in a sack. "And a pint of that Hot Damn, while you're at it," the guy said. Jake saw his hands shake as he gave the clerk the money. Jake now remembered the guy, he'd seen him once at a meeting, sitting against the back wall like Jake.

"There but for the grace of God…" thought Jake as the guy walked out of the store and Jake stepped up to pay for his doughnuts.

"Anything else?" asked the clerk.

"A pint of Lauder's scotch," Jake heard himself say. "Make that a fifth. A fifth of J&B."

CHAPTER TWELVE

Emma was in Claudia Silverstein's office. She sat in the chair and observed the office—the throws, the pottery, the original artwork, the carefully textured layers throughout the room. Homey yet modern, warm yet professional. Claudia sat in her chair across the room, watching her silently.

"Well, I wasn't sure I was going to come today," Emma finally said.

"This must be very hard for you," reflected Claudia. "You have mixed feelings. Maybe we could spend some time investigating what went on last time. We've both had some time to think about it."

"Fair enough. But I haven't been entirely honest. And I need to be. I owe you that. I owe myself that."

Claudia didn't say a word, just raised her eyebrows, lowered her head and looked over the rim of her glasses.

"I believe I have a very serious crush on another therapist who lives in Grand Rapids. I've told you that much already. But what I didn't tell you is that this therapist is a woman."

"Oh? I see. I wonder what made it so hard to tell me that?"

"Goddamn it, Claudia, it's not so easy on this end, you know?"

"You're angry with me for not being able to anticipate your emotions or not knowing how you felt."

"I'm angry, I'm angry, I'm angry at myself for not having the courage to face this a long time ago."

"So these are feelings you've had for some time?"

"Yes. I had them in high school, but I thought it was just being a teenager. I acted on them in college. But I thought it was the pot or the other girl. And ever since then, I've just suppressed it."

"Physical attraction to women?" asked Claudia.

"Yes. But it feels like it's more than that. It's not just physical. It's, it's hard to describe."

"How would you know to describe it? Have you ever talked with anyone about this before?"

"No. Not the attraction. I've told a few people now that I'm gay. Frank knows."

"So that's why he wants you to move out?"

"Yes. I don't blame him. He feels like our whole marriage was a sham. He's humiliated. I've been such a coward." Emma started to cry.

Claudia offered her tissues. "Will you stop with the deprecation? Maybe it was brave to stay in a marriage for a long time knowing that it wasn't for you?"

"Maybe," sniffed Emma. "I am so sorry I have to hurt him. And I told my friend, Betty. And she accepted it just fine. I don't know what I was expecting."

"What were you expecting?"

"I thought I'd be rejected. I thought she'd hate me. I thought she wouldn't want to work with me anymore."

"Now where do you suppose you got the idea that who you decided to love would be unacceptable?"

"Oh, here comes the therapy cliché. It had to be Mom and Dad."

"Well? Was it?"

"Yes," answered Emma. "They're not to blame."

"Emma, before you defend them, why don't you talk about how they convinced you it wasn't okay to be you."

"They had high expectations. Anything I did wasn't good enough. My mother was so depressed. And they drank, and fought, and drank. God, I've gone over this so many times with you," Emma looked at Claudia. Claudia shrugged. "I kept thinking that if I worked hard enough, if I was smart enough, if I was good enough, if I was *enough* enough, maybe she'd—"

"Maybe she'd what?"

"Maybe she'd get better."

"And?" Claudia arched her eyebrows.

"Maybe she'd love me."

"So," Claudia leaned forward, "you've been longing for the love of a woman for a longer time than high school."

"You don't think that this is connected to my mom?"

"Heavens no. Why would I think that? I've just been trained in Freudian analysis, before spending the rest of my career researching Attachment Theory."

"I'm serious, Claudia."

"I thought we were past being serious," answered Claudia.

"Now what the heck does that mean?" asked Emma.

"Nothing. I'm just wondering about the timing of all of this."

"How do you mean?" asked Emma.

"Okay, so you have a teenage crush on a girl. You get high with a co-ed and, what, make out?"

"Yes."

"And then your feelings lay dormant until after your mother dies. Doesn't that strike you as—interesting?"

Emma sighed.

"You're suggesting that it's more than a coincidence? It makes sense, I guess, intellectually. It doesn't make sense. I'm not sure I can say—"

"Emma," asked Claudia, "I'm going to ask another question that doesn't make sense, and I don't want you to get caught with it at that level. Just go with what answer comes to you, intuitively. What age were you when you picked up the responsibility of your mother's emotional life?"

"Two or three. But don't all children develop that mutuality of trying to care for their caretakers?"

"Yes, and most mothers have it together enough to let their children know that it's not their job."

"And maybe my mother didn't?"

"Maybe she was too depressed?" suggested Claudia. "Too hurt? Too drunk? Too wounded? Maybe she felt lost."

"Well, in that case, I'm certainly my mother's daughter. Except for the drunk part."

The women were silent for a moment. Emma looked at Claudia and wondered what she was thinking. Claudia seemed reflective and was gazing out the window of her office.

When she looked back at Emma, Claudia suggested, "Maybe this is where your woundedness comes from and maybe this will be the source of your healing, as well."

"So, does that mean you believe I'm not gay?"

"Let's not even get into that. I don't want you to feel you have to protect anything or defend anything here with me. Your feelings are very raw and tender."

"So you won't tell me," said Emma.

"Emma, if you want to know what I believe, I'd have to say that I don't know what makes people gay or straight. I think sexuality is very complex and there are probably various factors, from genetics to upbringing. But certainly attachment is an important variable. That doesn't negate your experience, your hopes, your longings to be loved, and to be fully loved by a woman. An experience you don't allow yourself to explore until—"

"After my mother dies. I see your point. My dreams were trying to tell me something important. It's so strange. A man in my dream group was dreaming of polluted lakes and being chased by a Samurai, and he was just diagnosed with cancer."

"Oh, that's terrible. I'm sorry."

"Yeah, well, it's like he knew and didn't know."

"We're always in light and darkness. We can't possibly be conscious of everything we're capable of being conscious of," said Claudia and leaned back in her chair.

"So what do I do, Claudia?"

"You know I never give that kind of advice."

"But you're suggesting that my feelings for Dylan, that they may be based on almost a pathology."

"No. I'm not. I'm suggesting there are dynamics at play that might be lending urgency to this, and maybe you needn't act impulsively before fully exploring them. I mean, this is the first I've heard of Dylan. As a woman, that is."

"Impulsively?"

"It's a lot to walk away from—a long-term marriage, not to mention the impact on your son, the possible impact on your career."

"I've thought about that. A lot. And I'm sorry I didn't talk with you about this sooner. Now it feels too late."

"Maybe. Maybe not. We're out of time. Shall we set up another appointment?"

"I can't decide. Let me think about it."

Holly is dreaming about sitting in front of a stack of magazines. Each magazine is filled with pictures of babies. She's working on a collage, a collage that is meant to be a huge picture of babies, babies, nothing but babies. Holly has a pair of scissors and is cutting out pictures of the babies, some of them pink and cooing, wrapped in blue blankets, the babies looking like something out of a Renaissance painting, like Raphael, and her sense is that the babies are coming alive, looking at her and winking, grinning broadly, and she's smiling back at them, even as she takes her scissors and carefully traces their images, cutting them out of the magazines and placing them carefully, lovingly in a pile on the table where she's working. It was a big stack of magazines.

I should have some black and white photos, *Holly thinks, and pages through the stack. She frowns as she sees a magazine that has a red title over a black and white picture on the cover, "True Crimes Against Babies." She recognizes the picture on the cover; Gordon Thomas, the mustached baby that she'd seen in her dream.*

Holly places the magazine aside and thinks about looking into another magazine, wanting to keep with the theme of cute baby pictures, not "true crimes," but now the magazines somehow change and they all contain office furniture or hunting equipment or financial statements, none of which held any interest to Holly and her intended collage.

The magazine of "True Crimes Against Babies" seems to gain more interest to Holly as she glances over at it, again and again, and finally thinks, What the heck, it's only a magazine.

Holly opens the magazine and looks at the front page. She expects to see a table of contents, but instead there is a bibliography that looks like her graduate course in child development. There were books listed on psychology, Piaget, Erikson, other developmental theorists.

She turns the page and a picture of Gordon looks out from underneath the title, "Remember Me?" is the headline. His eyes look like he had been crying. He was standing in a kitchen, holding an empty jar of peanut butter. There were feet in the corner of the picture. The feet of a woman, high heeled and wearing stockings. She must have been laying on the floor. *Holly wonders if she were asleep, or passed out, or dead, and then,* That must be his mother, *before turning the page. She sees a series of pictures, cigarette burns on a toddlers arm, a six-year-old boy smoking cigarettes, an eleven-year-old holding a can of Bud Lite.* That's my brand, *thinks Holly before she turns the page.*

Holly sees each picture of the boy's life, each picture of him still sporting a mustache, as he grew older and more hardened. He's just a baby.

She turns a page and sees a picture of herself, standing in a bathroom, looking down into a bathtub at a drowned baby. The picture is black and white, but otherwise looks exactly like a dream she'd had before. One of her worse fears.

"Why Couldn't She Have Stopped It?" asks the headline. She looks at the print to try and read the article, but it blurred. There was a phone under the water, next to the baby. It was ringing.

Holly woke up, panting, and heard her own phone going off. She was disoriented and didn't know for a minute where she was. On the fourth ring she got to the phone.

"Holly? It's Jake."

"Jake. Shit. You woke me up."

"I'm sorry. I thought you'd be up by now."

"What time is it?"

"It's about eight a.m. Aren't you working this morning?" asked Jake.

"Yeah, but I'm going in late. I'm sorry. I'm a little groggy. I just had a hell of a nightmare."

"Oh. I'm sorry. Are you okay?"

"Yeah. Give me a minute. Can I call you back?"

"Yeah. But Holly?"

"Uh huh?"

"I bought a bottle."

Holly was quiet for a moment and thought about pinching herself. Was this a dream? Had Jake just said he had bought a bottle?

"A bottle of what?"

"A bottle of scotch."

Was he asking her out on a date? Of course not. He was in trouble.

"Jake? Where are you?"

"I'm sitting outside your place."

"Oh. Look. Give me two minutes and come in. But do me a favor? Leave the bottle in the car."

Holly got up and went to the bathroom. She pulled on some jeans and a sweater, brushed her teeth and put on a Spartan cap. Then she went to the door and let Jake in.

"Hey," said Jake.

"Hey yourself," answered Holly.

"So you're having nightmares?"

"So you bought a bottle?"

"I guess we could talk."

Holly's next move surprised herself. She wrapped her arms around Jake's neck and pulled him down so that her face was next to his. She smelled cigarettes and aftershave. And then she kissed him. She kissed him so hard that she was surprised at the impact of it. It seemed like something electric passed between them, a small chemical bomb exploding behind her eyes, she held him closer and felt him squeeze her in response. They kissed and held each other in the doorway of her house, before they finally released and she looked up at him with surprise and saw the same expression looking back at her.

"I guess you'd better come in," she said.

"I guess I'd better," he answered.

They stood in her living room, kissing. Holly started to pull away but Jake pursued her. She felt herself becoming drunk on the kissing, a rapture passing over her. Jake's hand reached beneath her sweater and found her breasts, and her nipples hardened. Holly reached down and felt his erection, and heard him moan. She pulled him into the bedroom, and he took off her sweater. She stepped away from him, covering her breasts with her hands. She watched the expression on Jake's face. A mixture of gratitude and longing. She brought her hands down and undid the button on her jeans. Jake pulled off his shirt and quickly slipped out of his pants. They reached the bed at the same moment.

He entered her, and she came almost immediately. Holly was lost in an ocean of sensation and emotion. Jake kissed her passionately while he made love to her in long, slow strokes. She orgasmed a second time, and at her third climax, Jake came, too. They lay in a heap, gasping, stunned. Holly said, "Wow."

"Yeah," Jake said.

She could feel he was still hard, and soon, he began to move inside her again…

After they'd made love the second time Jake said, "What are we going to say about this?"

"Who needs to know?" asked Holly.

"Yeah. You're right. You know what? I don't feel so much like drinking anymore." He was holding Holly in his arms.

"Neither do I," answered Holly.

"Tell me about your dream," suggested Jake.

"Naw. I can't remember most of it. Do you want coffee?" asked Holly.

Jake kissed her shoulder and remembered, "You have to go to work. I just got off."

"I'll say. Twice you just got off."

"Oh, yeah. I think—"

"I think this was wonderful," said Holly, putting a finger over Jake's lips. "Don't worry about it."

Jake smiled and kissed her again. Then they made love again.

"I'd forgotten how much I missed sex," said Holly when they were done.

"Has it been that long?" asked Jake.

"Since before I got in the program."

"Wow. How long is that?"

"Five years."

"Wow. That's amazing. You were married, right?"

"Yeah, I'm divorced. The last man I was with was, well, it wasn't my husband, but I wasn't sober. Someday I'll tell you the story. How about you?"

"Sexual history? I don't have any STDs, if that's what you're worried about."

"No, I, well, that's a relief."

"But I haven't dated anyone seriously for a year or two now."

"Bad break up? Or too busy drinking?"

"Uh, both?"

"Now, what about that bottle?"

"I don't know. It was the weirdest thing. I had no plan at all to buy it. I was just standing in line at the QD, buying a couple of chocolate doughnuts, and the next thing y'know, I was asking for a bottle of scotch."

"You know what? It's cunning, baffling, and powerful."

"Alcohol?"

"Yup. And so's this," Holly said as she leaned over and kissed him.

"Chemistry?"

"Yeah, chemistry."

Holly called in sick and made Jake breakfast. She made him promise her he'd throw the bottle away and call his sponsor. Jake agreed, but not before he asked if it might be okay to keep it until the holidays.

Marianne walked through her day like a charm. She was back to wearing make up, and had done her workout at 5:00 a.m., just like she did before her "crisis." She made her meetings, answered her email, scheduled a lunch, made it through a stack of paperwork and reports and was nearly caught up from the time she missed, when she noticed the time.

The staff was starting to leave at around 5:00 p.m. The secretary asked Marianne if she needed anything before she went home. Marianne said, no, she was just planning to stick around for a little bit longer and get some of these reports in the mail. Her secretary offered to help for a little while longer, but she also needed to get home to help her daughter get her costume ready for the Christmas pageant. Marianne said, "Don't bother, don't worry. It's nothing I can't take care of myself."

After they had all gone Marianne locked herself in her office and looked out the window. It was already dark, the days now ridiculously short, and a line of headlights could be seen staggering down Washington Avenue, a block and a half from the Capitol building downtown. Marianne pulled a disc from her briefcase and opened it up, taking it out, and putting it in her laptop.

The screen brightened and the logo appeared, "Last Will and Testament." Marianne began to work on the document. She felt lighter and lighter as she did so, almost as though she could float away. She smiled and sang Christmas carols as she filled out the forms.

Mason was looking over his lists of movies. Mona was writing Christmas cards at the table and he was poring over the lists that he had made.

"I thought I'd have time to watch all these films again, but now I may have to be a little more picky."

"Oh, Buster, you don't know how much time you'll have."

"You're right. I can't help but have these kinds of thoughts. And when I do, I feel like I'm filled with self-pity. Pity is a strange word, isn't it? Comes from Pathos, no doubt."

"Whatever you say."

"But everything goes through that filter. 'I'm dying.' I think about going to a movie or a play or a concert, and then I think, 'I'm dying, is this really worth the time?' It doesn't matter what it is. Everything is held up and measured against my mortality."

"How are you feeling?" asked Mona.

"That's the other thing. I'm feeling fine. If it wasn't for the loss of my appetite, I wouldn't even know that I was sick."

"So," Mona set aside the Christmas card she was working on, "what do you want to do?"

"Now?"

"No. You've made the point, and the doctor said the same thing. You may only have a few weeks, maybe some months left. And we don't know how long before you—"

"Get sick," said Mason.

"Yes, get sick. So, what do you want to do?"

"Well. I think I'd like to visit London again. Wouldn't you like to go?"

"Yes, Buster, I'd love to go. Do you want to make the arrangements?"

"Sure. I'll get online and go to one of those travel sites. Sometimes you get a good deal."

"What about the timing? I know that once we traveled to London for Christmas, but you know that never really felt like Christmas to me."

"You're right. Christmas at home, and we'll get the family together."

"Good. When do we do London, then?"

"Sometime after Christmas. My Dream Group only has a few meetings left."

"You've gotten a lot out of that group, haven't you?" asked Mona.

"I've really—I'm not sure I could say that I've enjoyed it, but I've enjoyed meeting the people. It makes me feel lucky."

"How so?" asked Mona.

"Everyone in the group seems very unsettled. And anxious. It's made me realize how lucky I am, how lucky I've been, that I've had a life where I've done what I've wanted to and been with people I love. Especially you, Mona. I haven't regretted a minute."

"Oh, Buster," said Mona, with a tear in her eye. "You've always been a terrific liar."

"No, really. I may not have said it often, but now's the time to tell you, to tell everyone how much they've meant to me."

"You'll have to stop. You'll make me cry."

"Okay. I will. So I thought that after the holidays would be good, after the group is over. I'd like to go to the few groups we have left."

"Good. Well, make the arrangements. Make sure we stay someplace nice."

Mason got up and went into the study and turned on the computer. He clicked onto a travel Website and looked at a calendar. *Leaving in mid-January would be workable. The weather in London would be cold, but certainly warmer than Michigan in January.*

When it came time to click on the number of tickets, Mason considered buying one round trip and another one way. He purchased two round trip tickets to London.

Then he wrote a letter to Mona that she wouldn't find until after he'd died.

The first week of December found a thaw. Emma used the break in the cold to run outdoors, but the skies were relentlessly grey and then the rains came, and any snow that was left melted away. She returned to the gym.

Driving to her office, Emma thought that the Christmas lights and other decorations in the neighborhood looked out of place in the rain and gloom. Emma realized that she wasn't feeling any holiday cheer. The group was meeting again for their tenth meeting, and she was surprised at her own ambivalence towards seeing everyone.

On the one hand, she felt relieved about coming clean— *"coming out," wasn't that the phrase?* At the same time, she was experiencing a nearly unbearable grief about letting go. To see clients in the midst of this was difficult. To see clients in so much pain—she just wasn't sure she was up to it.

At the start of the group, Emma lit a candle and placed it in the center of the table that sat between everyone. She wasn't sure why she was doing it, but she was glad she did. Everyone was quiet.

"Let's start with a check-in. How is everyone doing?" She looked at their faces, seeing who might start.

Holly started. "I'll go. I've been having messed up dreams again. I know that I'm dreaming about dead babies again, but I haven't been able to remember them. And I want to remember. I need to."

"I have some techniques in mind to help with remembering. Shall we go over them now?" asked Emma.

Marianne said she thought that would be helpful.

Emma noticed that the group had elected purposefully *not* to talk about Mason. Or maybe, just not *yet*.

"Okay. Well, set your alarm a few minutes early, maybe just ten or fifteen minutes and have a pen and paper next to your bed. Wake up and just start writing. Also, if you wake up in the middle of the night, you'll have a chance to write. Once you get into the habit you'll start to identify when you're dreaming, and you'll also be able to remember the dreams by the activity of writing them down immediately upon waking. Is that clear?"

Holly said, "I know I'm dreaming something, but if I don't get to it right away, it's just gone. Why would that be?"

"I'm not sure," said Emma. "I am aware that the sleeping, dreaming brain is taking a very different chemical bath than is the waking brain, so there may be a connection."

"How is it different?" asked Mason. Emma noticed that he was still interested, still wanting to learn. It made her feel reassured in some way that she couldn't quite put her words around. She addressed Mason's question.

"Well, again, I'm sorry but I'm just not sure. I'm aware that there are studies that have researched the differences and what occurs in sleep."

"So dreams have a function? Other than psychological?" said Mason.

"There has been some suggestion that dreams are involved in storing memory, or moving memory back and forth between long term and short term. But, can I make a suggestion?"

Jake nodded. "Go for it."

"There's a lot of interest in the nature of the dreaming mind, and this discussion started as something that might be helpful to Holly, but now we're sidelined."

"Well, this is a dream group, isn't it?" asked Marianne.

"Yes, but—" said Emma.

"We're avoiding something," said Mason.

"I think so," said Emma.

"Denial," said Holly, "is the first stage of grief."

"Good point," said Emma. "What's the elephant in the room?"

"Me?" asked Mason. "Am I the elephant?"

"No, Mason," said Jake, leaning over and touching his knee. He was shocked at how bony it was. "You're not an elephant. On the other hand, I am the Walrus. Coo coo ca choo."

"I think what Jake means is that you're not the elephant; it's your news that's the elephant."

"I'm missing something," said Marianne. "What's the elephant?"

"It's a term that gets used in the recovery field," said Holly. "It means, there's an elephant in the room and nobody talks about this huge thing that no one can really miss."

"So our elephant is Mason's illness?" asked Marianne.

"Yes," said Emma. "So let's talk about it."

There were several long moments of silence before Jake made an elephant trumpeting sound. Everyone laughed.

"Okay," said Jake. "I'll go. I think it completely sucks."

"Yeah," agreed Marianne. "I do too. It completely sucks."

"You're looking better and better," said Jake to Marianne. "You got the lipstick thing going on again," he pantomimed, drawing lipstick around his kisser.

"Hey, hey!" said Holly.

"Sorry," said Jake. "Yeah, it sucks, but what are you going to do about it? I don't want Mason to die. I don't think Mason wants to die. I don't want to die, but I'm going to. Someday. We all are."

Marianne agreed that that was true. Sooner or later.

"I don't think that's the point," said Holly.

Jake disagreed with her. "I think it's exactly the point. The human condition completely sucks. I don't like a lot of stuff about being human. Death is a big part of that. So is being a drunk. I don't like being a drunk."

Emma was surprised at how passionate Jake was about this point, but also thought it was a good sign to see him so expressive.

"You're not a drunk," said Holly. "You're an alcoholic. In recovery."

"I'm a goddamn drunk," said Jake, "and I'm a drink away from being a drunk, and I'm always going to be a drunk. It's a life sentence. You know that, Holly."

"So you're saying—" offered Emma, but Jake interrupted her before she could offer a reflection.

"You can't make that empathic reflecting statement now, Emma Davis. I'm telling you how I feel about Mason's disease, and I think it sucks, and I think I have something I can connect to it, and what I want to know is how do you feel about it?" He looked directly at Emma. She was thrown off guard.

"Well, I—uh—"

"Emma, you don't need to say anything," said Mason.

"I don't mind," she said. "And I will, but I want to hear from the rest of the group, first."

"Cop out!" said Jake.

"Jake!" said Holly, looking furious with him.

Marianne entered, and supported Jake. "You know, Jake is right. You keep us baring our souls, Emma, what about you?"

"Okay," said Emma. "I think it sucks, too. I think that life is short. And I don't know you well, Mason, but," she felt a tear run down her cheek, "I think you're really a wonderful person. And you have so much to offer. And I think about you and your condition, every day. Several times a day. I can't get it out of my mind."

"You're telling me," said Mason and the entire group joined in a laugh. "May I talk?"

"Certainly," said Emma, sniffing.

"First of all, thank you all for your expression of support. Sucking, I think, is the consensus. And I agree. But, this is life."

Mason hesitated and looked each group member in the eye as he continued, one after another. "And a part of life is death. So, I'd like to finish this group and then travel to London. And I'll tell you something very strange. And I want you all to hear this, very carefully."

"What?" asked Jake. "Say it."

"I've never felt so alive. I don't take a moment for granted. I love every sight I see. I've never been so fond of the Christmas lights. I've never enjoyed watching my old movies so much.

There is so much in life to enjoy and to love. Just knowing that my death is imminent, everything seems so sweet."

"I think I know what you mean," said Marianne.

"Mason," said Holly, "I'm going to miss you."

"I'm not dead yet. I'd appreciate it if you treated me like I was alive, and until the group is over, or until I can't make it to the group anymore, I want to be treated like anyone else."

"I can do that," said Jake.

"Good," said Mason.

"Still sucks," said Jake.

"Yes, it does," agreed Mason.

After they talked about some of the dreams they'd been having, Emma looked at Marianne. She commented that, like Jake, she also noticed that Marianne was wearing makeup again. She wondered what had changed for Marianne.

"I am enjoying my life," she said. "A lot like what Mason described. I'm back to working out and doing my work."

"So what changed?" asked Emma.

"I decided that life is short, so you might as well enjoy it."

"Great. We met after the group last week, and you seemed so depressed," said Emma.

"I'm great at working through. I'll still see the psychiatrist you recommended." Marianne did look better. There was something that still bothered Emma, but she decided it was probably her own stress. People went through mood changes all the time.

"I'm glad you're feeling better," Emma said.

"And I'm doing okay," said Jake, "not that anybody is asking me. Still sober. But I did buy a bottle of booze."

"You did what?" asked Mason, incredulous.

"Yeah, I bought a bottle. I didn't drink it though."

Emma asked, "Jake, do you know why you bought the bottle?" She wasn't pleased when Holly answered before Jake could speak.

"Actually, it's not uncommon for alcoholics in early recovery to be very ambivalent. Going back and forth."

"I can answer this, Buttercup," said Jake. "I bought a bottle on complete impulse. But I didn't drink it. I had a talk with Holly, instead. A really good talk. A really, really good talk."

Emma looked at Holly, who was now blushing. "Oh, really?"

"Really," said Jake.

Holly spoke up. "Not really really, just really. It was good. For Jake. To talk."

"So I decided to dump the bottle," said Jake.

"What did you buy?" asked Mason.

"J&B."

"Did you dump it yet?"

"I will tonight," promised Jake.

Mason said, "Jesus Christ, don't do that. Give it to me."

"Seriously?"

"Yes. I'm not the one in recovery. I'll follow you home. Unless you have it in your car."

"Actually I do."

"Good thinking," said Holly. She noticed Emma's eyes were still on her.

The following morning Marianne went about her daily routine until she reached work. She told her secretary that she didn't want to be disturbed, not even for board members, and then searched the Web until she found a site that gave information on medication. She looked up several medications and took scrupulous notes. She then left work, and went to meet with the psychiatrist whom Emma Davis had referred her to see.

Marianne described her symptoms, some of which were true and some of which had been falsified, and then requested a certain medication that addressed these specific symptoms. The doctor wrote her a prescription for these meds.

Marianne then drove to see her family doctor and asked for a strong pain reliever, claiming that she had a sore back from exercise. Her doctor prescribe both Vicodin and muscle relaxants, a bonanza of meds that were more than Marianne had hoped for.

Marianne then drove to an urgent care facility, where she complained of various aches and pains and received another prescription for pain killers.

Marianne filled the first prescription at her local pharmacy, the second prescription at the local Meijer's grocery store, and the third at a Rite Aid. At each location she made sure to pay cash.

Marianne went home, put the medications in a shoebox at the bottom of her closet, and slept a dreamless sleep. She felt happy and fulfilled.

Emma finally got out of bed after a nearly sleepless night. She had been having trouble sleeping since she had decided to move out. She kept looking at the clock, thinking that her gym would open at 5:00 a.m. Frank had been staying in a hotel. Emma didn't ask where he was staying.

Emma had an early morning appointment to keep. After lifting weights and working on a cardio-machine at the gym, she got to her office and was surprised to see Jake sitting in the waiting room.

Jake reminded her that this was the follow-up appointment that they'd agreed to have after she had written the note for him to return to work.

"So how is it going?" asked Emma.

"I think pretty good," answered Jake. "I haven't drank anything in over a month now, in spite of buying that bottle."

"Right," said Emma. "What did you end up doing with that bottle?"

"I gave it to Mason, like he asked. I ended up driving over to his house. It's amazing. He has such a huge library of movies. DVDs and tapes and also reel to reel—he even has an old projector. He's all set up. We had a good visit."

"Sounds like it. You two made a connection."

"Yeah. Turns out we're both collectors. I told him about my jazz collection of old vinyl, and he seemed really interested."

"You're really excited about his interest in you."

"Y'know, I noticed that myself. I think it's because my dad never seemed to care that much about me. Well, I don't know if that's really true, but he was so busy working all the time, I think I just decided he didn't care."

"That's an interesting distinction," said Emma. "Whether someone cares, or whether they can show it, have the skills to, or whatever, those are two different things."

"Yeah," said Jake, looking her over. "You look pretty tired."

"Long night," said Emma.

"I know what you mean. Most of my nights are long. But then, I work most nights. Strange though, I'm really starting to sleep much better."

"Jake, I wanted to ask you a question. I wonder about you and Holly."

"I thought you might notice something between us. Is it that obvious?"

"Only to the trained eye," Emma said, smiling. "How long have you two been seeing each other?"

"Just started. I mean, we're friends, obviously, but it's just started being something more than a friendship. Does that mean we can't be in the group anymore?"

"No, I don't think so," said Emma, "but it's good for us to talk about it. Doesn't the A.A. group have some rule about not getting involved in the first year?"

"It's more of a guideline," answered Jake, pulling a stick of gum out of his khaki's. "But Holly mentioned that to me, too."

"So why did you decide to get involved?"

"I think that it wasn't much of a decision. It really just happened."

"I see."

"So work is okay, my dreams are improving, my love life is looking up, I'm not drinking. Should be good news, right?"

"I hear the *should* word, Jake. What's the problem?"

"The guy stalking Holly, the Gordon guy, he's been renting a lot of space in my head."

"He knocked you over."

"Yes, he did."

"He assaulted you. And her."

"That's right."

"I can see why you'd be upset. Are the police doing anything about it?"

"Last time Holly talked with them, they said that she'd be more likely to see him before they did, so she should just keep her eyes peeled and call them right away if she sees him. In the meantime, they're doing more drive-bys, just cruising through the neighborhood now and then looking for anything suspicious."

"So have you noticed them doing that?"

"Yeah. I also haven't seen him at all since Thanksgiving."

"Maybe he split. If he's smart."

"I think he is smart. But I also think he holds a grudge. And I think he doesn't like to be the one who runs away."

"What does your A.A. program preach about this kind of situation, Jake?" asked Emma.

"They say that alcoholics cannot afford resentments or to nurse grudges."

"Do you talk with your sponsor about this?"

"Yes."

"And what does he say?"

"He says to let it go, and let the police and God handle it. Not in that order."

"Okay. Sounds like good advice."

"I guess."

"Jake, I wonder if you've given any thought to ongoing therapy?"

"Not really. Do you think I need it?"

"Well, that's another question, but I'll address it. I've looked up some research, and people in early recovery tend to do better if they're involved in therapy."

"More than the Dream Group?"

"Yes. Something just for you. Something to address your thoughts and feelings around not drinking, handling life without alcohol, being in this new relationship."

"I'll think about it."

"Okay. That wouldn't necessarily be with me. I can make a referral to someone who knows alcoholic issues."

"Sounds strange when I hear you say it. Alcoholic issues. Like I have some kind of disease. Which, I guess I have."

"Think about it Jake. I'm glad you're working so hard to stay sober."

"You and me both."

After Jake left Emma emailed this message to Dylan:

Dylan,

Things are progressing fast. Frank wants me to move out before the New Year, and I'm looking for apartments. Needless to say, you're on my mind constantly. I'm hoping I can see you before the holidays.

Talk soon,
Emma

CHAPTER THIRTEEN

Mason is dreaming about London again. He is making plans to travel. He needs to get to the British Museum, a place he'd been before, to visit the Tabula Rasa. He is looking at maps to find the best line of the Tube to reach the museum, but the paper keeps changing in his hands, so that now he's looking at a map, but in a few moments it becomes a cartoon, then an article, then a sheet of blank paper holding fish and chips. He eats a piece of fish and can taste the salt and vinegar.

Mason sets the paper down and decides that he doesn't need a map to get to the museum. He's aware that he is near Kensington and, as long as he can find the Tube, he can maneuver his way there. He strolls down the street and notices people walking, most of them people he recognizes from his childhood in French Lick. There is his old football coach, who Mason knew had been dead for years, walking with a pair of ducks on a leash.

Mason hurries past and sees the tunnel that leads to the underground Tube. He's on board the subway without being aware of how he paid the fare. He's hopped aboard the first train that came along, without checking to see which direction it was going. Oh, well, *he thinks,* this feels right. *If he's going the wrong way, he'll just double back. He might as well enjoy the trip. He departs the train to head towards the British Museum.*

Once through the front door, Mason *is surprised to see the same movie theater that he went to in Chicago, where he had seen the John Ford picture,* Tie A Yellow Ribbon. *Choking up as he approaches the theater, he realizes he can buy the ticket again, go into the theater again, and have the same sensation of awe and awakening, the same satori, the realization that the world held something more for him than his town that this grand narrative called film was opening a path for him to build a life around.*

As a child, Mason *had no language for this, just a feeling, a sort of a thrill in the pit of his stomach, something that connected with him in such a visceral manner that he could never fully wrap words around it.*

Now as he stands outside of the theater, Mason *steps forward to purchase a ticket but is startled as he sees the figure in the red traditional armor of the Samurai standing behind the counter. He can't see the face, but an armored hand motions towards* Mason, *inviting him to buy a ticket.* Mason *steps forward and reaches into his pocket. He removes three stones. Two are black and one is white. He gives these to the warrior. He watches the helmet nod up and down, as if in approval, and then receives a ticket for the movie. The ticket is a large sheet of paper, and looks more like a certificate than a movie pass, but* Mason *walks into the theater. He notices that the man taking the tickets is the same Samurai.* Mason *gives him the ticket, and the man unhitches the velvet rope and allows* Mason *entrance into the theater.*

He is alone in the theater. He seats himself in a plush velvet seat, exactly in the middle of the theater. That's when the Samurai walks on stage. Mason *is sitting much closer now, in the front row, just a few feet away from the warrior.*

The Samurai takes out his long sword and places it on the ground. He takes out his short blade and Mason wonders if he is to witness the warrior commit Sepuku, the ritualized form of suicide that involved disembowelment. But the Samurai removes his helmet and Mason looks upon the face of Akira Kurosawa.

Mason watches as Kurosawa removes all of his armor and lays it at Mason's feet. Mason knows that Kurosawa can speak English. He also knows that Kurosawa is dead. Mason registers amusement to see subtitles that appear below Kurosawa's face as he spoke.

Kurosawa: *This armor is frightening. It can protect you on your journey.*

As Mason began speaking, he spoke in perfect Japanese. His words, too, appeared in subtitles.

Mason: *But I am here to see a movie. I'm at the end of my journey.*

Kurosawa: *No, your journey is just beginning.*

Mason: *Do I need to keep the armor?*

Kurosawa: *You have it to wear. You will have a day when you give it away; give it away as a gift, a gift to another traveler. You'll see. You'll know when you get there.*

Mason: *Where am I going? How will I find my way?*

Kurosawa: *How did you find your way here? You'll know how to find your way. You also don't need to know where you're going. The trip will find itself.*

Kurosawa turns to leave and Mason realizes that he is already on the movie screen, walking across the Southwest landscape that opens the

John Ford motion picture. Only now Mason can track Akira Kurosawa walking across a corner of the screen.

Mason thinks, I wish I had told him how much I liked his work, *but even as Mason has this thought the figure of Kurosawa, now almost tiny in the corner of the picture, turns towards him, nods, bows, and continues walking.*

There was a cold snap and the wind had begun really whipping down the streets of the city. Jake was glad he wore his down coat after he left his home. He was on his way to meet with his sponsor.

Jake found his sponsor, Nick, sitting in a corner of the Mexican restaurant in East Lansing at 8:00 p.m.

"Thanks for agreeing to do a dinner instead of a lunch," said Jake. "This is actually my breakfast."

Jake looked over the menu quickly and ordered the Enchiladas De Jocoque. Nick had a plate of nachos. Jake ordered a cola and Nick said he'd stick to water. Jake eyed the picture of Margaritas at the next table.

"Yeah, it's all around, isn't it?" asked Nick.

"I guess so. Funny thing is, I can't tell you what's on those couples' plates, how much of it they've eaten. But I see the pitcher of drinks, I can make a good guess of how many glasses are left, I notice that it's the guy that pouring and he's drinking twice as fast as the girl."

"I noticed the same thing."

"That never changes?"

"Not much. Sometimes I don't notice it at all. But I'm meeting with you right now, and I'm thinking about how you're doing. So, how are you doing?" asked Nick.

Jake looked up and smiled. "I think I'm doing okay. I've been noticing that alcohol is just what you guys say it is, 'Cunning, baffling, and powerful.'"

"I heard a rumor that you bought a bottle."

"Yeah. I did. I talked about it with Holly and I also mentioned it in a meeting. So I'm not sure who you heard it from."

"Well, one thing that's important, is that I didn't hear it from you."

"What do you mean by that?"

"You didn't call me."

"No, I guess I didn't. Until we set up this dinner. So, what does that mean?"

"Just notice it. I'm supposed to be the guy who helps you with your drinking problem, but you don't call me when you're about to buy a bottle."

"No. I did talk with someone in the program about it."

"Who? Holly?"

"Yeah."

"How deeply are you involved with Holly?" asked Nick. He took a nacho chip and dipped it in salsa while Jake measured his answer.

"What? What do you mean?"

"Jake, A.A. is a very small community. It's unlikely that you're going to get into a relationship with someone in the program and not have that noticed."

"So, okay. I'm involved. So what?" Jake had a look on his face like the guacamole was sour. But there was no guacamole on the table.

"Geez, Jake, you don't have to get so defensive. If you would just be upfront with me about this stuff, I wouldn't have to guess, and we wouldn't go around in these circles. Let me ask you a question. Do you want to stop drinking?"

"Yes. Absolutely."

"And do you trust yourself?"

"Yes. I think so."

"Who bought the bottle?"

"I did."

"Do you know why?"

"That's been something I've been thinking about for a long time."

"And?" asked Nick.

"And I have a few ideas. I'd just gotten off work. I was tired and hungry. I was lonely."

"You know about HALT? Don't let yourself get too hungry, angry, lonely, or tired?"

"I've heard about it."

"So what did you do with the bottle?"

"I talked with Holly about it, I talked with someone in the program about it, I gave it away to someone in the Dream Group that I go to every week."

"You didn't drink?"

"No. I didn't drink."

The food came and both men dug into their dinners with gusto.

"So why did you ask me about whether I trust myself?" asked Jake, between bites of his enchiladas.

"Well, you trust yourself, but you also bought the bottle."

"I see what you mean. Keep talking."

"Do you trust me?" asked Nick.

"I guess not. Not yet."

"What do you think will happen if you do?" asked Nick.

"I don't know. Become an A.A. clone."

"I know what you mean. That's what I worried about, too."

"And?" Jake waited patiently. He really wanted to know the answer to this.

"It probably happened," Nick laughed. "I don't know. I just know that very slowly I started to give myself over to the program. And very slowly, one day at a time, I started to change. But one thing's for sure: I've never had to drink again. So what I'm asking you, is if you believe that it might be possible for you to get this 'cure' that A.A. promises, if you give yourself over to a few suggestions."

Jake asked, "What kind of suggestions?"

"Well, meetings for one thing. Would you be willing to go to a meeting every day for the next ninety days?"

Jake took a bite of his enchiladas, took a swig of the cola, motioned to the waiter for another glass, looked back at Nick and said, "Okay."

"Good. That would be a ninety and ninety. Ninety meetings in ninety days. Call me every day, too?"

Jake sighed. "Okay. But if you want me to stop seeing Holly—"

"I'm not going to ask that. It's a little late to put the genie back in the bottle. Just notice what comes up as a result of it. Try to go to meetings that Holly doesn't attend. Keep your recovery separate from that relationship as much as possible, okay?"

"Fair enough. One more thing." Jake looked at Nick.

"What's that?" Nick asked.

"Are you done with your nachos?"

Holly woke up and rolled out of bed and got on her knees. She bowed her head and prayed, yawned, stood up and put on her big fleece sweater. She started her morning routine, bathroom, coffee, reading and writing. She was about the get dressed for work when the phone rang. It was her supervisor.

"Holly, I thought you might want to know that the police picked up Gordon last night."

"Oh, that's great. When did you get the news?"

"I'm here at the office, and there's a message for you that I thought you'd like to hear right away."

"Thanks, that's a relief. Any more information? When will he be charged?" Holly asked.

"I don't know any of that stuff now, but I'll let you know as soon as I can. The DA's office will probably want to talk with you, at some point, about whether you want to prosecute for stalking. Between that, the assault on the kid, the assault on your friend, he could be gone for a while."

"Thanks, Frank. I'll be in the office soon."

"Take your time."

Holly hung up the phone and then called her sponsor to give her the news. Then she called Jake to tell him, but got his voice mail. She left a message.

On her way to work she stopped and picked up some donuts for the staff. She felt like celebrating.

After arriving at work several of her colleagues mentioned how good she looked, and she realized that she was smiling, singing, joking.

She called the DA's office later and found that the paperwork hadn't gotten to the jail yet. She called and had it confirmed that Gordon Thomas was in fact incarcerated, was likely to be charged on several counts, and there had been no contacts to have him released on bail. Since he was considered a fugitive, he wasn't likely to be released before his trial.

Jake was driving home after his shift at the psych ward. It had been a quiet night, and Jake had had a chance to do a good deal of reading. He used to take a nap on his breaks, but now he read. And he requested the job of sitting at the front desk. Every now and then, a patient would awaken and need to come to the desk and ask for something—a glass of water or just to talk for a few minutes before going back to bed. But most often, Jake read.

Jake started taking books with him to work after he had stopped drinking for a couple of weeks. He was interested in reading. It was the first realization that drinking had in some way incapacitated him intellectually. Jake was surprised at that insight, because as often as he reflected that this drinking was probably not doing his liver or kidneys or stomach any good, he'd never thought about the impact the drinking might have on his favorite organ—his brain. Well, maybe his *second* favorite organ.

Jake had brought two books to work last night. A collection of Mary Oliver's poetry, which Holly had loaned him, and an Elmore Leonard novel. Both were easy to read in small chunks and so were perfect for reading in five or ten minute clips at work. Jake reflected on his drive home that the gritty streets of Lansing reminded him of the crime-scapes of Leonard, whom

Jake had read was a Detroiter. And the grey skies reminded him of Oliver's poetry. Both the writers, he thought, lived in their senses and told their tales through the senses. Jake looked at the ashtray in his car and wondered, *If I've stopped drinking, how hard would it be to stop smoking?* Then he thought of Mason and his cancer. Jake started to cry.

What's happening to me? Jake wondered. He noticed that he cried easily and at times for little provocation. He had planned to go home but found himself driving to the A.A. club on the East Side of town. When he got there he bought himself a long john and a cup of coffee and sat down at a booth near a window. He saw the snow falling on the commuters on their way to work, as he was winding down from his long night.

One of the guys he saw a lot at meetings, he thought his name was Don, came up to him and asked to sit down. Jake said "Sure."

Don was a big beefy guy with a large gut. He looked to be about four days away from a razor, and Jake reflected that you could take that more than one way. Don had dark circles under his eyes, a big mustache, and a crew cut.

"How's it going?" asked Don.

"Not bad," answered Jake. Then decided to tell the truth. "I find myself crying at the drop of a hat."

"It's rough early on. It gets better," said Don.

"People keep saying that," said Jake.

"That's because it's true. I remember my first three months. I felt like I was walking around without any skin. It was really raw. I had to keep from killing myself and that's no joke."

"Jesus. I'm not suicidal."

"Well, just in case you're wondering. A lot of us don't believe there's life after drinking. The only way to know it for sure is to give yourself some time."

"I'm doing that. It's just not easy."

"So what's happening in your life?" asked Don.

Jake was surprised that someone he knew in such a peripheral way could seem so interested in him. He started to talk about his job, he talked about the books he had in the car. Don told him about Lawrence Block's detective series that featured an alcoholic protagonist. Jake talked about jazz, and then he mentioned Mason again and got choked up.

"This guy means something to you, doesn't he?" asked Don.

"I didn't think so, but yeah, he does."

"It's hard for men to get close to each other. What about your dad?"

"I hardly knew him," said Jake. "He was a drinker, and he worked hard. Mostly, I knew to stay out of his way when he was home. Which wasn't often."

Don nodded and looked at his watch.

"A meeting's about to start. You want to go?"

"Yeah. That's why I'm here."

On Saturday Emma went for an early swim, then started looking at apartments. She went to her office and looked at several listings online. She had an idea of what she could afford and, after paying for her own insurance, the rent on her office, and other bills, it wasn't much.

With more than a little dread, she drove from complex to complex. She started in Okemos, trying to avoid the main roads, which were crammed with Christmas shoppers. Emma saw one apartment after another. Each trip from her car to the rental offices seemed desolate to her. She'd walk across the frozen concrete, avoiding icy patches, and heard her boots scuff along the salt-stained pavement of the parking lots. Every one she visited had cheery Christmas music playing, the holiday lights, stockings hung over the office windows. She felt less than cheery.

Emma worked her way west, through the listings in East Lansing. She desperately wanted to avoid student housing and the more expensive apartments. She'd heard horror stories of the new condos in downtown East Lansing that had sold at six figures, only to have students use them as dorms. She'd heard of the professional neighbors or even retirees sharing hallways with kids who would party all night, urinate in the stairwells, puke in the halls, and generally wreak havoc.

Emma found a cluster of older red brick buildings on the far west side of the city, still in East Lansing but clearly catering to a more mature population. The only students living in the apartments were grad students. Emma found a small, two-bedroom, with windows that looked out over the courtyard, trees, and black squirrels scampering on the grounds below. The rooms seemed tiny.

The woman who had showed her the apartment asked her if she had any questions. Emma asked how much. The answer surprised Emma. It was within her means. At that moment, standing in the kitchen that seemed more like a galley than an actual room, Emma saw a bright red cardinal light on the tree branch just outside the window. The crimson feathers contrasted with the snow draped black bough it rested on.

"I'll take it," she said.

"Just like that?" asked the apartment manager.

"Just like that. When can I move in?"

"We'll need to clean it, you can probably have it in two weeks."

"Okay. That'll work fine," said Emma. Then she realized that two weeks to the day would be the day after Christmas.

"Can I have it a few days earlier?"

"I suppose so. In a rush?"

"I have a situation. I need to be moved in by the holidays."

Emma returned to her gym after finding the apartment. It had taken about four hours, and even though she had already swam that day, she decided to work out on some weights for a while. Then she sat in the steam room until she couldn't stand it. And then she took a cold shower and went home.

There were two messages on the machine. One was from her son Nathan, telling her and Frank that he'd be home after his last final on Tuesday. The other one was from Frank.

Emma called Frank on his cell phone, and he answered on the first ring.

"Hi. I noticed you called," she said.

"Yeah. I was just getting some work done, and stopped by the club and saw you lifting, and I called home. I mean, I knew you wouldn't be there."

"Oh," said Emma, "I didn't see you. You should've come by."

"I didn't want to bother you."

"You wouldn't have. I would like to see you. I was going to call you, anyway. Nathan is coming home from school on Tuesday."

"Yeah. Have you told him yet?" asked Frank.

"No. I haven't. But I was thinking maybe we should talk. I mean, it's been a couple of weeks since we had our last conversation."

"Right. Good idea. I've missed you, Emma."

"Well. I found an apartment. It's near here. They'll let me have it before Christmas."

"Did you hear what I said?" asked Frank. "I miss you."

"Frank, I would be lying if I said I didn't miss you."

"Well, do you have any second thoughts? Do you have to do this?"

"I don't know. I don't want to hurt you. I don't want to hurt Nathan."

"You don't have to, you know. I can, I don't know how to say this, but if you need time, time to explore your feelings, or even, if you need to experiment—I mean, I've got a lot invested in this marriage; I can be flexible."

"What are you saying?" asked Emma.

"I'm just suggesting that there might be options."

"I see. Well, we should talk about this in person."

"Okay," said Frank. "What are you doing tonight?"

At the mall on the north side of town Marianne was doing her Christmas shopping. She had decided on this mall as opposed to any others because they had a Pottery Barn, and she had decided to purchase her staff gift certificates.

Marianne felt a little tired, having spent this Saturday at the office, putting in her regular hours, getting caught up on her numerous tasks.

Why didn't I ever learn to delegate? she asked herself. She stopped at the Starbucks and bought herself a large coffee before doing her shopping. Then her eye caught the Schuler bookstore, and she made a decision to walk through the store before finishing her work shopping.

Marianne started towards the audio books. She'd never had time to read, but found that she could put on a book while working at her tasks, and kill two birds with one stone. She was looking at the latest audio book by Covey and mouthing the words, *Sharpen the Saw*, when she heard her name called out by someone.

A younger woman was standing with a stack of books in her arms, dressed in a navy wool winter coat and bright red scarf. Marianne took a moment to see that the smiling woman was Holly from the Dream Group.

"Marianne! I thought that was you. Hi!" said Holly.

"Yes. Hi Holly. You're doing quite a bit of shopping, aren't you?"

"Well, I love the holidays. Don't you? And I have a lot of people in my life and my favorite gifts are books. I find it fun to try to match up people with books. Like my nephew, I'm getting him a science fiction, this book on chocolate is for my sponsor, and I've even found a book for Jake. Oh, Jake's here, too. Did you see him? He's in the back of the store, listening to the jazz CDs."

"No. I didn't see him. Are you two—?"

"Together? Well, kind of yes; we came here together, yes. You should go over and say hi. Jake thinks a lot of you."

"He does? I'm a little surprised."

"Yeah. He admires how hard you work. Your ambition. You know, it's really something."

"Yes. I suppose. I'll go say hello to him. Back in the jazz section?" asked Marianne.

"I'll take you there," said Holly, shifting the books in her arms, then deciding to set them down on the information desk and ask the clerk if she might leave them there for "just a second."

Marianne and Holly walked up behind Jake who was intently listening to a Dave Holland Big Band CD, with the jewel case in one hand and the other fingering through a stack in the shelves. He was wearing a jean jacket and smelled like cigarette smoke.

"Hey," Holly said loudly, tapping Jake on the shoulder, "look who's here."

"This is great," Jake said even more loudly, waving the CD over his shoulder. "I've got to get this." Turning, Jake saw Marianne and his face broke out into a big smile.

"Wow. Marianne. Wow."

Marianne blushed. She surprised herself.

Jake jerked the headphones off his head. "Doing some shopping, huh?"

Marianne said, "Yes. I have a few things to pick up for my staff, so I thought I'd go to Pottery Barn."

Holly squealed, "I *love* the Pottery Barn. Oh, you can do the thing I do with books, match the gift to the person's personality."

"That's a good idea. I don't have their personality profiles with me, though."

"Wow, what's that?"

"Oh, we had a consultant come in a couple of years ago, and he gave us all personality tests," explained Marianne.

"Well, you don't have to go that far, do you?" suggested Holly. "Just think of what they like."

"Good idea," said Marianne, starting to back away. Then she heard Holly nearly explode.

"Oh, *my Gawd*, I can't believe this! Look who's over at the DVDs—it's Mason. Oh, *my Gawd!*"

"Yeah, it is," said Jake.

Holly grabbed both Jake's and Marianne's wrists and led them over to where Mason had been asking a clerk to open a DVD display for him.

"Mason! Dream Group!"

"Rule number one: don't talk about Dream Group," said Jake.

"Well, look at this. Did you three all go out together?" asked Mason.

"No," said Marianne. "Holly and Jake were here together and she bumped into me."

"What a weird coincidence. No, it's—what would Jung call it? It's—"

"A miracle?" asked Holly.

"Karma?" suggested Jake.

"Yeah, you could both be right. Or fate or destiny," laughed Mason. "No, it's 'synchronicity.'"

"Cool. I remember now," said Jake. "What are you getting?"

"Oh. I wanted to get a copy of *Akira Kurosawa's Dreams* for Emma Davis. She's been so helpful, hasn't she?"

"Oh, Mason, that's so nice. She'll love it. You're so sweet. Isn't he sweet, Jake?" said Holly.

"Yeah, Mason. You're sweet. Only you'll make us all look bad. I wasn't going to get her anything."

"Neither was I," said Holly. "Well, one more gift won't kill me. Hey, what are you two doing for dinner? Jake and I are going to go over to the new rib joint. You want to join us?"

"Oh, I'm afraid not," said Marianne. "I need to be going. Finish my shopping."

"My wife is somewhere around here," said Mason. "We were planning to go to a show, but, you know what, I think we'll join you two. Marianne, can't you come, too?"

"I really shouldn't," she said.

"Why not?" asked Jake.

"Jake, don't be rude," said Holly, then looked at Marianne. "Please come. If you don't have anything better to do."

Marianne took a breath and said, "All right. I'll do it."

Jake and Holly laughed and Mason said, "Dare I eat a peach?"

Jake said, "Isn't that an Allman Brother's album?"

"T.S. Elliott," said Mason. Then, as Holly went to pay for her books, Mason took Marianne by the elbow and said, "You know, I really wouldn't ordinarily say this, but these are extraordinary times for me. You should really lighten up and learn how to enjoy yourself."

Marianne blanched.

"See what I mean?"

And then they all went to dinner.

Frank had offered to have dinner with Emma at their house, but Emma had asked to meet in public again. He offered to come and pick her up, but she thought it wiser to drive separately. They agreed to eat at one of the new restaurants at the mall on the north side of town. Emma was distracted on her way to the Italian restaurant and passed the driveway that led to the restaurant. She was turning around in the parking lot of another restaurant when she noticed Holly and Jake get out of Holly's car. They were laughing, and waving at some other people who were getting out of an SUV further down the lot. Emma noticed that the other people were Mason and Marianne, and a woman that she didn't recognize.

"That's weird," she said.

When she met Frank at the restaurant they'd chosen, Emma was distracted.

"Thanks for coming to meet me," said Frank. He gave her a hug and she hugged him back.

"Sure," she said, "how've you been?"

"Well, that's like asking someone in a funeral home—"

"Yeah, you're right. I'm sorry. This is rough. Rough for both of us."

Frank got a table, and they sat down. The waiter asked for their drink orders and Emma ordered a glass of Merlot. Frank decided on a martini.

"So I didn't ask you, how you've been?" asked Frank.

"It's been rough, just like you. I mean, probably different from you, but—"

"You found a place, you said?"

"Yeah. It's not that far from our place, just about a mile away. The apartments, the red brick places next to the cleaners."

"Oh. Did you put a deposit down?"

"They didn't require one until I get the key. There's paperwork, and I didn't want to do it today. They'll let me have it before the holidays. Just like you asked," said Emma. She took a long pull on her wine, which had just arrived.

The couple ordered. Emma took the salmon salad and Frank ordered the lasagna.

"I told you I wanted to talk to you about something. But before I do, I just want you to know that anything I've said, anything that has been hurtful, Emma, I didn't mean it. You mean the world to me, you know? I've just been scared. I never thought, I mean I've known lots of people who have gotten divorced, but I never, never in my wildest dreams, thought it could happen to us."

"It's not you, Frank," said Emma.

"I know it's not me. But can you imagine how this feels? How it looks? God, I sound so melodramatic."

"I know what you mean. I'm sorry. I appreciate what you said about the hurtful comments. I—you know, you mentioned that you wondered how this would look. I think about that, too. I mean, my work, I'm supposed to keep families together."

"There's the irony," winked Frank.

"And I wonder if I can possibly continue to even work in the field. I had a strange thing happen on my way here.

My entire Dream Group was meeting in the parking lot in the restaurant next door."

"Wow. Maybe they're planning an intervention on you," suggested Frank.

"That's not funny. I mean, I don't know why they'd be getting together behind my back."

"People lead lives outside of therapy, honey. That might be news to you."

"I know that, Frank. God, you make me sound so self-involved."

"I would never suggest that. Here's the food. Let's eat."

The couple began to eat, and Emma noticed for the first time in a week she actually felt hungry.

"Have you been eating?" asked Emma. "You look like you've been losing weight."

"Yeah, I've lost about fourteen pounds. How about you? You look anorexic."

"I haven't gotten on the scale, but all my clothes are loose. I haven't had an appetite, but right now I'm famished."

"It's me. It's my influence on you. See, if we can eat together, we can live together, don't you think?"

"We'll always have pasta," laughed Emma. "God, I haven't laughed since Thanksgiving. Before Thanksgiving."

"See. This is what we need. More of this. We should shelve the divorce and just eat out more."

"Frank, I don't think—"

"I was joking. Geez. Lighten up. But now that we're talking," Frank leaned closer. "Here's what I was going to suggest. Let's just say, for the sake of argument, that you are a lesbian or bi-sexual."

"For the sake of argument, I'm with you." Emma reached for a second slice of bread. She was surprised at how hungry she was.

"So, let's just say you really do prefer women. Does it necessarily have to follow that we get a divorce?"

"Well. What are you suggesting?"

"I've been thinking, obviously. What if we have an 'open' marriage?"

"Say again?"

"An 'open' arrangement. You sleep with whomever you want. We stay married. We live together. I could be in a different room—or you. Whatever. Why disrupt our lives? Why hurt Nathan?"

"As crazy as that sounds, I'd be lying if I said I hadn't considered it myself."

"Why didn't you tell me?"

"Because I was closed off. I couldn't tell anybody about these feelings of mine. I just thought I could bury them."

"Didn't work, huh?"

"No. And they intensified after my parents died."

"Talk to Claudia about that?"

"I may be taking a break from Claudia."

"Oh. Kicking everybody out of your life, now? Just you and Betty and whoever your new squeeze is?"

"No. Well. This is new for me. I don't know who to trust."

"Maybe you could start by trusting someone you've lived with for twenty years."

"I'm thinking of trying to trust myself for a change."

"Touche," said Frank.

The couple ate in silence for a time. Emma was struck that she really was hungry. And the wine felt good.

"So, I'm liking the idea about possibilities," said Emma.

"Good. You do what you like. I can't change that."

"But I'm tired of living a lie."

"Emma, how do you know? Let's say you dump me, crush Nathan—"

"Frank, please."

"Okay, 'disappoint' Nathan, and you move in with Miss Thang, and you discover, it ain't for you. What then? You've bet the farm on an impulse. See, this way, you can—"

"Hedge my bets," said Emma, finishing Frank's words.

"Exactly," said Frank.

"Let's look at dessert."

"Oh, no. Not until you answer me."

"You know me better than that, Frank. I'd never let you blackmail me out of a cheesecake."

They both ordered dessert and coffee.

"So think about it. Don't say 'yes' and don't say 'no.'"

"Okay. I'll think about it. But one thing I do know, Frank."

"What's that?"

"I will always want to be your friend."

"That's a start."

"You're a good guy."

"The 'good' part isn't the problem, is it?"

"No. It's the—"

"Guy part," they both said at once and laughed again. Emma started to cry.

"I think I should go now."

"Can I come home? Never mind. Forget I said that. We made good progress here tonight. At least we're talking. I have football to watch later tonight. The bowls have started."

"Did the Spartans get into a bowl?" asked Emma. "I've been so distracted I didn't even notice," she said as she dried her eyes with her napkin.

"Nope. Not this year. Next year."

"I've heard that before," said Emma. "Thanks for dinner."

That night, as Marianne sleeps, she finds Mason waiting for her in her garage. He's dressed in pajamas.

"I know where you're going," she says. "I've been where you're going, I can take you there."

Marianne takes a pebble from her shoe and watches it hatch like an egg. A black oily fluid that oozes from the crack.

"Take this and eat of it. When you eat it, think of me."

Marianne awoke with a start.

The second week of December was ridiculously cold. Emma made sure to have some hot drinks ready when the group arrived. Mason, looking gaunt, accepted a coffee cup just to hold it in his hands. Holly had a decaf, and Jake, going to work later, took a "leaded." Marianne declined. Emma made herself a tea.

After reminding the group that this was their eleventh meeting, Emma asked if anyone had anything to report.

"Yeah, we met without you Saturday night," said Holly, with a mischievous grin.

"Really?" said Emma.

"Didn't I tell you that would be her response?" asked Jake.

"Yes, you did. But it isn't what she's thinking."

"Holly, you've acquired new powers," said Emma.

"What do you mean?"

Mason suggested that Holly had become a mind reader, and Emma told him that he was correct. Holly mentioned that if she were Emma, she'd be wondering if the group had gotten together to talk about her.

Emma said she assumed that her clients might talk about therapy outside of the office, but that, unless they wanted to talk to her about it, it was none of her business.

"We were actually trying to find a less expensive way to talk about our dreams," said Jake.

"Which we're not doing now," pointed out Marianne.

"Actually, Emma," explained Mason, "it was a strange set of coincidences, or 'synchronicity,' as Jung would call it. Holly and Jake were at the bookstore, doing some Christmas shopping, as was I, and they ran into Marianne. And then the three of them saw me. So we all went to dinner together. And my wife, of course." Emma noticed that Mason's voice had changed. It seemed coarser, like some of the lubrication was missing from the pipes.

"It was fun," said Jake. "We hardly talked about dreams at all. Not that there's anything wrong with talking about dreams."

"So it was really a coincidence. Well, I sometimes think it's a small world, but then I remind myself, that it's really a small town. So, you all had a good time?" Emma was relieved it turned out to be a coincidence.

"Yes," said Marianne. "I had a good time. It almost surprised me."

"You don't get out enough," said Jake.

"Jake is right," said Mason. "Marianne is taking herself much too seriously. Speaking of which, you look particularly tired tonight, Emma. Are you all right?"

"I'm fine. Just the season, you know how busy it gets."

"Yes. I do," said Mason. "Well, as far as 'checking-in' goes, my wife and I have decided to put off going to London until after the holidays. Maybe I told you already. I want to finish this group. I'm still blessedly pain free, I feel tired and weak sometimes, but I've been able to focus and write a little."

Holly said, "That's great. I have good news, too. The guy that was stalking me got arrested, finally."

Holly talked about being relieved. The group conjectured about how long a sentence Gordon might have, and whether or not there would be an actual trial, and whether or not Holly or even Jake would need to testify.

Jake spoke of his commitment to the ninety meetings in ninety days, and Mason in particular told him what a fine thing he was doing.

Emma asked how everyone else felt about Jake's progress, and Marianne thought it was a good thing. Holly said, "I think it's Jake's deal. I hope he can make it."

Jake looked at her with his mouth open and said, "Wow. That sounds pretty cold."

"That's just the way it is. I've heard promises from newcomers before. Today's miracle is tomorrow's relapse. We'll see. I'm not dissing you. I'm just saying it's easy to talk the talk."

"You want to see me walk the walk."

"Exactly." Then Holly winked at him.

Emma asked Marianne how she'd been doing. Marianne admitted feeling better, but related that her dreams were a little more disturbing. Yet she couldn't remember them. She wondered if the anti-depressants could be making her have strange dreams?

Emma thought that might be possible. She noticed that Marianne still hadn't revealed much of herself in the group. She asked Marianne what being in the group had been like.

"It's been different. But I feel hopeful now," said Marianne.

"How bad did your depression get?" asked Holly.

"Well, how bad do they get? It got really bad. I felt—"

"Hopeless?" asked Holly.

"Yes."

"Suicidal?"

"Never. But, like I said, I'm feeling much better now."

"So," said Emma, "who has a dream?"

"I have a dream," said Mason.

"Just like Martin Luther King," said Jake.

"I suppose so. I was in London and I went to a theater, and it turned out to be the same theater that I went to as a child in Chicago. And guess who is speaking in the theater?"

"You?" asked Emma.

"Didn't you say it was all me? Well, if that's the case, it was me in my disguise as Kurosawa."

"Your favorite," said Holly.

"Yes," said Mason. "And it turns out that he was the Samurai I kept seeing in my dreams, the one I was running away from."

"This is so cool," said Jake. "What did he say?"

"He said that my journey was just beginning. And he gave me his armor. And he told me to give it away, that I would know when and where and to whom I should give it."

"That's beautiful," said Holly.

"So, Emma," said Mason, "that's why I want to give you this gift. It's a gift of appreciation. It's a DVD of *Akira Kurosawa's Dreams*. Do you have it?"

"No," said Emma, reaching to take the DVD that Mason offered her. Her eyes became misty. "This is very thoughtful. This is very moving."

"Are you going to cry again?" asked Jake.

"I think I might."

"Please don't start," said Jake. "I've been crying like crazy. We'll all start."

"So," said Holly, "Mason, is the armor—?"

Mason said, "I have no idea. There's a gift that Emma Davis gave me. I don't have to understand it all. I just need to appreciate the power and the beauty of the image—*dream appreciation* instead of *dream interpretation*, right?"

"You got it," said Emma.

CHAPTER FOURTEEN

Jake had met Nick, his sponsor, at a coffee shop the following day. Nick bought them both a cappuccino and asked Jake how it was going.

"It's damn cold; that's how it's going," answered Jake.

"Yeah, it is that," said Nick. "How's it going with the meetings?"

"Good. I mean, I go every day. And the funny thing is that I'm starting to look forward to them."

"Great. What do you look forward to?"

"I don't know. It's sure not the coffee. God, that stuff is like hot piss."

"I know. That's why we're meeting here, not there," said Nick with a broad smile.

"I think it's the people. Or the stories. The stories are amazing, you know? I heard a guy talk the other day, his daughter had died, recently, and here he was at a meeting, and I thought, 'Wow, if he can do it—'"

"'—so can I.' Yeah, I know what you mean. We share our experience, strength and hope with each other. Believe it or not, Jake, someone in the room is drawing the same kind of lesson from you."

"From me? How so? Who?"

"I don't know. Nobody specific. But I'm sure that it's happening. People feel inspired by people who keep coming back. It's important. And you keep coming back."

"Well, I guess so."

"What else is new?" asked Nick.

Jake looked around the coffee shop, which was almost empty. There was someone reading a paper in the corner and someone with their nose in their laptop. He wondered how to answer Nick. He wondered what to tell, and what to keep to himself.

"Oh, work is fine," said Jake. "Census is down, so I can bring books in to read. I'm really enjoying reading. I'm loving music, too."

"Still in the Dream Group?"

"Yeah. It's funny, I'm not dreaming quite as much. I don't know about that. It's still hard for me to get to sleep."

"That takes some time. I didn't get good sleep the first year I was in recovery. I hate to say that, it may have even taken longer than a year."

"I hate hearing that."

"It might not be that bad for you. Anyway, one day at a time."

"Yeah. One day," sighed Jake.

"Still seeing Holly?" asked Nick.

"Yes. Yes, I am. I think—" Jake was quiet.

"Go ahead, you think what?"

"I think it's none of your business. In a polite, kind of way." Jake smiled at Nick.

"I know what you mean. Sponsors tend to poke their noses into every corner of your life. Especially early on. And keep in mind, you are free to fire me at any time for any reason at all. But I want you to know, I'm not asking for details, I'm not asking you to gossip, I'm not asking for anything other than what you might end up drinking over. And for that, it's important to keep the lines of communication open. Make sense?"

"Well, yeah, but I'm not crazy about it."

"Say more about that."

"I just don't know what to say. It seems private."

"So did your drinking a few weeks ago."

"Yeah, but this is different."

"Right. There's another person involved."

"Now that you put it that way—" said Jake.

"You know, Jake, I've known Holly for years. And she's a big girl. She knows what she's getting into. Though, I'll have to admit, if she were a guy going out with a woman that was a newcomer, it would be viewed a lot more critically."

Jake looked at Nick and frowned. "What do you mean?"

Nick hesitated, then said, "Guys have been banned from the Al-Anon club for preying on newcomers. It still happens. But this place shouldn't be a pick-up joint."

"You think there's a double standard?"

"Maybe. But that's not my point. I like Holly, I don't want to see her hurt. My unwritten contract with you is to help you learn how to live without drinking. So, addicts and alcoholics often turn to other means to help them with how they feel. It could be food—"

"I've gained seven pounds in two weeks," said Jake.

"—or TV, or the computer, or spending, or sex or—"

"Okay, I see what you mean."

"We don't have much of a sense of moderation. And getting into a relationship, especially early on, there's no sense of moderation. Usually people kind of 'lose themselves' in each other. And you're still in the middle of trying to find yourself."

"I still think it's a fine line."

"Okay. Fair enough. I'm not telling you not to see her. We're clear about that, aren't we?"

"Yeah."

"Just consider keeping an open mind and letting me know how it's going, if you run into any bumps. I don't want you to feel sheepish in talking about it, when problems come up."

"Oh, you think there will be problems?"

Nick looked at Jake as if to explain, then realized he was being sarcastic. He smiled at Jake, and Jake smiled back.

On the day that Emma told her son Nathan that she was leaving his father, the sun was out, and it was the first time Emma had seen Nathan in weeks. He'd seemed healthy and heavier than when she'd seen him last. She met him at home, and he'd arrived with some new winter clothes and a request for some money to buy Christmas presents.

On the day that Emma told her son Nathan that she was leaving his father, Emma had seen a few clients in the morning, but couldn't get it out of her mind what lay ahead, in terms of the talk she needed to have with Nathan.

On the day that Emma told her son Nathan that she was leaving his father, she had called her husband Frank and told him that she was going to proceed with her plans to move out, that she still cared for him but had to be true to herself. That she was sorry.

On the day that Emma told her son Nathan that she was leaving his father, she called Claudia Silverstein to set up another appointment and had a long talk with her on the phone before Nathan got home.

On the day that Emma told her son Nathan that she was leaving his father, she had gone for a walk on the path near the river, where she often ran, and wept.

On the day that Emma told her son Nathan that she was leaving his father, she went home and baked his favorite cookies.

After telling Nathan that she was leaving, and why she was leaving, Nathan told her that he loved her no matter what. Then he left home to see friends and Emma wouldn't see him again for two days.

Mason walked down the sloping street of Sunset Lane. He loved to walk. Even though his gait was slowed and it was cold—just below freezing he guessed—he still enjoyed the sensation of the sun on his face. He noticed how low in the sky the sun hung, the squirrels scampering from yard to yard, the birds on the branches. As he walked past each house, he could have named each of his neighbors, and usually list the past owners of the last thirty years. This had been his home for a long time. He could walk from here to campus without noticing a single detail, but today he noticed everything he could.

Walking to his front door he pressed the palm of his hand against the wood. He recognized his house as an old friend. It was a protector, a host, a witness, and a holder of his life and the life of his family for a generation.

As he walked into his home Mason noticed Mona knitting an afghan in the living room. He also smelled cigarette smoke. He sat down in the chair across from her without taking his coat off.

"Cold, dear?" she asked.

"I'm always cold these days. Are you smoking again?" he asked with a frown.

"Just a little." Mona smiled at him. "Leave it alone, Buster. This is between me and Virginia Slims."

Mason nodded, his mouth open, a wordless response. He could never make Mona do anything against her will, yet somehow she had always given him the impression that he was always right. He wondered how she did it. However she did it, it worked.

"I was thinking, on my walk, I was thinking of getting one more article out."

Mona looked up from her knitting, her lap a riot of red, black and gold fabric. "What's the topic?" she asked.

"I'm thinking about an article on dreams and film."

"Films that are about dreams?"

Mason sat back in the chair. "No, more like films are to the culture as dreams are to the individual."

"Films are the culture's way of dreaming? That's an interesting idea. How so?" she asked.

"There's an old quote by Lao Tzu, he said he'd dreamed about being a butterfly, but when he woke up he wondered if he might be a butterfly, dreaming about being a man," said Mason.

"I like that," said Mona. "What's a dream and what's real?"

"Yes. Do we dream about our lives or are our lives manifestations of our dreams?"

Mona pursed her lips. She was used to being Mason's sounding board, and her questioning helped him to clarify and define the scope of his writing.

"So give me an example. How does this apply to films? Work one out for me."

"Okay," said Mason, leaning forward. "Let's take *Gone with the Wind,* for instance. This film was a near archetype for the World War II generation. It resonated with them as a metaphor of a time when people were arising from the ashes of the Great Depression. And the sense of personal drama being played against a backdrop of history, the sense of personal loss as a necessity. Scarlett O'Hara's initial selfishness was like a frame of the Jazz Age, before the Depression. See, if an individual had this dream, the connections between real life and the dream would be obvious."

"It doesn't really have a happy ending though, does it?" asked Mona.

"No, it doesn't. But it does have hope. And dreams don't always have a happy ending. The ones that stick with us are often the ones that are the most distressing."

"You have a point there, Buster."

"So," Mason reflected, "If an individual had a dream like *Gone with the Wind*, we could appreciate these themes in their own life: romance, choice, coming of age, love, loss, determination, and mission. What if that individual felt moved to volunteer to fight a war against fascism? Did the dream inspire the action, or was the action predetermined by the spirit of the dream?"

"You'll have to work on that part. Maybe quote some philosopher. You're good at that," suggested Mona, her eyes returning to her knitting.

"Or how about a dream, I mean a movie from the next generation? Like *The Godfather*?"

"Another blockbuster."

"Well, those are the dreams, the films that most people related to. So, Coppola was telling the story of a young idealistic man, who wished more than anything to break away from his family's history of blood and corruption, but found himself drawn into the midst of it by his own love and loyalty, and finally by a wish for revenge. It's a morality tale, written in the soil of Vietnam and played out against America's backslide into colonialism."

Mona interrupted him. "But wasn't *The Godfather* released before Vietnam was over?"

"Right," said Mason. "But Coppola did something unheard of in those days. He made a sequel. Like—" his eyes lit up, "Like a recurring dream!"

Mona smiled at him.

"The themes are generational, destiny versus free will, the need to choose, and the cost of choosing against our best, highest selves."

"Another nightmare," said Mona. "But why is that film so popular with men?"

"Probably the father thing," said Mason. "All men want to live up to their father's legacy, or try to live it down. Sometimes both. For Pacino, I mean Corleone, it was both."

"You might be on to something," said Mona. "So what if America was a person, and they had a recurring dream like *The Godfather*?"

"These would be pretty dark dreams. They're really like a warning: What happens when you betray your ideals? It's just a series of betrayals. And it ends, the second movie, it ends with brother killing brother. It's practically Old Testament."

"The third one didn't do so well, did it?" asked Mona.

"You never saw it, did you?"

"No, Buster, I did not. I got tired of all the blood."

"Thematically the finale is of a piece with the other two films, but it was flawed in a number of ways. The script was supposed to be operatic, but it ended up grandiose. Pacino overacted horribly. Just chewed up the scenery. And as much as I like Sofia as a director, she didn't belong in *The Godfather*. But, like I said, the themes are in line. The cost of corruption is nihilism."

"You've lost me there, Buster."

"Put more bluntly, once you get in bed with the devil, sooner or later he's going to want to screw."

"Isn't that the truth. Say, Buster, do you mind if I smoke?"

Mason opened his mouth, looked at Mona, then shrugged his shoulders. "Why not? I already have cancer."

Holly was making cookies with her sponsor at Holly's house. The warmth of the oven, the Christmas carols playing on the radio, and the small Christmas tree on the table in the living room were all cozy reminders of the season.

"So how's it going with Jake?" asked Martha.

Holly told Martha she thought Jake was really taking the program seriously. He seemed committed to staying sober.

"Are you guys going to meetings together?"

"Only on the weekends. Since he works midnights we're really on opposite shifts from each other. So we can't see each other as much as we'd like to. Or maybe it's just enough."

"How are you feeling about it?" said Martha as she began frosting a batch of sugar cookies.

"Oh, well, part of me says 'take it slow' and another part of me says 'I'm in love,' so what's an alcoholic to do?"

"Usually we'll go with what feels good," suggested Martha.

"Do you think that's wrong?" asked Holly.

"No, not wrong. It's just worth watching. The thing I always watch in my relationships—and I've had plenty of failed relationships, let me tell you—is that my heart overrules my head. Every time. And I always end up wishing I had listened to my head."

They kept frosting cookies and Holly went to change the station on the radio. She stopped when she heard a Bonnie Raitt tune.

"By the way, congratulations," said Martha.

"For what?" asked Holly.

"For being in a relationship, as hard as it always is and as difficult as they are. Even though they haven't worked for me—or at least not yet—I just wanted to congratulate you because this is the best time of all, the early days. It's like being drunk on love, isn't it?"

"Yeah, I guess so."

"Are you ever not thinking about Jake?" asked Martha.

"Sometimes. Sometimes in meetings, or at work."

"So how's work? That guy still locked up?"

"Yeah, he is. And he should remain locked up for a while, is what they're suggesting. I got word from the prison that they're going to do a psych eval on him. They're suspecting OCD because of his behavior in prison."

"OCD?" asked Martha.

"Oh, obsessive compulsive disorder. It's a psychiatric diagnosis. He has to do certain rituals and can't bend them without freaking out."

"So that's why he was stalking you?"

"I don't know. I think he was stalking me because he was an asshole."

"But I bet it's a big relief. Does it make your job easier?"

"You know, it's a funny thing. At first I felt really happy, giddy. But I've been thinking, 'What a horrible way to make a living.' I mean, this is important work and somebody has to do it, but it doesn't have to be me, does it?" asked Holly.

"Does it?" asked Martha.

"What do you mean?"

"I'm Catholic. I know what penance is," said Martha.

"What are you suggesting? You're starting to sound like my therapist."

"Well, I was wondering if there was anything that you never talked about in your fifth step. I mean, you had a very typical kind of fifth step, but I've wondered from time to time if you've kept any secrets."

"Why would you say that?" asked Holly, incredulous.

"I don't know," said Martha, innocently, frosting another cookie. "All these nightmares you've had. Dreams of dead babies and being persecuted. Made me wonder if there was something you've been ashamed of and never talked about." Martha looked Holly in the eye and said, "Know what I mean?"

Holly dropped her knife and got a faraway look in her eye.

"Oh, my God," Holly said.

"What?" asked Martha.

"Oh, my God. There is something. It wasn't even like I was hiding it, it was just something I never thought I'd ever talk about."

Holly began to cry.

"Holly, you need to talk about it. All the literature in A.A. talks about how we need to let it out. No more secrets."

"I know, I know," said Holly.

"If you keep it inside you could drink over it."

"I know, I know."

Martha gave Holly a tissue and went over and gave her a hug. "C'mon. This really upsets you, doesn't it?"

Holly took a deep breath. Before she started talking she blew her nose.

"When I was a student, I was doing an internship in another county, for the state, working with Protective Services. I went with another worker, we went out to investigate a case and the worker was interviewing the mother. I was talking with a little boy, who was about five years old. And he told me about something. He told me about how his mother would sit on him sometimes and how he couldn't breathe. But he made me promise not to tell. He told me not to tell because his mom would hurt him."

"Isn't that normal?" asked Martha.

"Yes. But I didn't tell. I never told the worker. She cleared the mom, and I never told her what happened."

"So what happened to that case?"

"I don't know. I have no idea. I don't know if that kid was okay, or scarred, or killed, or what."

Martha sighed. "Do you know why you didn't tell?"

"I don't know," said Holly.

"You were raised in an alcoholic household, Holly. You were used to not telling secrets."

Holly started sobbing again. "But it was my job to tell. I can still see his face. He was so scared."

Martha held Holly at arm's length and said, "Holly, you have to pull yourself together here."

Holly started to sniff.

"Okay. Now you've told someone. How's it feel?"

"I feel ashamed."

"What are you going to do about it?" asked Martha.

"I don't know."

"Well, in the program we have to make direct amends, wherever possible. So what's your amends?"

"I don't know."

"Okay. Let me think." Martha got up and took another batch of cookies from the oven and set them on the counter to cool. Holly dried her eyes. Her breathing slowly evened out and she held the gaze of her sponsor. Finally Martha spoke.

"Do you remember the name of the family?"

"Yes."

"How long ago was this?"

Holly let herself think. She had been a student, which meant she was still married and still drinking. She thought about the year she graduated and subtracted a year from that.

"It was ten years ago," she said.

"So, you can find out if there have been other new cases filed against the mom, using your contacts and the stuff you have access on with the computer?"

"Yes."

"So do that. And look up that boy and find out if he's getting the kind of care that he needs, make sure he's okay."

"I can do that." Holly looked at Martha and marveled at her strength and wisdom. She thought, *I'm lucky to have her in my life.*

"And then don't keep secrets."

"Okay. I can try to do that."

"There is no 'try,' there is only 'do' or 'not do.'"

"Yes, Yoda," said Holly, smiling.

"So when are you going to do this?"

"Tomorrow at work. No more secrets?"

"No. No more. Not one. Boundaries, yes, but secrets, no."

"Okay. I have always felt guilty that I never returned your Kasey Chambers CD," said Holly.

"You have that? I've been looking all over for it. That's right, I gave it to you after the party, didn't I? So give it back, won'cha?"

Jake was sitting in an A.A. meeting at the Alano Club.

The room was half filled with about a dozen men and five women. Four cafeteria-style tables were been pushed together to make a rectangle, in the center of the room. There were about twenty wooden chairs around the table and then another thirty or so that circled the outside wall. About half the seats at the table were taken, with a few people sitting against the wall.

Jake was just off work and feeling tired. He had coffee in a Styrofoam cup and was chewing a plastic straw to keep from smoking. He decided to attend a non-smoking meeting today, which was new for him.

He was listening to the chair of the meeting start her sharing to get the meeting going. She was a woman in her early thirties and nicely dressed. First there was the prayer, then the readings, then the woman spoke.

"I'm Anne and I'm an alcoholic."

"Hi, Anne," recited the group. Jake smiled. He couldn't get over how corny it seemed. He also recognized that when they did it for him he felt welcomed.

"This is a topic meeting and I've been trying to think about what to talk about, and I decided that a good topic would be 'resentments.' Bill W. wrote that 'Resentments are the number one offender' in terms of triggering alcoholic's relapses or even 'dry drunks,' and I think that's true for me.

"The other day I was going to a store in East Lansing and I went into a parking lot. Well, I had just pulled in and the ticket had just been issued from the little meter machine, when a guy pulls in behind me and I hear this 'beep.' I was pissed off right away and I'm looking in my mirror thinking, 'Come on, give me a break!' So I pull in, but I watch where this guy is going. And he parks just a few cars away, so I decide to get out and give him a piece of my mind. But I catch myself, and think, 'Y'know Anne, maybe he thought he knew you, which would be another explanation for why he would be honking at you.'"

"So I decide to give him the benefit of the doubt and I walk up to him, and he's just some young college kid and I say, 'Excuse me, do you know me?' And he's looking a little sheepish, and I think 'Gotcha!' cause he knows now that he's been the asshole."

"So he says, 'No, I don't think so.' And I say, 'Oh, well I thought that YOU thought that you must know me,' and now I'm feeling like De Niro in *Taxi Driver*, you know, like, 'You lookin' at me?' and the kid is starting to back away and I'm feeling really good about myself, like, 'Thought so, punk!' And I go about my way, but then I'm thinking, 'Anne, you're confronting total strangers in parking lots. Is that what the program teaches you?' so I almost go back to make an amends, but decide that I should just leave him alone."

"So later in the day I have to go back to the same store to get some other present that I missed and I pull into the same lot, press the same button, a ticket comes out and I can't believe it, the same obnoxious 'beep!' So I turn around, half expecting to see the same car, and there's no one there! It's the sound the machine makes when the ticket comes out!"

"So, 'What does this have to do with alcoholism or recovery,' you ask? Just this: I made it all up in my head. I made it up that someone was disrespecting me, I made it up that someone was doing something at my expense, I made it up that someone was victimizing me. I made up the whole thing, out of a 'beep' that a machine made. And I thought, 'If I do that with a beep, what do I do with a sigh or rolling eyes, or someone's tone of voice, or something else that has hardly anything to do with me? So, I think that's the point. We alcoholics can be overly sensitive. Our thinking can get out of whack and we can start looking outside of ourselves for a target. So with that, I think today we'll start outside the circle and go to the new guy. How's it going, Jake?"

The group mumbled, 'Thanks Anne,' to acknowledge her lead, then shifted in their chairs to look at Jake.

Jake always hated this moment. He was trying to listen to what was said in the meeting, while figuring out what he was going to say. And then, when his time came, he would become blank. Now, that everyone in the room seemed to be looking at him, he seemed surprised that it was his turn. He decided to go with the first thing on his mind.

"Oh. I'm Jake, I'm an alcoholic," said Jake and the group said, "Hi, Jake."

"I would usually just pass, but something about what you said caught me. Maybe it was the movie reference, because Travis Bickle has always been one of my heroes, which is probably a character flaw in itself. But it made me think of another line in another movie—the first *Batman* with Jack Nicholson, where he's the Joker. And Batman has just come and messed up his day, which, of course, involved mayhem and robbery. But he says, 'I have found a name for my pain and that name is Batman.' I always thought that was profound. So I try to watch that. Because I do have a lot of resentments and I haven't gotten as far as the steps that start dealing with that. I just try not to drink every day and so far it's working. I come to a meeting every day and I don't drink that day. That really works. But one thing I'm finding out, I'm filled with all kinds of emotion. I didn't have a clue. I get sad. I get scared. I get really pissed off. And it would be really easy to blame someone rather than just 'deal,' y'know? So that's all I got."

"Thanks, Jake," said the group.

After the meeting Jake went home and pulled out his "Ballads" CD that he'd burned from his LP. He threw it on his system, and as Monk's "Ask Me Now" began to play, he made some tea. He had picked up one of the Detroit newspapers and the local paper, and slipped them in his microwave, setting it on high for one minute. The papers came out hot. He spread out on the couch with his tea, his long legs draped over the length of his couch, the hot papers in his lap.

Jake took his time with the papers, growing drowsy as he perused the Detroit Sports page—another disappointing year for the Lions, but the Pistons looked good. Once he got to the Lansing paper he was beginning to nod out. In the court section he barely noticed that William Thomas was held over at a hearing for a trial and he wondered if this was the Gordon guy who had been pestering him and Holly.

It didn't take long, somewhere between Mingus' "Goodbye Pork Pie Hat" and Bill Evan's "A Child Is Born," Jake dozed off lying on the big couch. Soon he was snoring.

Jake is floating in a boat, the music is the water around him and the water is the music, and his boat is made of newspaper. He's carried from conscious thought to the random images of dreams, then he gives himself to it, almost with a smile, gives himself up to drifting in the ether, how much the experience of sleep reminds him of drugs without drugs, of time without time.

His boat is caught in a current, and buoyed along a river beneath the city, a labyrinth of tunnels that make him think of a scene from Lon Chaney's Phantom of the Opera, *amazing how much Lansing can seem like the underground of Paris, but he is floating downtown. He can't tell how he knows it is downtown, but he knows there is a river that he will cross, and knows somehow he must cross over and that the police station, city hall and the Capitol building will all be coming soon, just drifting, until he notices the gumball lights of an entrance that has to be LPD—the Lansing Police Department. Jake floating towards it, wondering if he might be called to explain himself, but the boat moves into the small inlet and Jake finds himself carried in, the boat seeming to direct itself. He sees against the stone walls torches that illuminate another figure, and it is Gordon, trying to start the engine of a big fan boat he has seen in the swamps of Florida. He wonders if there might be alligators in the sewers of Lansing. His boat has apparently docked close to that of Gordon Thomas's and he notices that Gordon is so engaged with starting his motor that he hasn't seen Jake, and Jake has the element of surprise, and there is a big gun made of bone, that looks like a pirate's pistol, but slightly longer, almost the length of a sawed off shotgun, next to Gordon's legs. And Jake reaches over and picks it up before Gordon looks down at him with a look of surprise and raw hatred. Jake aims the gun at Gordon and says, "It's over. Give up."*

Gordon says, "You should have killed me when you had the chance." He reaches into the pocket of his orange jump suit and pulls out a large bowie knife. Jake knows immediately that he is going to pierce the paper of his boat and that he will sink. Gordon reaches down and cuts his boat and Jake feels the cut of the knife across his chest, even though he hasn't been cut himself, he sees the red line extend from left to right, nipple height. He peels it off like a string of licorice and says, "Eat it," to Gordon, but Gordon says "That's yours, I've got my own." Jake feels the boat sinking. I have one shot, *thinks Jake as the boat sinks. He wonders if the water is deep or cold and he holds the red line in one hand and the gun in the other. He just can't pull the trigger. Jake is sinking further into the water* and he startled awake. Then he wrote it down.

The week before Christmas caught Michigan in a snow storm. The blizzard dumped six inches of snow over the city, which wreaked havoc with drivers. Emma would have cancelled the group if the snowing had continued, but by the evening, the main roads were cleared and Emma checked her messages to see if anyone had cancelled. No one had.

Mason was wearing a heavy, down coat, and Emma felt touched that he'd shown up. Marianne was next, followed by Jake and Holly, who arrived together.

At the start of the group, Emma complimented the group on fighting the snow. It was a sign of their commitment that they had showed up at all. It occurred to her that the group had become important to them in some way, even to Marianne, who was still ambivalent about sticking with it.

Emma mentioned that she was open to canceling the group that was scheduled between Christmas and New Years, but everyone said they'd just as soon meet. Jake mentioned that he was going to get some overtime hours, since some of the hospital staff would be traveling over the holidays. Jake also mentioned that he had a dream he'd like to discuss.

During the rest of the check-in, Marianne wondered if being on anti-depressants might effect one's ability to dream. Emma offered to stick around after the group was over to look up side effects in her physician's desk reference manual. Marianne said that would be helpful.

Emma noticed that Marianne seemed lighter in her moods. She thought that the meds must be helping.

Then she asked Mason how he'd been feeling.

"I've been writing," he said, "which is good and also bittersweet, because I was thinking about how much more I'd like to do, but this is probably my last article. It's on dreams, and I'll bring you all a copy before our last group."

Emma said she'd really like to see it.

"I'm also beginning to feel some pain," Mason said, and grimaced. "I'm not in pain at the moment. I'm just remembering. I'm on painkillers and I have access to a morphine patch, if I want it, but I'm trying to resist that and stay as alert as I possibly can. I'm tired. I'm not eating."

"I thought you looked a little drawn," said Jake. Emma noticed his voice crack with that last word.

"That's a good word for it," said Mason. "I look at my reflection and I'm surprised, although I don't know why I should be. The doctors have been helpful, but it's really just a matter of time. It's always been just a matter of time. But, having said that, it's a matter of time for all of us—and all of you as well. I just have a better sense of how much time there is left for me. And I'm still—it's difficult to say—mixed. I get sad, and sad isn't really a good word for it. Despair is a good word. And at other times I feel so lucky to draw another breath, to see the snowfall, to feel the air in my lungs, to hear a child's voice. It's an amazing miracle, life is. And I've lived a blessed life. So, enough about me, I came tonight to hear your dreams."

Emma asked if anyone had any response to what Mason had said.

"Yes," said Marianne. "I'd like to say that I wish I could do something for you."

"You have," said Mason. "You have done something for me. Just by being here."

"Somehow, it just doesn't seem like enough," said Marianne.

"You know what I'm realizing?" asked Mason. "It's all that there is. Just being present. Showing up for each other, that's really the stuff life is made up of."

Holly sighed and said, "You seem so brave to me."

"This isn't bravery," laughed Mason. "Please don't make me into a hero. This is just showing up for life. You know, death is a lot like life, you just face it the way you do another day, I think. But I appreciate your thought, Holly. You're a sweetheart."

Jake said that he didn't know what to say. Mason nodded his head at Jake, and Jake began to cry.

Holly moved to comfort Jake, but Emma caught her eye and shook her head.

"Holly, it's okay. Jake's okay."

Jake started to weep. "It doesn't feel okay," he said. "It hurts."

"Where does it hurt, Jake," asked Emma.

Jake pointed to his chest.

"That's right," said Emma, her voice soothing. "Right in the heart. It's just pain, Jake, good clean pain. It won't kill you. Just feel it. Feel it and let it go."

Jake took a deep breath and stopped his sobs. "I'm sorry."

Mason said, "No need to apologize. I know what you mean."

The group laughed and Emma said, "The pain that is connected to grief is just another version of love. I think it's important to feel it, to express it."

Marianne, with tears in her own eyes, said "So feelings are—"

"Natural," finished Emma. "And they help us. Even the hard ones. That's why I think it's important to try to feel what they are and hear what they're telling us."

"I see. I'm touched," said Marianne, dabbing her eyes. "I'm not sure how to express it and it seems really strange to me, but I have come to care for you, Mason, and you, Jake, and Holly, and even Ms. Davis. And this has happened over such a very few meetings. I'm not sure why."

"It's not uncommon," said Emma, "in this kind of group, where we're letting ourselves be vulnerable with each other, where we're revealing so much of ourselves. And this has been—"

"Pretty intense. I think it's been life and death. I think about getting the news of Mason's cancer and Jake getting into recovery," said Marianne.

"It has been intense, hasn't it?" said Emma. "It was so touching to hear of you all going to dinner the other night."

"That was a gift," agreed Mason. He opened his mouth to speak. The rest of the group edged forward to hear what he was about to say. He became aware of the silence and smiled.

"But, that's what life is, isn't it?" Mason asked, finally. "Getting something you hadn't planned for? Or not getting what it was that you thought you wanted?"

Emma realized that everyone in the group had wet eyes except for Mason. She decided to forge ahead. "Jake, you said you had a dream you wanted to discuss?"

Jake was looking at Mason. He absently groped his jacket pockets and then remembered.

"Yeah. I wrote it down, but I didn't bring it with me. But that's all right. I remember most of it." Jake looked up at the ceiling and started to remember his dream. "I was in a boat, made of newspaper and it was floating in a subterranean chamber under the streets of Lansing, heading towards the Capitol building. And I had to pass the police station. And the guy, Gordon Thomas, the guy who had been stalking Holly and attacked us both, he was like escaping from the police station. He was wearing an orange jump suit and he was trying to get away in a boat, one of those boats that just skims the water, like in the everglades, with a big fan on the back—"

"We know what you mean," said Mason.

"Anyway, he didn't see me, and I snuck up behind him and took his gun, and it was just a big old pirate pistol, but it was made out of bone. Then he saw me and took out a knife and I wanted to blow him away, you know? I just wanted to shoot him and for some reason, I couldn't." Jake was frowning.

"Do you know why you couldn't?" asked Holly.

"I'm not sure."

"Think about it," said Emma. "Or better yet, feel about it. The answer you come up with doesn't even have to make sense."

He closed his eyes for a moment and took a breath. "Because it would be wrong. You shouldn't kill. You shouldn't ever kill," said Jake.

"Okay. Good. Anything else?"

"No," said Jake. "The dream ended there."

"Any thoughts?" Emma asked the group.

"I have some thoughts," said Jake, "but I wanted to hear from you and everyone else before I went into what I thought."

Emma asked the group what they would have made of this dream, if they had it themselves. Marianne was the first to answer.

"I would have been frustrated. I think that any time, in a dream, where I can't accomplish what I've set out to do, I think of that as a kind of a failure."

"Okay, who else?"

Holly said "Well, I know this guy a little bit and to me it would have been a nightmare."

"Was it to you, Jake?" asked Emma. "Was it a nightmare?"

"Well, I'm kind of an expert on nightmares, because I've had so many," he smiled, "and on the grand scale of things, I would have to say no."

"Okay," said Emma. "So we have 'frustration' and we have 'fear.' Mason, do you have any thoughts?"

Mason looked thoughtfully at Jake. "I think it would have been about not killing someone, like Jake just said. The dream was taking him deep, into an area he'd never been, and there was his arch nemesis, with some kind of ancient weapon, which Jake wielded and he finally just couldn't literally pull the trigger. It's like an archetype. You can't kill your enemy, because he's that thing deep inside you. It's what you fight all the time. He can't die as long as you're alive. And this guy represents that for Jake. He's cruel and crazy, and Jake is wonderfully kind and only a little crazy."

Jake smiled.

"Okay," said Emma, "Jake, what do you think?"

"Oh, no, Emma. You didn't tell me what you thought."

"Oh, my associations were much like what you've heard so far. Only, I was very interested in the boats."

"The boats?" asked Jake.

Emma said, "You're on a boat made of newspapers. It is what carries you. Are you much of a reader, Jake?"

"Yes, I am. More so, a lot more so, now that I've stopped polluting my brain."

"Interesting. And did your boat have a motor?"

"No. It just seemed to know where to go."

"And his boat, Gordon Thomas's?"

"Was the power boat."

"But that's not how you described it," said Emma.

"It skims the surface," said Jake.

"Which means—" she prompted, leaning forward.

"There's no depth," Jake said, and his eyes got big.

"Exactly. My association was that there is one way of being in the world, Gordon Thomas's way, which is suitable in the swamps and the shallows, but your vessel is meant for a deeper way of living, which seems intuitive and yet based on knowledge."

"You get all that from the boats, huh?" asked Marianne.

"Just my associations. Doesn't mean that they're right."

"Or even that there is a right answer," said Holly.

"Exactly."

There were a few moments of silence, and again Emma noticed the ease the group had developed in their own reflection. The silence was palpable and respectful.

She looked at Jake and nodded her head, and he said, "I thought, a lot like Mason, although he put it better than I'm able. I thought about the shadow self—that Gordon is a part of me that I can't kill, a part that feels anger and is something of a pirate. I can't fully take on the pirate role, but I can't kill it, either."

"I like that," said Emma.

Holly said that there was something she'd like to talk about.

The group all turned their attention towards her. Emma thought Holly looked a little pensive.

"Well, I think I've had a breakthrough. At least, something like a breakthrough. I think there is something that I haven't been honest about for a long time, and I think that my dead baby dreams have been connected to this situation I had when I was a student. There was a case, I don't need to get into all the details, but there was a case involving child abuse, where I should have reported something in an investigation, and I didn't. I think, now I know, I was scared."

"I think it's interesting that you have worked so hard to be fearless," said Mason.

"What do you mean?" asked Holly.

"This whole situation with the guy that Jake was dreaming about, I've been struck by how much courage you've displayed."

"I guess I have," said Holly.

"So, what helped you make this breakthrough?" asked Emma.

"I was talking with my sponsor, and it just kind of popped out."

"Had you forgotten it?" Emma asked.

"No. In fact, I think about it a lot."

"But you've decided to start talking about it."

"Talking about it, and I want to look this kid up and see if he's okay and see if there's anything I can do."

"Why now?" asked Emma.

"Because if he's—"

"No, I'm sorry, I wasn't clear. Not about the boy, but what shifted inside of you that you can talk about it now?" clarified Emma.

"I'm not sure. There's a saying in A.A.—'We're only as sick as our secrets.' And this was a secret that had me. And I was tired of holding on to it."

"You felt ashamed," said Emma.

"Yes, I did."

"How do you feel now?"

"Better," said Holly. She took a deep breath and unconsciously stroked her red hair. "I think about what Marianne said, about how close I feel to all of you. And what everyone has faced up to. How Jake is working on his recovery, and I know firsthand what a bitch that is. And Mason, I can't even imagine how hard that would be. So, if you're all working so hard to face something, why can't I face my shame?"

"Well put," said Emma.

"You didn't mention what I'm facing," said Marianne.

"Well, you don't usually tell us what you're facing," said Holly. "I'm sorry, I hope that wasn't too blunt. I know you're depressed. But you keep us out, out of your life. I feel like I know what's going on, though. It's written all over your face." Holly looked at Marianne and said, "You're scared as hell."

"I guess you're right," said Marianne.

"But I don't know why," said Holly.

"I guess I'm not sure myself. I do know that I went through a very dark time, very recently, and I started to take the anti-depressant medications and I'm feeling better. I'm starting to feel more hopeful."

"Maybe, I don't mean to be pushy," said Holly.

"No, go ahead, say it."

"Maybe you can start trusting us. Maybe you can open up a little."

"Maybe so," said Marianne. "Let me think about it."

"You can sleep on it," suggested Emma.

The next morning the snow lay on the ground like a blanket. Inside the large Department of Social Services building, Holly's cubicle sat in the middle of an enormous room, in the midst of dozens of other cubicles. The air was filled with the buzzing of phones and conversations, and in the background was Christmas Muzak. Holly was at work finding the boy. Since she remembered his name, had a good idea of his age, and had access to files on all past clients of the agency, she had high hopes of being able to find him. She also had contacts who still worked in the rural county, where she'd been working at the time.

Holly also had something else going for her. She was an investigator.

She first looked up Phil Hooks but found nothing. Next, Holly looked up the parents. Norm and Elaine Hooks. Norm was deceased, but this wasn't all that long ago. After finding out the date of his death, she searched the obits online and found that there were requests for donations to the American Lung Society. Another smoker, she guessed. A "Phil Boone" was listed as a surviving son, but there was no mention of Elaine.

Elaine Hooks was a little harder to find, and it was her temper that her son Phil was trying to avoid. She'd been remarried to an Arthur Boone, and he was employed by General Motors. There had been no further cases open on Elaine or Arthur.

Holly tried looking for Phil Boone, wondering if Arthur had adopted the boy. Again, no luck. Nothing on the State of Michigan record, anyway.

Holly realized that she was avoiding the obvious. She knew that Phil would be fifteen years old and the good news was he wasn't in 'the system,' not a part of any investigation, not institutionalized. All good news.

Holly called the school counselor at Howell high school. Howell was about forty-five minutes from Lansing, but had become a bedroom community of Detroit, even though it was fifty miles away. She knew that some schools had already started their holiday break, but with luck, she might be able to reach the counselor. Her luck was good.

The counselor was not immediately in, and Holly left a voice message. Then she started returning phone calls from her stack of unanswered voice mails. While she was setting up a meeting with an attorney where she was scheduled to testify, Holly saw a call come in from the Howell area code. She interrupted the attorney to ask, "Can I call you right back?"

Holly was anxious when a male voice said, "This is Steve Jones from Howell school district. You called, and I called you back."

Holly bent the rules a little bit. She explained that she was involved in an investigation and was ruling out victims of a possible abuse case. She asked if Phil Hooks was a student at the school.

The social worker at the school said that was protected information but Holly reminded him that it wasn't in the case of a Protective Service investigation. Steve Jones said, "Yes, he is a student here."

Holly wanted to say, "Is he okay?" but restrained herself to ask if Mr. Jones had any contact with this student.

Mr. Jones said that he did and that there was nothing spectacular or notable in the student's conduct, nor did he notice any symptoms of abuse.

Holly thanked him for the information and then called Martha.

"He's alive and he's in high school and he's okay," said Holly. "Or at least, a school counselor thinks he's okay."

"Great. Are you relieved?" asked Martha.

"Yeah. A little. Do you think I should visit him, or pay for therapy, or do something—"

"Heroic? No, not at all," said Martha. "I think that this amends is a living amends, and that means you change how you are today. You don't stir up trouble from the past. This might be more damaging to him today, for you to go to him, than it would be for you to leave it alone."

"Do you really think so?" asked Holly.

"Holly, how would I know? I don't have any idea. I just think that you've been torturing yourself over this situation for a long time and it turned out that the kid survived and you survived and maybe you should just let it go and do your job the best you can."

"I guess you're right. Okay. Thanks Martha."

After Holly hung up with Martha she thought about the boy, Phil Hooks, and thought about the number of times that she didn't look the other way, didn't give up or cover up, stood in the face of angry and sometimes dangerous parents or other adults who were harming children. Maybe she'd been wrong sometimes. But she knew that in her career, she tended to err on the side of being overly thorough, and she had never glossed over or turfed out a case.

Holly took out a pen and wrote the name "Phil" on a piece of paper, then tore the name out of the page until it was little more than a couple of inches long. She opened her desk drawer and pulled out a small aluminum box that had held Altoid breath mints, which she had painted red and in white acrylic had written the words "God Box." She placed the name in the box, where it joined several other small slips of paper.

CHAPTER FIFTEEN

For Jake, work was busier than usual. First,there was an admission. Then a patient was up and wanted to talk—a depressed gentleman who was scheduled to start electro-convulsive therapy the next day and wasn't sure he had made the right decision to go along with the therapy. They talked for nearly a half hour before he went back to bed. Then one of the schizophrenics on the locked ward began to act up. The youngest psych tech on the shift had been scheduled back in the locked area and didn't have enough experience to know how to talk the patient down. Now it escalated to the point where the tech had pressed the "panic button."

The panic button, as it was informally called, set off a buzzer and flashing lights and meant that someone was in a life or death situation. Jake saw the lights flash first, which meant that the buzzer would start in the next few flashes. To keep the rest of the thirty eight patients on the floor asleep, Jake knew he needed to hit the button in the next few seconds.

Jake moved across the lobby to the big locked door in just a few long strides, silently except for his keys jingling on his belt, then in his hand. The charge nurse appeared at the door and said "Jake?" as his hand went to the door. He motioned her and said, "I've got it. Don't worry."

As Jake entered the dark hallway that was the intensive care area of the psych hospital, he immediately heard some commotion in the day room. As he turned the corner he took in the scene in a glance. Francis, the new tech, was standing on a table in the center of the room. He was holding a chair in front of him like a lion tamer. The schizophrenic patient, a young, athletic looking male with flowing dark hair, was on all fours and was growling like a dog.

Jake hit the button maybe a second before the buzzer was going to start. His first words were to the tech.

"We need to keep things quiet for the other dogs!" he whispered intently and then to the patient, "Isn't that right, boy?"

The patient snarled at Jake but looked a little confused that Jake was intervening towards the other staff person and not him.

"I think I have a biscuit here," said Jake as he reached in his pocket. To Francis he said, "Why don't you get down off that table, real slow, and put down that chair?"

Francis lowered the chair to the floor and then climbed off the table, opposite where the patient was now sniffing the air, with one hand raised as a paw.

"I must have left the biscuit with my friend. Francis, tell Judy to bring back a nice Thorazine dog biscuit and I'll help this doggie warn the others when strangers approach. That okay with you boy?" asked Jake.

The patient began to softly bark.

"Good boy."

After the nurse had given the patient another shot, the new tech asked Jake, "How did you know what to do?"

"You know, it's just a lot of experience. I've spent years and years working with schizophrenics, and I learn pretty quickly what's going on in their world and just enter into it to maneuver around. Like that guy thinking he was a dog."

"Right. He came crawling into the day room."

"So he wakes up in the middle of the night, and he's disoriented. Hell, he's psychotic, and he thinks he's a dog. So, what is he?"

"He's not a dog."

"No, not to you or me, but he thinks he is. And if he is, and he sees a stranger in his territory—"

"He'd want to defend it," said Francis.

"Yeah. So he needs to know you aren't a threat. He sees you getting ready to defend yourself and it's 'fight or flight,' y'know?"

"So you didn't act scared or aggressive."

"Being calm, no matter what, is half the battle."

After work Jake was tired. Not tired so much, he realized, as exhausted. He went to his morning meeting and was relieved to see Nick at the club. Then he remembered it was a Saturday morning.

As usual, the club was smoky. He saw Nick sitting at one of the booths with some writing in front of him. Jake bought a cup of coffee, nodded at some of the people he recognized, and approached Nick.

"How's it going," said Nick, more as a statement than as a question.

"Ehhh," replied Jake in a kind of non-committal grunt.

"Fucked up is fucked up," said Nick.

"You know what makes me sick and tired?" asked Jake rhetorically, about to go off into a rant.

"I think I have a good idea. It's why you're here, isn't it? It's why we're all here. Have a seat. We have a few minutes before the meeting."

Jake sat down and looked into the Styrofoam coffee cup. The steam at the top of the coffee was swirling. He thought for a moment and then began to speak.

"Besides being alcoholic. I'm sick of my job. I'm sick of babysitting newbies who don't know anything about anything about schizophrenics. I'm sick of seeing doctors walk in and pick up a couple of hundred dollars for spending three minutes asking patients if they're sleeping, while I'm making less than a tenth of that an hour."

"Hate your work? Join the club. Most people do."

"Thanks for the sympathy, Nick," said Jake with a sneer.

"Oooh, that's a little hostile."

"Well, maybe I'm a little pissed off. I'm just starting to realize that I've spent ten years of my life in this dead-end job while the friends I started with have gone on to grad school and now they're therapists or psychiatrists or lawyers, and I'm living in a stinkin' four-room flat—" His voice was getting louder.

"Jake, I'd like to you take a breath," suggested Nick.

Jake breathed, but his eyes had a new intensity.

"Okay, I know this is hard to accept, but all alcoholics start to realize how much of their life they've pissed away once they've been in the program for a little while," said Nick, in a near whisper.

"That's not what I wanted to hear."

"What did you want to hear?" asked Nick.

"That my situation is—"

"Different?" asked Nick.

"Well, yes." answered Jake.

"Or how about 'special'? Does that fit?"

"Okay."

"There's nothing special about your suffering Jake. There's nothing different than anyone else's. Listen to people around the table today. Your suffering is ordinary," said Nick.

"That doesn't seem right. It doesn't seem fair."

"No, it doesn't. Believe me, we—all of us, every damn one of us—come in here thinking we're special cases. And we're not. Here's an exercise, if you're open to it."

"Okay," said Jake, now smiling sheepishly. He looked over his shoulder. No one seemed to be listening. In fact, most people were moving into the meeting room.

"Repeat this like a mantra every time you start complaining," suggested Nick, "'It's not about me.' Now you try it."

"It's not about Nick," answered Jake.

"See, that's why you have to practice it, because it's hard. 'It's not about me.' Now you try it."

"'It's not about me.' Do I have it right?" asked Jake.

"That's good. You get an 'A' for the morning."

"Is there anything I could do for extra credit?" asked Jake.

"Only if you're willing to leave Holly alone for a few months," said Nick.

"Ouch."

"I'm sorry. That was probably out of line. Your relationship with her bothers me, mainly because I'm afraid for both of you."

"Is it really that bad?" asked Jake.

"It's not 'bad.' Not like morally bad. It's not that. It's just that, relationships forged in the fire of early recovery are usually, well, they quite often lead to relapses."

"I'm listening in my head, but inside I'm saying, 'It's not about me.'"

"I knew this would backfire. C'mon, the meeting's about to start."

Gordon Thomas sat in his cell in the downtown police station. They were supposed to move him to the jail in Mason, but he'd heard a cop mumble something about overcrowding *or what not*, and he'd have to cool his jets in the downtown pokey.

They weren't letting him go, that was for sure. And he'd better find a way to get himself out quick.

Before they find the body.

Gordon stretched out on the thin jail mattress and looked over the cell. The iron bars, the windowless room, the flush ceiling and concrete floor, not even the toilet looked like an opportunity for escape.

Why didn't she just listen?

He heard the sounds of the cops, bullshitting about the holiday, no Santa for perps. He counted the times the doors opened or closed. He counted their steps and even their words. He counted the number or bars to his cell or the years he'd have to serve if they found her body before he escaped.

He was almost sure they hadn't found the body.

Gordon was pulled over for a stupid speeding ticket, and the cop, damn his luck, the cop had asked him to blow and said he saw a beer can in the back seat and had called for back up.

That's what happened, Gordon thought. *The cop got me for speeding, called in my license and found the warrant and called for help.* He didn't think to make a move with two armed troopers, but they also didn't look at the car like it was a crime scene. They didn't look in the trunk for a knife or for any blood evidence.

He'd changed his shirt, and his pants. But then Gordon remembered his goddamned boots.

He needed a plan.

So far no one had said anything about murder. The security was the same for anyone in a drunk tank. If they could just, *please God,* send him a woman transport officer or maybe a little guy.

If he could get out of this orange jump suit. *How the hell do you not stick out in downtown Lansing wearing this clown outfit? Wasn't there a clothing store nearby? Just pop in, grab a big top coat and run out? That could work. Knock down the first guy that gives me shit.*

Thinking about knocking guys down, Gordon remembered that pansy in the parking lot on Thanksgiving when he'd almost had the red head. That little piece of tail was almost his, and damned if she hadn't almost run him over. *Little spitfire.*

Gordon felt his pulse quicken when he thought of her. Before he was caught, he had been spending more and more time shadowing her. Holly. Holly Masters. The red head. He was almost sure she hadn't seen him. Maybe once or twice. It was a game he'd played as a kid, when he first learned to drive. Pick out a pretty girl at random and then see if he could follow her all the way home without her noticing. Then he'd started to think about following her inside, so he'd quit that little game. But now it was back. He would follow the red head around, imagining what it might be like to be with her, the things they could do together, the things he could do to her.

Of course, she wouldn't admit she wanted it. Probably call it rape. Gordon thought about killing her. What that would feel like. He'd never killed anybody before Brandi. It was different than he'd thought. He hadn't felt anything.

He didn't want to think about that. *Brandi was a good girl, just a little mixed up. Not any more. Poor Brandi.*

Gordon blamed the one person who was responsible for screwing up his life and Brandi's, and now he'd probably spend a life in jail because of her: Holly Masters. The red head. Little Missy. Little Spitfire. He knew where she lived, what she drove, where she worked—and even the name of her pussy boyfriend. Once he got out of this jail and by God he could do it, there would be one stop between here and the Canadian border. One thing he should have done a while ago.

Gordon heard the door at the end of the hall open and two officers, one man and a woman, stopped in front of his cell.

"Mr. Thomas," the woman said, "here are your clothes. You can change since we're going to take you to court."

He smiled at the officers and tried out his best *kiss-ass* voice. "Thank you, officers. Will I be able to go?"

"That'll be up to the judge," said the man. He was a little bigger than Gordon. Both of the officers were armed. "You've got a few charges against you. Operating a vehicle while drinking, plus some outstanding domestic charges."

"Shoot, I thought that had been dropped. I guess I screwed up pretty bad, huh? I'm sorry to put you officers through all this at the holidays and all." Gordon wondered if he could get himself to cry but decided that might be too much.

After he'd changed into his jeans and shirt he pulled on his boots. As close as he could tell there was no blood on them.

When the officers returned to the cell the man said to Gordon, "We're on our way to Mason. We usually handcuff our prisoners but you seem like an easygoing guy, and this is the holiday. Are we going to have any trouble?"

"No, sir, surely not. I'm just a good ol' boy and I don't want to make matters any worse."

They walked him through the station, using the back halls. The place was flooded with cops until they reached a garage.

"Wait here," said the male officer as he walked across a row of police cruisers and Gordon noticed the door maybe sixty feet away. It looked like it opened to an alleyway. The female officer was the only thing between him and freedom, and maybe thirty seconds before her partner pulled up in a car. He had to decide whether to flat out run or hit her first.

As Gordon stepped closer to the woman he shifted his weight and brought up a hard right, landing the sucker punch on her jaw, noticing the lights go out in her eyes before she even began to fall. He heard a voice across the garage yell out, "Hey!" as he started his sprint across the floor of the garage, the knob of the door opening in his hand and he was in the alley with three ways to go. He couldn't even believe his luck as he chose to run towards the street, nearly home free.

He was surprised at how close he'd come to not making it. He was surprised at the thought that crossed his mind as he rounded a corner and saw another alleyway to freedom: *Poor Brandi.*

On Christmas Eve, Emma had two clients scheduled in the morning. The first one cancelled and then second client came a little late and left a little early. She noticed Betty had left her a card in the kitchen of their offices. It had a picture of a child with their tongue stuck to a metal flagpole in the winter. It read "Happy Holidayth," and inside Betty wrote:

To my dearest friend,

I'm so sorry about your predicament. I know you to be a wise, caring soul, so I know that you will do what is right and what you need to do. Remember, everyone involved loves you.

I hope you can do what will make you happy.

Love,

Betty

P.S. Merry Christmas

As she drove to her home Emma listened to the Anonymous 4 singing Yule songs on her car stereo. The snow was falling gently around her house, and she saw that both Frank and Nathan's cars were in the driveway.

Emma and Frank and Nathan made a meal together on Christmas Eve. They listened to music, they told stories and reminisced. They looked at pictures and opened presents. They had built a fire and were drinking a glass of eggnog when Frank said, "You know, Emma, you don't have to do this."

Before Emma could respond Nathan said, "Yes, she does, Dad. Mom should have a life that makes her happy. You two will always be friends, won't you?"

Frank looked down into his drink.

"I can't imagine a day when I don't love your mother," he said, tears welling in his eyes.

Emma said, "Frank, thanks."

She looked at the two men of her life and said, "I love you both so much. And you and I, Frank, we have a bond, a partnership, that won't end as long as Nathan is alive."

She wanted to make sure Nathan heard this. She took Frank's hand in her own and held her other hand out to Nathan.

"I promise you that I'll always think of you as my partner and the father of my son and treat you with respect and dignity."

Nathan let go of her hand and said, "Well, I'm tired. I'm going to bed." Emma wanted to ask him to stay up for awhile, but she let him go.

After Nathan left the room Frank asked Emma when she was planning to move.

"I'll get on it right away. How's the day after Christmas?"

"That will be fine," said Frank, and went off to bed.

Emma thought about going to bed, but instead put on her big winter coat and took a quick walk around her neighborhood.

She had a lot of tears to cry, and she didn't want to do it at home. She didn't want to burden her son with any more of her pain.

Holly had spent Christmas day with family out of town. Her parents had come back from Florida and were visiting her aunt, her mom's sister, in Saginaw. Holly had driven there for the day, and by the time she had driven back to Lansing it was dark. It wasn't hard to get dark in Michigan in late December. Dark was easy. The days were ridiculously short, with sunrise occurring just before work and darkness falling before you left work for the day. Those few hours of light were precious, and Holly welcomed every moment of sunshine.

She looked into the grey sky and thought about how she'd describe these clouds. Cloudy didn't quite get it, because there were no distinct clouds. It was as though someone had just painted the sky grey. The sky was a great skullcap of grey. The contrast between the grey sky and the snow on the ground that covered the dormant sugar beet fields started to blur as Holly drove the two lane highway that connected Saginaw to Owosso. She turned up the hip-hop mix she was playing, and opened a window for a few minutes to wake up. She bought a cup of coffee at a drive-through at a fast food joint in Owosso and made the next forty-five minutes of the trip without a problem. By then it was dark.

Holly could make out the outline of the woods in the distance and thought about the deer. She'd heard, from the guys at work, that this had been a bad year for deer hunting, and she herself had seen fewer deer on the hoods of cars than she had in previous years. Bad year for hunters. Good year for deer. Or maybe not. She wondered if there were fewer deer. How could there not be? *We've been hunting them relentlessly for years*, she thought.

Holly found herself thinking the way Jake talked. He seemed so dark, so cynical and skeptical. He would say something about hunting, about how "fucked up" man is that he would need to kill as a sport. Or, what did he say the other day about the economy? He had said that since the automobile industry started pulling out of Michigan and opening factories in Mexico, the only growth industries in the state were gambling and corrections. Holly smiled, thinking about his cynicism.

That would make her job harder. It was already hard enough. Holly wondered whether she needed to stay working in this field. She'd known a couple of lifetime P.S. investigators, and they seemed so hardened. They were really good at their jobs, but it looked like it cost them. Holly wondered if she needed to stay.

What a crazy idea, she thought to herself. *As if I need to stay in this job. Like I don't have a choice.*

Did my family need me to be an investigator? Her parents still drank, but they seemed happier now than they did when Holly was a little girl. Why would that be? Retirement and living in Florida seemed to agree with them, as did a family reunion. *Maybe they've made it work.* She wished Jake could have come with her, that they could meet him and he could meet them. What would he have said?

I was a snoop before I was an investigator, she thought ruefully. Holly remembered as a child, realizing that something was wrong. It wasn't just her parents, it was wrong with her as well. She was unhappy, and shy, and burdened with her parent's unhappiness until it had become her own. Until she had discovered drinking.

And drinking worked, she thought. She had gotten through high school with fewer concerns, had started to hang out with the cool kids, had started to date, and was high functioning enough that she got great grades. Holly remembered her first blackout was early in her drinking. After that, she had tried not to drink too much or too quickly. She worked hard to control her drinking during her college years as well.

It's a miracle I graduated, Holly thought. Then she thought normal drinkers probably didn't have to struggle to control their drinking. That had been an early sign.

Holly angled her car onto Highway 69, and the dark patches in the road worried her. She'd experienced the black ice of Michigan on the roads before, sailing merrily along at sixty or seventy miles an hour and suddenly feeling a total loss of control. She slowed her car to fifty-five. Car after car passed her, and one SUV honked as he drove by.

"Yeah, Merry Christmas, motherfucker," she yelled over her own stereo. But the East Lansing exit was ahead, and she pulled off to drive into town on old M-78 rather than stay on the highway. Michigan drivers were so aggressive, that's what her roommate in college had said, and she had been from Baltimore.

Snowflakes began to fall as Holly drove into town on Saginaw Street, which became Grand River, and then Oakland Street in the matter of a couple of miles. Holly felt relieved. Christmas nights were always a strange time. All the anticipation of the day worn out, all the gifts open, all the meals and the visiting done *and, now what?* As a teen, she had gotten into the habit of going to a movie on Christmas night and thought she might do the same today. Jake was going to work a double shift over Christmas Eve, but then again, he didn't need to work again for the next two nights so he might be up for it.

Holly called Jake on his cell phone.

"What's up?" she asked.

"Just off work. Thought I'd hit the Ala-thon at the club, eat a turkey sandwich or something," Jake answered.

"Oh, I brought some food home if you're hungry. I'm just a couple of blocks away from my place, but I can come over and make you something to eat."

"If you come over now, I know what I'll be eating," said Jake.

"I'll be right there," Holly said with a smile.

Then she called her home to see if there were any messages from her sponsees. One girl, a new girl she had met at a meeting last week, had called to check in with Holly, just as Holly had asked her to and then there was another call from the Lansing Police Department.

"This is Officer Troy from the Lansing Police Department. I wanted to call to warn you that William Gordon Thomas has escaped from the Mason County Jail and since he had been stalking you and threatening you in the past, we do have a duty to warn. I don't even know if you're in town or not, but if you're around and want some police protection, we would supply that for you. We'll do some drive-bys and monitor your house. So give me a call back at..."

Holly replayed the message again. "Shit," she said, out loud.

A few days after Christmas, Emma began preparations for moving. She contacted a local moving company she'd found in the Yellow Pages. She'd seen their moving vans over the city for the past few years. She just never thought she'd need to do this herself.

Emma game-planned what she'd need. Some basic cooking supplies. The apartment came with a refrigerator and oven, and there was a washer and dryer downstairs. *Just like college,* she thought. She remembered seeing other people her age. She found herself second-guessing and constantly reassuring herself.

She made a list of what she could take and what to leave. The bedroom set from the guest bedroom, she'd talk to Frank about whether he'd rather have her take that than the master bedroom furniture. Her bedroom at the apartment was so small, no way could it fit a king sized bed, much less the dresser.

And she'd need a couch or loveseat and a couple of chairs for the living room. And book shelves. She wouldn't touch anything in Frank's entertainment center, but she would take the radio and CD player. No TV. That would be an intentional loss.

There was new carpeting in the apartment, but Emma recalled not liking the color in the bedroom and wondered what it would take to refinish the floors. She'd have to look into that. And get some boxes from the grocery store, boxes for books and CDs. Mainly books.

Shelving. That's something she'd need. And packing her clothes. She was making lists like mad.

Frank walked through the room. Emma felt tempted to cover up what she was writing, and then caught herself feeling guilty.

"Frank, I'm getting ready to move and making a list of what I might need and I was wondering about taking the guest bedroom furniture—the bed and that little dresser. Do you have a problem with that?" she asked.

"From what I understand, you are entitled to half of what we have here. I'd like to fight you over it, I really would, but I have spoken with an attorney, and I know how the fight will end already. So, you can buy new stuff, I'll have to buy you out of the house, or you can take half of what's here."

"I won't be able to fit it in the apartment where I'm moving, it's about a quarter, less than a quarter of the size of this place."

"I see. Well. I'm still hoping you'll move and then be back after a while. I'm willing to wait. I've thought it over. If it takes a few months, a year, more than a year. What ever you need, Emma."

"Frank, don't—"

"Don't what? Don't care? Don't wait? Don't stop loving you? I tell you what—you do what you need to do, I'll do what I need to do. Fair enough?"

"Yes. So the furniture in the guest bedroom, and I'll need a few things from the kitchen, we should have enough—"

"Emma, take whatever you need. All that can be replaced. The only thing that can't be replaced is you." Frank turned and walked out of the living room.

"I'm such an asshole," she said. Then she went back to making her list.

At the same time Marianne was working in *her* house. She'd spent most of Christmas day in her office, finishing up projects and putting things in order and writing directives.

Marianne was bringing out the pictures of her family and arranging them on her living room table. The phone rang but she didn't answer it. She heard the voice of her secretary on the answering machine.

"Marianne? Hi, this is Marci. Happy Holidays! I wanted to let you know that even though we have the day off I went in to the office and I saw the gift you left me. It was so beautifully wrapped. The rest of the staff all have the same boxes on their desks, and I wanted to say, 'Wow,' I mean you really outdid yourself on this. These pots and pans must have cost hundreds of dollars, just my gift alone, and you purchased, well, a whole lot of them. So, I'm the only one in the office today, but I would expect you'll be getting more of these calls, as people come in this week. And thanks for the note, too. You're very kind and very generous."

Marianne smiled. She had purchased a stainless steel set of pots and pans for each of her staff members. Sure, it had cost her a couple thousand dollars but it was what she had wanted to do. It was how she wanted them to remember her.

Marianne got her pills out of the medicine chest and lined them up in single file in front of the pictures on the table. By her own estimate she would hardly need all of them, but to be on the safe side she planned to take them all. She opened a good bottle Chablis to help it all go down. She put on some music, the *Greatest Hits of Andrew Lloyd Webber*, and was dressed in her favorite business suit.

It was afternoon. Any last calls to make? Any last minute detail? A note. She hadn't written a note. She took a long pull from the glass of wine, and then began to write.

At the same time Jake wrote in his notebook:

Journal entry #44. One entry for every day of sobriety. Going where no Jake has ever gone before—entering into the galaxy of 'reality.' This realm seems to have strange creatures like I've never seen before. One beauty that I'll call 'Holly' has entered my ship. Or, more precisely, I've entered her vessel. More than once. Multiple times. We both seem happy about this.

Fleetship commander Nick has expressed concern over my entering the SS Holly. He thinks this may be premature. It is the only thing premature about our joinings, let me tell you. I find our encounters to be precisely what the doctor ordered.

Speaking of doctors, have little to report in the line of dreams. Slept like a dead man last night, after said encounter with Holly.

The alien being known as Gordon has escaped his prison pod. This is a concern for the entire Federation, but more specifically to Holly and myself, since this cretin has launched an attack on us both in the past. If he is wise, he will be looking into a galaxy far, far away. But I don't know if he's wise. I know he has a tendency to be obsessed.

Hey, me too. I get obsessed by Holly, as well. But not to the point of stalking or threatening. Which is his gig, I guess. I'll just keep on system alert until I can get his coordinates.

Shit! Have to turn over the Mingus disc. There is a life form on this planet that I would have to label "jazz." The life form, not the planet. This form inhabits individuals and has a symbiotic relationship, to the extent that the host becomes jazz itself. It is usually found in musicians, who attempt to play a certain kind of music, but has been known to occur in listeners as well. I am showing signs of this type of possession, but know of no cure. Nor do I want one.

Okay, time to call Holly and go to a meeting.

CHAPTER SIXTEEN

Emma started her move by going to her apartment and giving it a good cleaning. She also brought along some candles to welcome in the spirits, a boom box and some of her favorite music, Bach and the Beatles, and was sitting on the floor of the living room. Emma was trying to get a sense of colors, placement of furniture, and the like when her cell phone rang.

Emma considered letting it go to voice mail but she answered.

"Guess who?" It was a woman's voice.

"Uhhh, I give up? Oprah?"

"No, silly. It's Dylan. Where are you?"

"I'm in an apartment. I'm in *my* apartment. Why? Where are you?"

"I'm in East Lansing."

"No shit?" asked Emma.

"No shit. I'm at the Beaner's on Grand River with a double caramel latte and I was thinking, 'What could I cut all this sweetness with,' and then you came to mind."

"I didn't know you would be in town."

"I am. And I'm just a few blocks away. What's your address, Emma? I'm on my way."

"Oooh, well, I don't know."

"What do you mean, you don't know? You don't know your address or what?"

"Yes. Both. I'm sorry, Dylan, you just surprised me."

"Don't you like surprises? Cause I'm afraid I have lots of them."

"No. Yes. I don't know. Let me step out. Okay, I'm at 1116 between Grand River and Abbott. The red brick building. I'm apartment #65."

"Okay. I'll be right there."

"I'll stand outside and wait."

Emma saw her breath but stood outside in her turtleneck, folding her arms to keep herself warm. The weather had turned warm, a winter thaw, and the snow was melting and a fog had appeared, rolling across the lawns in front of her building. She *was* surprised Dylan was here. She hadn't thought this out. She felt a mixture of excitement and anxiety and apprehension.

Dylan's red Mustang came rolling across Grand River Avenue and pulled into the small parking lot, and she waved at Emma. Dylan was striking in a red scarf, a splash of blond hair running across her smart black leather jacket and black jeans.

They embraced in the front yard and Emma resisted the urge to look around at who might be watching.

"C'mon in," she said.

"How are you?" asked Dylan.

"I'm great. No. I'm—" Emma walked into the apartment, and Dylan closed the door. Dylan caught her in a clinch and kissed her passionately.

"I'm a little better now. I don't think I've ever been kissed like that," said Emma.

"There's more where that came from," said Dylan.

"Yeah, well, I could use a little bit more of that," and she kissed Dylan back. After a few moments she said, "Can I take your coat?"

"Not unless you have a bed. It's colder in here than it is outside," said Dylan.

"No. Nothing's moved yet. I was just—" Emma stepped away from Dylan, "looking at the place and trying to get a vision. A vision of what it might look like."

"What does a dyke's apartment look like?" asked Dylan.

"Well, I was wondering what *my* apartment might look like," said Emma.

"That's what I said."

"You're bold today," smiled Emma.

"And you're not?" asked Dylan.

"I don't know. I wasn't expecting you. I'm still in a little bit of, I don't know, getting through the holidays, and spending my last Christmas with Frank and our son—"

"This is an Andy Williams moment. I'm sorry. I feel a bit foolish."

"No, Dylan, no. I didn't mean—I'm thrilled to see you."

"Well, I came here very specifically to jump your bones. You'll either have to turn on the heat or we'll have to find a room."

"Wow. Okay. Wow. Dylan. I need to have a second, okay? I'm sorry, I'm just—"

"You having second thoughts?"

"No. No. It's just really sudden and you're coming on really strong."

"Stronger than Vodka. That's me," said Dylan. "I don't know what you had fantasized about life after marriage, but if I'm included, you should know what I'm about."

"Okay. I can get that. I am a little more cautious."

"Bullshit, Emma. You just left your husband to have an affair with a lesbian woman. Nothing cautious about that. You getting cold feet? Should I go?"

Emma took a step back. She was taken aback at Dylan's boldness. But she really didn't want her to go.

"No. Please don't. Let's get out of here. I have the day off. In fact, I don't have to be anywhere until tomorrow for my Dream Group. Let's go."

"Where?"

"Anywhere. Anywhere. Let's go to Ann Arbor. There's a lot of great restaurants there. Or we could go get a room in Traverse City," said Emma.

"That's almost a four-hour drive," Dylan smiled as she said it. Emma looked Dylan in the eyes, noticed them sparkle in a kind of sexy challenge, and felt a rush of warmth through her entire body. She stepped up to Dylan and kissed her again.

"Great. You have a car," Emma said. "We can go up and get a room for the night."

"Anyplace but here, huh?" asked Dylan. "We can slow this down, you know? You've heard the joke about lesbians dating, haven't you?"

"I'm not sure."

Dylan kissed Emma and then asked, quietly, "How do you know a lesbian couple is on their second date?"

Emma could barely catch her breath. "I don't know. How?"

"There's a moving van in the driveway."

Emma laughed and asked Dylan, "You want spontaneity? Let's just get in the car and drive. It'll give us a chance to talk. I want to get to know you better."

"Okay," said Dylan. "Which direction?"

"Flip a coin. Heads is Ann Arbor, tails is Traverse City."

"Tails."

Holly dreams of snow. She walks in woods, which she recognizes as a park. Somewhere she'd gone as a kid, riding her bike on the trails to smoke cigarettes, then weed, a place where she went parking when she was in high school, a place she hasn't revisited in years.

Holly walks across an opening, knowing there is a trail on the other side, if she can remember which part of the woods, a trail that will lead her back home.

She finds herself at the edge of a pond that's solid ice. At least, it looks solid. She walks around it, but the more she walks, the bigger the pond becomes.

She walks onto the ice and notices the woods seem farther away, not closer. She's far into the pond by now and doesn't think it wise to turn back, but the ice seems solid here.

She sees Jake, coming towards her on a snowmobile.

"Go back!" she yells. She's confident the ice will hold her, but not so sure about anyone more than her alone and certainly not a snowmobile.

Jake doesn't appear to hear her and she begins to wave her arms at him, motioning him to stay away. She can see a smile on his face and knows he has confused her warnings with a welcoming. She begins to shake her head back and forth and sees Jake begin to slow down. He climbs off his machine and begins walking towards her. "Go back!" Holly shouts. But Jake keeps walking and smiling. He is wearing a long leather coat, open down the front and Holly notices something that looks metallic as he comes closer. She sees that he is weighted down with weights and she starts to panic and walk backwards as he approaches her.

Holly slides on the ice and falls backwards, feeling herself hit her elbows hard against the ice and hearing a crack in the ice as she lays there, Jake approaching, still smiling and she says, now meekly, imploringly, "Go back. Please, you have too much on you, go back. Please."

The ice cracks and Jake still seems completely unaware of the danger, as he tries to pick Holly up off the ice. Then she hears the crack become a crash, as they both fall under the ice and into the water.

Holly is aware, first, how clear it is under the water. Then she notices Jake's expression change from pleasure to fear. She sees him reach out for her and she instinctively takes his hand before realizing that he's sinking and now he has her wrist and forearm in his grip. She is going down with him. The water is deep, and they are dropping rapidly.

Holly holds her breath.

Holly woke up gasping and pushing away from Jake, who was asleep but waking up and holding her wrist in his hand in the embrace of sleep.

"You okay?" he said.

"Yeah," Holly gasped. "Just need some space." She pushed away from Jake and got out of bed.

Jake was still groggy. "Want to talk about it?"

"No, go back to sleep. I just want to write it down. Go back to sleep."

"We can talk about it," said Jake, already going back to sleep.

Tonight, thought Holly, *tonight at group we can talk about it.*

Emma returned from her overnight in Traverse City with Dylan feeling disoriented. She was rarely so spontaneous. They'd talked about their families, food, therapy, dreams, their work, their hopes, their fears. The only thing better than the talk was the sex. But Emma realized that even without the sex, she was swimming in some pretty deep waters with Dylan. She was falling deeper and deeper in love. Dylan drove back to Grand Rapids after dropping Emma in East Lansing, and they made plans to see each other on the weekend.

She worked through her schedule seemingly without effort. By the time the group met, Emma was starting to feel tired. She caught a reflection of herself in the mirror above her desk and smiled.

As the group started, Emma noticed that only Jake was smiling. Mason was thinner and had a grey pallor to his skin, almost as though he'd smudged his cheeks with ash. She was amazed he made it to group. Marianne and Holly both looked somber.

"So, how was everyone's holiday?" Emma asked.

"Quiet," answered Marianne.

Mason said, "Pretty good. Family time. Everyone came to see me. I'm quite the celebrity, suddenly."

"All your family?" asked Holly.

"Pretty much. My brother's whole family came from French Lick and we got along famously. It was a good day. A good weekend."

Jake asked Mason how he was feeling.

"Not as well. I'm starting to experience some pain and that is really not great. But I've got morphine, which I'm taking and every now and then I, well, Jake, maybe you know something about this, I hallucinate."

"Yeah," said Jake. "Sure. I mean, I've tripped before."

"I wasn't thinking that way, but now that you mention it, I was thinking more along the lines of working with people who are hallucinating."

"Oh, yeah," said Jake, and Emma noticed him blushing.

"So it's got me thinking about the difference between dreams and hallucinations, too. Do you know the difference, Emma?" asked Mason.

"To tell you the truth, I haven't given it much thought. Or any thought, prior to this moment."

"Okay, I've taken us far afield. But to get back to your original question, the holidays were just fine."

"Jake, why don't you go next?" asked Holly. Emma noticed Holly's hands gripping the edge of her seat. Her knuckles were white.

"Okay," said Jake. "My holidays were okay. I spent a lot of time working. A lot of the staff wanted time off. So I was working with people who were hallucinating. Of course, that's almost every day. And I spent a lot of time with Holly. And Holly got some bad news."

Everyone looked at Holly.

"Yeah, that creep that was stalking me broke out of jail." she said. Marianne gasped and offered Holly a place to stay.

"Thanks. I hadn't thought of that. Maybe." She smiled at Marianne. "Let me think about that, because I was thinking of staying some place else, but he knows where my sponsor lives and he knows about Jake."

"If he's smart," said Mason, "he'll be miles and miles away from here. Once he's caught, he'd be a fool to do the same thing again."

"Well, it's certainly scary," agreed Emma. She felt a chill go through her. "How are you doing?" she asked Holly.

"Actually, I'm okay. I'm less scared than I was before. And I agree with Mason, something tells me that it won't be an issue. But I did have a dream that I want to talk about."

"Good," said Jake. "She wouldn't talk to me about it."

"Well, partly because you were in it."

"Okay, well let's do a general check-in. Holidays were good, how are you all doing?" asked Emma.

"Did I mention that I'm in pain?" said Mason with a smile.

Emma smiled and noticed how everyone responded to Mason. He had their hearts.

"Yes, you did," said Marianne. "I—I brought you a present, Mason. But don't open it here." She brought a small gift-wrapped box from her purse. He shook it and it rattled. Mason pursed his lips and made a face.

"Candy corn?" he asked. Marianne shrugged. "Thank you, you shouldn't have. To answer your second question, Emma, this is strange. A strange time in my life. Because I know it's ending, and soon. And it looks like London may be out of the question. Which is fine. Because life isn't about places. I don't know if that makes sense. I go between feeling very profound and like I don't make any sense at all. And, ironically, I don't dream. I sleep a lot, I'm tired a lot. But I hallucinate while I'm awake."

"What do you see when you're awake?" asked Emma.

"When I hallucinate? I saw the ships on the great lake, once, looking into my back yard. Sometimes I see John Wayne or cowboys of some sort in the distance."

"A posse?" asked Holly.

"Maybe so. Maybe they're looking for me. That roundup in the sky. I'm sorry, gallows humor, it's just that for some reason, things seem funny. Maybe it's the drugs."

"Well, this is a switch. I had to give up using, and you get stoned as hell," said Jake.

"Yeah, isn't that something? But I'm really happy, just happy to be here. I would just be content to listen to you all. I'll let you know if I see any cowboys."

Marianne put up her hand. "Well, there's something I need to talk about. I was thinking a lot about what Holly said to me last time. How I'm closed off from you all."

Holly started to apologize, but Marianne cut her off. "No, you were quite right. And I need to start talking about it. If I could tell you a dream I had?"

"Sure," encouraged Emma.

Marianne began, "I dreamed I was outside and looking at the sunset. Actually, I couldn't see the sunset, I could just see the tops of trees. You know how they look this time of year, all the leaves gone, barren, and the sunset was actually behind me, because I could see the tops of these trees and the sun illuminating them, and it was so beautiful." Marianne's voice choked up and a tear appeared at the corner of her left eye and rolled down her cheek without her wiping it away. "I realized this life is filled with too much beauty, too much for my heart to hold, and I could only hope—"

Holly offered her a tissue. Marianne took one and thanked her. She continued, "I was looking around to find someone to show this to, and I didn't see anyone, but I noticed the building I was in front of, and I assumed it was my work, but it was, it was like a library, but it was also a church. It's hard to describe. But I knew it was full of people, people who were learning, people who were worshipping, people who loved each other, and I thought, 'Isn't it time I went in?'"

The group was silent.

"What a beautiful dream," said Emma.

"Yes, isn't it?" said Marianne, dabbing her eyes dry. "And I don't even need to talk about it. It's like you said, Emma, I'd rather just appreciate it. The dream, to me, is just *hope*. You know? And what I wanted you all to know, I wanted you to know how close I came to giving up hope. I've been thinking of suicide."

Mason looked at the box in his hands. Now he knew what the box contained.

"I didn't let you know what I was thinking and I came so far as to get enough pills, and the right kind of pills to do the job and I really thought, I mean I was right there, ready to do it, and I thought, 'May as well see the new year,' and I went to sleep and I had that dream. So, before you lecture me, Emma—"

Emma shook her head.

"Oh, I know," Marianne said. "I know you wouldn't. I was just—"

"Afraid," Holly had finished her thought for her.

"I suppose so. But what I was about to say, is that I know I've got to change. My life is a little dead-ended, interpersonally. And I need to do something else."

"That's a brave realization," said Emma. "Do you know what it is?"

"I thought I might start by getting into therapy. And, if it's all right with you, Emma, would you take me on as a client? Because there are some things I need to talk about and put behind me, and I really want to be a part of life."

"I think that would work," said Emma. "We can talk about it a little more after the group is over. Good for you, Marianne. Good for you."

Jake related an anecdote he'd heard about suicide survivors.

"You know, Marianne," he said, "from working on a psych unit, I've met a lot of people who have tried to kill themselves. And I don't even know if this story is true, but I heard about a survey they did with people who jumped off the Golden Gate Bridge. Now, this bridge is huge. It's like the Mackinac Bridge. People splatter when they hit the water. But every now and then, someone survives the fall."

"And?" asked Holly, motioning with her hands to hurry Jake along.

"And, they asked the survivors what they were thinking on the way down. And they all thought, pretty much, the same thing."

"What did they think?" asked Marianne, after a pregnant pause.

Jake looked her in the eye and said, "They all thought, 'I wish I hadn't done this.' So, in their last moments, they chose life."

Emma told Marianne that they would make a plan should Marianne begin to get those feelings again.

"Oh, I'm not feeling that way now," said Marianne.

"Right," said Emma, "but sometimes those feelings will come back, so we should make a plan." She'd been impressed by Jake's ability to reach Marianne, his style of connecting with her seemed so matter of fact and easy. *I wonder if he ever thought about becoming a therapist?*

Marianne agreed to meet after the group.

Emma asked if anyone had a reaction to what Marianne had just said, or her dream.

"I didn't know you were that desperate, Marianne," said Jake. "I mean, I feel almost selfish, that I didn't get to know you better or couldn't see it."

"You couldn't have seen it. I keep really well-hidden."

"Yeah, I guess for lack of a better word, my pain was so evident that everyone in the group saw it right away and I had to do something to deal with it."

"Right," said Emma. "But your symptom, your drinking, well, it was something that got harder and harder to hide."

"I loved your appreciation of beauty," said Mason. "And I love aesthetics. And the church/library combo you have. I would guess that you worship learning and are realizing that there is something new for you to learn."

"Yes, I see that," said Marianne.

"And there are others who are also learning," said Holly, "and you want to join them. I also just wanted to say, I can identify with the 'dark night of the soul,' facing down that decision: Am I going to live or am I going to die? It's the feeling I had early in recovery, when I knew I couldn't go on drinking. And it is a life or death thing."

"Yes," said Marianne. And then she twisted in her seat and made a face like she'd tasted something sour. "Listen, enough about me. We'll run out of time and you said you had a dream," she said to Holly.

"Yes," said Holly. "Speaking of life and death. I had a dream last night. I was on the ice, and Jake was speeding towards me in a snowmobile, and I was worried whether the ice might hold me alone. Well, I couldn't get him to hear me. And he came out, and we crashed through the ice—I feel like this is really personal and I should've told you this dream before coming to group, Jake. I'm sorry."

"No, that's cool. Go. Tell it."

"Well, you were reaching out to me. It's like you were wearing something that was weighing you down, and I reached out to you, and you grabbed me and the next thing I knew, we were sinking like stones, and I woke up, I couldn't breathe."

"So what do you make of it?" asked Emma.

"I think Jake and I need to have a talk."

After group, Jake and Holly had their talk. They went back to the coffee shop where they'd met for the first time after the group. Jake had to go to work soon and ordered a house blend with a shot of espresso. Holly ordered a decaf latte. It was cold out, and the couple initially held the coffee cups in their hands to warm up before taking the first sip.

Holly broke the ice. She told Jake she wanted to still be friends, still see each other at meetings, but she felt they should no longer date, shouldn't call each other, and definitely no sex, not for a year. Jake looked at her and said, "Is that what you want?"

"It's what I need," Holly said. She stood up, bent over and gave him a quick kiss on the lips. "I'll be around, okay?"

"And then she walked out of my life," he said, watching her walk out the door.

Jake went to work feeling miserable. It was only an hour away from New Year's Eve and the census on the psych unit was very low, less than ten patients. They were overstaffed and Yvonne, the charge nurse, told him he didn't need to stay for his shift. Jake was mulling this over when the elevator pinged and a giant bear of a man walked across the floor.

At six foot seven, and close to three hundred pounds, Edward was hard to miss. Wearing a large black leather topcoat made him even more conspicuous.

"You son of a bitch!" said Jake as Edward walked towards him, a large smile on his face.

Edward wrapped Jake in his arms and easily lifted him off the floor. "Mr. Pooh!" he said, in a voice that resonated like aged bourbon.

"How the hell are you man? What are you doing here?" asked Jake as Edward lowered him to the floor.

"Well, I am an alum, aren't I?" asked Edward.

By now the other psych techs and the charge nurse had come out to see what was up. Yvonne recognized Edward and told the others that he was okay to visit the unit.

"Edward Jenkins, your old partner in crime, Jake. What has it been? Five years?" she asked.

"Eight. Eight years," answered Edward.

"What brings you up here?" she asked.

"I'm back in the state for the holidays. My home, well, you wouldn't remember, but my home was in Southfield and I decided to come back to Lansing, see if any of my old college buddies were still around. Then I thought, maybe I'll pop up to the hospital, see if I recognize anyone and the first face I see is Jake's here."

"Good to see you, Edward. I just released Jake for the night, so he's all yours."

Jake rode down the elevator with Edward. "Where'd you park?" asked Jake.

"I got a ride from a friend. They were going to meet me at Pasquale's," answered Edward.

"Pasquale's is closed."

"Oh, shit. I should have checked. Maybe we'll just go to the White Spot."

"White Spot's closed, too," answered Jake. These were two bars that had been located just a couple of blocks from the hospital. It was also in a particularly rough area of Lansing, a place that had more than a fair share of muggings and assaults and even an Uzi drive-by, in previous years.

"What's open?" asked Edward.

"So where's your friend, then?" asked Jake. He suddenly felt nervous. Here he was, just broken up with Holly, and his old drinking buddy shows up out of the blue. "Do your friends have a cell phone?"

"Oh, they'll be okay. If the bar's not open, they'll just go home."

"Okay. Well, I've got my car, over here in the lot."

"Listen, Mr. Pooh, have you got any pot?"

Edward had called Jake Mr. Pooh for as long as Jake remembered. Jake didn't know why.

"No. No, I don't. Sorry. Jonesing?" asked Jake.

"Not really. I just thought about the old days."

It was below zero and both men exhaled plumes of breath, visible in the crystal night air. They got in the car and Jake suggested the Mexican restaurant down the street.

"That would work," said Edward.

"Where are you staying?"

"No plans to stay."

"Okay."

They pulled into a parking lot that had enormous potholes and was ice slick. There were only a handful of cars.

"They might be closing. Let's see," said Jake as they got out of the car.

"We close in an hour," said the waitress. She had a stud through her lower lip and a rose tattoo behind her left ear.

The restaurant seemed cold and dimly lit. Tile floor, stucco walls with Mayan influenced paint job. There were only a few people in the place, three guys at the bar, an older couple in a booth.

"Let's take a booth," said Edward. He ordered a pitcher of margaritas.

"I'm not drinking," said Jake. Then, to the waitress, ordered a diet cola and a plate of nachos.

"You still want the pitcher?" asked the waitress.

"Yeah. He might change his mind, after he sees how much fun I'm having." After the waitress had left Edward said, "This is a big change. Is it because you're driving?"

"Naw. Well. Yeah. Any reason's a good reason not to drink."

"A.A.?"

"You always did cut to the chase, didn't you Edward? What are you up to?"

"I was living in Cinci. Got married. You know that. You were there. Jesus. Got a job at the correctional facility, running psych tests."

"Cool. Things are good?"

"Oh, so so."

The waitress arrived with the drinks. "Your nachos will be up in a minute. You guys mind cashing out? I'm due to go home soon."

"Sure," said Edward and peeled off a twenty dollar bill.

"Let me contribute," said Jake, reaching for his wallet.

"No, I've got it. Least I can do," said Edward.

Jake gave the waitress a five-dollar bill. "This is for you."

Jake watched Edward pour the lime green drink in a salt-rimmed tumbler and drain it in two long gulps. Then he poured another. Jake watched his old friend's face while he drank and felt a shiver run down his spine. He resisted salivating.

"Sure you won't join me?"

"No. Looks good, but no." Jake took a long pull at his cola. He imagined tasting tequila. The pitcher of Margaritas really looked good.

"So, you didn't answer my question. Are you doing A.A.?"

"How'd you guess?" asked Jake.

"Something different about you. I tried it, for a couple of months, about a year or three ago."

"Oh, yeah? I didn't know that," said Jake.

"Wasn't for me. Too much like a cult," said Edward, taking another sip.

The waitress came back with the nachos and Jake asked if she'd get him another diet before she left.

"Sure you don't want a pitcher?" asked Edward, joking. The margaritas were half gone.

"So what made you go to meetings?" asked Jake. He was trying to focus on his nachos and not make eye contact with the pitcher.

"Problems. I lost my license. Both my driver's license and my license to practice."

"Jesus, Edward, I'm sorry. I had no idea."

"Yeah. That wasn't the worst of it. I lost Beth, too."

"All over drinking?"

"No. It was, well, drinking was a factor, but it wasn't the thing. I'm just not cut out to be a nine-to-five guy. You know. I'm more like you. That's why I thought, maybe, we could hang out, we could, y'know, relive some old times? Hit up Mac's bar. 'Auld Lang Syne,' y'know?"

"Well," Jake said and ate a fistful of nachos, "I'll have to give it some thought. Where are you staying?"

"I don't have any plans, as of the moment."

"Jesus, I thought you said a friend—"

"Well, it was a cabbie. He was friendly, though."

"Edward. Do you need a place to crash?"

"No, man," he said, smiling. Then he said, "Okay, if you insist."

Jake smiled. "You haven't changed much, have you?"

"Mr. Pooh, Mr. Pooh. Remember the night we did acid?"

"Which night?"

"We went and saw the Art Ensemble at the Kiva."

"Oh, yeah, that night. I peed my pants at the pizza joint after, laughing so hard."

"Yeah, you were saying—"

"That the concert was still playing, only now they were playing the kitchen—"

"And Karl was straight and he thought it was the acid talking—"

"Yeah, and I went into hysterics and peed myself. Yeah, I remember."

"Do you have any acid?" asked Edward.

"No, man. I don't have any acid."

After the nachos and drinks were consumed, Jake told Edward he would put him up for the night.

On the way to the car Edward started looking up and down the street.

"Can we stop and get some beer?" he asked.

"You know, I'm sorry Edward, but I'm not that long sober. It would be really hard for me to have any in my place right now."

"All the more reason to have it. Life is short. Do what you want."

"You're the devil," said Jake. "But seriously man, no. I can't do it. And I'm kind of going through something right now with a woman I've been seeing. So—"

"Oh. Sorry to hear it. You were always one for the ladies, though, Mr. Pooh."

"Yeah, Edward. You and me both. And look where we are. Put out like the cat."

Holly took the phone call early on New Year's Eve. She had caller I.D. but the caller had blocked their number. She usually screened her calls but this time she let it go, wondering if it might be Jake. She knew she had asked him not to call her, but…

There was no answer when she picked up the phone. She said "Hello?" but there was nothing but dead air on the other side of the phone. She could hear traffic in the background, like the caller was near a highway.

"Hello?" Holly hung up after her second greeting and felt sick. She thought she should leave her house but the phone rang again. It was Jake's cell number.

"Hello?" asked Holly.

"Hi Holly, it's Jake. Listen, I know you asked me not to call you, but I have a friend in town, and he's a little hung over, I think I might—he slept on my couch last night."

"I thought you had to work last night."

"I did. They sent me home and this guy, an old drinking buddy, he showed up out of the blue. I think he might be homeless. I don't know how he got to town, or what. We went out to El Azteco."

"Did you drink?" interrupted Holly.

"No, I didn't. But he did. And then I brought him home to sleep it off and I guess I'm not sure what to do."

"Jake, did you call your sponsor?" asked Holly.

"No. But that would probably be a good idea. He might need a place to stay. He wants me to go out with him tonight to celebrate old times."

"So he's not interested in getting sober."

"He asked me if I had any acid, Holly."

"Okay. That answers that. Dump him, Jake."

"What? That seems heartless."

"If it's him or you, who do you choose?"

"Just like you dumping me?"

"I didn't dump you, Jake. Damnit! I put you on hold for awhile. I'm—I'm crazy about you Jake. And that just scares the shit out of me. I don't want to sabotage your sobriety, and I don't want you to make me out to be someone I'm not."

"What do you mean, Holly?"

"In early recovery, sometimes people grab hold of something or someone, like in desperation. I just—can we just give it some time, Jake?"

"I really wish we could have talked about this in person. Could we meet, or—"

Holly was perturbed, then she remembered the hang up call from a minute ago.

"Jake, listen, did you call me, like just a couple of minutes ago?"

"No."

"Well, somebody did and then they hung up."

"Uh oh." There was a moment of silence on the line. Then Jake spoke the words they were both thinking. "Holly, get out of there."

"Do you think?"

"Yes. Get out of there. Tell you what, I'll meet you at the club. Get out now."

"What about your friend?"

"I'll leave him here. Just go. Get out of your house right now."

"He knows I go to the club."

"Okay, that joint you took me for breakfast, with Nick. I'll meet you there. I need some breakfast anyway but go, Holly. Go right now."

"Okay," said Holly and hung up the phone.

Before Jake could get out of the house Edward weaved around the corner of the living room and peered into Jake's bedroom. "Subzub?" he asked, a nonsensical thing the two of them used to say to each other when buzzed.

Jake said, "Listen, Mr. Ed, I have to go. My friend is in trouble. She was being stalked by a dude. Hey, listen, could you come with me?"

"Subzub?" asked Edward.

They piled into Jake's car and drove the few blocks to the restaurant. It was a mom and pop, ham and eggs joint off Michigan on the edge of Lansing, just a of block before East Lansing began.

It was bitterly cold and Jake noticed he was shivering, but wasn't sure if it was from the cold or the fear of confronting Gordon again.

They parked on the side of the building and Jake said, "We'll wait here to watch for her." Jake kept the car running, hoping the heater would kick in. He was quiet, scanning the lot, the street. Then he looked at Edward who was sitting and smiling at him.

Edward asked, "What about this dude?"

"He's been stalking her. He's obsessed with her since she investigated him for child abuse. And he was in jail and he escaped. Oh, yeah, he also got physical with me."

"Oh, yeah? You guys fought?" asked Edward.

"Sort of. He just kind of pushed me down."

"Big fucker?"

"Not as big as you, Edward, but nasty. Really nasty."

Both Jake and Edward lit up cigarettes and cracked open their windows while waiting. Jake had just thought that they should probably call the cops, when he saw Holly pull into the lot.

"There she is," said Jake, watching as Holly pulled in towards the restaurant but on the opposite side where they had parked. Just about forty feet behind Holly another car pulled in and parked next to where Jake and Edward sat. Jake recognized Gordon, even though he had shaved his head and was driving a different car. He could tell that Holly didn't know she'd been followed.

"And here *he* is, Edward, this is the guy. Are you ready?"

"What are we doing?" asked Edward.

"Stop him from hurting Holly," said Jake as he opened his door.

Jake walked around the rear of his own car and behind the car Gordon was in, careful to avoid the rear view mirror. Gordon had his eyes on Holly, and Jake thought he probably hadn't intended to make a move in a public parking lot.

On the other hand, Gordon was insane.

Jake had a moment of panic as Holly got out of her car and waved towards him. At the same moment Gordon craned his neck to see Jake standing behind his car in the blind spot, Jake looked towards Holly, and pointed into the car with one hand while pantomiming a cell phone call with the other. What happened next unfolded fast:

Gordon started getting out of his car. Jake moved up behind him before he could stand up completely. He kicked at Gordon's left knee and heard him grunt. Gordon still got out of the car. Jake looked for something big to hit him with and ended up using his right fist, hitting Gordon as hard as he could. He hurt his hand, badly, but was relieved to see Gordon fall. Holly was making her call.

"That all you got?" asked Gordon, getting up off the ground. "Glad to know that you took your best shot, cause that's all you get," he said.

Edward was now standing behind Gordon, with the car door between the two men. Gordon was reaching into his winter coat and Jake said, "Do it now!" and before Gordon could turn around, Edward slammed the car door shut on Gordon, hitting him at his knees, chest and back. Jake could hear a 'whoosh' sound as the air was knocked out of Gordon and a slight grunt as he fell to the ground again.

"That motherfucker isn't getting up," said Edward as Gordon writhed on the ground. Edward slammed the car door shut like an exclamation point.

"Watch his hand," said Jake, as Gordon's hand was still in his coat.

"What'cha got, big guy?" asked Edward, pulling on his arm. The strength of Edward's grip actually assisted Gordon with getting on to his feet. Edward, startled, slipped on the ice and fell to the ground.

Gordon's hand emerged, holding a box cutter. He didn't say a word. He raised his arm to take a swipe at Edward's throat. Jake launched himself forward, springing from his heels through the length of his long legs, his forehead aimed at Gordon's face, his left hand gripped around Gordon's wrist.

Jake felt himself fall, while holding Gordon's wrist. He felt them fall together, all in a heap. He saw stars, then red, and for a moment black. Then he heard a number of people surrounding him, and Holly saying, "I've got the knife!" and hearing sirens in the background and then passing out again.

When he woke up, Jake was still on his back in the parking lot. There was a paramedic applying smelling salts. Edward and Holly were standing behind the young female paramedic, and Gordon was in the back of a patrol car.

Jake looked at his hand and it was throbbing in pain, but he could open and close his fist and he knew nothing was broken. He'd never hit anyone before. He noticed some blood on his shirt and wondered if he'd been stabbed.

"You broke his nose," said Holly, "with your head. He bled pretty hard."

Edward said, "Just like old times, huh?"

Jake just smiled. The police asked them for their statements and after they were done, they all went to the other side of town for breakfast. After meeting Holly, to Jake's surprise, Edward agreed to attend a meeting and go to the A.A. New Year's Eve dance. Jake was almost disappointed, because now *he* wanted a drink. He ate pancakes instead.

CHAPTER SEVENTEEN

On January second, Emma moved into her apartment. She had spent New Year's day painting the walls of her place and Dylan had come down from Grand Rapids to help. She'd chosen colors that felt right to her, a lilac for her bedroom with a deep purple accent wall that Dylan had spent the day intentionally smudging. A cheery yellow for the kitchen and a soft chocolate for the living room. She felt encouraged by how well it all went together, and she felt hopeful for the first time in weeks.

The following morning she woke up, alone, in her new bedroom. She went into the second bedroom, which she'd converted with some secondhand furniture into a small office. She put on some Bach, sat at her desk, opened her laptop and began to write.

Today I'm living with the solution. Today is the start of something new in my life—as new as these colors I've surrounded myself with—as new as the snow that fell outside last night. I feel alive. I feel like I can breathe. I was struck by how much pain—absolute agony—I went through leaving Frank. I worried myself sick about how it would affect Nathan. I still don't know that. But now—I'm thinking that I'll be just fine, that Nathan will be fine, too. Even Frank, God bless, Frank, even Frank, will be able to move on. Today I'll focus on the little blessings I have—my health, my work, and the chance to love and be loved. Not just out of choice, but through who I am, who I have always been and now I've allowed myself to fully become. Why did I wait so long?

I'm not out of the woods yet. Of this I'm sure. There is grieving to be done. There's a whole lifetime to reconfigure. But I can start inside of these walls and I can choose the colors of my life for the first time in my life. I'm okay. I'm really okay.

That day Edward caught a bus back to Detroit. He said he'd be going to meetings again in Detroit, trying to find some people to hang out with this time, instead of sitting in the corner, judging, waiting for his chance to leave and get back to the bar.

Jake was relieved that his old friend was gone and took the time to close his curtains and nap before work. Jake's dream came in fits and starts, mainly images of the last couple of days, *a mix of Edward, drinking, sometimes sitting next to him in a meeting, his big smile like a Cheshire cat's. Images of Holly, getting into a car, getting out of a car. And sometimes images of Gordon, but these are far away and dimmer.*

Jake sees Holly at a cabin up north. There is a clearing, some sand, beach grass, and woods in the distance. Somewhere, nearby, there is water. He is leaving a log cabin, with Holly in front of him. Jake has bags packed on the porch and sees Holly getting into her car and starting it up.

"Holly! Holly wait!" Jake yells as he notices that Holly is putting the car in gear, but isn't he supposed to be with her?

"Holly!" Jake yells again as he steps off the porch and drops his baggage. Holly starts to drive. Jake starts running, wondering if she knows he's here, or if this was intentional. Could she be leaving him?

"Holly!" he yells again as he notices her accelerating. He's gotten close to the car. If he jumps he just might catch the bumper.

And he leaps. His fingernails catch the edge of a plastic runner next to the bumper and the trunk. He's amazed that his feet fly out from under him and he is suddenly parallel to the ground. Holly seems to be driving even faster. He can see Holly looking into the driver's side of the rear view mirror, making eye contact.

Jake feels the car accelerate ever faster and Holly looks away. The car is speeding towards the woods and Jake knows he can't hold on forever. He is going to have to let go.

His fingers ache and slip, Jake has no choice, it isn't even letting go, just a release and he finds himself airborne. He is parallel to the ground and he seems to be maintaining his speed but he can't catch the car. The car is turning now, turning to follow the curve in the road, but Jake is flying straight ahead. He still isn't falling, still not losing either speed or height off the ground, but Jake realizes he is approaching a stand of pine trees. He knows his velocity is certain to cause an awful crash, his head smashing into a tree. Jake pictures it, but again realizes, Wait a minute, I'm flying," and turning in the air, he doesn't fall but he turns and he lifts his arms before him and he flies upwards and continues to fly like Superman, and even though he's not faster than a speeding bullet, he's going as fast as the car that dropped him off and he's gaining altitude and flying above the trees. Can he follow the road, find Holly's car? That doesn't seem to matter anymore, because he was flying, actually flying!

Emma greeted the group on their first meeting of the New Year, and the second to last time the five of them were scheduled to meet. Everyone was dressed in jeans, even Marianne, and Mason had a large Russian fur hat on his ashen face. He told her his wife had dropped him off and Jake volunteered to take him home. Mason accepted.

"This is supposed to be our second to last meeting," Emma began. "If there's anything we haven't talked about," she said, "if there's any dream you've left out undone, if there's anything else you want to do as a group or to say to each other, make sure to bring it up. Let's do a quick check-in with every one before we get started. Who will go first?"

Mason started. He looked thinner and his voice was deep and gravelly when he spoke.

"I think I'll go first," he said. "I've really enjoyed this group, first of all. I haven't liked, very much, what has been happening to me, but I have gotten a lot of things from the group." Mason smiled and reached over and patted Jake on the knee.

"I tend to live in a land of ideas. I watch movies and think about them. The same with dreams. There is something in the dreaming life and the study of dreams that is about self-reflection. Being where I am at this point of life, and by that I mean the end, I have another perspective. What I mean to say is that I'm thinking more and more in terms of relationships and in terms of the spirit. Ideas are just nothing much if they don't mean something to someone else. Anyway, that's what I've been thinking."

Mason chuckled. "So, I haven't had too much to dream— I'm on a lot of medication and I'm not experiencing much pain, but I can tell something is happening to me. I'm very weak and tired. I feel like the whole body is shutting down, which it is, according to the hospice people who come to visit and care for me. They've been wonderful. Part of what I want to say is, not really an apology, but a matter of how things are progressing. I'm not sure I'll be able to make it to the next group."

Holly spoke immediately, "We can come to you."

"Yeah, that's a good idea," Jake agreed.

"Emma, is that acceptable?" asked Marianne. Then she got a look of deliberateness on her face and added, "Actually, it doesn't matter, does it? We'll just do it with you or without you."

"No," said Emma, "it's certainly acceptable. We can meet at Mason's, if it's okay with him. I'm sorry I didn't consider it first. Mason, is there anything else you'd like to say?"

"Well, I'll warn Mona," said Mason with a smile. "I've had my struggles, but you all have as well. It's been really great to watch young love at work. It's been great to watch everyone confront their demons. You all seem happier. Even you, Emma."

"Thank you, Mason. Who's next?"

Holly volunteered to speak next. "First off, I love you, Mason."

"Thank you Holly. I love you, too."

"And I would like to visit you, if it's okay. Do you have any visitors?"

"Plenty. Family, colleagues. Students. Mitch Albom hasn't shown up, yet."

Holly continued. "It's been a tough week for me. I had a talk with Jake and we're not seeing each other now, except in the context of this group or in meetings."

"Does it feel okay to talk about that here? With Jake here?" asked Emma.

"I—I am not sure. If it doesn't feel okay, I'll stop. Are you okay with it, Jake?"

Jake hesitated before answering. "Am I okay with not being able to talk with you without a group present? No. I wish we could talk alone. But that's not part of your new 'rules.' So I'll take what I can get."

Emma wasn't sure how to handle this and then wondered if anything really needed "handling." Holly and Jake seemed to be sorting out their boundaries and their feelings on their own.

"I hate to hurt you," said Holly. She looked at Mason, who was looking at the floor. She looked at Marianne. "I hate to hurt Jake," she said softly. "I am more afraid of hurting him, and myself, by getting too involved, too quickly, at this point of his recovery. It's taboo in A.A. They call it 'the thirteenth step' and there is a good reason for it."

Holly took a deep breath. Jake was looking at her and she reached over to touch his hand, then drew back. "So, this week. Jake saved my life, again. The guy that broke out of prison was following me, and Jake and his friend helped to knock the guy out while the police came."

"Oh, my God! Are you okay?" Emma was shocked.

"I'm fine. I was worried that Jake might have a concussion."

"I'm fine," said Jake.

It took the two of them some time to tell the story and answer questions from Marianne, Mason, and Emma. At the end of it, Holly said, "So, I'm grateful to Jake for saving me, again. And I love Jake. Jake, I love you."

Emma noticed that Jake had tears in his eyes.

"Jake, what's going on with you?" she asked. She remembered how, a couple of months ago, he could barely tolerate any emotions.

He took a deep breath and said, "I feel bad. I just feel bad." His voice was full and he made direct eye contact with Emma. She decided to follow her instincts.

"Where do you feel it?"

"All over. In my chest."

"Is it painful?"

"Yes."

"A stabbing pain or a dull pain?" Emma asked.

"I feel like I swallowed a rock."

"Let it out, Jake," advised Mason.

"Not right now," Jake answered and he shut his eyes.

"On a scale of one to ten, what number is the pain?" asked Emma.

"Well," Jake answered, "I'm sure it's not like what Mason is feeling."

"What's going on with me is going on with me," Mason snapped. "You do your own pain and I'll do mine."

Jake opened his eyes and looked at Mason. He seemed a little startled. Holly said, "That's what I'm trying to get across. You just have too many needs right now, Jake. You have to give yourself time to heal before this will work."

Jake looked at Holly and said, "But I love you."

"I love you, too, Jake. But you need—"

Emma directed Holly. "Can you talk about yourself? What *you* need?"

Holly paused. "I need to know I'm doing the right thing. I need to know I'm not screwing someone or something up. I've been thinking about what I've learned in this group. I've learned that I operate out of a sense of guilt. That's what my dreams were telling me. I move into what others want of me, instead of me moving where I want to go and doing what I need to do for myself. I've never known that in recovery. I mean, I stopped drinking, and *that* was a blessing. But I never knew *this* about myself. My dreams were telling me, but I needed you all to help. Not that any of you ever said that to me or pointed it out to me, but you helped me to see it. Because, in recovery, we focus on our spiritual development, but I didn't look into what message I was giving myself, over and over, and I was persecuting myself. I was crucifying myself. I mean, what kind of shit is that? So, I've decided to stop. I'm not going to beat myself up. I'm going to listen to what I want and need. I'm not going to compromise myself. I'm not going to give up on myself. That's all."

Emma nodded. She thought this was a good moment to move on.

"Marianne?" she asked.

"I thought you'd want to do Jake next," suggested Marianne.

"Let's give Jake a minute."

"Okay," said Marianne. "Well, to fill the rest of you in, I met with Emma after the group last week. We talked about my suicidal feelings, and we had an additional session. There is something that happened, something that happened to me when I was a child, and we don't need to go into it here, but it was something that I've never talked about and never dealt with, and I've made a lot of choices based on that trauma. And I've made the decision now to deal with it. I'm going to talk with Emma on a regular basis, and she told me about an EMDR, is that right? Eye movement therapy that helps you deal with trauma. Because, I've just sealed myself into a little box of loneliness. I thought I was protecting myself. It turned out to be a tomb. So, I've joined a church and decided to take a class, because my dream—"

"The library that was a church," remembered Mason.

"Right. Well, the church I'm not so sure about but don't want to go back to the church of my childhood and I want something a little more open and liberal. And the class is a Latin dance class. I love to work out, but it's something I've always done alone. So I'm going to try this. I thought about joining a health club, too. I've been spending too much time alone at home. Anyway, life is better."

After Emma asked if anyone had reactions to what Marianne was reporting, Mason gave her some encouragement. "I think you're on the right track. I'm happy for you. Life has a lot to offer. I feel like we've just passed each other, heading towards that dark portal."

"I think I know what you mean. I'm moving in the opposite direction now."

Emma turned to Jake and asked, "Okay, Jake. How's that rock you swallowed?"

"Before, when you asked me, it was an 'eight.' Now it's a 'three.'"

"What does that tell you?"

Jake waited for a moment and then said, "That feelings aren't permanent."

"Exactly," said Emma. "Feelings come and go. Like the weather. It's okay to feel."

"I know," said Jake.

"A part of you knows," said Emma. "And maybe the rest of you is learning."

"Okay," he said. "It's been a hard week for me as well. I found something with Holly that is—that was—so beautiful."

"Why talk about it in past tense?" asked Emma.

"It's over."

"That's not—" Emma hesitated and looked at Holly. "Holly, correct me if I'm wrong, but that's not what I heard Holly say."

"What?" asked Jake.

"I didn't hear her say 'it's over.' I heard her say 'it's postponed.'"

"Is that true?" asked Jake, looking at Holly.

"Jake, *yes*. Didn't you hear me say that I love you? Didn't you hear me say that I honor your recovery and see that you need time? And I need to give you that time? Didn't you hear me say that this was hard for me as well?"

"Apparently not," he said with a smile.

"What do you hear now?" asked Emma.

"Well, that Holly loves me. And that she cares about my recovery. And that's why we should wait."

"That's it," agreed Holly.

"And how do you feel?" asked Emma.

"Good. I'm not used to being cared about that way."

"You experienced boundaries as rejection," suggested Emma.

"I wouldn't have put it together that way, but now I see what you mean."

"So, sometimes it's hard to hear what others are really saying, and sometimes it's hard to interpret their true intent, and sometimes it's hard to tolerate your own feelings."

"Yeah. I'm a mess."

"You're in early recovery," said Holly. "Give yourself a break. That's exactly where I was in early sobriety. I didn't know up from down."

"So this is normal?"

Emma said, "Yes. For early recovery, it's perfectly normal. It will change. You have to learn how to deal with your own emotions and learn to deal with people as they are, and not your projections, or fears, of what they are."

"Okay," Jake exhaled. "I can do that. By the way, I had a dream. I was being dragged after a car that Holly was driving, but then I had to let go and I started to fly."

Emma looked at Jake and asked, "Jake?"

"Emma?" He looked back at her, his eyebrows raised. *Still the smartass*, she thought.

"You're going to be just fine. You know that?" She smiled at him.

"Yes," Jake answered. "Yes, I believe I do know that."

By the following day Mason's home had received several phone calls. Jake had called to ask if it would be okay if he came to visit. Emma had called to see if it would really be okay to hold the last group at his home. Holly had called to ask if she might bring over a comforter she'd like to give Mason as a present. And Marianne called to ask if Mason would receive her as a visitor. The visits were scheduled by Mona, who told them to drop by for short visits in the afternoon, to stay for ten or fifteen minutes, that Mason was usually very tired but he'd love to see them.

Mason was having a dream while Mona was taking these calls. *He dreams about his dad and growing up in French Lick Indiana. In the dark of the night he looks out on the stars from his back porch, as he did so many times as a child, and sees the stars brighter than ever. He realizes that his father stands at his elbow.*

"Where you been, Dad?" asks Mason.

"I had to go up ahead. There was somethin' in the road. Cleared it away."

"Oh," says Mason, finding a voice that sounds young to him, younger than he remembered being for a long time.

"We've got a trip to take," says his dad.

"I know," nods Mason. "Are we leaving now?"

"No, son. But soon. Are you scared?"

"A little."

"I was, too. It's a fine trip. You won't be afraid once we start. Heck, all the pain is on this side of the fence, you know what I mean?"

"Can I take anything with me? Do I need to pack anything?" asks Mason.

"You'll want to. You'll want to take it all, but you can't take anything with you. Now, you have a job to do before we go. You know that?"

"Yes, Dad."

"Lock up the house for the night and then get ready to see who you need to see, say what you need to say, do what you need to do. Can you do that?"

"I think so, Dad."

"Okay son. I'll be back. When you see me again, we'll take the trip."

"Will we use the truck, Dad?"

"If that's what you want. Oh, and your sister will be with me, too. You remember her, don't you?"

On the day Emma moved the rest of her things into the apartment, it was bitterly cold. The air seemed to crystallize and the hairs in her nostrils froze after being outside for a moment.

Emma arranged to meet with the movers early. They were moving some furniture, while she took a couple of loads of books and clothes in her car. Betty had offered to help, and when Emma returned she saw Betty was in the house. A feeling of reassurance washed over her, and images of her and Betty working together, playing tennis, drinking coffee, talking, all merged to remind her that she wasn't alone in this.

The home looked strange with the chair and sofa missing from the family room. Emma walked into the kitchen where Betty was talking with Frank, hearing their voices as she approached. She could hear the tone of their voices before hearing their words. Betty sounded conciliatory, Frank sounded tired.

"I think the place I'll need the most help now, Betty, is at my condo. Just a little help unpacking," said Emma.

"Sure. You want me to drive over now?" asked Betty.

"That would be great. It's not locked. I'll be right over."

After Betty left Frank looked at Emma.

"You don't have to do this, you know," said Frank.

"I don't think I can talk about this now, Frank. This isn't easy for me."

"If it's not easy, then don't do it. Maybe that's a sign."

"You—Frank, please, let's talk again in a few days. This part, we just have to get through this part."

"You're not taking any of the appliances?" asked Frank, moving across the kitchen.

"No. The condo has all that stuff. It's old, but it all works. There's a washer and dryer in the basement of the place. You'll have to come visit."

"I doubt I'll be doing that."

"Okay. Maybe we'll talk in a few days."

Frank looked like he wanted to say something but then stopped himself. He looked out the window and then spoke.

"Emma, I didn't want it to come to this, but I've got to proceed with the divorce if you leave here. If you leave here today, the divorce is started. Don't plan to come back. Don't plan to talk with me without my attorney present. I'm going to be aggressive. You won't get anything from me."

Emma looked at Frank. She realized that this was his last card. "Do what you have to do, Frank. I'm doing what I have to do."

Frank looked her in the eyes.

"You don't make enough to live on. Do you know that? Once you start paying your own health insurance, and I'll hold you to paying for half of Nathan's tuition, you'll be ruined financially, Emma. You'll have to change your lifestyle."

"I think that's the point." She regretted it, the moment it left her lips. She'd hoped to do this without animus. Now she'd blown it. She avoided Frank's eyes, but heard his voice as a hissing whisper near her.

"Fuck you Emma. Fuck you. You'll never make it without me."

Emma turned her back on Frank and walked out the door. She didn't cry but she remembered Jake describing the rock in his throat. She got in her car and got ready to drive away.

Nathan drove in behind her, just before she was able to pull out of the driveway.

Emma got out of the car and he backed up, and pulled to the side.

"Didn't mean to block you in," Nathan said.

"I'm just about to go, Nathan. You want to come see it?"

"Maybe later. Do you need help?"

"I've got the movers. And Betty's helping, too."

"Good," said Nathan. He rocked back and forth on his heels. Emma was struck by how much he'd grown in the last few months.

"Nathan, I'm not leaving you. You know that? I have a second bedroom. My home is your home. I'd like you to come over and set it up for yourself, just how you'd like it."

"Okay, Mom. I'll come by this weekend. Before this weekend. I have to get back to school by next week."

"I know. Nathan, I'm sorry about this."

"Yeah. Well, it sucks."

"That's about right," said Emma, and walked over to her son and hugged him. The tears released as she held him. They were both crying.

"We've got to stop this. Our tears will freeze," she said, laughing.

"Okay. That's fine by me. I'll go inside now," said Nathan.

"Okay. I love you. I'll call you tonight and we'll set up a time. Come over anytime."

"I'll call you, Mom."

After she moved, Emma felt restless. She would start to open boxes and put her things away, try to put a picture on the wall, try to find something she had thought that she'd packed, realize that she hadn't, and begin to cry. She called Dylan, who asked, "You want me to come there, or do you want to come here?"

Emma was in Grand Rapids within a couple of hours, after quickly packing an overnight bag.

Dylan lived in an old home in East Grand Rapids and had done a good job of refurbishing it. She had hardwood floors and brightly painted walls with original artwork. She was wearing jeans and a baggy sweater when Emma arrived. She kissed her hello and led her to her living room. She'd made a fire.

"I didn't think it would be this hard," Emma cried to Dylan. "And that's with knowing that it was going to be damn hard!"

Dylan was just a listening ear. She made tea for Emma and made few comments. Mostly, she listened. After a while, she asked if Emma would like to go out or stay in. Emma said she didn't feel like going out.

"The world feels like such a dark place right now," Emma said, sipping her tea. "I didn't mention this before, but I have a client who's in the process of dying. It's such a dark time of year anyway."

Dylan asked her if she considered getting back into therapy.

"I've actually set another appointment with Claudia," answered Emma. "She's someone who I've known for a long time and she knows me better than anyone, I think."

Dylan sat next to Emma and took her hand. "I want to get to know you better than that. I want to get to know you, and I want you to know that I can tell this is hard. It's impossibly hard. My divorce was the hardest thing I've ever had to do and I didn't have any children involved. So you take all the time you need. I'll just follow your cue, Emma. Move slow, we'll move slow. You want me, though, just let me know, I'm right here."

Holly had been sleeping, after a long day of work. She'd tossed in a DVD and fell asleep before she was twenty minutes into it.

Her alarm went off and she looked over and hit the snooze button. She was aware of dreaming, but couldn't remember what about. She looked outside and saw that snow was falling, again.

"Florida," she said out loud. "or Mexico. Maui," she intoned and fell back asleep—

Now on a beach. The sun is warm and the beach, a pristine khaki, the water a turquoise blue, with palm trees swaying behind her. Holly is dressed in the same pajamas that she wore to bed last night. Baggy sleep pants and an orange T-shirt. She's still in bed.

"Bed on the beach," she says, a smile growing on her face. She knows she's dreaming. She knows she can change the picture if she wants. The picture is good, but it was snowing, just outside the dream, and she wants to just stay here for a few moments.

She sees something in the sky. A bank of clouds, moving fast from the horizon, towards her. Holly feels a tug of anticipation.

There is a figure, on the clouds, a human figure, who Holly recognizes as Ellen DeGeneres, sitting on a lawn chair and wearing the same baggy sleepers and orange T-shirt that Holly is wearing.

"Hi, Holly!" Ellen calls from the clouds.

"Hi! Ellen?" asks Holly.

"No, Holly. I'm God. Your Higher Power, if that's what you prefer. Yahweh. Budda, Allah, I'll answer to anything. Even Ellen if you like."

"Wow. Well, you look just like—"

"Somebody you'd feel good talking to. That's me. Did you know that I don't have any specific form?"

"I always thought that."

"I know."

"What are you doing here?" asks Holly.

"Interesting question, Holly. I've always been here. You're doing something different to contact me. What are you doing, Holly?"

"Umm, sleeping? Dreaming?"

"Uh huh. What else?"

"I'm cleaning up my life. I am cleaning up an old mess, I'm forgiving myself. I'm taking care of myself."

"Uh huh. Anything else?"

"I—I found a man, and I think I'm falling in love."

"That's great!"

"So, God, tell me how it's going to work out?" asks Holly.

"That's not how it works, Holly, you should know that."

"You don't give away any endings?"

"There aren't any 'endings.' The way it works out is how it's working right now."

"Yeah. Wow. Well, right now, I'm giving him some time."

"Is that what he needs? Or what you need?"

"I think, maybe, both."

"Cool. Holly, something is coming—"

"Revelations?"

"No, that's whack. Some nut jobs added that to the Bible to scare people."

"So what's coming?" asks Holly.

"Gotta go, Holly. Remember, I'm always right here."

"God! Hey! Ellen! What's coming?" Holly cries as she sees the clouds slip towards the horizon, over the sea. Then she sees a turtle crawling out of the ocean, and begin to crawl to the high weeds just to the north of where Holly lay in her bed.

"Here turtle, turtle, turtle, here turtle," Holly sang in a child like voice, only to be interrupted by her alarm going off.

"Wow!" Holly said after waking up. She didn't write it down. She didn't have to. This was a dream she knew she'd remember for life.

Emma sat in the chair opposite Claudia.

"So, it's been a while," said Emma.

"Yes," answered Claudia. "How have you been, Emma?"

"Oh, that's a big one. I guess that's why I'm here. Well, I made the decision to leave Frank. And then, I left him."

"I'm sorry," said Claudia, "and congratulations."

Emma laughed.

"Yeah, it has both of those qualities. At times I feel like celebrating, sometimes I feel like I'm at a funeral."

Claudia smiled and her eyes showed compassion. She waited for Emma to continue.

"It's amazing to me, that I spent so many years pretending. I am with Dylan, I've seen her a couple of times, and it's new, but it just feels so right. Even the difficulties feel okay."

"What are the difficulties?"

"Well, she wanted to push things at first. I wanted to go slow. I have a lot on my mind. She's become respectful. But I know, absolutely, this is no bed of roses. But it feels right."

"How do you know?" asked Claudia.

Emma looked down at her fingers, started to fold her hands in her lap, then instead held them in front of her, her fingers splayed like she was seeing herself for the first time. Her eyes were moist and clear, and a large smile grew across her face.

"Well, that's hard to explain. How do you know you like Chinese food but not hamburgers? How do you know you like the Beatles but not the Stones?"

"So it's a taste?" asked Claudia.

"Yes, maybe. But it runs deeper than that. It's like, how would I say this? It's, you know, I spent years and years with Frank. And we worked really hard on the relationship. Well, you know that."

"Yes, I do."

"And he wasn't a bad man. Still isn't. But I never felt like I was where I was supposed to be. I couldn't ever feel settled. Now, when I'm with Dylan, I mean, just being with her, just talking, or driving together, or making love—"

"Oh, it's gotten to that point?" asked Claudia.

"Yes. And that's wonderful, too. But all of it, just being with her, I feel like I'm, I'm home."

"Yet, you said there were some difficulties."

"Uh huh. But the home, the home isn't where she is, necessarily. I'm not making this clear, am I?" Emma sighed.

Claudia shifted in her chair and reassured her client. "That's fine. You're figuring it out yourself. This may be the first time you've tried to put this together and put language to it," said Claudia.

"That's true enough. I'm home in here," Emma said, pointing towards her heart. "I'm doing the things that I've been meant to do. I'm being myself. I don't know how else to put it. I am what I am. Like Popeye." Emma smiled.

Claudia smiled back at her. "How are Frank and Nathan taking it?"

"Frank is going to fight. Legally, he says. I didn't want it to come to this. Maybe he'll back off, maybe not. Doesn't matter."

Claudia said, "You say that now, but if things get rough economically—"

"I know. It's going to be hard. You know what he said to me?"

"No. What did he say?"

"He said 'You're never going to make it without me.' What do you think of that?"

Claudia raised her eyebrows. "What do you think of it?"

"I think he's scared. I think he's afraid he's never going to make it without me. I think that's what he wanted to say, but he was too afraid to say it that way. So it came out as a challenge, instead."

"That's what I thought," said Claudia. "How about Nathan?"

"I think we're going to be okay. On the day I moved out we talked a little, and he seemed warm and supportive. I'm sure this is a shock to him."

"Probably. But it sounds like he wants you to be happy?" asked Claudia.

"I think that's it. We're going to talk again, soon. He hasn't seen the place yet, but I want him to know that he should think of it as a 'home base'—my home will always be his home."

"Yes. Have you been coming out to any of your friends?"

"You know, Claudia, that's one thing that's really been hitting me. Betty knows. She helped me move. She's my best friend. But, other than clients and the people I see in passing at the MAC, my world is really pretty sparsely populated."

"How do you feel about that?"

"I want more friends. I want a bigger social circle. I was always a part of Frank's group, but I was also always a bit of an outsider. I was always the liberal one, the artsy one, the—"

"The gay one," said Claudia, smiling.

"Yeah. That, too. The gay one. So, I don't know what to do. I don't know if I make new gay friends or what."

"This is all quite new to you."

"Yeah. It hit me the other day that I could move, I could move anywhere. With my parents dead, my sibs all live far away, my son is in college—"

"Doesn't Dylan live in Grand Rapids?" asked Claudia.

"Yes. So, I will definitely be visiting G.R. more often. That makes sense to me. I could do anything. Things feel opened up. There's that freedom. At the same time, I don't want to do anything hasty."

Emma looked over at Claudia and said, "Thanks for taking me back. I'm sorry that I was so difficult. I was scared and angry and, I think I was projecting. I just thought you disapproved."

Claudia said, "I didn't 'take you back.' You just gave me a call and came back on your own. I didn't go anywhere."

"You know what I mean," said Emma. "I'm sorry I was a handful."

"Comes with the job, you know?" said Claudia, her hand waving in the air. *C'est la vie.*

"Yeah. I know."

Marianne visited Mason after work that same day. Mason was sitting in the sunroom of his modest home in East Lansing. It was clearly a professor's home, thought Marianne, full of books and a room that seemed completely devoted to DVDs and videos and movie reels and projectors.

Mona directed Marianne to the room where Mason sat, and she mentioned that Mason was doing okay with short visits, suggesting no more than ten minutes or so.

"That will be fine," said Marianne. "I just wanted him to know I'm thinking of him."

Mona said, "Your group is so wonderful. Mason talks about it and looks forward to it all the time."

"Well, the group is almost over."

"He mentioned that. I understand you've talked about meeting over here," said Mona.

"Yes, if that won't be an inconvenience."

"I think that'll be fine. Emma called to make sure it would work. Of course, things could change," said Mona.

"Of course," said Marianne.

When Marianne entered the sun room she noticed that Mason was dressed in pajamas and a bathrobe.

"I'm sorry I'm so casual," said Mason, not rising but motioning with his hand for Marianne to sit in the seat next to him. "I'm practicing my Hugh Hefner look. How am I doing?"

"You look fine, Mason," said Marianne, smiling stiffly.

"And you're a liar," said Mason.

"Mason, you behave yourself!" said Mona.

"I will. I'm just a little more, 'uncensored,' you might say," said Mason.

"I'm fine," said Marianne to Mona. "I'm used to him from group."

"Okay. I'll leave you two alone for a moment. Ring the bell if you need anything, Buster," Mona said, motioning to a small hand bell that rested on the TV table next to Mason.

Once Mona had left Marianne looked at Mason. "How are you doing?" she asked.

"Well, like shit, a lot of the time," he said. "I realize I'm dying. I wonder what that's going to be like. Sometimes it doesn't seem real. Most of the time it seems too real. You always know someday you're going to die, but then, the reality of it hits you like a son of a bitch. It's pretty amazing."

"When I thought—" Marianne hesitated. She looked out the window into the snow in the yard.

"When you were going to kill yourself," said Mason, completing her sentence. He was looking directly at her. Marianne looked into his face.

"Yes, well, when I was planning on suicide, the idea seemed like an escape. It seemed wonderful. Like a vacation you never had to return from."

"And your pills are helping you to live?" asked Mason.

"They seem to be helping. Yes."

"You gave something to me, in the group."

"Well, that was a little awkward, but I was thinking, if you needed an alternative, if the pain gets too bad, well, there was enough to do the job."

"You know, Marianne, I have more than enough pain killers on hand. I have enough to kill myself, anytime I want. But I appreciate the gift. Seems like a strange gift, don't you think?" He smiled.

"I suppose so," said Marianne. "I didn't think of it as a gift, so much."

"But you gift wrapped them. Don't you see?"

"Yes. But only because—I guess I don't know why I did that."

"Well, this isn't therapy. You don't need to explain yourself."

"No," Marianne looked at Mason and smiled. "You've been a good friend."

"I hardly know you," said Mason. "But thanks."

"You, you made a difference to me. That night, before Thanksgiving, when we all went out to dinner."

"Yeah. That was a good time," said Mason.

"Yes. And you said something to me," said Marianne.

"I think I told you to loosen up, or some damn thing."

"You did. And it made a difference. I just wanted you to know that. It made a difference."

"What difference do you suppose it made?"

"It made me start taking my anti-depressants, for one thing, just for a few days, they started to work, and it helped me decide to wrap up these pain killers, and give them to someone who, someone who might need them."

"Well, that was thoughtful. You're a beautiful woman. Did you know that, Marianne?"

At that moment Mona walked in and said, "I think it's time for the visit to end. Mason has other visitors today, and he needs his rest."

"Of course. Good to see you, Mason," said Marianne. "If there's anything I can do—"

"You know, there is something," said Mason.

"What?" she asked, leaning closer.

"Go out and enjoy yourself. Have a good time. Eat some ice cream. Have an orgasm. Tickle your fancy."

"Buster!" said Mona.

"He's okay. I know what he means," said Marianne, with a smile on her face.

"I mean exactly what I say. Go out and live, okay?" said Mason.

"I'll do it, Mason. See you soon."

And she left.

Emma dropped by later in the afternoon. She brought some flowers and a guided imagery CD and heard the same protocol as Marianne had earlier in the day from Mona.

"Hello, Mason," Emma said, walking into his sunroom. Mason was wearing the same pajamas and robe.

"Hi, Emma. Emma Davis," he said, and held her in his gaze. Mason smiled and his eyes glazed over for a moment before he spoke again. "What a pleasure. Please, have a seat."

"It's good to see you. Your home is just what I pictured," Emma said, seating herself in the easy chair that was next to his bed. "It's full of books and warmth and movies. Just what I thought."

Mason looked at Emma and winked. "I guess I did all right, you know?"

"I guess you did," she answered. "One reason I wanted to come by is to check on what we talked about earlier. About the group meeting here. I wanted to be respectful."

"Yeah, sure. It's fine with me, and I talked with Mona about it and she's okay with it, too. I'm not sure I'll be awake for all of it. I seem to go in and out, know what I mean?"

"Yeah. I do. We can take it a day at a time. Okay? And we probably won't stay very long," said Emma.

"Good idea," said Mason. "Marianne was here earlier today."

"I think the whole group plans to come by one time or another," said Emma.

"Say goodbye, maybe. I try to think of wise things to say to people, but I'm mainly just a little more blunt than usual."

"Are you dreaming?" asked Emma.

"I should have known you would have asked that," said Mason, smiling. "I had a dream about my dad. I don't remember anything else. Just my dad."

"Where's your dad?" asked Emma.

Mason pointed up.

"You miss him?" Emma asked.

"Every day. Not for long, though."

"Are you in pain?"

"Every day. Not for long, though."

"That's a good answer, isn't it?" asked Emma.

"We do what we can. You're a good kid, y'know?"

Emma smiled. "I do what I can. See you Thursday, okay?"

"Can do."

Emma came back to her apartment and turned on the stereo. She was playing some Bach—the *Rostaprovitch Cello Sonatas*, and was about to light some candles. She was feeling weary from even a short visit with Mason and then the buzzer chimed. She went to the door and turned on the intercom.

"Who is it?" she asked.

"Nathan."

Emma buzzed him in and walked into the hallway to greet him. At first she was startled, because he looked so much like his father did at that age. She gave him a hug and welcomed him into her place.

"Let me turn this off; it's kind of dreary," Emma said as she switched off the stereo.

"It looks nice," Nathan said. "I like the colors."

"Yeah, well, it's small, but it is kind of nice, isn't it? Let me show you your bedroom."

Emma took Nathan into an empty room.

"Wow. This room isn't even painted."

"No. I wanted to keep it empty. It's your choice, what you want to do with it. I thought, sometime we'd go shopping. Pick out some furniture, a bed, maybe a TV. I can't afford to do it all at once, but—"

"Wow, thanks. Yeah, we'll have to do that."

Emma's throat constricted when she heard how blank his words felt.

"How about this weekend?" Emma asked.

"Could be," said Nathan.

There were some moments of silence. Emma began to talk again, nervously.

"I didn't paint it because I thought we might do that together, some weekend. I've got a bunch of colors that compliment the rest of the place, but are a little more masculine, so you get a choice of what color you might like."

"Thanks, Mom."

"Come on in the living room and have a seat. So, tell me, how's your Christmas break coming? When do I get a chance to meet your girlfriend?"

"When can I meet yours?"

Emma blushed, but answered the question immediately.

"We have to have this talk, don't we? I'm embarrassed that I haven't—" Her words were halting. She tried not to look out the window, to keep her eyes on Nathan.

"Yeah, I know."

" All this seemed like it happened very suddenly, since you left for school. But I've known, most of my life I've known."

Nathan just nodded. He looked like he was about to cry.

"And Dylan? She comes around every so often. I'm sure you'll get a chance. So, how are you doing, Nathan? Seriously."

"I'm not so sure. I guess I'm doing okay. My grades came in. I have a 3.5, which isn't as good as I was hoping, but you always said that college would be tougher than high school."

"Do you like it?" Emma felt herself on the verge of losing control. She knew she was trying to make this an ordinary visit. She knew it wasn't. Nathan answered her.

"Parts of it. The part about being away from home is, kind of good and kind of hard. I didn't know you and dad would be—" and Nathan began to cry. Emma did as well.

"I'm sorry," she said as she sat down next to her son and put her arm around his shoulders, and pulled his head down next to hers. "I never meant this to hurt you and I knew it would. If there was any other way—I love you so much."

"But you don't love Dad," said Nathan, now on the verge of sobbing.

"No, Nathan, I do love your father. I love him as your father. I love all of our history. It's just that, he wasn't right for me. I had to pretend. And I just couldn't do it anymore."

Nathan pulled away and wiped his eyes with the sleeve of his pea coat. He refused a Kleenex when Emma offered one.

"Sorry, Mom."

"It's okay, honey. Believe me, I've cried a lot over this. I'm not done, not by a long shot."

"Are you happy, Mom?"

"I am, sweetie. I'm sorry that I'm hurting you and your dad. That makes me really sad. But I'm doing something I think I should have done a long time ago. But then I wouldn't have had you, and if that was the main reason I was with your father, well, then it was worth every moment."

"Why didn't you take the cat?" he asked.

"Honey, I thought I'd leave Cleo with your dad. For now, at least. He might need the company more than I do."

"Okay. I've got to go."

"Oh, so soon? Would you like to go to a movie, or get a bite to eat?"

"I'm supposed to meet with my friends. We're going to see that new movie about the island."

"Oh. Well, good. I'm glad you could visit. I'm glad we could have a talk. You have to go back after the weekend. Would you like to schedule a time to set up and go shopping?" Emma couldn't help but feel disappointed.

"Dad and I are going to the State game."

"Oh? Football?"

"Football's over, mom. Hockey."

"Oh. Well, keep in touch, okay? I'll call you. Maybe sometime soon, okay?"

"Okay. Bye, Mom. I love you."

"I love you, too, sweetie."

Jake saw Holly in the Sunday morning meeting at the A.A. Club. It was on the third step, and Jake enjoyed hearing people talking about their decision to go with the solution. After the meeting he stepped outside and smoked a cigarette.

Holly walked out and had Martha at her side.

"Morning, Jake. Good meeting?" said Martha.

"Yeah, it was."

"Why are ya smokin' out here? All the smokers are inside," said Martha.

"Because it's too smoky in there," said Jake.

"We're going out to breakfast. Want to come?" asked Martha.

"Naw. I'm meeting Nick later. Have you got a minute, Holly?"

Martha looked at Holly and said, "I'll meet you over there, okay? Want me to order for you?"

Holly told her to go, she'd just be a minute.

"How are you doing, Jake?"

"I'm good. I wanted to tell you something. And I didn't want to talk to you through the meeting, if you know what I mean."

"Yeah, I hate when people do that."

"Well, I just wanted you to know, first off, I've been giving a lot of thought about A.A. and not drinking, and I wanted you to know, I'm *in*."

"Well, good. I didn't think you were '*out*.'"

"No. But, I've been, kind of just checking this whole thing out, and thinking maybe I'd stay, maybe I'd leave. But I'm finding something here I've never found before. It's almost like a healthy family. Or at least, a healthier family than mine was."

"I know what you mean. Well, good. I hope it's not just on my account," said Holly.

"I'd be lying if I said that you weren't a big part of it. I'm still crazy about you."

"Jake, maybe we'd better not—"

"No, I won't go there. Sorry. That isn't what I meant for this to be about. I just wanted you to know, that part of the decision is you, but another part is that I just feel a hell of a lot better."

"Yeah, once you stop poisoning yourself on a daily basis, its amazing how much better you feel."

"Right. And I know that it's a Higher Power, it's not me, but Holly, I know that you helped me. You helped me at a time when no one else could reach me. I needed someone, something, and you were there. So thanks."

"Oh, thank you, Jake. Twelve step work, well, it's not work. I'm glad you're making it."

"Yeah. Me, too. And one other thing, I've decided to go back to school. Seeing Edward made me realize that I've always wanted to get my Ph.D. And I was thinking, 'Yeah, but I'll be almost forty before I get it,' but then I thought, 'I'm going to be forty anyway, so, why not?'"

"Jake, that's great news," said Holly. "Listen, I don't want Martha to wait too long. Are you sure you don't want to join us?"

"Naw. Nick. Remember?" He took a pull on his cigarette.

"Right. Jake, I miss you. See you around, okay? And thanks for sharing." Holly took him in her arms and gave him a kiss on the lips. "I'm waiting for the day, Jake. I'm waiting for the day."

CHAPTER EIGHTEEN

After breakfast, Holly returned home and started taking down her Christmas decorations. She looked at her computer and for a moment it looked like a servant awaiting her command.

"Why not?" she asked out loud.

She looked up the Masters in Social Work program at M.S.U. She saw that she could easily make the deadline for applying. She wondered if the state would chip in for the tuition.

Holly clicked over to her MSU Credit Union bank account. Then she checked the balance in her checking and her savings accounts. She'd been trying to stash away some cash for a rainy day fund, and saw that her balance was over five thousand in savings.

Then she looked at tuition again.

She checked the State of Michigan Website to check benefits, and looked at tuition reimbursement. The state would reimburse 100% if the employee worked two years past graduation. Holly started to think it over.

I don't have to stay in investigations, she realized. *Adoptions would be cool. Someone could be happy as a result of my work, instead of trying to kill me or giving me nightmares.*

Or maybe I could become a therapist, and hang out my own shingle, like Emma. Maybe someday I could start a private practice with Jake. Wouldn't that be something?

Holly called Martha.

"I'm thinking about going back to school," she said.

"I was wondering how long that would take you," answered Martha.

"What do you mean? You knew this before I did?"

"Well, it's not hard to figure out. You're not exactly thrilled doing the job you're doing. It's draining, it's dangerous, and then you hear Jake talk about going back to school—"

"And it's suddenly seems possible. Yes. In fact, the more I talk about it, the more excited I get."

"That's great. What do you need to do?"

"I need to write a statement, fill out some paperwork, get my finances in order. I need to stay with the state for two years after I get my degree."

"Are you up for that?" asked Martha.

"Yeah, I've already thought about it. If worse comes to worse, I can always switch to another department."

"Okay. Well, do it!"

"Okay. I'm getting started this afternoon."

Emma slept in the living room of her new condo, on her couch, for the first three nights. She still had to put her bed together and had thought that this wouldn't be a problem. She was mechanically inclined enough to put it together. She just hadn't gotten around to it.

On the fourth night, Emma decided to do it. She went to a store in the shopping mall near her condo, bought some new sheets, blankets, pillowcases and other bedding she'd need. Then she picked up the small wrench she'd need to put the bed together.

Emma had chosen a bed from the mattress store across town. She had looked at a few beds and realized she could spend thousands of dollars on a bed frame. She had decided on a really good mattress and box spring, and going with a faux brass frame that made a square shape around her entire bed. She could hang screens, or lights, or fabric over the frame of the bed. It seemed fun and she could afford it.

Emma got the instructions out of the box and began to put the bed together. It was awkward, and she had wished that she had asked for help, as it was difficult to hold the bars while also wrenching the parts together. She managed. Emma always managed.

When she had finished she wrestled the box spring, then the mattress onto the frame. By this time she was sweating. Her body was conditioned to think once she had exerted itself she would be working for a good hour, so by the time she had put on her sheets and bedding, she was almost dripping wet.

Emma took a quick shower and made some decaf tea. She read some poetry from her Mary Oliver anthology and got into bed. She thought about calling Dylan but decided against it. She looked at another poem. This one had a line that caught her attention. The poet was describing burying her parents:

> This lead thing that you carried
> I will not carry

With that thought, Emma went to sleep.

She dreams that she's in an old house. The house looks Southern. It just feels like New Orleans. Some kind of creeping decay, a kind of ruinous rot spreading through the place.

Emma walks into a dining room. There are cobwebs and every surface is covered by a thick layer of dust. A large wooden dining table fills the center of the room, underneath a hanging chandelier. Her mother enters the room, wearing a white dress that is frilly and yet practical. Her mother is wearing her hair up, in a bun, like she did when Emma was young.

"Mom? Emma asks.

"Yes, dear? Do you want your dinner?"

"No, Mom, is Dad here?"

"He should be down shortly."

Emma sees her father walk into the dining room and sit at the head of the table. He's wearing a pin-striped suit, a three piece, with a vest, and she can see a chain for a watch drape itself across his abdomen. He's as thin as ever, but his hair is pure silver now. And he was pale.

"Dad?" asks Emma.

"What is it? Are you going to the dance tonight?"

"Yes, Daddy." Emma feels so much younger. She has to will herself not to talk like a child. "Dad, I'm—is Mom going to come in?"

"Dorothy, come in now," says her father. Emma's mother came into the room. "Our little girl has something to say to us."

"Mom, Dad, I've got something to tell you," says Emma.

"Go ahead, dear," her father motions for her to continue.

"Is anything wrong, dear?" asks her mother.

"No. Well, I'm not sure if it's—no, it's not wrong. Well, I just needed to let you know, that I've decided to make a change."

"Changing what, dear?" asks her mom. "Changing jobs? Or your hair color? The grey is starting to show a little."

"No, not that. I'm moving, for one thing."

"Moving is a good thing. Property values in your neighborhood have risen steadily, I'm sure," says her dad.

Emma clears her throat. "It's more than a move. I'm leaving Frank."

"Oh, no, dear. That's terrible. I'm so sorry. Is he cruel, dear? Does he beat you?" asks her mother.

"No. That's not the problem. The problem, well, it's not a problem. The situation is that I'm gay."

"I'm gay too. Aren't you gay, Mother? But that's not a reason to leave your husband. We're all happy and gay and we'd like to be happier, but that's no reason to leave your husband," says Emma's father.

"Well, we're using the word differently, I think. Let me explain. I've known, I've always known, that I was different from other little girls. I've always dreamed of being with other girls, the way boys dream of being with girls. Of being with girls and marrying girls. I've always wanted to love girls. I'm not like other little girls. I was never able to tell you. I was afraid you wouldn't love me. And now that you're dead—"

"Wait a minute, dear," says Emma's mother. "What are you saying?"

"You're dead. You know that, don't you?"

Emma watch as her parents began to fade out before her eyes.

"Oh, no, I didn't mean to have you disappear. I just thought you should know. You're not dead. Come back. You're not dead. I was just kidding."

And Emma woke up calling out "You're not—you're not dead. Come back," out loud, a low murmur that sounded quieter and more pathetic in the quiet of her little bedroom.

"Whew," she said. She got up and wrote the dream down. She'd talk with Claudia about it later. Or maybe not. She wouldn't be able to sleep for the rest of the night.

Before his shift at the hospital was over, Jake called Mason's home and spoke with Mona. He explained who he was and asked if it would be okay to visit. He could hear Mona's voice whispering and then she came back and said, "Mason would be happy to see you." It was only a ten-minute drive from where Jake worked.

After Mona let him in, she ushered him into the bedroom. There was a hospital bed in the center of the room, with a couple of easy chairs and some folding chairs set up. Jake noticed a group of yellow balloons tied to an IV drip, "We Love You Grampee," and a shelf full of greeting cards and flowers. Mason lay in the bed with his eyes closed.

Mona gently shook him and Jake said, "No, don't bother him," before Mona looked back at him and said, "He asked me to wake him for you." After Mason opened his eyes Mona left the room. Mason looked at Jake and motioned to the chairs that were set up in the room around the bed.

"The room is all ready for our group tomorrow night," said Mason. He tried to sit up, and when Jake tried to help him he waved him away. He just lay back on his pillow.

"I hope I can hold out that long. I'm not getting out of bed anymore. This thing…" said Mason, and he didn't finish the thought.

Jake took the cue. "Listen, I won't stay long. I just wanted to stop in and say 'hi.'" He stood for a few moments, waiting for Mason to say something. He suddenly didn't know what to do with his hands, or his eyes. He felt his throat tighten.

Mason pointed to a chair. "Why don't you sit down? Stay with me for a minute."

Jake sat. He watched Mason breathing. Mason had shut his eyes, then opened them again. "Still here?"

Jake laughed. "Yeah. Want me to go?"

"Not yet. We're not ready. Stay for a minute."

He didn't respond to Mason's comment about "not ready." Jake was used to working with schizophrenics or patients who were tapped into an inner reality that made no sense to onlookers. He knew when not to intrude. He sat and watched Mason, and felt calmer. At the same moment he felt a huge bubble of tears starting to form deep in his chest. He didn't say a thing.

Mason began to talk, with his eyes still shut. "I thought you were such a smartass, when we started. You know what? I thought that you'd just fuck up. And then you did, and I wasn't surprised. You know what surprised me, Jake?"

"No, sir. What surprised you?" answered Jake.

"You didn't give up. I was ready for you to give up. I gave up on you. You didn't give up on yourself. Did you know that?"

"Still have that scotch I gave you?" asked Jake.

Mason opened his eyes. "Yeah, I do. Haven't touched it. Why? Want it back?"

"No, sir. I don't. I surely don't. I'm glad I gave it to you," said Jake. His eyes were filling with tears.

"Jake, will you get Mona?"

Jake stepped into the hallway. Mona was in the room just off the hallway. She had a box in her arms. "He wants you," Jake said.

Mona walked into the room. "I brought what you asked for, Buster," she said.

"Give it to Jake," Mason said.

Mona gave Jake the box and he saw that it was packed with DVDs. Ken Burn's Jazz series. Documentaries on Miles Davis, Charles Mingus, Thelonious Monk. Concert footage on Coltrane.

"I want you to have these, Jake. I know you like jazz. Mona doesn't like it so much, do you?"

"No, Buster, I do not," she answered.

"Jake. Take these. I wish I could give you more. You gave me a lot."

Jake was struck. The tears were rolling down his cheeks.

"You don't have to talk, Jake. Just sit down here and cry with me for a moment. I can't cry anymore. Too doped up. Will you cry here with me?"

Jake sat at Mason's bedside and bawled like a baby. Mona stepped into the hallway.

Jake was shocked at his sobbing, yet he couldn't seem to stop it. He was incapable of speech. He was embarrassed and ashamed, yet he couldn't stop it. In some distant corner of his mind he knew this was about a lot more than Mason. It flashed through his mind to drink, but he knew he didn't want to do that. He knew he would get through this. And sure enough, after just a couple of minutes, his sobs subsided. Mason didn't seem to mind. His eyes were closed until Jake stopped. Then Mason opened them, and Jake wondered if he'd winked, or if it was his imagination.

"Okay, I think you're done. Get ready. Time to go. Take the movies with you okay?" said Mason.

Jake was sniffling and he got up, picked up the box, and leaned over to kiss Mason's forehead.

"Thank you, Mason."

"Get out of here, smartass."

Marianne studied her planner that she had downloaded onto her laptop, and looked at her schedule. She didn't know how she was going to do it.

She had signed up to take Latin Dance lessons and had also signed up to volunteer at Hospice. She wanted to get more involved with the community and she'd wanted to do something that would feed her soul and let her move her body, but she didn't know how she was going to squeeze these activities in with her work load.

Marianne counted the hours she had devoted to work. Arrive every morning at seven a.m. and leave every night at six p.m. and usually either work through lunch or have a working lunch. Eleven hours a day. Fifty-five hours a week. Then work on projects at home on weekends. And nights. Marianne realized she was probably working an excess of sixty-five hours a week. She would have to cut back on work.

But then how will it get done? she wondered.

Then she had a revelation. *How would it have gotten done if I had killed myself? I didn't worry about it then. Now that I'm thinking of living, maybe I can take the same approach.*

Marianne cut her Saturday hours in half, moved her daily schedule from seven thirty to five and scheduled hour-long lunches on a daily basis. Then she got online, just as her secretary had advised her, and joined a couple of dating services. *It's time for me to live, time to find time to live my life.*

Emma woke up early and decided to go for a run. She knew she was closer to the bike trail along the river than when she lived with Frank. She put on her form-fitting running outfit and wondered if she had stretched it out in the wash before noticing that she must have lost weight. She threw on a baggy MSU sweater and a snowcap and was ready to roll.

The air felt good on her face, cold, crisp, and clear. There was light in the eastern sky as Emma made her way through her new neighborhood down to the bike trail. Even though there was some snow on the trail, she had been eager to run. Being careful about avoiding icy patches, she kept up a relaxed pace. The trail seemed pristine, snow covering the wooden path along the river side, the river still running quietly, and she ran with a shortened stride to help her center of balance in case she slipped.

We're still in the Garden, she thought as she looked at the steam rising off the river. There were ducks in flight, from down river. Emma kept an eye on her watch, knowing she couldn't go too far. She had to work today. And this was the final meeting of her Dream Group.

Reflecting on the weekend, Emma knew that she needed to make an appointment with an attorney to discuss the divorce. She wanted to put that off. She wanted to see Dylan. She missed Dylan.

Emma wondered about the past few months since she'd started the Dream Group.

My God, I've moved out of my house, and each member of the group has faced their own crisis. Each one of them did have a secret—Holly's shame, Marianne's depression and suicide, Jake's drinking, Mason's cancer. It's amazing.

She kept running, now turning back and heading home to her condo. *And we've all made it. Except Mason. Mason isn't going to make it. But who knows? Maybe his involvement with the group was a blessing. Maybe it's what is helping him over these last few days.* Emma felt herself choke up.

She could hear the traffic of I-496, the major artery that cut through Lansing and curved into 127, heading north just before East Lansing. At one point, the off ramp and the running trail were mere feet from each other, separated by a chain link fence and some railing. Emma always hated this. She felt vulnerable and exposed running so close to cars traveling seventy miles an hour, just a few feet away.

Emma wondered about the wisdom of doing the group at Mason's that night. She'd have to call and confirm with his wife. *What was her name again?* All these questions about appropriate boundaries started in her head and she wondered if her colleagues would approve. *Was this really 'best treatment'? Was this really in the best interest of each of the clients?*

She crossed from the path and ran up the residential street that took her back to her condo. There was probably less than a mile of her run to finish. Her stride felt good, her arms pumping vigorously, and she thought of Nathan's visit. *It's a start,* she thought, as she rounded the bend.

The home stretch is where Emma would usually put on her kick, and finish strong, but something made her slow down today. *Emma, are you getting old?* She slowed down to a walk and held her hands on her hips as she walked the last couple of blocks to her condo.

Emma looked up into the trees behind her condo, as she cut through the back, and saw a flutter of sparrows lighting in a tree across from her place. And, in the midst of the snow, she saw a brilliant red flame on a branch, alone. A cardinal. In the winter. The bird sat still on the branch but the contrast of the crimson against the white was breathtaking to her. She knew enough about the bird to know that cardinals mated, his other must be near by. *And there she is.* Emma saw the muted colors on a branch, just below.

Emma breathed deeply the winter air of the Michigan morning. Inexplicably, a tear ran down her cheek. She couldn't put words to it. She couldn't describe how or why she knew. But she realized in that moment that she was going to be okay.

Since every one in the group had visited Mason before the group on Thursday night, they all knew where he lived. The agreement had been to meet at Mason's home at 7:00 p.m., stay for a short time, and finish the group at Emma's office.

Emma was the first to arrive. She wanted to check in with Mona. She saw that a hospice nurse was present. Emma felt like an intruder. There were flowers piled in the living room and stacks of cards unopened. The little home seemed so solemn and still. She told Mona that the others would be there shortly, but that she would tell them to go if Mona felt this to be an imposition.

"He wanted this," Mona said. "I think if you keep it short. We've gone with twenty-four hour care. It's close. He's really close. And he hasn't woken up since he went to sleep yesterday. But you're welcome to meet in the room with him. Let me know, will you, would you let me know if he wakes up? I want to see his eyes again, if I can," said Mona.

Emma embraced Mona. "Of course. We'll only stay a little while."

Jake was the next to come, followed by Marianne. Holly arrived just a minute before 7:00 p.m. Emma explained that it appeared that Mason was in a coma and that their meeting might be shorter than anticipated. Everyone indicated that they understood.

As they filed into the room, the nurse left. There were four chairs, two on either side of the hospital bed, which had been lowered so that people could see each other over the top. In the center of the room was Mason. He was drawn, thin, and grey. Holly almost gasped to see him, and Marianne clutched her hand. The bouquet of yellow balloons from his grandchildren had been tied to the bedpost, over his head.

Emma sat near the head of the bed on Mason's left and Jake sat opposite her on Mason's right. Holly and Marianne took seats at the foot of the bed.

The lighting was muted and they sat and listened to Mason's breathing. It was slow and labored.

Emma's eyes filled with tears. "Does anyone, does anyone have anything they want to say?" She felt at a loss of words herself.

"Hi, Mason," said Holly. "We're here. The group is here."

Marianne just shook her head. Jake reached over and took Holly's hand. Emma was saying, "Well, we all came together to talk about dreams. It has struck me what a profound time this was in everyone's life. All of your dreams were so powerful, and it was, it was an honor that you chose to share them with me and with each other. I wanted you all to know that this group, it was a total surprise to me. I had no idea how meaningful it would become to each of you, and to me. Dreams are pictures, pictures of feelings, pictures of our lives. You all helped each other read your dreams. This has been a group about beginnings and endings. And, I'm amazed at each one of you. Thank you, thank you for the honor of being a part of your lives over the last few weeks."

The group sat silently.

"I think we should go," said Marianne.

They all nodded. Then they stood up at once, and saw the circle. Jake was holding Holly's hand, and he reached down and took Mason's hand in his left. Holly caught Marianne's eyes with hers, and reached across the bed and took Marianne's left hand with her right. Emma looked across at Jake, and with her right hand found Mason's left hand. And Emma felt Marianne take her left hand. The circle was complete. Then Emma heard Jake's voice, soon joined by Holly's, and then her own and Marianne's, saying:

"God, grant me the serenity, to accept the things I cannot change, the courage to change the things I can, and the wisdom to know the difference."

Then they left. After a few minutes they were all back at Emma's office.

Emma arrived first and let the other three in. They filed into her office without a word. Emma thought the word *procession* and inwardly acknowledged the ritual the group was performing.

After everyone sat down they all looked to Mason's seat, which was empty. Finally, Emma spoke.

"That was pretty powerful."

"I'll say," said Marianne.

"It was beautiful," said Holly. Her eyes were still red from crying. "I don't know what I expected, maybe to be scared or sad. But I felt so peaceful. Especially during the prayer."

"That was a nice touch," said Emma. "Thanks, Jake."

"I didn't plan that," he said. "It just happened."

"So," asked Emma, "does anyone have any thoughts, feelings? Dreams?"

"Just one," said Marianne. "You thanked us, Emma. I want to thank you. This group may have saved my life. Literally."

"Yeah, thanks," said Holly. "This whole experience, the group, it was so much more than I'd bargained for. It was really impactful. I have been a part of groups before. Well, in the Twelve Step world, you're a part of a group, like, constantly, but this group has really been special and you made it special."

"Thanks," said Emma. She realized that she was really going to miss the group's meetings. "It's meant a lot to me, too. It's hard to summarize it all."

"I'm glad that we kept meeting," said Jake. "There was a time, about halfway through, I didn't think this was going to work. What happened?"

"I don't know," answered Emma, honestly. "I know that our instinct, as humans, is survival first. And then, love, evolution, change. We tend to move towards growth."

"Until we die," said Marianne.

"Who knows?" said Holly, looking at Marianne.

"I wanted to say that I am amazed," said Jake. "I got into this group as a lark. I read about it on a flyer at the hospital, or was it the paper? Anyway, I thought, 'What the hell?' I never intended to stop drinking."

"Well, the group wasn't about your drinking," said Emma.

"No. But it was. Because, my dreams were telling me something that my brain couldn't accept any other way. I couldn't take in that I was an alcoholic. I was in trouble. And you guys helped with that. And I apologize for being a pain in the ass. I'm still a pain in the ass. I'll probably always be a pain in the ass. But something has shifted. I was stuck before, and now, I'm not. So, thanks."

"How are you with Mason's death, Jake?" asked Holly.

"He's not dead yet, Holly. But I said my good-byes." Jake looked out the window, and Emma could see that he was remembering a private moment. He looked back at Holly and said, "It was nice we could see him as a group."

They spoke for a few minutes more, making the kind of small talk people make when they're waiting for an ending that they hope won't arrive. And then they talked about that for a while, too.

Finally, Emma said it was time to end.

"One more thing?" asked Jake.

"Sure," said Emma.

"I may be out of place here, but I'm hoping you're okay."

Emma blanched. "How do you mean?"

"Well, again, tell me if I'm out of line, but it's been clear, that you're going through some heavy shit yourself."

"Really?" asked Emma. She started to cross her hands in her lap, then stopped herself.

"Yeah," agreed Holly. "It's written on your face. I'm thinking it's gotten better lately."

"Now that you mention it," said Marianne, "I've seen it too."

"*Really?*" asked Emma.

"Now," said Jake, "maybe it's none of our business, but I just wanted you to know, you can't talk with me about your problems, but I'm hoping you're taking care of yourself."

Emma took in a deep breath. She continued to be surprised by what was communicated in the consulting rooms of therapy. Messages she wasn't conscious of delivering.

"Thanks, Jake. I am. And I didn't know it showed, but I'm really okay. You all made a change during the course of these past few months, and so did I. And that's all I'll say about it. But thanks for caring. If any of you should want to call back again, you have my number." She looked at Marianne. "And we have a meeting next week." Marianne nodded and smiled.

"Well, Jake and I are going to see each other regularly at meetings," said Holly.

"Sometimes," he reminded her.

Emma encouraged Jake to continue with some individual treatment, that she'd seen some research that suggested that early recovery was usually more successful if it was augmented by treatment. She gave him the name of a colleague.

Finally the moment came for them to say their goodbyes. They each left her office, giving Emma a hug, and went back to their homes. Emma stayed in her office for longer than usual and noticed that, for now, it was more familiar to her than her condo. She lit a candle and put on some music and sat in her chair. She wondered if she should start a new Dream Group. Maybe in the spring.

Mason died within the week at his home. He had come out of his coma, briefly, the day of his death. His children were around him and had begun to sing a song from an old western,

> "Happy Trails, to you, until we meet again,
> Happy Trails, to you, keep smilin' until then..."

Mason opened his eyes, briefly, looked at his family and smiled.

That night, Mona was alone with him, listening to the sound of his breathing, growing into a raspy, slowing rhythm. She had told him, more than once, to let go. To go into the light. She had told him that she loved him, but that she would be okay without him, that he needed to go ahead, and she told him that she would find him on the other side.

She fell asleep in the chair next to his bed, and then, near midnight, Mona woke up. The room was silent. Mason was no longer breathing. She touched his hand. He was still warm. But he was no longer breathing. She kissed his lips and said, "Goodbye, Buster," before she called the children and the nurse.

Emma's voice:

Last night I woke up from a dream. In the dream I was walking down a street. I didn't know where I was but it was night and I was alone. I was supposed to meet Mason but I couldn't find him.

I woke up and felt acutely alone. I got up and had a drink of water and looked out my back window of the little kitchen in my condo. I saw how the moon illuminated the snow in the courtyard and no one was around. I wasn't scared. I wasn't even lonely. I just felt alone. And I was. It was 3:00 a.m.

This morning I woke up to that same feeling. I wonder if it's what I didn't want to face all those years with Frank. Maybe it's just existential angst.

Now it all seems like a dream. How could I have guessed that this past fall would have given birth to this new life? This new love?

I thought when my depression began that I was finally about to pick up the legacy of my father. I remember writing in my journal that I was writing a book of lies. It was my life that was a lie.

On pure intuition, I had formed a circle of seekers and each one found something that had haunted their dreams.

Marianne found hope. Isn't that all depression is, after you take away the studies of serotonin and brain waves? I'm afraid we confuse the map with the territory. The symptom with the problem. The problem is the loss of hope.

I've seen that dead look in the eyes of my clients. A dead carcass sort of look. I've seen it in the mirror, looking back at me.

Medications do help. They can save your life. But you always have to go back and find the wound. For Marianne, it was her response to a broken relationship. Freud would suggest a daddy complex—all those years waiting for an unavailable man. Why else go after an unavailable male? Why take so long to see the writing on the proverbial wall?

What am I saying? I should look into my own recently-emerged closet for that answer. But now Marianne has hope and hope can build into faith. Possibilities emerge.

Jake was haunted, too. The most haunted. He almost brought the whole group down, yet, just like in Marianne's dream, he became an emotional leader for us. An example of facing your demons, of courage and recovery.

I've known several alcoholics in recovery. They seem amazing to me. Honest, sometimes compulsively so, and helpful. Especially with each other. They are like a tribe, or a huge extended family. Jake will be fine with them.

Holly still worries me. She reminds me of myself in so many ways. Maybe it was her duel with shame that seemed so familiar. Or the solution she seems intent on forging. A life devoted to helping others. I don't know that I've ever met anyone in this field who wasn't a "wounded healer."

Thank God she escaped her demons. Both the shame of her past and her stalker.

And Mason. Where are you now? I wished I'd been wrong about your dreams. Now you are with my mom and dad. May you all rest well. I wonder if death is another awakening? A new, longer life? Maybe this life is the dream?

So what did we learn? Hope, courage, awareness? I feel like Dorothy in Oz. What did I learn? That there's no place like home?

Except I left my home. And I'm afraid I broke the hearts of every man who ever loved me. That is the truth of this. Did I help anyone who truly matters to me? Is it all a facade, a lie? These thoughts still crowd my mind.

But, I found my own heart and I've found my own home and, within it, I've found love and faced my own shame and found courage and hope and awareness. And I will be here for my son and I will treat his father with dignity and respect and I will survive and thrive.

Last night I woke up from a dream and couldn't go back to sleep. I know I was awakened, that the dreamer in me woke me for some reason, some healing reason. I go for a run, I write in my journal, I wait until a decent hour to call Dylan. But my dreams are no longer nightmares.

This began as a book of lies and it became a purse full of dreams. I became aware. My dreams guided me and the dreamers I met encouraged me to hope and have the courage to make a change.

Thank God for change. That ability to change my mind, and to change my life.

My dreams have become like Mason's dreams of travel. How thoughtful of him, to leave me his dreams. In many of my dreams today, I am with Dylan, seeking adventure in far away cities, New York, Paris, giving talks on, what else? Dreams. This is one dream I will work to make real. One dream to come true.

ABOUT THE AUTHOR

Michael Stratton is a psychotherapist, speaker and consultant. He operates a private practice in East Lansing, Michigan. Stratton has presented on dreams in locations from Maui to Mackinac. He's trained therapists from San Francisco to New Jersey. He pursues his love of music by hosting a weekly jazz radio show. A founder of Monkey Business Consulting, Stratton has established a national presence. Learn more at www.mikestratton.com. Everybody Dreams is his first novel.